Progressive

Music

Theory

Grade Two

By

Andrew Scott

2

Distributed By

Australia

Koala Publications Pty. Ltd.
4 Captain Cook Ave
Flinders Park 5025
South Australia
Ph (08) 268 1750
Fax 61 - 8 - 352 4760

U.S.A.

Koala Publications Inc.
3001 Redhill Ave
Bldg. 2 # 221
Costa Mesa
CA 92626
Ph (714) 546 2743
Fax 1 - 714 - 546 2749

U.K. & EUROPE

Music Exchange,
Unit 2,
Ringway Trading Estate,
Shadow Moss Road,
Wythenshawe,
Manchester M22 6LX,
Ph (061) 436 5110

I.S.B.N.   **0 947183 30 2**   **(Progressive Music Theory — Grade Two)**
I.S.B.N.   **0 947183 10 8**   **(Series)**

60 min Stereo Cassette Available

All the examples in Progressive Music Theory Grade Two have been recorded onto a 60 min. stereo cassette.

You can listen to each example and hear how the theory of music relates to its performance. The cassette is an ideal companion to this volume because it brings written music to life, and clearly illustrates the relationship between notes written on the page and how they sound. It also includes recordings of all the aural test examples in the back of this book, which is an invaluable aid for ear training.

Available from all good music stores, or direct from the addresses below.

U.S.A. - $9.99 (Ca. residents add tax)
Koala Publications Inc.
3001 Redhill Ave.
Bldg. 2 # 221
Costa Mesa
CA. 92626
Ph. (714) 546 2743

U.K. - £ 5.95 (includes V.A.T.)
Music Land
9 St. Petersgate,
Stockport.
Cheshire SK1 1EB
Ph (061) 474 7104

AUSTRALIA - $13.99
Koala Publications
4 Captain Cook Ave
Flinders Park
South Australia 5025
Ph (08) 268 1750

If ordering direct please add $1.00 or 50p. postage per item.
Payment by cheque or money order.

Introduction

Progressive Music Theory Grade 2 has been designed as an introduction to music theory, and assumes that you have studied and understood all the material in **Progressive Music Theory Grade 1**. It incorporates the following special features: —

* co-ordinating cassette available which allows you to listen to what you're studying;

* suitable for students of any musical instrument or style;

* structured in a carefully graded, lesson-by-lesson approach;

* questions at the end of every lesson, with fully explained answers at the back of the book;

* presented progressively and logically, with easy to understand wording and definitions;

* topics covered include:

> - A and D Major Scales and Chords
>
> - Intervals
>
> - Harmonic Minor Scales
>
> - Relative Majors and Minors
>
> - Triplets
>
> - $\frac{6}{8}$ Time
>
> - Musical Form
>
> - Lyrics
>
> - Terms and Signs

* contains glossary of musical terms;

* Aural Training Section helps develop your listening ability.

* popular, well-known tunes are used throughout to illustrate the information given. A list of these pieces can be found in the index.

Contents

Lesson 1   **page 6**
Review of Major Scales 6
The G Major Scale 6
The D Major Scale 7
The D Chord 8
Tonic Triad of D 9
The A Major Scale 9
The A Chord 10
Tonic Triad of A 11
Key Signatures 11
Scales over Two Octaves 12
Questions 12

Lesson 2   **page 15**
Minor Scales 15
Harmonic Minor Scales 15
The A Harmonic Minor Scale 15
Sequence of Intervals 16
The A Minor Chord 16
Abbreviations for A Minor 17
Minor Keys 17
Relative Major and Minor Keys 17
Relative Major and Minor Scales 18
Relationship between A Harmonic
    Minor Scale and C Major Scale 19
Questions 19

Lesson 3   **page 21**
Intervals Measured in Semitones 21
Major, Minor and Perfect Intervals.....22
How to Recognise Intervals by Ear ...24
How to Recognise Intervals
    from Music 29
Writing Intervals above Given Notes .30
Writing Minor Intervals 31
Questions 32

Lesson 4   **page 33**
The E Harmonic Minor Scale 33
The E Minor Chord 33
The D Harmonic Minor Scale 35
The D Minor Chord 35
Relationship between Keynotes of
    Relative Majors and Minors 36
Summary of Relative Majors
    and Minors 37
Questions 38

Lesson 5   **page 41**
The Dotted Eighth Note 41
Triplets 42
The Eighth Note Triplet 42
Notes and Rests Summary 43
Questions 44

Lesson 6   **page 45**
The $\frac{6}{8}$ Time Signature....................45
How to Count $\frac{6}{8}$ Time
    Slow Tempo 45
    Fast Tempo 46
Strong Beats in $\frac{6}{8}$ Time 47
Notation of Notes in $\frac{6}{8}$ Time.............47
Notation of Rests in $\frac{6}{8}$ Time 49
Simple Time Signatures 51
Compound Time Signatures 51
Summary of Time Signatures 51
Examples of Slow and Fast $\frac{6}{8}$ 52
Questions 53

Lesson 7   **page 55**
Musical Form 55
Binary Form 55
Ternary Form 56
Song Form 57
Questions 57

Lesson 8   **page 60**
Setting Words to Music 60
Questions 61

Lesson 9   **page 62**
Terms and Signs
    – for Volume 62
    – for Performance 62
    – for Speed................................64
Other Performance Terms 65
Questions 65

Answers to Questions **67**

Aural Training Section **78**

Glossary of Musical Terms ... **83**

General Index **88**

Index to Songs **88**

Lesson 1

Review of Major Scales

A Major scale is a sequence of notes that follows the familiar pattern:

Do   Re   Mi   Fa   So   La   Ti   Do

The order of the intervals between each note always conforms to the following arrangement:

Tone   Tone   Semitone   Tone   Tone   Tone   Semitone

Semitones occur between the third and fourth scale degrees, and between the seventh and eighth scale degrees. All the other intervals are tones.

The first four notes can be grouped together to form a lower tetrachord. The second four notes form an upper tetrachord.

Example 1.   G Major Scale

The semitone intervals are marked with slurs.

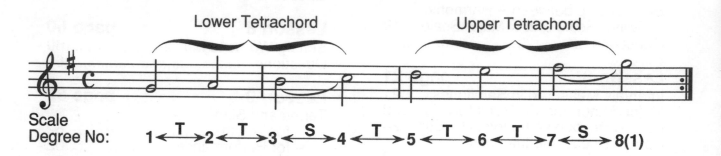

T = Tone
S = Semitone

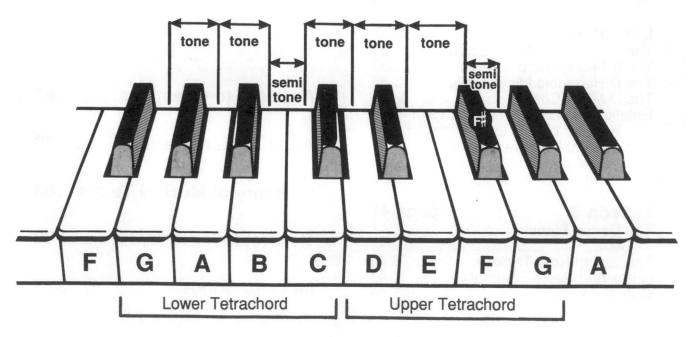

The D Major Scale

The D Major scale contains two sharps, F♯ and C♯.

To create this scale, start on a D note, which is the fifth note of the scale which has one sharp, G Major. Use the same notes as the G Major scale, but sharpen the seventh note (C) of the D Major scale to maintain the pattern of tones and semitones.

Notice that the upper tetrachord of G Major is the same as the lower tetrachord of D Major. The upper tetrachord of D Major is the lower tetrachord of G Major with the second last note sharpened.

Example 2. D Major Scale

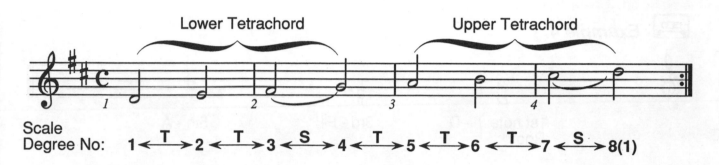

Scale Degree No: 1 ←T→ 2 ←T→ 3 ←S→ 4 ←T→ 5 ←T→ 6 ←T→ 7 ←S→ 8(1)

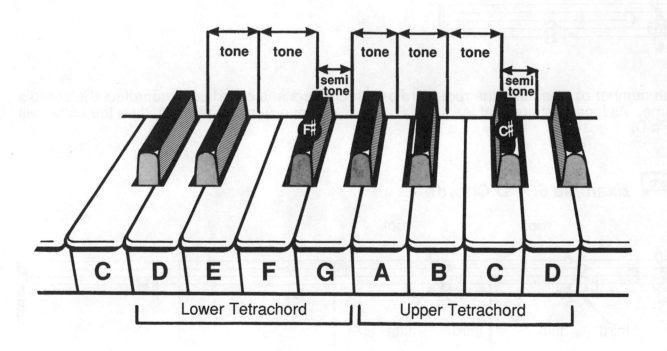

The D Chord

In Progressive Music Theory Book One, Lesson 9, you learnt that a Major chord contains the first, third and fifth notes of the Major scale of the same name. Thus the D chord contains the first, third and fifth notes of the D Major scale. These notes are D, F#, and A.

 *Example 3.*   **D Major Scale**

1st   2nd   3rd   4th   5th   6th   7th   8th(1st)

 *Example 4.*

1st note ⎫ - D   3rd - F#   5th - A
Root   ⎬

 *Example 5.*   **D Chord**

The number of times that the root, third or fifth appears in a chord does not affect the chord's name. As long as there is at least one D, one F# and one A in any position, then the chord will be a D.

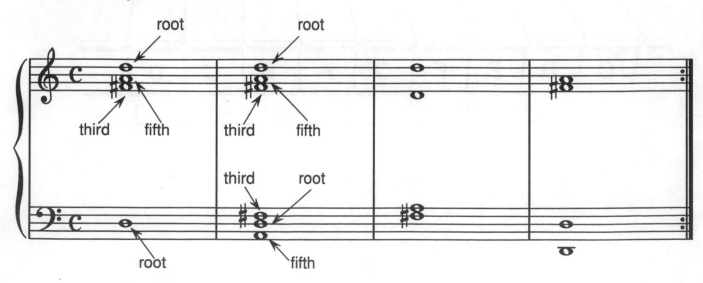 *Example 6.*   **D Chords**

Tonic Triad of D

You have seen in Progressive Music Theory Book 1, page 66, that a TONIC TRIAD is a chord which contains three notes in very specific positions. The notes which a tonic triad contains are:

1 - the root note (also called the tonic), as the lowest note;

2 - a note that is an interval of a third above the root (the third), and

3 - a note that is an interval of a fifth above the root (the fifth).

In the key of D Major the tonic note is D, the third is F♯ and the fifth is A.

The tonic triad can be written in several positions on both the treble and the bass staves. Example 7 shows some of the possibilities.

Example 7. **Tonic Triads of D Major**

The A Major Scale

The A Major scale contains three sharps, F♯, C♯, and G♯.

To create this scale, start on an A note, which is the fifth note of the scale which has two sharps (D Major). Use the same notes as the D Major scale, but sharpen the seventh note (G) of the A Major scale to maintain the pattern of tones and semitones.

Example 8. **A Major Scale**

The sharp sign for the G♯ note is written on top of the treble staff.

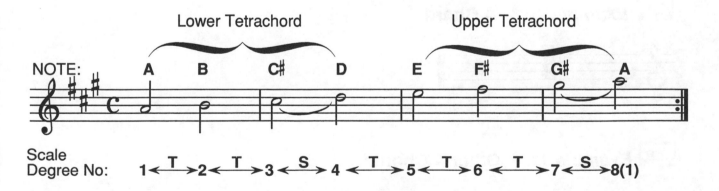

Notice that the upper tetrachord of D Major is the same as the lower tetrachord of A Major. The upper tetrachord of A Major is the lower tetrachord of D Major with the second last note sharpened.

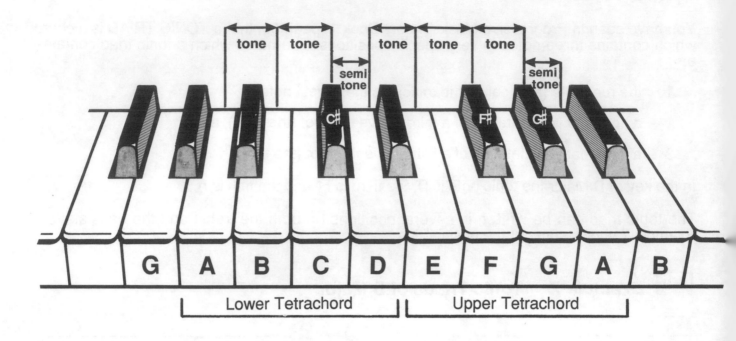

The A Chord

The A chord contains the first, third, and fifth notes of the A Major scale. These notes are A, C♯ and E.

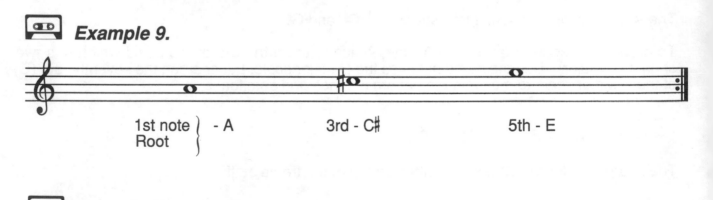

Example 9.

| 1st note ⎱ - A | 3rd - C♯ | 5th - E |
| Root ⎰ | | |

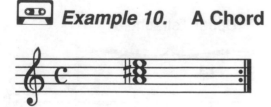

Example 10. **A Chord**

Example 11. **Other A Chords**

Tonic Triad of A

In the key of A Major the tonic note is A, the third is C# and the fifth is E.

Example 12 shows some of the possible ways to write the tonic triad of A Major.

Example 12.   **Tonic Triads of A Major**

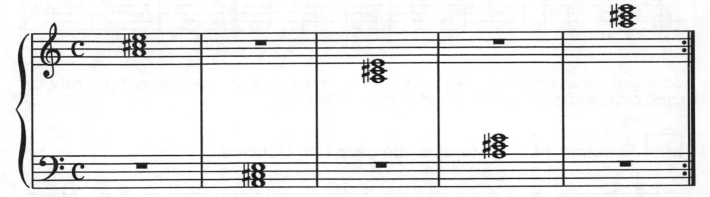

Key Signatures

The key signatures for the five scales you have studied so far are as follows:

C Major   **F Major**

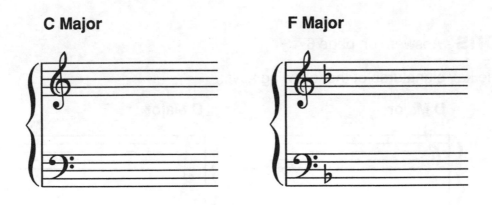

G Major   **D Major**   **A Major**

Scales over Two Octaves

Sometimes it is necessary to write scales over two octaves. To do this, write one octave of the scale, then use the last note of that scale as the starting point for the second octave.

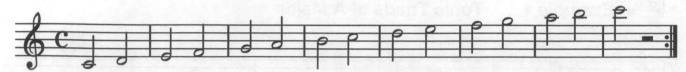 *Example 13.* **C Major Scale over Two Octaves**

When you are writing two-octave scales across both staves, it will look neatest if you make the notes change from one staff to the other around Middle C.

 *Example 14.* **A Major Scale over Two Octaves**

Questions - Answers on page 67.

1. Write the key signatures of the following keys:

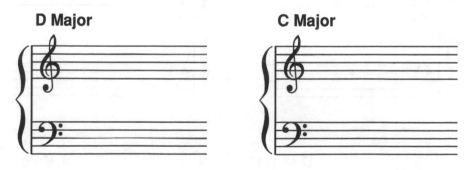

D Major   **C Major**

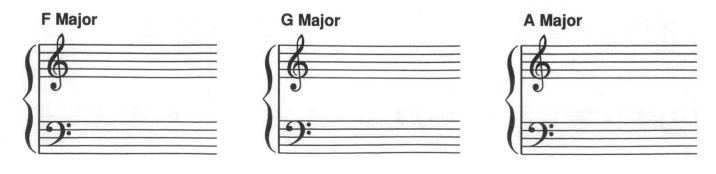

F Major   **G Major**   **A Major**

2. Write one octave ascending in quarter notes of the following scales, using the correct key signature on the staves provided. Mark the semitone intervals with slurs.

A Major

D Major

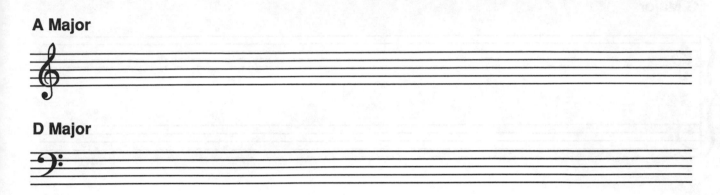

3. Write one octave ascending and descending in half notes of the following scales.

C Major

F Major

4. Give the names of the keys which have the following key signatures, and write a tonic triad for each key on both staves.

5. Name the notes which make up the A chord and the D chord.

6. Write the names of the following chords:

14

7. Write two octaves of the G and D Major scales ascending in half notes on the grand staff.

G Major

D Major

8. Write two octaves of the C Major scale descending in whole notes on the bass staff only.

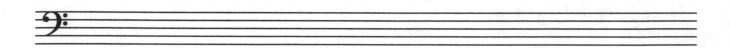

Lesson 2

Minor Scales

There are several different types of Minor scales, such as the Harmonic Minor, Melodic Minor, Natural Minor (also known as the Pure Minor) and Dorian Minor. The only Minor scales you will be studying in this book are HARMONIC Minor Scales.

Harmonic Minor Scales

Just as there are twelve Major scales, each starting on a different note, so are there also twelve Harmonic Minor scales.

The A Harmonic Minor Scale

The A Harmonic Minor scale has the same key signature as C Major - no sharps or flats. Although there is a G# in the scale, the sharp sign is always written in front of the G, as an accidental, not in the key signature.

Example 15.   A Harmonic Minor Scale

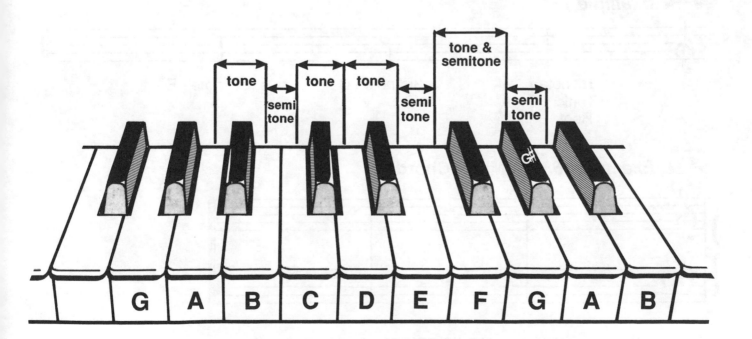

Sequence of Intervals in a Harmonic Minor Scale

The order of tones and semitones in a Harmonic Minor scale is different from that in a Major scale. In a Major scale, semitone intervals occur between the third and fourth notes, and between the seventh and eighth notes. There is a tone interval between each of the other notes.

In a Harmonic Minor scale, semitone intervals occur between the second and third notes, the fifth and sixth notes, and the seventh and eighth notes. A tone interval exists between the other notes except for the sixth and seventh, which are separated by an interval of three semitones (or a tone and a half, or a tone and a semitone).

These patterns are the same for all Major and Harmonic Minor scales. They can be summarised as follows:

Major Scale:

Tone	Tone	Semitone	Tone	Tone	Tone	Semitone

Harmonic Minor Scales:

Tone	Semitone	Tone	Tone	Semitone	Tone-and-a-half	Semitone

The A Minor Chord

The A Minor chord is built by using the first, third and fifth notes from any A Minor scale.

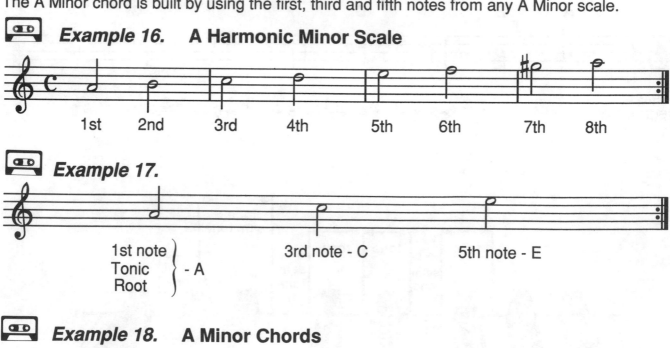

Example 16.   A Harmonic Minor Scale

1st   2nd   3rd   4th   5th   6th   7th   8th

Example 17.

1st note
Tonic   } - A
Root

3rd note - C   5th note - E

Example 18.   A Minor Chords

The chords in Example 18 are TONIC TRIADS of A Minor.

Example 19. **A Minor Chords in Other Positions**

As long as there is at least one A note, one C and one E, the chord will be A Minor.

Abbreviations for A Minor

The most common abbreviations for writing the words "A Minor" are as follows:

Am   **Amin**

Minor Keys

In Lesson 7 of Grade 1 you learnt that when a piece of music mostly contains notes from a certain scale, the piece is said to be in the key that corresponds to that scale. Thus if a piece of music mostly contained notes that are found in the C Major scale, you would say that the piece was in the key of C Major.

When a piece of music contains mostly notes that are found in a Harmonic Minor (or some other kind of Minor) scale, the piece is said to be in a Minor key.

Although there are several different types of Minor scales, there is only one kind of Minor key. Thus, the term "key of A Minor" is used to refer to a piece which uses notes from any of the different A Minor Scales.

Relative Minor and Major Keys

When a Major key and a Minor key have the same key signature they are said to be RELATIVE to each other.

The key signature for C Major is the same as the key signature for A Minor - no sharps or flats. Thus, A Minor is said to be the relative Minor key of C Major. Also, C Major is said to be the relative Major key of A Minor.

In short: **The relative minor key of C Major is A Minor.**
               The relative major key of A Minor is C Major.

When you need to determine the key of a piece of music, keep four things in mind:

1. The key signature (if available) indicates either a Major or a Minor key;

2. The scale from which most of the melody notes are drawn has the same name as the key you are looking for;

3. The last note of the melody is frequently the keynote (tonic);

18

4. The presence of an accidental is often an indication that the piece is written in a Minor key.

Examples 20 and 21 are illustrations of pieces written in the key of A Minor.

Example 20.   **Go Down Moses. Key of A Minor**   Traditional

Example 21.   **Adagio in Am**   J. B. Loeillet

Relative Major and Minor Scales

The key signature for a Major scale is the same as the key signature for its relative Harmonic Minor scale. The key signature for the C Major scale, no sharps or flats, is the same as the key signature for its relative Harmonic Minor Scale, A. So the A Harmonic Minor scale is said to be the relative Harmonic Minor scale of C Major. Also, the C Major scale is said to be the relative Major scale of A Harmonic Minor.

Relationship Between A Harmonic Minor Scale and C Major Scale

Harmonic Minor scales begin on the SIXTH note of their relative Major scales and use the same notes, except that the SEVENTH note of the Harmonic Minor scale is sharpened.

The A Harmonic Minor scale begins on the sixth note of the C Major scale, A. The notes in both scales are the same except for the seventh note of A Harmonic Minor, G, which is sharpened (or raised) by a semitone to become G#.

Example 22.   C Major Scale

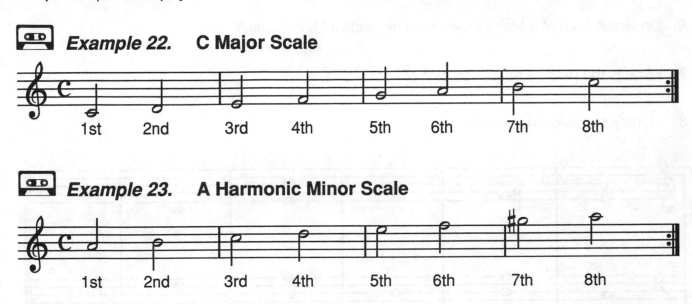

Example 23.   A Harmonic Minor Scale

Questions - Answers on page 68.

1. Write the A Harmonic Minor scale in quarter notes, ascending and descending, over one octave on the treble staff.

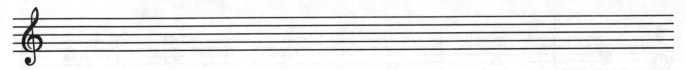

2. Write the scale again in the same way on the bass staff.

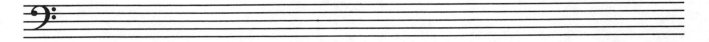

3. Write the A Harmonic Minor scale in half notes, ascending over two octaves, starting on the A below Middle C.

4. Give the order of intervals in a Harmonic Minor scale.

5. Write a tonic triad of A Minor once on each staff.

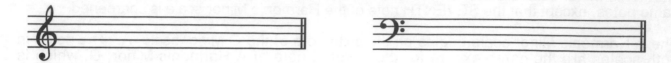

6. On which note of a Major scale does its relative Minor begin?

7. What is the relative Major key of A Minor?

8. Identify the following chords:

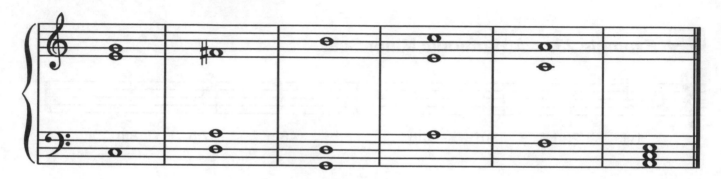

9. Name the following intervals:

Lesson 3

Intervals

In Lesson 8 of Book 1 you were introduced to the following intervals.

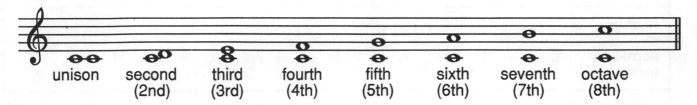

| unison | second (2nd) | third (3rd) | fourth (4th) | fifth (5th) | sixth (6th) | seventh (7th) | octave (8th) |

This lesson shows you some more intervals, and tells you how to classify them more accurately.

Intervals Measured in Semitones

On the keyboard diagram below you can see the interval of a fourth is marked between the C and F notes, and between the A and D notes.

The number of semitones between C and F is five, as is the number of semitones between A and D. All intervals of a fourth contain five semitones. If you start on any note on the keyboard and count up or down five semitones, the interval between the first note and the last will be a fourth. To say that two notes are a fourth apart is a short way of saying that there are five semitones between them.

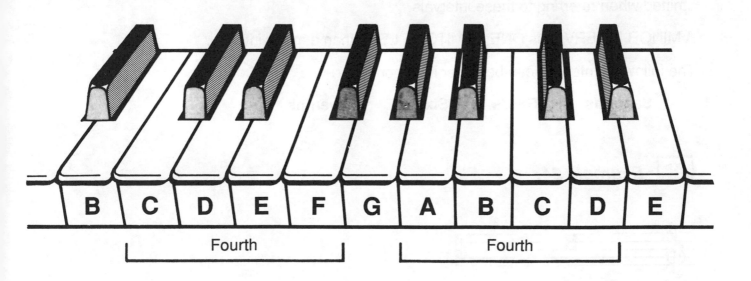

All intervals can be measured by the number of semitones they contain.

The table below records the number of semitones in each of the intervals you have learnt so far.

Interval	unison	second (2nd)	third (3rd)	fourth (4th)	fifth (5th)	sixth (6th)	seventh (7th)	octave (8th)
Number of semi- tones	0	2	4	5	7	9	11	12

You already know how to name intervals by NUMBER, e.g., 2nd, 3rd, 4th and so on. Now you are going to learn to distinguish them by QUALITY as well.

Major, Minor and Perfect Intervals

Where the upper note occurs in the major scale which begins on the lower note, the interval is either MAJOR or PERFECT.

Intervals which can be Major are:

Seconds　　　**Thirds**　　**Sixths**　　　**Sevenths**

Intervals which can be Perfect are:

Fourths　　　**Fifths**　　　**Octaves**

Perfect intervals are so named because they occur in both Major and Minor scales between the tonic and the fourth, fifth or eighth notes of the scale. The term "perfect" is frequently omitted when referring to these intervals.

A MINOR INTERVAL is ONE SEMITONE LESS than a major interval.

The following intervals can be either Major or Minor:

Seconds　　　**Thirds**　　**Sixths**　　　**Sevenths**

 *Example 24.*

Example 24, the interval C to E, is a MAJOR THIRD, because the upper note (E) occurs as the third note of the major scale which begins on the lower note (C).

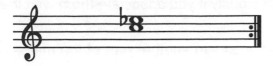

Example 25.

Example 25, the interval C to Eb, is a MINOR THIRD, since Eb is one semitone lower than E, making the interval C to Eb one semitone less than the interval C to E.

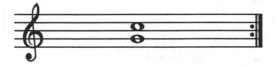

Example 26.

Example 26, is a PERFECT FOURTH, because the upper note (C) is the fourth note of the major scale which begins on the lower note (G).

The following tables summarize the intervals you have just learned.

Intervals which can be Major or Minor	Intervals which can be Perfect
2nd 3rd 6th 7th	4th 5th 8th

Interval	Unison	Minor 2nd	Major 2nd	Minor 3rd	Major 3rd	Perfect 4th
Number of semi-tones	0	1	2	3	4	5

Interval	Perfect 5th	Minor 6th	Major 6th	Minor 7th	Major 7th	Perfect 8th
Number of semi-tones	7	8	9	10	11	12

The interval of six semitones is discussed in a later book.

How to Recognise Intervals by Ear

You can learn to recognise each of the intervals given previously if you associate them with the first and second notes of the following melodies.

An asterisk (*) after a song title indicates that the interval occurs in another part of the melody.

	SONG	
Interval	**Ascending Interval**	**Descending Interval**
Unison	Home on the Range Twinkle, Twinkle Little Star Camptown Races	
Minor 2nd	Just a Closer Walk with Thee Ode to Joy (Beethoven) The Song of the Marines	Joy to the World Beautiful Dreamer All Through the Night
Major 2nd	Brother John (Frère Jacques) Major Scale Goodnight Irene	Mary Had a Little Lamb The First Noel We Three Kings
Minor 3rd	Greensleeves Little Brown Jug Mary Ann	Lightly Row Girls and Boys, Come out to Play For He's a Jolly Good Fellow
Major 3rd	When the Saints go Marchin' In Pop Goes the Weasel Michael Row the Boat	Summertime Goodnight Ladies Beethoven's Fifth Symphony* (3rd and 4th notes)
Perfect 4th	Here Comes the Bride Aura Lee While Shepherds Watched Their Flocks	I've Been Working on the Railroad The Can-Can A Little Night Music (Mozart)
Perfect 5th	Twinkle, Twinkle Little Star* (2nd and 3rd notes) Scarborough Fair* (2nd and 3rd notes) Star Wars Theme* (4th and 5th notes)	Mary Ann* (2nd and 3rd notes) Big Ben* (3rd and 4th notes)
Minor 6th	Go Down Moses Symphony No. 40* (Mozart) (9th and 10th notes) The Liberty Bell (see page 49)	All Things Bright and Beautiful The Blue Bells of Scotland (see page 58, bars 2 and 3)

	SONG	
Interval	Ascending Interval	Descending Interval
Major 6th	Hush Little Baby My Bonnie Lies Over the Ocean	Nobody Knows the Trouble I've Seen Down by the Riverside* (2nd and 3rd notes)
Minor 7th	The Can-Can* (see Example 44)	The Can-Can* (see Example 45)
Major 7th	Irish Folk Song* (see Example 46)	Sharp Turn* (see Example 47)
Octave	The Blue Danube* (see Example 48)	Hot Cross Buns We Wish You A Merry Christmas* (see Example 49)

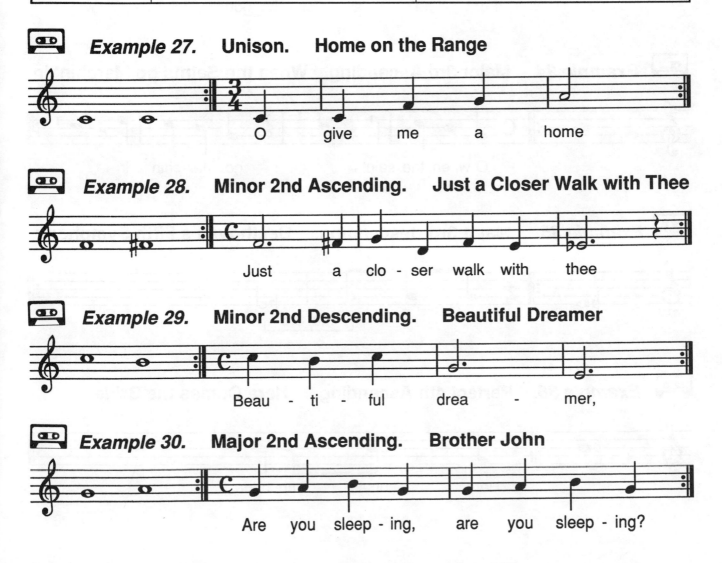

Example 27. **Unison.** **Home on the Range**

O give me a home

Example 28. **Minor 2nd Ascending.** **Just a Closer Walk with Thee**

Just a clo - ser walk with thee

Example 29. **Minor 2nd Descending.** **Beautiful Dreamer**

Beau - ti - ful drea - mer,

Example 30. **Major 2nd Ascending.** **Brother John**

Are you sleep - ing, are you sleep - ing?

Example 31.   **Major 2nd Descending.   Mary Had a Little Lamb**

Ma - ry   had   a   lit - tle   lamb

Example 32.   **Minor 3rd Ascending.   Greensleeves**

A - las,   my   love___   You   do   me wrong

Example 33.   **Minor 3rd Descending.   For He's a Jolly Good Fellow**

For,   he's   a   jol - ly   good   fel - low

Example 34.   **Major 3rd Ascending.   When the Saints go Marchin' In**

O when the saints   go mar-chin' in

Example 35.   **Major 3rd Descending.   Beethoven's Fifth Symphony**

maj 3rd

Example 36.   **Perfect 4th Ascending.   Here Comes the Bride**

Here   comes   the bride

Example 37. Perfect 4th Descending.
I've Been Working on the Railroad

I've been work - ing on the rail - road

Example 38. Perfect 5th Ascending. Twinkle, Twinkle, Little Star

5th

Twin - kle twin - kle lit - tle star

Example 39. Perfect 5th Descending. Mary Ann

5th

All day, all night

Example 40. Minor 6th Ascending. Go Down Moses

Example 41. Minor 6th Descending. All Things Bright and Beautiful

All things bright and beau - ti - ful

Example 42. Major 6th Ascending. My Bonnie Lies Over the Ocean

My bon - nie lies ov - er the o - cean

Example 43. Major 6th Descending.
Nobody Knows the Trouble I've Seen

No - bo - dy knows the trou - ble I've seen

Example 44. Minor 7th Ascending. The Can-Can

m 7th

Example 45. Minor 7th Descending. The Can-Can

m 7th

Example 46. Major 7th Ascending. Irish Folk Song

maj 7th

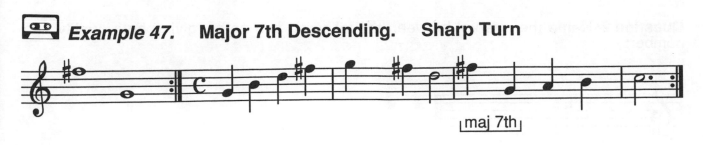

Example 47. **Major 7th Descending.** **Sharp Turn**

maj 7th

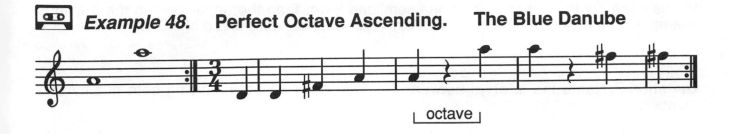

Example 48. **Perfect Octave Ascending.** **The Blue Danube**

octave

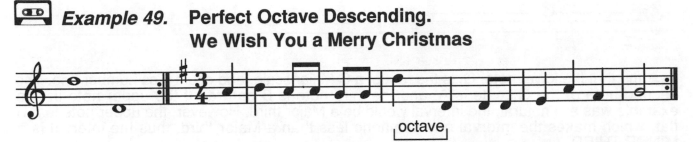

Example 49. **Perfect Octave Descending.**
We Wish You a Merry Christmas

octave

We wish you a mer-ry Christ-mas and a hap-py new year.

How to Recognise Intervals from Reading Music

In Grade 1 you learnt how to name the interval between two written notes by assuming that the lower note was the tonic of a Major scale. Counting that lower note as the number 1, you counted up the scale until you reached the upper note. The number of the upper note gives you the name of the interval.

Question 1: Name the interval between the following two notes, giving both quality and number:

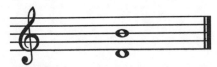

Answer: Assume that the lower note, D, is the root of a D Major scale. Counting D as number one, E is the second note, F♯ is the third, G the fourth, A the fifth, and B the sixth. Thus the interval between D and B is a SIXTH.

We have determined the NUMBER of the interval - it is a sixth. We also need to know its quality - whether it is Major, Minor or Perfect.

If you refer to page 22, you will see that when the upper note occurs in that Major scale which begins on the lower note, the interval can be either Major or Perfect.

In this example, the upper note, B, occurs as the sixth note of the D Major scale, which starts on D, the lower note. Since the only intervals which can be perfect are fourths, fifths and octaves, the interval between D and B is said to be a MAJOR SIXTH.

Question 2: Name the interval between the following two notes, giving both quality and number:

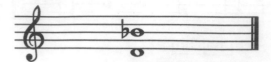

In this example the upper note is one semitone lower than the upper note in the previous example. The previous interval was a Major sixth, so this example is a MINOR SIXTH.

Question 3: Name the interval between the following two notes, giving both quality and number:

Assume that the lower note, G, is the root of a G Major scale, and count it as number one. The second note of the G scale is A, and the third note is B natural. If the upper note in this example was a B natural, the interval would be a Major third. However, the upper note is a B flat, which makes the interval one semitone less than a Major third, thus the interval is a MINOR THIRD.

How to Write Intervals Above Given Notes

To write a note which is a specified interval above a given note, proceed as follows: Let the given note be the root of a Major scale, then count up the degrees of that scale until the required interval is reached.

Question 4: Write the note which is a Perfect fourth above the following note:

Answer: The given note is a C. The note which is a Perfect Fourth above C is the fourth note of the C Major scale. The notes of the C scale are: C, D, E, F, G, A, B, C. The fourth note is F, so the answer is:

Writing Minor Intervals

To write Minor intervals, first find the note which would form a Major interval of the same name, then write the note which is one semitone lower than the first note.

Question 5: Write the note which is a Minor third above the following note:

Answer: First find the note which would form a Major third interval above the given note, A. The note which is a Major third above A is the third note of the A Major scale, which is C♯. Therefore the note which is a Minor third above A is the note which is one semitone lower than C♯. This note is a C NATURAL, or C.

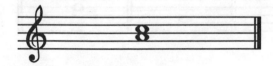

Question 6: Write the note which is a Minor seventh above the following note:

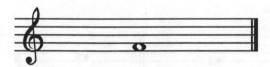

Answer: First find the note which would form a Major Seventh interval above the given note, F. The note which is a Major seventh above F is the seventh note of the F Major scale. The notes of the F Scale are F, G, A, B♭, C, D, E, and F. The seventh note is E. Therefore the note which is a Minor seventh above F is the note which is one semitone lower than E. This note is E♭.

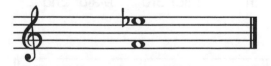

Questions - Answers on page 69.

1. Name the following intervals, giving both quality and number:

2. Write notes above the notes given to form the following intervals:

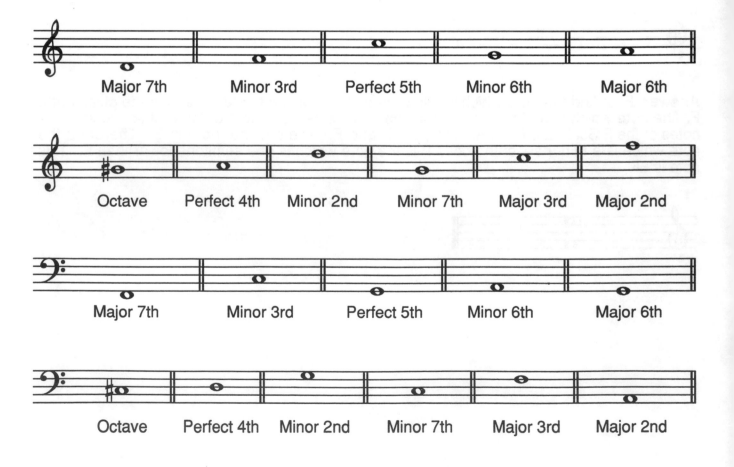

Lesson 4

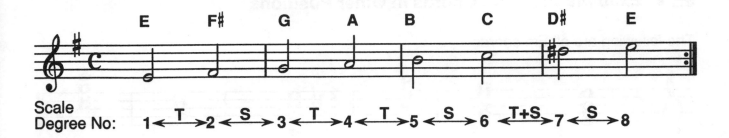

Example 50. **The E Harmonic Minor Scale**

As with all Harmonic Minor scales, the sharp sign for the raised seventh note (in this case D♯) is written on the staff in front of the note, not as part of the key signature.

This scale has one sharp in its key signature, the same as G Major. Therefore E Minor is the relative Minor key of G Major.

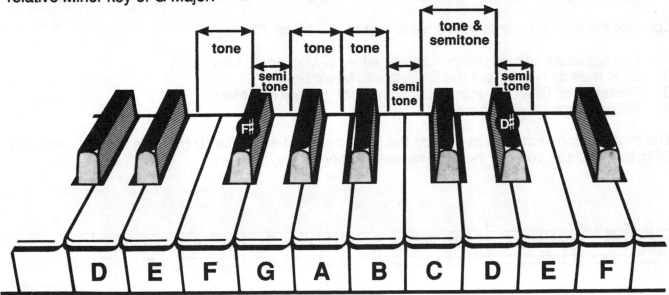

E Minor Chord

The Em chord contains the first, third and fifth notes from the E Harmonic Minor scale.

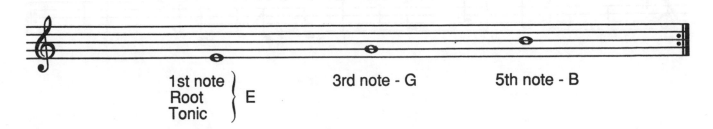

Example 51.

1st note
Root   E
Tonic

3rd note - G   5th note - B

34

 *Example 52.* **Em Chord**

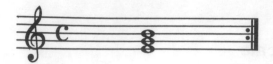

The chord in Example 52 is in the tonic triad position.

 *Example 53.* **Em Chords in Other Positions**

The following are all Em chords:

 *Example 54.* **Greensleeves.** **Key of E Minor** Traditional

Look for the four indicators in this piece that reveal to you the key:

1. Key signature of one sharp indicates either G Major or E Minor;
2. Most melody notes from the E Harmonic Minor Scale;
3. Presence of D♯ as an accidental, not part of the key signature;
4. Melody ends on an E note.

The three melody notes from outside the E Harmonic Minor scale (D naturals in bars 4 and 12, C♯ in bar 14), add color to the tune without altering its key.

📼 *Example 55.* **The D Harmonic Minor Scale**

The raised seventh note in the D Harmonic Minor scale is C#.

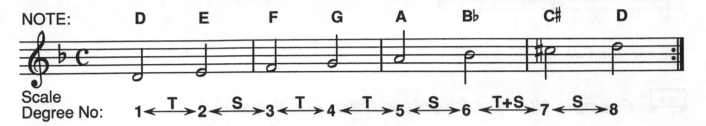

This scale has one flat in its key signature, the same as F major. Therefore, D Minor is the relative Minor key of F Major.

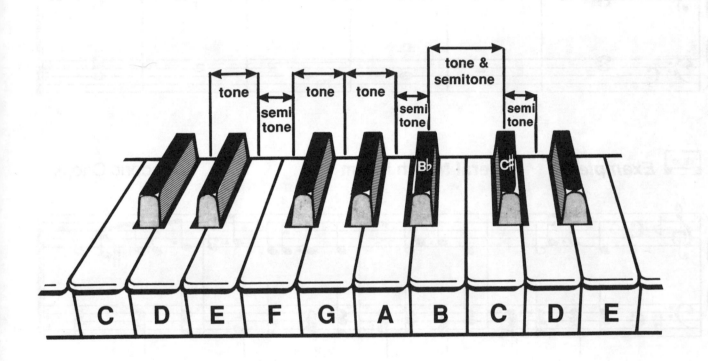

D Minor Chord

The Dm chord contains the first, third and fifth notes from the D Harmonic Minor scale.

📼 *Example 56.*

1st note ⎫
Root ⎬ D   3rd note - F   5th note - A
Tonic ⎭

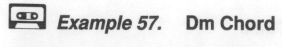

Example 57.   Dm Chord

The chord in Example 57 is in the tonic triad position.

Example 58.   Dm Chords in Other Positions

The following are all Dm chords:

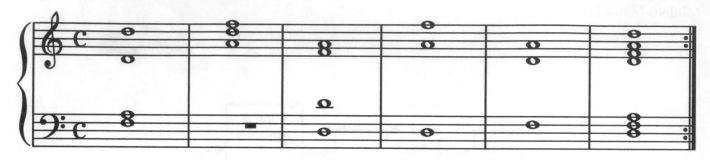

Example 59.   Funeral March in Dm   Frederic Chopin

Relationship Between Keynotes of Relative Majors and Minors

You have seen that the name (or keynote) of a Major scale's relative Minor can be found from the sixth note of the Major scale. For example, the sixth note of the C Major scale is A, which is the name of C Major's relative Minor.

Another way to establish the keynote is to count three semitones below the name of the Major scale. So, to find the name of the relative Minor of C Major, just count three semitones down from C. The third note is A, which is the name of the relative Minor of C.

This pattern also works in reverse. To find the name of a relative Major scale, just count up three semitones from the first note of the Minor scale. E.g. suppose you have the key of E Minor and you want to know the name of the relative Major. Count three semitones up from E and you arrive at G, which is the correct answer.

There are 3 semitones between the keynotes (names) of Relative Major and Minor scales.

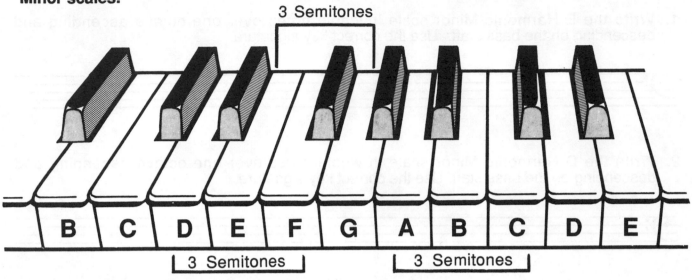

Summary of Relative Majors and Minors

Major Scale or Key	Key Signature	Relative Minor Scale or Key
C		A
G		E
F		D

Questions - Answers on page 70.

1. Write the E Harmonic Minor scale in whole notes over one octave ascending and descending on the bass staff. Use the correct key signature.

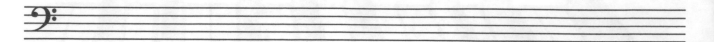

2. Write the D Harmonic Minor scale in whole notes over one octave ascending and descending on the bass staff. Use the correct key signature.

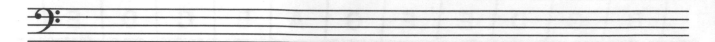

3. Name the keys of the following examples. Some examples have correct key signatures, others do not.

(d)

(e)

4. Identify the following intervals, giving both quality and number:

5. Write tonic triads for the following keys:

Em   **F**   **Dm**   **A**

6. Name the keys of which the following chords are tonic triads:

7. Identify the following chords:

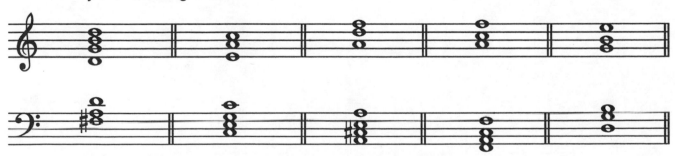

8. Which notes from a Minor scale does a Minor chord contain?

9.   Write notes above the notes given to form the intervals named below:

Perfect 4th   Major 6th   Minor 7th   Minor 2th

Major 3rd   Perfect 5th   Minor 3rd   Major 7th

Lesson 5

The Dotted Eighth Note

A dot placed after a note extends its time value by one half.

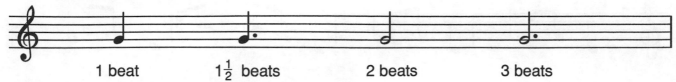

A dot placed after an eighth note lengthen its value to three quarters of a beat (or three sixteenth notes).

A dotted eighth note is frequently accompanied by a sixteenth note.

$\frac{3}{4}$ of a beat + $\frac{1}{4}$ of a beat = 1 beat

How to Count the Dotted Eighth Note

When you count the dotted eighth note, remember that it is equivalent to three sixteenth notes tied together.

📼 *Example 60.*

| Count: | **1** e and **a** | **2** e and **a** | **3** | **4** |
| Written: | **1** e + **a** | **2** e + **a** | **3** | **4** |

It is often easier to feel than to count the dotted eighth-sixteenth note combination.

Example 61.   **Here Comes the Bride**   R. Wagner

Triplets

A TRIPLET is a group of three notes of the same beat value played in the time of two of those notes.

The Eighth Note Triplet

An EIGHTH NOTE TRIPLET is a group of three eighth notes played in the time of two eighth notes.

Example 62.

The numeral and curved line which indicates that the notes are to be played as triplets should be written above or below the beam which connects the three notes, not near the note-heads, so that the curved line will not be mistaken for a slur.

Example 63.   **Amazing Grace**

Notes and Rests

The following table summarizes the notes and rests you have learned.

Note	Value	Rest
𝅝	**Whole Note** 4 Beats	
𝅗𝅥.	**Dotted Half Note** 3 Beats	
𝅗𝅥	**Half Note** 2 Beats	
𝅘𝅥.	**Dotted Quarter Note** $1\frac{1}{2}$ Beats	
𝅘𝅥	**Quarter Note** 1 Beat	
𝅘𝅥𝅮.	**Dotted Eighth Note** $\frac{3}{4}$ of a Beat	
𝅘𝅥𝅮	**Eighth Note** $\frac{1}{2}$ a Beat	
𝅘𝅥𝅮 ³	**Eighth Note Triplet** $\frac{1}{3}$ of a Beat	
𝅘𝅥𝅯	**Sixteenth Note** $\frac{1}{4}$ of a Beat	

44

Questions - Answers on page 71.

1. How many eighth notes are there in
   (a) a whole note;
   (b) a dotted quarter note;
   (c) a dotted half note;
   (d) a quarter note?

2. How many sixteenth notes are there in
   (a) a dotted eighth note;
   (b) a half note;
   (c) a whole note;
   (d) an eighth note?

3. Write the time signature at the beginning of each of the following bars.

4. Name the following chords:

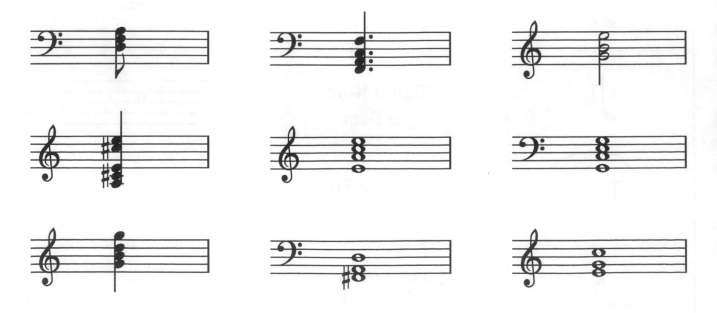

Lesson 6

The Six Eight Time Signature ($\frac{6}{8}$)

You have seen in Lesson 4 of Grade 1 that the number on the top half of a time signature tells you how many beats there are in each bar.

In $\frac{6}{8}$ time, the **6** tells you there are SIX BEATS PER BAR.

The number on the bottom half tells you what kind of beats they are.

In $\frac{6}{8}$ time, the **8** tells you they are EIGHTH NOTE BEATS.

How to Count $\frac{6}{8}$ Time

In $\frac{6}{8}$ time, the notes are organised into two groups of three eighth notes.

Do not mistake the groups of three eighth notes for triplets. In $\frac{6}{8}$ time the three eighth notes are played in the time of three eighth notes. If they were a triplet there would be a figure 3 to indicate this, and the three eighth notes would be played in the time of two eighth notes.

Slow Tempo

If the tempo (or speed) of the piece is slow, it is best to count every beat, starting with 1 and ending with 6 in each bar.

Example 64. Slow $\frac{6}{8}$

Count: **1 2 3 4 5 6   1   2   3   4   5   6**   etc.

A note with a value of two eighth notes can be represented by a quarter note.
A note with a value of three eighth notes can be represented by a dotted quarter note.

Example 65.   **We Three Kings**   Traditional

Fast Tempo

In a fast tempo, the six eighth notes in each bar are too fast to count individually. In this situation you will find it easier to feel and count only TWO beats in each bar: the first eighth note and the fourth eighth note. You can think of the eighth notes as PULSES, instead of beats, and use the term "beat" to mean "a group of three pulses."

This is why the notes in $\frac{6}{8}$ time are grouped in batches of three eighth notes - so that your eye can easily see where the beats fall when the tempo is quick.

When you are counting two beats per bar in $\frac{6}{8}$ time you are counting the eighth notes three at a time. The beat value is then three eighth notes, or a dotted quarter note.

Example 66.

This example illustrates the grouping of eighth note pulses into beats. In fast $\frac{6}{8}$, three eighth note pulses make up one beat.

Example 67.   The Irish Washer Woman   Traditional Irish

Example 68.   Row, Row, Row Your Boat   Traditional

Strong Beats in $\frac{6}{8}$ Time

The strong beats in $\frac{6}{8}$ time fall on the first and the fourth eighth notes, whether the tempo is fast or slow. The first eighth note beat is stronger than the fourth.

📼 *Example 69.*

Here are eight bars of $\frac{6}{8}$ time played on a drum kit in a medium tempo. You will be able to hear each of the six eighth notes, as well as accents on the first and fourth eighth notes, which give this rhythm a feeling of either two beats in the bar (three pulses per beat) or six.

The hi-hat cymbal outlines the six eighth notes of each bar, with the bass drum emphasising the first and the snare drum playing on the fourth.

The hi-hat cymbal is written on top of the bass staff and is indicated by the symbol ♩.

The snare drum is written in the E space, and the bass drum in the A space.
It is more important to listen to the rhythm being played than it is to follow this notation.

Notation of Notes in $\frac{6}{8}$ Time

Rule 1

In $\frac{6}{8}$ time, the notes are organised into two groups of three eighth notes. See Example 64.

Rule 2

A note with a value of two eighth notes can be represented by a quarter note (see Example 65), except where it would cross the third and fourth eighth notes, in which case it should be replaced by two eighth notes tied together.

📼 *Example 70.*

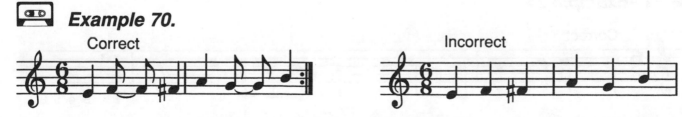

Rule 3

A note with a value of three eighth notes can be represented by a dotted quarter note (see Examples 65 and 66), unless the note would cross the third and fourth eighth notes, in which case it should be replaced by a quarter note and an eighth note tied together.

Example 71.

Rule 4

Notes with values of four and five eighth notes can be represented by combinations of eighth, quarter and dotted quarter notes, provided that no note crosses the third and fourth eighth notes.

Example 72.

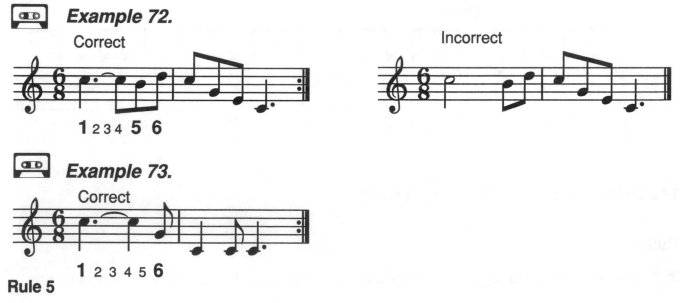

Example 73.

Rule 5

A note with a value of six eighth notes can be represented by a dotted half note.

This is the only situation in $\frac{6}{8}$ time where a single note can be used across the third and fourth eighth notes.

Example 74.

Notation of Rests in $\frac{6}{8}$ Time

Rule 1

An eighth note rest can be used to represent silence with a value of one eighth note.

Example 75. **The Liberty Bell**

John Sousa

Correct

Minor
6th

Rule 2

Silence with a value of two eighth notes can be represented by a quarter note rest (see Example 75, bar 4), but only across the first and second eighth notes, or across the fourth and fifth eighth notes. In any other locations use two eighth note rests.

This rule is slightly different from the rule which applies to quarter notes, which can be used anywhere except across the third and fourth eighth notes.

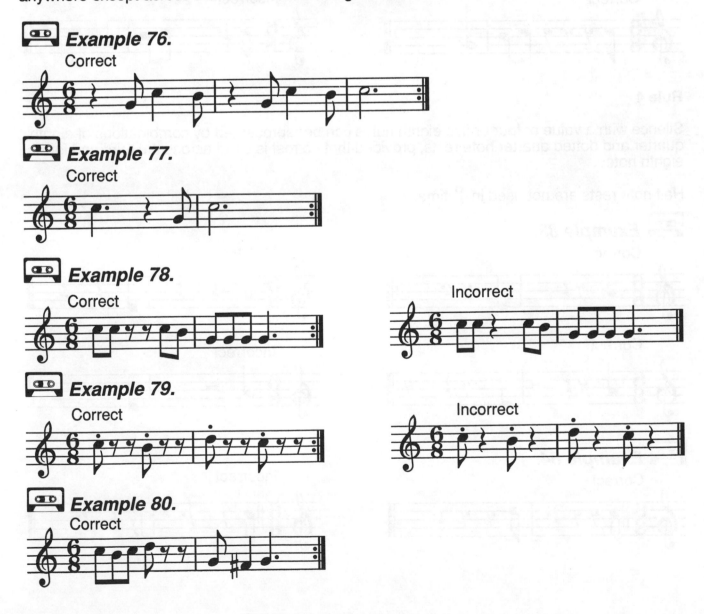

Example 76.

Correct

Example 77.

Correct

Example 78.

Correct   Incorrect

Example 79.

Correct   Incorrect

Example 80.

Correct

50

Rule 3

Silence with a value of three eighth notes can be represented by either:

(a)   a dotted quarter note rest, provided that it is not placed across the third and fourth eighth notes or

(b)   a quarter note rest and an eighth note rest, provided that the quarter note rest does not cross the third and fourth eighth notes.

Example 81.

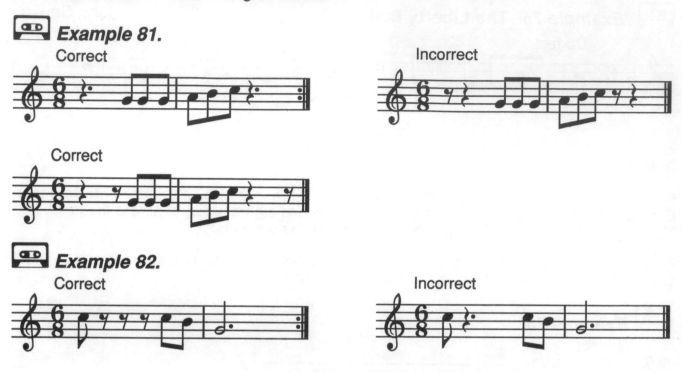

Example 82.

Rule 4

Silence with a value of four or five eighth notes can be represented by combinations of eighth, quarter and dotted quarter note rests, provided that no rest is used across the third and fourth eighth notes.

Half note rests are not used in $\frac{6}{8}$ time.

Example 83.

Example 84.

Rule 5

Silence with a value of six eighth notes (a whole bar of silence) can be represented by a whole note rest.

This is the only situation in $\frac{6}{8}$ time where a rest can be used across the third and fourth eighth notes.

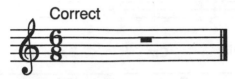

Correct

Simple Time Signatures

The time signatures you have learnt before this lesson - $\frac{2}{4}$, $\frac{3}{4}$, $\frac{4}{4}$ and **C** - are what is known as SIMPLE TIME SIGNATURES, because the beats are counted in quarter notes. You also learnt the terms duple, triple, and quadruple, which mean that there are two, three, and four beats per bar respectively.

Compound Time Signatures

Examples 66 to 68 in fast $\frac{6}{8}$ time show why $\frac{6}{8}$ time is sometimes referred to as a COMPOUND time signature. The six eighth note pulses can be compounded (or made up) into two beats containing three pulses each, giving each beat the value of a dotted quarter note.

Note the difference between a compound time signature and a simple time signature. In a simple time signature the beat value is one quarter note. In a compound time signature the beat value is one DOTTED quarter note.

The tempo of the piece determines whether you count six beats per bar or two. If it is slow, count six beats per bar. If it is fast, count two beats per bar, remembering that each beat contains three pulses.

Because of this method of counting two beats per bar $\frac{6}{8}$ time can be referred to as COMPOUND duple time.

Summary of Time Signatures

Simple Time	Symbol	Beat Value	Beats Per Bar
Simple Duple Time	$\frac{2}{4}$	quarter note	2
Simple Triple Time	$\frac{3}{4}$	quarter note	3
Simple Quadruple Time	$\frac{4}{4}$ or **C**	quarter note	4

Compound Time	Symbol	Beat Value	Beats Per Bar
Compound Duple Time	$\frac{6}{8}$	dotted quarter note	2

52

Example 85.   Slow $\frac{6}{8}$

The Pleasure of Love

Traditional French

※ Refer to page 62 for an explanation of the sign above bar 1.

Example 86.   Fast $\frac{6}{8}$

Mexican Hat Dance

Traditional Mexican

Questions - Answers on page 72.

1. Write the time signature at the beginning of each of the following bars.

2. Fill the following bars with eighth notes on the G line.

3. Use rests to complete the following bars. Refer to page 26 of Progressive Music Theory Grade 1 if you have forgotten how to do this.

54

4.   Explain the difference between simple time and compound time.

5.   Rewrite the following examples, correcting any errors.

Lesson 7

Musical Form

FORM in music refers to the occurrence of patterns or sections of music within a piece.

Binary Form

One of the most common types of form is called BINARY FORM. A piece of music written in binary form will have TWO sections of approximately equal length, usually four or eight bars. The first section can be designated PART A, and the second PART B.

The structure for binary form can be summarized as A B. Example 87 is an example of a song in binary form. Part A lasts from the first note of bar 1 to the last note of bar 8. Part B lasts from the first note of bar 9 to the last note of bar 16.

The beginning of Part A is indicated by the symbol A and Part B by the symbol B .

Example 87.   Row, Row, Row Your Boat   Traditional

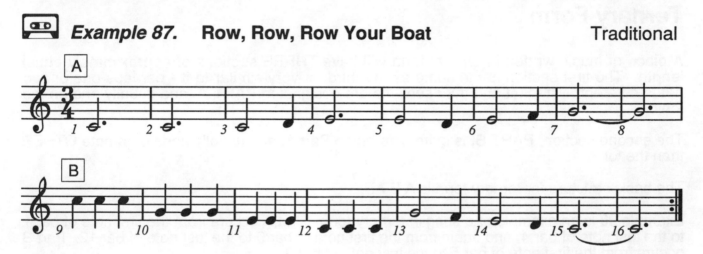

Anacrusis

Sometimes Part A begins with an anacrusis. When this happens, Part B may (but not always) begin within a bar. Notice how the markings for each part are written over the first note of that part.

Example 88. Clementine   Traditional

Other Features of Binary Form

The last note of Part A is usually NOT the tonic. Part B usually ends on the tonic. Example 87 illustrates this, as do Examples 88 and 89.

Example 89.   **Midnight Blue**   Ludwig van Beethoven

Ternary Form

A piece of music written in ternary form will have THREE sections of approximately equal length. The first section is the same as the third, or very similar to it - perhaps one or two notes different. The first and third sections are designated PART A, and usually end on the tonic.

The second section, PART B, is quite different to Part A, and usually ends on a note OTHER than the tonic.

The basic structure for ternary form is A B A.

Example 90 is an example of a song in ternary form. Part A occurs from the first note of bar 1 to the last note of bar 4, and again from the first note of bar 9 to the last note of bar 12. Part B occurs from the first note of bar 5 to the last note of bar 8.

Example 90.   **Twinkle, Twinkle Little Star**   Wolfgang Mozart

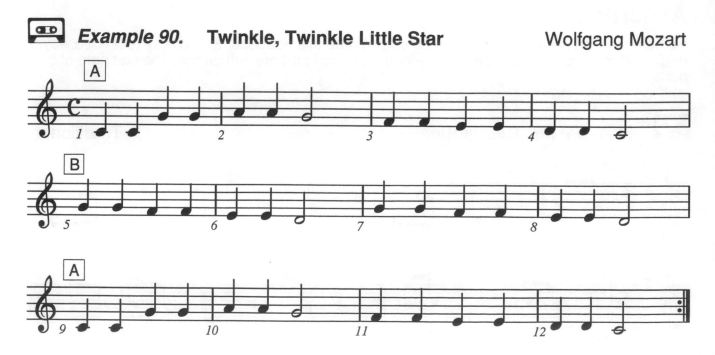

Song Form

If Part A (or a slight variation of it) is repeated before Part B occurs, this is said to be a variation of ternary form call SONG FORM. Song form has the structure of A A B A.

Example 91 is an illustration of ternary form where Part A is repeated with a minor variation before the B section.

Example 91. **O Susanna**

Stephen Foster

Questions - Answers on page 73.

Name the form of the following melodies, and mark each section by writing the letter A or B over the first note of each section. If the melody is ternary, state also whether it is in song form.

1.

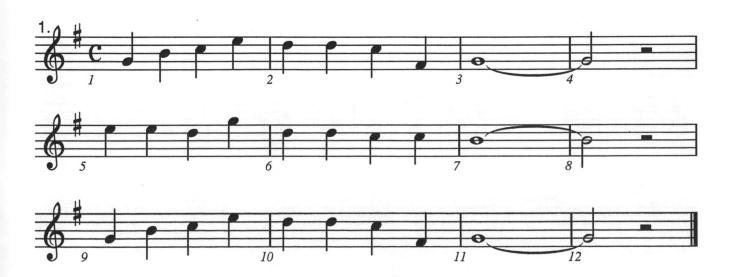

58

2.

3. **The Blue Bells of Scotland** Traditional Scottish

4.

Lesson 8

Setting Words to Music

Words which have music written for them are called LYRICS. When you want to set words to music, it will be useful if you can first divide the words, or syllables of those words, into rhythmic groups.

⌷ *Example 92.*

> With rings on her fingers and bells on her toes,
> She shall have music wherever she goes.

When you read Example 92 aloud, you will notice that certain words and syllables are said with more emphasis or accent than others. For example, the word "with" is less accented than the word "rings". Also, within the word "fingers", the first syllable "fin -", is stronger than the second syllable "- gers". Using hyphens to divide those words with more than one syllable makes the verse look like this:

> With rings on her fin-gers and bells on her toes,
> She shall have mu-sic wher-ev-er she goes.

If you write an accent sign (>) above each accented syllable, the verse will appear as follows:

>   >   >   >   >
> With rings on her fin-gers and bells on her toes,
> >   >   >   >
> She shall have mu-sic wher-ev-er she goes.

Finally, you can put a bar line in front of every accent.

> | > | > | > | >
> With | rings on her | fin-gers and | bells on her | toes,
> >   >   >   >
> | She shall have | mu-sic wher - | ev-er she | goes.

Notice that the first word, "with", is unaccented, which indicates that when the music is written for these lyrics it will begin with an anacrusis. Also, there are three syllables in most of the bars, which suggests that the music should be in $\frac{3}{4}$ time.

It is not necessary to have the same number of syllables in each bar. Example 93 is one possibility of a melody that goes with these words.

⌷ *Example 93.* **Rings on Her Fingers**

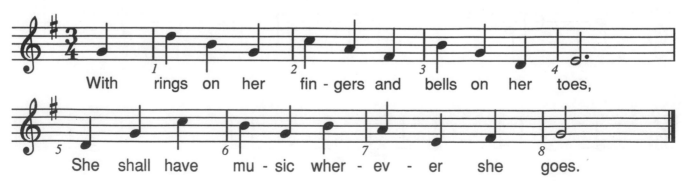

The purpose of this lesson is to show you how to take the first step in setting words to music, so the following examples concentrate on marking accented syllables.

Example 92 featured a grouping pattern of one strong syllable followed by two weak ones. Another common grouping pattern in lyrics is one strong syllable followed by one weak one, which suggests a time signature of $\frac{2}{4}$ or $\frac{4}{4}$. Example 94 illustrates this.

Example 94.

I could sit down here alone
And count the oak-trees one by one.

When you place accent signs over the accented syllables and bar lines in front of those syllables, the verse looks like this:

$$
\left|\overset{>}{\text{I}}\ \text{could}\ \right|\ \overset{>}{\text{sit}}\ \text{down}\ \left|\ \overset{>}{\text{here}}\ \text{a-}\ \right|\ \overset{>}{\text{lone}}
$$

$$
\text{And}\ \left|\ \overset{>}{\text{count}}\ \text{the}\ \right|\ \overset{>}{\text{oak}}\text{-trees}\ \left|\ \overset{>}{\text{one}}\ \text{by}\ \right|\ \overset{>}{\text{one.}}
$$

Questions - Answers on page 76.

In the following two line lyrics, place hyphens between those words that have more than one syllable, and bar lines before each accented syllable.

1.   The   passer - by   shall   hear   me   still

      A   boy   that   sings   on   Duncton   Hill.

2.   So   sweet   love   seemed   that   April   morn

      When   first   we   kissed   beside   the   thorn.

3.   Go   to   the   pantry,   open   the   door,

      Take   out   some   food   to   give   to   the   poor.

4.   I   wonder,   bathed   in   love   complete,

      How   love   so   young   could   seem   so   sweet.

5.   O   for   the   joy   and   the   fun   of   the   fair,

      But   how   can   I   go   if   I've   nothing   to   wear?

6.   A   poor   life   this   if,   full   of   care,

      We   have   no   time   to   stand   and   stare.

Lesson 9

Terms and Signs

The following are some commonly used signs and terms.

Terms and Signs Relating to Volume

	Italian Word	English Translation
pp	**pianissimo**	very softly
mp	**mezzo piano**	moderately softly
mf	**mezzo forte**	moderately loud
ff	**fortissimo**	very loud

Terms and Signs Relating to Performance

Da Capo al Fine

DA CAPO AL FINE (or D.C. AL FINE) means play from the beginning to the word "fine" (finish).

Example 95.

The Segno

𝄋 This symbol is called a SEGNO, which means sign. It is a place marker.
DAL SEGNO (or D.S. AL SEGNO) means go back to the sign (which occurs earlier in the piece.)
DAL SEGNO AL FINE means go back to the sign and play to the word fine.

Example 96.   The Wedding Waltz

Andrew Scott

(See also example 85 on page 52.)

The Fermata

This symbol is called a FERMATA which means pause.

It means sustain the note for as long as you feel it is effective.

Example 97.   For He's a Jolly Good Fellow   Traditional

Mezzo Staccato

Written   Played

When notes have both dots and a curved line drawn under or over them, it indicates that they are to be played MEZZO STACCATO, which means slightly detached. Ordinary staccato means that you hold the note for half its written value, mezzo staccato means that you hold it for THREE QUARTERS of its written value.

Example 98.

The Repeat Sign

Repeat dots are written in the 2nd and 3rd spaces of a staff. Dots on the LEFT of an end barline indicate that you play the piece again from the beginning, or from a pair of dots placed on the RIGHT of an end barline.

Play bars 1 to 4, then repeat from the beginning.

Play bars 1 to 4, then repeat bars 3 and 4.

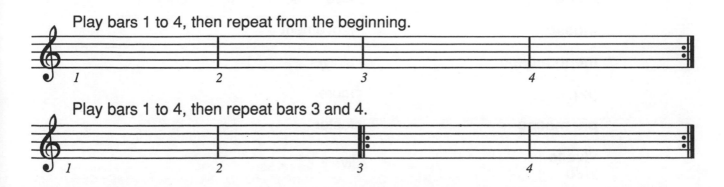

64

Accent Signs

> ∧ These symbols are called ACCENT SIGNS, and tell you to play the note more forcefully than other notes in the same passage. This sign, > , can be placed either above or below the note, near the note-head, whereas this one, ∧ , is always placed above the note.

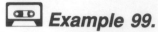 *Example 99.*

The Tenuto Sign

The TENUTO SIGN is a kind of accent sign that tells you to sustain the note for a little longer than is written. The note is accentuated by "stretching" it a little. Tenuto signs are always placed as close as possible to the note-head.

 *Example 100.*   **Habanera**   Georges Bizet

Terms Relating to Speed

Italian Word	English Translation
allegretto	moderately fast
allargando	becoming broader, slowing down
largo	broadly
lento	slowly
meno	less
mosso	movement
meno mosso	slower
piu	more
piu mosso	faster
vivace } vivo	lively

Other Performance Terms

Italian Word	English Translation
cantabile	in a singing style
leggiero	lightly
maestoso	majestically
poco	a little
sempre	always
senza	without
sostenuto	sustained

Questions - Answers on page 76.

1. Give the meaning of each of the following terms:

> vivace
>
> allargando
>
> lento
>
> leggiero
>
> maestoso
>
> meno mosso
>
> senza
>
> diminuendo
>
> mezzo staccato
>
> sostenuto

2. Give the Italian and English names of the signs in the following bars and explain their effects:

(a)

(b)

3. Arrange the right hand column so that the correct meaning is opposite each term.

pianissimo	broadly
mezzo piano	slowly
fortissimo	movement
largo	very softly
lento	moderately softly
meno	in a singing style
mosso	very loud
meno mosso	lively
piu	without
piu mosso	sustained
vivo	slower
cantabile	less
maestoso	always
poco	a little
sempre	majestically
senza	more
sostenuto	faster

4. Add to the following score the signs or terms that are listed below:

(a) the key signature for D Minor;
(b) the time signature;
(c) the term which means that the melody is to be played broadly;
(d) the sign which tells you to increase the volume between bars 1 and 4;
(e) the sign which tells you to pause on the note in bar 6;
(f) the term which tells you to return to the original speed;
(g) the sign which indicates that the notes in bar 5 should be played slightly detached;
(h) the sign that tells you to repeat the piece from the beginning.

Answers

Lesson 1

5. A Chord - A, C#, E.

    D Chord - D, F#, A.

6.

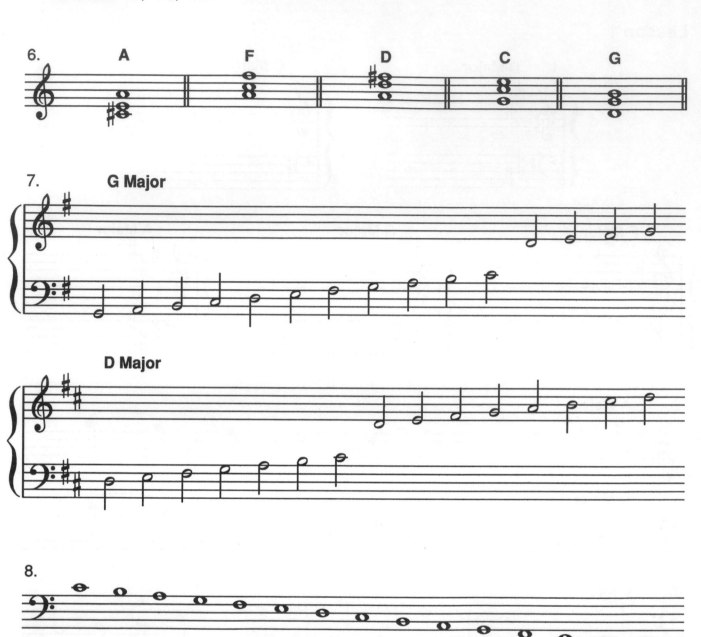

7. **G Major**

    D Major

8.

Lesson 2

1.

2.

3.

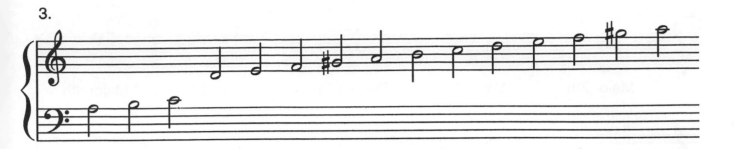

4.   Tone, semitone, tone, tone, semitone, 3 semitones, semitone.

5.

6.   A minor scale begins on the sixth note of its relative Major.

7.   C Major is the relative Major key of A Minor.

8.

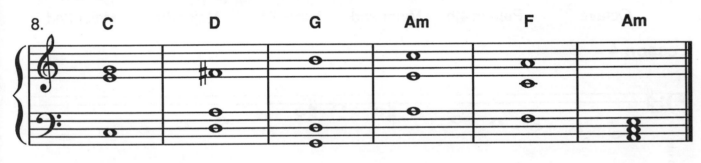

9.

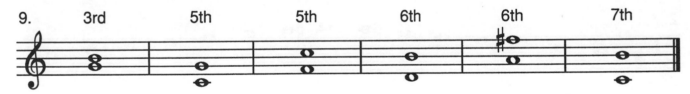

Lesson 3

1.

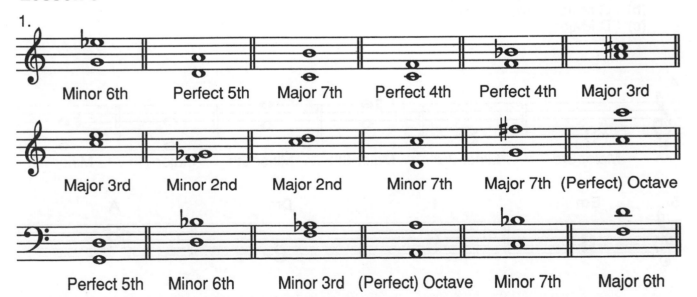

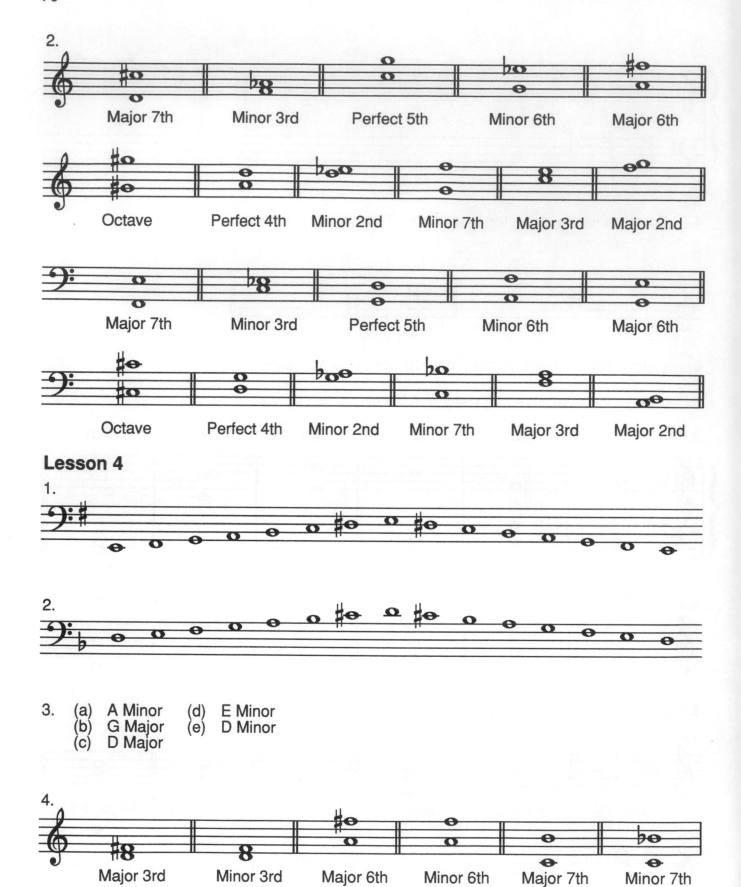

2.

Major 7th   Minor 3rd   Perfect 5th   Minor 6th   Major 6th

Octave   Perfect 4th   Minor 2nd   Minor 7th   Major 3rd   Major 2nd

Major 7th   Minor 3rd   Perfect 5th   Minor 6th   Major 6th

Octave   Perfect 4th   Minor 2nd   Minor 7th   Major 3rd   Major 2nd

Lesson 4

1.

2.

3.   (a)   A Minor   (d)   E Minor
     (b)   G Major   (e)   D Minor
     (c)   D Major

4.

Major 3rd   Minor 3rd   Major 6th   Minor 6th   Major 7th   Minor 7th

5.   **Em**   **F**   **Dm**   **A**

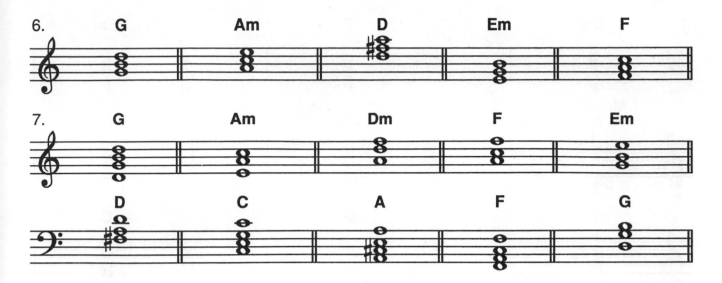

8. A Minor chord contains the first, third, and fifth notes from a Minor scale.

9.

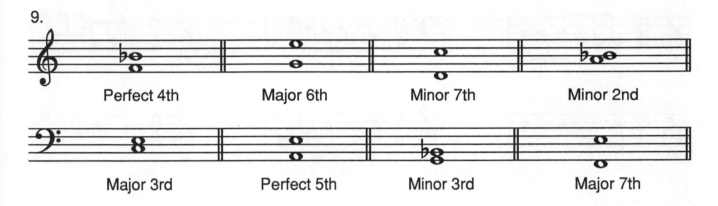

Lesson 5

1. (a) eight   (b) three   (c) six   (d) two

2. (a) three   (b) eight   (c) sixteen   (d) two

3.

Lesson 6

3. (cont).

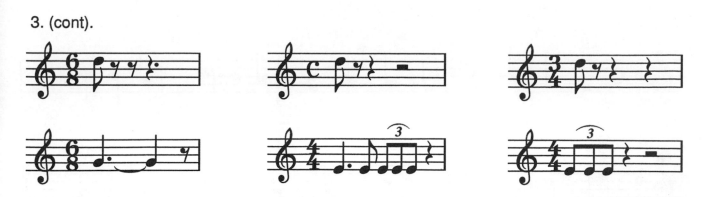

4. In simple time the beat value is one quarter note, in compound time it is one dotted quarter note.

5. (a)

(b)

(c)

Lesson 7

1. Ternary A

74

2. Binary

3. Ternary - Song Form

4. Binary

5. Ternary - Song Form

6. Binary

7. Binary

Lesson 8

1. The | pas - ser - | by shall | hear me | still,

    A | boy that | sings on | Dunc - ton | Hill.

2. So | sweet love | seemed that | Ap - ril | morn

    When | first we | kissed be - | side the | thorn.

3. | Go to the | pan - try, | o - pen the | door,

    | Take out some | food to | give to the | poor.

4. I | wond - er, | bathed in | love com - | plete,

    How | love so | young could | seem so | sweet.

5. | O for the | joy and the | fun of the | fair,

    But | how can I | go if I've | no - thing to | wear?

6. A | poor life | this if, | full of | care,

    We | have no | time to | stand and | stare.

Lesson 9

1. **vivace** - lively

    allargando - becoming broader, slowing down

    lento - slowly

    leggiero - lightly

    maestoso - majestically

    meno mosso - slower

    senza - without

    diminuendo - becoming softer

    mezzo staccato - slightly detached

    sostenuto - sustained

2. (a) Fermata, or pause, means sustain the note for as long as you think it will be effective.

    (b) Mezzo staccato, or slightly detached, means play the notes for three quarter of their written value.

3. **pianissimo** - very softly

   mezzo piano - moderately softly

   fortissimo - very loud

   largo - broadly

   lento - slowly

   meno - less

   mosso - movement

   meno mosso - slower

   piu - more

   piu mosso - faster

   vivo - lively

   cantabile - in a singing style

   maestoso - majestically

   poco - a little

   sempre - always

   senza - without

   sostenuto - sustained

4.

Aural Training Section

Second Grade

The following examples are provided to assist you in developing your ability to hear and analyse music. They are also useful as specimen aural tests.

Where the student is required to sing or hum a phrase, it may be necessary for the teacher to transpose each example down one or two octaves to bring them within comfortable range of the student's voice.

To gain the most benefit from the aural tests, do not look at the written music as you listen to the cassette.

On the cassette, each passage or phrase is played twice.

Rhythm

The student taps or claps a phrase after the teacher has played it twice.

Melody

The student hums or sings a phrase after the examiner has played it twice.

81

Pitch

The teacher plays two notes a major third or a fifth apart simultaneously, and the student hums or sings either of them.

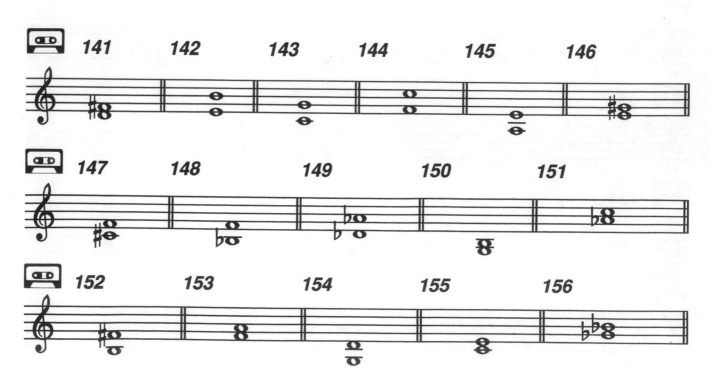

Glossary of Musical Terms

Accent - a sign, $>$, used to indicate a predominant beat.

Accidental - a sign used to show a temporary change in pitch of a note (e.g. sharp ♯ , flat ♭ , double sharp (𝄪) , double flat (♭♭), or natural ♮). The sharps or flats in a key signature are not regarded as accidentals.

Additional Notes - a note not belonging to a given scale. Can be used for improvising against most chords in a progression without sounding out of key.

Ad Lib - to be played at the performer's own discretion.

Allegro - fast and lively.

Anacrusis - a note or notes occurring before the first bar of music (also called "lead-in" or "pick-up" notes).

Andante - an easy walking pace.

Arpeggio - the playing of a chord in single note fashion.

Augmented - term usually applied to the fifth note of a scale or chord and which means that the fifth is raised by one semitone.

Bar - a division of music occurring between two bar lines (also called a "measure").

Bar Line - a vertical line drawn on the staff which divides the music into equal sections called bars.

Bass - the lower regions of pitch in general.

Blues Scale - consists of the 1st, ♭3rd, 4th, 5th, and ♭7th notes of a major scale.

Breve - a note with a value of two semibreves, i.e. eight beats in $\frac{4}{4}$ time.

Chord - a combination of three or more different notes played together.

Chord Progression - a series of chords played as a musical unit (e.g. as in a song).

Chromatic Scale - a scale ascending and descending in semitones.
e.g. C chromatic scale:

ascending: C   C♯   D   D♯   E   F   F♯   G   G♯   A   A♯   B   C

descending: C   B   B♭   A   A♭   G   G♭   F   E   E♭   D   D♭   C

Clef - a sign placed at the beginning of each staff of music which fixes the location of a particular note on the staff, and hence the location of all other notes. e.g.

Treble Clef   **Bass Clef**

Cliches - small musical phrases that are frequently used.

Coda - an ending section of music, signified by the sign ⊕

Common Time - an indication of $\frac{4}{4}$ time - four quarter note beats per bar.

Crotchet - same as quarter note.

D.C. Al Fine - a repeat from the beginning to the word "fine."

Diminished - term usually applied to the fifth note of a scale or chord and which means that the fifth is lowered by one semitone.

Dorian Minor - scale which begins on the second note of a major scale and uses the same notes as that major scale. e.g. D Dorian Minor begins on second note of C Major. Notes are D, E, F, G, A, B, C, D.

Dot - a sign placed after a note indicating that its time value is extended by a half. e.g.

      ♩ = 2 counts   ♩. = 3 counts

Double Bar Line - two vertical lines close together, indicating the end of a piece, or section thereof.

Double Flat - a sign (♭♭) which lowers the pitch of a note by one tone.

Double Sharp = a sign (𝄪) which raises the pitch of a note by one tone.

D.S. Al Fine - a repeat from a sign (indicated thus 𝄋)to the word "fine".

Duration - the time value of each note (see "Rhythm").

Dynamics - the varying degrees of softness (indicated by the term "piano") and loudness (indicated by the term "forte" in music.

Eighth Note - a note with the value of half a beat in ⁴⁄₄ time, indicated thus: ♪ (also called a quaver). The eighth note rest, indicating half a beat of silence is written: 𝄾

Embouchure - A French word that means the position of the lips when playing a wind or brass instrument.

Enharmonic - describes the difference in notation, but not in pitch, of two notes, e.g.

F♯ or G♭

Fermata - a sign ⌢ , used to indicate that a note is held to the player's own discretion (also called "pause sign").

Fill-Ins - a short lead riff played between one line of a lyric and the next, or between one verse and the next.

First and Second Endings - signs used where two different endings occur. On the first time through ending one is played (indicated by the bracket ⌐1. ‾‾‾‾ ; then the progression is repeated and ending two is played (indicated ⌐2. ‾‾‾‾).

Flat - a sign, ♭, used to lower the pitch of a note by one semitone.

Flattened - lowered by one semitone.

Form - the plan or layout of a song, in relation to the sections it contains -
e.g.   Binary form, containing an "A" section and a "B" section (AB).
       Ternary form, containing an "A" section and a "B" section and then a repeat of the "A" section (ABA). The verse/chorus relationship in songs is an example of form.

Forte - loud. Indicated with the sign 𝆑

Half Note - a note with the value of two beats in ⁴⁄₄ time, indicated thus: 𝅗𝅥 (also called a minim). The half note rest, indicating two beats of silence, is written:

Harmonic Minor Scale - type of minor scale which is produced by flattening the third and sixth notes of a major scale. E.g., the C Harmonic Minor scale - D, D, E♭, F, G, A♭, B, C, - is the C Major scale with its third and sixth notes flattened.

Harmony - the simultaneous sounding of two or more different notes.

Improvise - to perform spontaneously: i.e. not from memory or from a written copy.

Interval - the distance between any two notes of different pitches.

Intonation - the art of making each note perfectly in tune.

Key - describes the notes used in a composition in regards to the major or minor scale from which they are taken: e.g. a piece "in the key of C Major" describes the melody, chords, etc. as predominantly consisting of the notes C, D, E, F, G, A and B - i.e. from the C scale.

Keynote - same as tonic, the note after which the key of a piece is named. E.g., in the key of F, the keynote is F.

Key Signature - a sign, placed at the beginning of each stave of music, directly after the clef, to indicate the key of a piece. The sign consists of a certain number of sharps or flats, which represent the sharps or flats found in the scale of the piece's key: e.g.

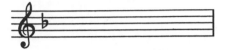

indicates a scale with B♭, which is F Major or D Minor. Therefore the key is F Major or D Minor.

Lead - the playing of single notes, as in a lead solo or melody line.
Leger Lines - small horizontal lines upon which notes are written when their pitch is either above or below the range of the staff, e.g.

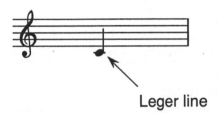

Leger line

Legato - smoothly, well connected.
Lowered - reduced by one semitone.
Lyrics - words that accompany a melody.
Major Pentatonic scale - a 5 tone scale consisting of the 1st, 2nd, 3rd, 5th and 6th notes of a major scale.
Major Scale - a series of eight notes in alphabetical order based on the interval sequence tone - tone - semitone - tone - tone - tone - semitone.
Melodic Minor - type of minor scale which features different notes in its ascending and descending sections. Produced by flattening the third note of a major scale for the ascending section, and using the flattened third, sixth and seventh notes for the descending section.
E.g. the C Melodic Minor Scale,
     Ascending - C, D, E♭, F, G, A, B, C.
     Descending - C, B♭, A♭, G, F, E♭, D, C.
Melody - a succession of notes of varying pitch and duration, and having a recognizable musical shape.
Metronome - a device which indicates the number of beats per minute, and which can be adjusted in accordance to the desired tempo.
e.g. **MM** (Maelzel Metronome) ♩ = 60 - indicates 60 quarter note beats per minute.
Minim - same as half note.
Minor Pentatonic Scale - a 5 tone scale consisting of the 1st, 3rd, 4th, 5th and ♭7th notes of a Harmonic Minor scale.
Mode - a displaced scale: e.g. playing through the C major scale, but starting and finishing on a D note.
Moderato - at a moderate speed.
Modulation - the changing of key within a song (or chord progression).
Natural - a sign (♮) used to cancel out the effect of a sharp or flat. The word is also used to describe the notes A, B, C, D, E, F and G. e.g., "the natural notes".
Natural Minor Scale - the most useful type of minor scale. Produced by flattening the third, sixth and seventh notes of a major scale. E.g., the C Natural Minor scale - C, D, E♭, F, G, A♭, B♭, C - is the C Major scale with flat third, flat sixth, and flat seventh notes.

Octave - the distance between any given note with a set frequency, and another note with exactly double, or half that frequency. Both notes will have the same letter name; e.g.

Passing Note - connects two melody notes which are a third or less apart. A passing note usually occurs on an unaccented beat of the bar.

Phrase - a small group of notes forming a recognizable unit within a melody.

Pitch - the sound produced by a note, determined by the frequency of the vibrations.

Pulse - a type of beat that is usually counted in groups rather than individually. E.g. three eighth note pulses are counted together as one beat in $\frac{6}{8}$ time.

Pure Minor Scale - same as Natural Minor.

Quarter Note - a note with the value of one beat in $\frac{4}{4}$ time, indicated thus, ♩ , (also called a crotchet). The quarter note rest, indicating one beat of silence, is written: ₹

Quaver - same as eighth note.

Raised - increased by one semitone.

Reggae - a Jamaican rhythm featuring an accent on the second and fourth beats (in $\frac{4}{4}$ time).

Relative - a term used to describe the relationship between a major and minor key which share the same key signature: e.g. G major and E minor are relative keys both having only one sharp (F♯) in their key signatures.

Repeat Signs - in music, used to indicate a repeat of a section of music, by means of two dots placed before a double bar line:

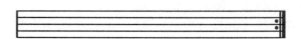

Rest - the notation of an absence of sound in music.

Rhythm - the aspect of music concerned with tempo, duration and accents of notes. Tempo indicates the speed of a piece (fast or slow); duration indicates the time value of each note (quarter note, eighth note, sixteenth note, etc.); and accents indicate which beat is more predominant (in rock, the first and third beats; in reggae, the second and fourth beats).

Riff - a pattern of notes that is repeated throughout a song.

Root Note - the note after which a chord or scale is named (also called "key note")

Root Position - type of chord voicing where the root note is the lowest.

Scale Tone Chords - chords which are constructed from notes within a given scale.

Score -   (a) music written on paper;
                (b) musical soundtrack for motion picture or stage play.

Semibreve - same as whole note.

Semiquaver - same as sixteenth note.

Semitone - the smallest interval used in western music.

Sharp - a sign (♯) used to raise the pitch of a note by one semitone.

Sharpened - raised by one semitone.

Sixteenth Note - a note with the value of a quarter of a beat in $\frac{4}{4}$ time, indicated thus, ♪ , (also called a semiquaver).

The sixteenth note rest, indicating a quarter of a beat of silence, is written: ♯

Slur - a change from one note to another without attacking the second note, indicated by a line drawn over or underneath two or more notes. Indicates that the notes should be played smoothly.
Staccato - to play short and detached. Indicated by a dot placed above or below the note

e.g. ♩ or ♪

Staff - five parallel lines together with four spaces, upon which music is written.
Syncopation - the placing of an accent on a normally unaccented beat: e.g.

Tempo - the speed of a piece.
Tie - a curved line joining two or more notes of the same pitch, where the second note(s) is not played, but its time value is added to that of the first note.

1   2

In example two,
the first note is held
for seven counts.

1 2 3   1 2 3   1 2 3 4 1   2   3   4

Timbre - a quality which distinguishes a note produced on one instrument from the same note produced on any other instrument (also called "tone color".) A given note on the trumpet will sound different (and therefore distinguishable) from the same pitched note on piano, violin, flute, etc. There is usually also a difference in timbre from one instrument to another.
Time signature - a sign at the beginning of a piece which indicates, by means of figures, the number of beats per bar (top figure), and the type of note receiving one beat (bottom figure).
Tonality - aspect of music that considers the key of a piece.
Tonguing - a technique used to punctuate notes, on wind and brass instruments to give them a definite start and finish.
Transposition - the process of changing music from one key to another.
Treble - the upper regions of pitch in general.
Treble Clef - a sign placed at the beginning of the staff to fix the pitch of the notes placed on it. The treble clef (also called "G clef") is placed so that the second line indicates a G note:

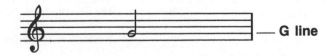

Triplet - a group of three notes played in the same time as two notes of the same kind.
Unison - to sing or play in unison - to sing or play the same notes.
Vibrato - subtle fluctuations in a note's pitch, adding expression to long notes.
Whole Note - a note with the value of four beats in 4/4 time, indicated thus ○ (also called a semibreve). The whole note rest, indicating four beats of silence, is written:

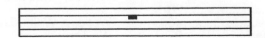

General Index

Accent - in lyrics 60
        - in performance 64
A Chord 10
A Harmonic Minor Scale 15
A Major Scale 9
A Minor - abbreviations for 17
        - chord 16
        - key signature for 17
        - relationship to C Major 19

Binary Form 55

Compound Time 51

D Chord 8
D Harmonic Minor Scale 35
D Major Scale 7
D Minor - chord 35
        - key signature for 37
Duple Time 51

E Harmonic Minor Scale 33
E Minor - chord 33
        - key signature for 37

Form - binary 55
      - song 57
      - ternary 56

G Major Scale 6

Intervals - measured in semitones 21
        - Major 22
        - Minor 22
        - number of 21
        - perfect 22
        - quality of 22

Keynotes - relationship between
          relative Majors and Minors 36
Key Signatures 17

Lyrics 60

Minor - intervals 21
       - keys 17
       - scales..15

Pulse 46, 47, 51

Quadruple time 51

Relative Major and Minor 17, 36, 37

Scales - Harmonic Minor 15
        - over 2 octaves 12
        - Major 6
        - sequence of intervals in 16
Simple time signatures 51
$\frac{6}{8}$ time signature
        - counting fast 46
        - counting slow 45
        - notation of notes in 47
        - notation of rests in 49

Table - of key signatures 11, 37
       - of notes and rests 43
       - of time signatures 51
Tetrachord 6
Tonic Triad - definition of 9
Triplet 42
Triple Time 51

Index to Songs

Adagio 18
All Things Bright and Beautiful 27
Amazing Grace 42

Beautiful Dreamer 25
Blue Danube, The 29
Brother John...25

Can-Can, The 28
Clementine 55

For He's a Jolly Good Fellow 26, 63
Funeral March 60

Go Down Moses 18, 27
Greensleeves 26, 34

Habanera 64
Here Comes the Bride 26, 40
Home on the Range 25

Irish Folk Song 28
Irish Washerwoman, The 46
I've Been Working on the Railroad 27

Just a Closer Walk with Thee 25

Liberty Bell, The 49

Mary Ann 27
Mary Had a Little Lamb 26
Mexican Hat Dance, The....................................52
Midnight Blue...56
My Bonnie Lies over the Ocean 27

Nobody Knows the Trouble I've Seen 28

O Susanna 57

Pleasure of Love, The 52

Rings on Her Fingers 60
Row, Row, Row Your Boat 46, 55

Symphony # 5 (Beethoven)..............................26

The Blue Bells of Scotland 58
Twinkle, Twinkle Little Star 27, 56, 62

Wedding Waltz, The 62
We Three Kings 45
We Wish You a Merry Christmas 29
When the Saints Go Marchin' In 26

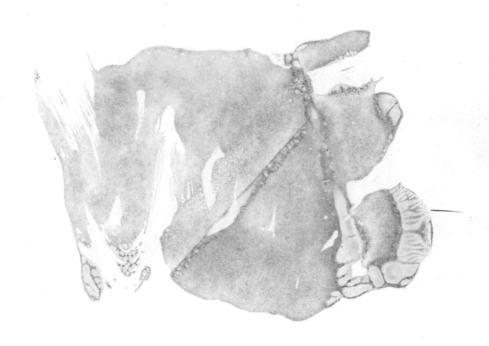

Go where the money is
a guide to understanding and
entering the securities business

Go
where the money is

a guide to understanding and entering
the securities business

LAWRENCE R. ROSEN

1969

Dow Jones-Irwin, Inc.
Homewood, Illinois

Library of Congress Catalog Card No. 68-56878
Printed in the United States of America

Introduction

The securities industry is one of the most dynamic in the world. Consider that the industry has an inventory valuation in excess of $500 billion dollars and over 20 million clients.

Participation in the securities industry brings one into the mainstream of life—every change in technology, the political situation, economics, taxation, and even investor psychology has implications that may be reflected in the values of stocks.

Those who choose to make the securities business their career may look forward to several rewarding aspects of the profession.

1. The nature of a securities representative is that of a financial counsellor and fiduciary. As such, the representative will find himself charged with responsibility to his clients and may expect to receive both respect and recognition from his clients for his professional services.

2. Every representative ultimately finds that a portion of his time is spent teaching—showing people how and why a particular investment program may help achieve their future goals. Thus, the securities profession combines features of the academic world with the dynamics of business.

3. The representative may look forward to receiving the gratitude of his clients through the years for having been instrumental in helping them put their financial houses in the order necessary to: a) educate their children; b) buy their dream house, yacht, or trips abroad; c) enter their own business; d) achieve a degree of financial independence; and e) retire with dignity and comfort.

4. The representative may look forward to receiving personal remuneration consistent with his efforts. The securities business offers unlimited horizons—earnings have no ceiling. Some representatives who develop supervisory and managerial abilities earn in excess of $100,000 per year and many earn between $15,000 and $50,000.

5. The securities business is in a constant state of flux—nothing is static. An individual with an inquisitive and challenging mind will be confronted with an endless number of new situations, developments, and problems. There is never a dull moment in the investment field.

One purpose of this book is to give the reader all the basic information that is necessary to understand the securities business. The material contained herein should be sufficient to help the reader pass the qualification examinations for registration as a registered representative which are administered by the National Association of Securities Dealers, Inc., or the Securities and Exchange Commission.

At the end of each chapter are a series of questions similar to those encountered on the NASD or SEC examinations. It is important to answer correctly at least 95 percent of these questions before continuing to the next chapter. The answers to all end-of-chapter questions are contained within the particular chapter. Reread the pertinent section and find the full explanations for any incorrectly answered questions. If this procedure is followed, one may enter the qualification examination with complete confidence of a successful conclusion.

A second purpose of the book is to give the reader a full background of the investment business, an understanding of which is important to any individual in formulating his own financial future.

The helpful suggestions and criticisms that have been made by several distinguished persons in the financial field have been of enormous assistance to the author. Particular thanks are due to Dr. Eugene Klise, Professor of Economics, Miami University; Dr. Fred Amling, Dean of Business, Rhode Island University; Mr. J. Burleigh, Qualification Examination Department, National Association of Securities Dealers; Mr. Allen Conwill, formerly Director of the Division of Corporate Regulation, Securities and Exchange Commission, and currently a partner in the law firm of Wilkie, Farr, Gallagher, Walton & Fitzgibbon; Mr. Arthur Lipper, President, Arthur Lipper Corporation, Member New York Stock Exchange; Mr. Melvin Lechner, Certified Public Accountant, formerly manager at Arthur Andersen & Co., and currently Assistant Vice President Investors Overseas Services; and Mr. Edward Cowett, General Counsel and Executive Vice President, I.O.S. Ltd. (S.A.), and coauthor of *Blue Sky Law*.

October, 1968   Lawrence R. Rosen

About the author

Lawrence R. Rosen was president and a director of Investors Continental Services, Ltd., a brokerage firm headquartered in New York City, which merged with Investors Planning Corporation of America in the fall of 1967. Both firms are subsidiary corporations of Investors Overseas Services (IOS), a financial giant in the international field, whose sales in 1966 exceeded one billion dollars. IOS owns an international complex of companies in the field of investments, banking, insurance, real estate and sales.

Mr. Rosen, who is presently vice president of IOS, attended Miami University (Ohio) under a Naval ROTC scholarship. He graduated with a Bachelor of Science degree and was elected to membership in Phi Beta Kappa, scholastic honorary; Beta Gamma Sigma, business honorary; and Omicron Delta Kappa, national men's leadership fraternity.

After seeing an extensive amount of the Far East with Uncle Sam as a finance officer on the flagship of the U.S. Seventh Fleet, Mr. Rosen joined IOS in Hong Kong and served as a registered representative in Japan.

Since 1963 Mr. Rosen, a Louisvillian, and his wife, Sue, a native San Franciscan, have made their home on the shores of Lac Léman in Geneva, Switzerland. The Rosens have a French poodle, Bijou, who accompanies them in their pursuit of two principal leisure activities, skiing in the nearby Alps and sailing.

Table of contents

1 Forms of business organization. Stocks and bonds   1

2 Financial statements   29

3 Analysis, economics, monetary and fiscal policy   47

4 Mutual funds and Investment Company Act of 1940   91

5 Securities Act of 1933. Securities Exchange Act of 1934.
  Other securities laws 121

6 SEC Statement of Policy and state laws 143

7 Investment banking 157

8 The over-the-counter market and registered stock exchanges 165

9 National Association of Securities Dealers (NASD) 191

10 Internal Revenue Code 235

General review questions 253

Answers to review questions 259

Bibliography 263

Index 265

1 | Forms of business organization
Stocks and bonds

The securities industry meets three basic needs of a free-enterprise economy. First, it provides a source of capital for the operation and expansion of business; second, it affords an orderly marketplace where people can buy and sell securities; third, it permits the public to share in ownership of the economy.

Consider the securities industry as a source of capital for business. Two individuals, George and John, develop a brand-new process for making widgets. After reviewing their plans, they feel sure that the public will buy widgets, which they can manufacture at a determined cost and sell at a price that will afford a reasonable profit. But to start manufacturing they need to invest approximately $100,000 in equipment and materials. And they must rent and equip a factory.

The problem, like most business problems is one of money. George and John just do not have enough money, nor do their friends and families. They take the problem to an investment banker, who after reviewing all their well-prepared plans decides that the project has merit. Through the investment banker, they arrange to obtain the needed capital—$100,000—by selling ownership in their company to the public in the form of shares of common stock.

The new stockholders have a meeting and elect a board of directors to supervise operation of the Widget Company. The board then elects John as president, with full-time responsibility for running its operations. After a year passes, the board of directors meets to consider the financial results, and it discovers that the company has earned a profit of $15,000 in its first year of operation. The board decides to pay a dividend of $10,000 to the shareholders, and retains $5,000 of the profit in the business for expansion.

The company soon discovers a tremendous market for widgets, but with their present facilities it simply isn't possible to manufacture enough of the product to meet the demand created by widget salesmen. John meets again with the investment banker to consider selling more common stock.

The investment banker explains that selling more stock is one means of raising the

1

additional money that is needed. If more common stock is issued, all the original stockholders can receive rights, which offer them the first opportunity to buy the new shares. Thus, each present stockholder may exercise his rights to purchase the new shares and maintain the same percentage of ownership that he originally had, or he may sell his rights to another person. Any person who buys a right can then exercise it by purchasing some of the new shares. Rights often allow stockholders to buy new stock at less than the current market value of the stock, so they have a value based on the right to buy at the bargain price.

However, the investment banker recommends that John also consider selling preferred stock to raise the needed $100,000. He explains that preferred stock usually calls for a fixed dividend per share. For example, if preferred shares are sold for $100 each, the dividend may be fixed at $6. The present (and original) common stockholders may benefit more by raising new capital through issuance of preferred stock rather than issuance of more common stock, because the Widget Company hopes to earn annually much more than $6 on each $100 received from the sale of the new preferred stock. Thus, the extra earnings over $6 will benefit the present common stockholders.

Preferred stockholders do have certain privileges or preference. The preferred stockholders, though limited to a $6 dividend, must be paid before any dividend can be paid to the common stockholders. And if Widget Company should go out of business the preferred stockholders would be entitled to receive their original $100 per share before any payment to common stockholders.

But the investment banker explains that there is a disadvantage to raising additional capital through issuance of common or preferred stock, since dividends are paid from profit left over *after* Widget Company has paid its federal income taxes. Dividends are not deductible from Widget's federal corporation income tax. If, on the other hand, the needed $100,000 is raised by selling bonds (I O U's), then the interest the Widget Company pays to the bondholders is deductible from taxes which could mean that even more profit is left for common stockholders. However, Widget Company could be forced into receivership or bankruptcy if it failed to pay the required interest to bondholders.

The problems of Widget Company are typical of those faced by companies the world over. The brief example given above serves only to introduce the subsequent detailed explanations of securities and the securities markets.

Proprietorship and partnerships

The Widget Company is a corporation. Often, however, new businesses start in a less complicated fashion, either as a proprietorship or as a partnership.[1]

1/ There are several other forms of business organization, including: syndicates, trusts, joint stock companies, mutual organizations, professional corporations, cooperatives, and real estate investment trusts. However, a discussion of these forms of organization is beyond the scope of this textbook. Readers interested in further details may consult Jules I. Bogen, *The Financial Handbook* (New York: The Ronald Press Company, 1968).

A *proprietorship* is a business owned by one individual. As the owner, he has exclusive control of the firm and is liable for all debts. Both personal and business assets of the owner are subject to attachment by creditors. Compared to a corporation, the proprietorship is relatively unstable, lacks continuity of management, and may have difficulties in financing expansion.

In a *general partnership*, two or more individuals are associated as co-owners of a business, and are jointly and severally (individually) liable for all debts of the firm. Each partner has unlimited liability for the debts of the business.[2] Partnerships are usually formed by a legal document known as "Articles of Co-Partnership" or by a partnership agreement. In most states, the statute of frauds requires a partnership agreement that extends beyond one year to be in writing. Each general partner has the right to commit other partners by his signature alone.

In a *limited partnership*, a general partner manages the business, and other limited partners exercise no management control and have no liability beyond the amount they have invested. Provisions of state law must be followed in order that a limited partnership be valid.[3]

Neither proprietorships nor partnerships issue stock. Stock is and must be issued by corporations. Corporate stock is defined as an interest in the corporate property, all of which is owned by the stockholders of the corporation.

Corporations

A corporation is a legal entity, operating under a charter granted by the state. Chief Justice Marshall defined a corporation as ". . . an artificial being—existing only in contemplation of the law." It is started by at least three people (incorporators) who obtain a charter[4] from the state, granting them, as an entity, certain of the legal powers, rights, and privileges of an individual. A corporation is, in effect, an artificial person. Characteristics of a corporation include the following.

Limited liability. Shareholders are generally not responsible for debts of a corporation, except for the amount of unpaid stock subscriptions. If one invests $5,000 in the stock of a corporation, normally the most one can lose is $5,000 if the corporation goes bankrupt. A creditor usually cannot force the owners of issued and paid-up stock of a corporation to repay a corporate business debt. On the other hand, owners of

2/ Generally, creditors of an insolvent partnership must exhaust business assets before satisfying their claims from the personal assets of partners. Personal creditors of partners have a claim against personal assets of partners prior to creditors of the partnership.

3/ Some items that should be included in a partnership agreement include: (*a*) kind of business to be conducted; (*b*) names of partners and the firm; (*c*) capital contribution of each partner; (*d*) method of dividing profits and losses; (*e*) duration of the partnership contract; (*f*) method of admitting new partners; (*g*) amount of time to be devoted to the business by each partner; (*h*) restrictions on the power of partners to act as general agents for other partners; (*i*) salaries to be paid to partners; (*j*) limitations, if any, on partners, withdrawal of profits; (*k*) procedure to be followed in voluntary dissolution of the partnership; (*l*) procedure to be followed on death or withdrawal of a partner, and provision for continuation of the business by the remaining partners; (*m*) method of valuation of a partner's interest in the event of his withdrawal from the partnership or on his death; and (*n*) provision for life insurance on the lives of partners for the benefit of the other partners.

4/ The charter might authorize the corporation to carry on: (*a*) a profit-making business, (*b*) nonprofit-making activities, or (*c*) public or governmental functions.

proprietorships and general partners have unlimited personal liability for their business debts.

Perpetual existence. Proprietorships and partnerships may cease to exist on the death or resignation of any of the principals involved; these factors do not affect continuity of a corporation's existence. Because a corporation never dies, it may be able to obtain continuous credit for expansion. Its owners may transfer stock to others with few formalities and without disrupting the business of the corporation.

Shareholders' ownership. Corporations are owned by the people who have invested in the stock of the corporation. Corporate stock can be purchased, usually in very small units. Shares may be classified as to the degree of risk assumed and the rights and privileges conferred on the owner.

Taxation. Dividends paid to stockholders of a corporation are generally paid from earnings that have already been subject to a federal (and possibly state) corporate income tax. Thus, most corporate dividends are subject to double taxation—the personal income tax and the corporate income tax. This subject is discussed in more detail in Chapter 10, "The Internal Revenue Code."

Closely-held corporations may elect to be taxed as partnerships if certain requirements are met. These corporations, called tax-option or subchapter-S corporations, do not pay corporation income tax but instead pass on tax liabilities to their stockholders, as in a partnership.

Some partnerships that have corporate characteristics may be determined to be "associations taxable as a corporation." In such cases, the partnership income is taxed twice, as if it were a corporation. Generally, it is presumed that a partnership is an association taxable as a corporation if any two of the following characteristics are present in the partnership.

1. Continuity of life.
2. Centralized management.
3. Free transferability of interests.
4. Liability for debts is limited to the property of the business.

The disadvantages of the corporate form of organization include:

1. Generally more costly to form (legally).
2. Possible double taxation of income.
3. Owners often segregated from management.
4. Extensive reporting to federal and state governments required.

The stockholders elect a board of directors to administer the affairs of the corporation.

There are several classifications of corporations. A *domestic corporation* is created under the laws of a particular state and is known within that state as a domestic corporation of that state. When a corporation transacts business in states other than that in which it is incorporated, it is known as a *foreign corporation* in such other states. A *holding company* is a corporation that owns the securities of another corporation, in most cases with voting control.

Corporate securities

Securities of corporations fall into two main categories—*stocks* and *bonds*. Stocks represent ownership; stockholders own the corporation. Bonds represent a loan that the corporation is obligated to repay (like an I O U). Of course, these are broad definitions, since there are many types of stocks (ownership) and bonds (debts).

Stocks

Every corporation must issue stock. Each issued and outstanding share represents a share of ownership of that corporation. There are several types of capital stock in a corporation. They are generally referred to as common stock or preferred stock.

Stockholder privileges. Stockholders of a corporation have certain privileges, including the right to:
1. Have a stock certificate.
2. Vote for directors and other important corporate matters.
3. Receive declared dividends.
4. Subscribe to additional shares in the future under certain conditions.
5. Transfer ownership.
6. Share in the proceeds of liquidation of the corporation.
7. Inspect the corporate records within reasonable limitations.

A stockholder is entitled to a stock certificate, which physically evidences ownership of a specified number of shares of the corporation's stock. The certificate shows:
1. The name of the issuer and the place of incorporation.
2. The number of shares authorized; the class of stock, if there is more than one class; and whether the stock is common or preferred.
3. The name, address, and number of shares of the registered holder.
4. The signatures (actual or facsimile) of the corporate officers authorized to sign the certificate.
5. In some cases, the names of the transfer agent and registrar.

When a purchase is made, the *transfer agent* of the company records in the corporation's stock record books the number of shares and the name of the new owner. The certificate of the former owner is canceled, and a new certificate is issued. The *registrar* is responsible for checking the transaction—that is, for making certain that the number of new shares issued is the same as the number of old shares canceled. After registration, the new certificates are sent to the stockholders. The registrar sees that all stock issued is valid and in compliance with the state charter under which the corporation operates.

For convenience in handling, many stock certificates are registered in *a street name* or in the name of a nominee rather than in the name of the actual owner. Stock in street name is stock in the name of the investment broker. Stock in nominee name is registered generally for convenience in the name of a person other than the owner or broker.

Ownership of common stock usually entitles the stockholder to vote at the stockholders' meeting on issues that affect fundamental policies of the corporation, including the election of directors of the corporation, who will then set management policies and select the officers and executives to carry out, or execute, the policies. Voting privileges fall into two categories—regular and cumulative.

In regular, noncumulative, or statutory voting, common stock ordinarily has one vote per share. *Noncumulative* voting enables a person or group that controls more than 50 percent of the outstanding voting shares to elect 100 percent of the directors. The owner of 100 shares of common stock would be entitled to 100 votes at a stockholders' meeting.

The stockholder has the right to attend the annual or any special meeting to vote his shares in person. If he cannot attend the stockholders' meeting, he still can vote by proxy. *A proxy* is a person to whom the stockholder gives a written authorization, like a power of attorney, so that the proxy may vote in the owner's absence at the stockholders' meeting. The authorization may require the proxy to vote either in a specific way or at his discretion.

Cumulative voting, a method of voting for corporate directors, enables the stockholder to multiply the number of his shares (e.g., 10) by the number of directorships being voted on (e.g., 12), and cast, if he chooses, the entire total (e.g., 120) for one director or a selected group of directors. A 10-share stockholder normally casts 10 votes for each of, say, 12 nominees for the board of directors. Without cumulative voting, these votes (120 votes altogether) would be divided 10 for (or against) each nominee. With cumulative voting, he may cast the entire 120 votes at one time in any manner he chooses. Cumulative voting allows minority stockholders to obtain representation on the board of directors, whereas in noncumulative voting a bare majority of the stockholders can prevent the minority from electing any directors. It is for this reason that cumulative voting is now required by law in some states. Corporate management normally selects in advance the directors to be voted on and recommends that shareholders vote accordingly.

If shareholders become dissatisfied with the existing corporate management, they may seek a change through a proxy fight, which occurs when the dissident group competes for the stockholders' votes. Management has an advantage in such a fight, since the corporation pays for its proxy solicitations while the competing group must pay their own expenses, unless they are successful in their proxy fight.

Some companies issue more than one class of common stock. The holders of a particular class of common stock may be limited in voting privileges, participation in dividends, or rights in liquidation of the company. However, each stock certificate spells out the rights and privileges of that particular stock issue. Such *classified common stock* is often divided into two classes—class A (nonvoting with first rights to dividends) and class B (voting).

Stockholders are entitled to dividends when declared. Dividends are payments determined by the board of directors of a company to be distributed pro rata (in proportion) among the shares of stock outstanding. Sometimes, a company will pay a dividend out of past earnings, even if it is not currently operating at a profit. For preferred stocks, the dividend is usually a fixed amount. On common stocks, the dividend varies with the performance of the company and the amount of cash available for distribution. The dividend may be omitted if business is poor or if the directors decide it is wiser to retain earnings in the corporation for expansion or for investment in improving facilities of plant and equipment.

There are three types of dividends—cash, property, and stock. Cash and property dividends are subject to income tax; stock dividends are not. Stock dividends are used by shareholders to adjust their cost basis (amount invested or paid for each share owned). *Cash dividends* are the most usual method of distribution and are expressed as so many dollars per share. Thus, an investor who owns 100 shares of ABC Company, which declares a $2 annual dividend, will receive $200. Rapidly growing companies may not wish to give up cash from the business to pay dividends and may issue a *stock dividend*. These are often expressed in percentages. For example, a 5 percent stock dividend would mean 5 new shares to the holder of 100 ABC Company shares. A 100 percent stock dividend is also termed a stock split. *Property dividends* rarely occur. These could take the form of bonds, preferred stock, stock of other companies (usually subsidiaries), or merchandise.

The common stockholder in some states or by virtue of the corporate charter has the common law right to participate in new stock offerings. Unless this right has been waived in the original charter, or by a subsequent vote of the common stockholders, the common stockholder has a *preemptive right* to purchase his pro rata shares in all new stock being offered for sale by the corporation *before* the stock is offered to the public. The preemptive stock right is intended to protect the stockholder's proportionate share of the voting power, the existing retained earnings account, and future earnings. Stockholders receive one right for each share of stock owned. As the new stock is usually offered at a price *below* current market price, rights ordinarily have a market value and can be actively traded. The life or duration of a right is usually a short period of time.

The theoretical value of a right may be calculated. Assume that a share is currently selling for $100, and that the new shares may be subscribed to for $89. Assume that 10 rights are necessary to subscribe to 1 new share at $89. The necessary formula is:

$$\text{Value of 1 right} = \frac{P}{R \text{ plus } 1}$$

P = Premium: the amount by which the share price exceeds the subscription price ($100 - 89 = 11$); R = Ratio: the number of rights required to subscribe to 1 share (e.g., 10). Thus, one right is valued, theoretically, at $11 divided by 11, or $1. Supply and demand in the marketplace may cause the rights' market value to differ from their theoretical value.

A *warrant*, like a right, is a privilege of buying shares of stock at a specified price under certain conditions. However, warrants usually have a longer life and, in some cases, are perpetual.

The stockholder normally has the right to transfer (sell) his ownership to another person without the consent of the corporation.

The common stockholder is entitled to share in the proceeds of liquidation of the corporation, after liabilities, bondholders, and preferred stockholders have been paid, in that order. Thus, common stockholders have the last claim on assets in liquidation of a corporation.

Stockholders have the *right of inspection* within reasonable statutory limitations of such records as: (*a*) the stockholder list, (*b*) minutes of stockholders' meetings, and (*c*) corporate books and records.

Preferred stock. Preferred stock has preference over common stock when dividends are distributed. In liquidation of the corporation, preferred stockholders have a limited prior claim on assets. Preferred stock rarely appreciates significantly in value; common stock can appreciate.[5] The dividend paid to preferred stockholders, like interest on bonds, is usually at a fixed rate. For example, a $5 preferred stock with a par value of $100 will pay a dividend of $5 per year. Preferred stock may have voting privileges, but often it does not.

Claims of both common and preferred stockholders (owners) are junior to claims of bondholders (creditors) or other creditors of the company. Preferred stock is senior to common; hence, common stock is known as a junior security. Common stockholders assume the greatest risk, but exercise greater control and have the greatest opportunity for growth if the company prospers. This growth may be in the form of increased dividends or through appreciation; that is, the increase in the market value of common stock.

There are various types of preferred stock, each varying according to the rights and privileges of the stockholders (owners), including: cumulative, noncumulative, convertible, participating, and callable.

When a company has *cumulative preferred stock* outstanding, it means simply that if the company omits to pay a dividend in any one year these dividends accumulate, and the arrears must be paid by the corporation *before* any dividend can be paid on common stock.

Noncumulative preferred stock has no privilege of accumulating dividends in arrears. Naturally, the preferred dividend for any given year must be paid before the dividend on the common stock is paid that year.

Convertible preferred stock can be converted, at the preferred stockholder's option, into a specific number of shares of common stock under certain stated conditions, which are fully disclosed at the time of issuance.

Participating preferred stock entitles the investor to regular preferred dividends, and in addition to or in lieu of such dividends the investor shares to a stated extent with the common stockholders any earnings that are to be paid out as ordinary dividends. Thus, depending on the circumstances that allow preferred stock participation, preferred shareholders may receive more than the normal specified rate of preferred

---

5/ Participating or convertible preferred may appreciate significantly.

dividend. Otherwise, preferred stockholders receive only a fixed rate of dividend, which does not fluctuate except in the event of default.

In comparison to common stock, preferred stock because of its fixed dividend does not usually react so strongly to market fluctuations. However, convertible preferred stock because of its privilege of conversion to common stock and participating preferred stock because it shares in common stock dividends do react more strongly to changes in the market.

Callable preferred stock can be called for redemption by the issuing company at a specific price and under specific conditions. The entire issue can be callable after a specific date at a stated price, or part of it can be callable, with the balance callable at a later date. Generally when an issue is called, a premium—an amount greater than the original issuance price—is paid by the company to the preferred stockholder or bondholder. However, the call price could be less than the market value at the time of purchase on the market.

Features applicable to both common and preferred stock. Cumulative, convertible, participating, and callable features generally apply to preferred stock. Other features or privileges may apply to both common and preferred stocks. For example, a *guaranteed* stock is either a common or preferred stock for which the dividend is guaranteed by a firm other than the issuer of the stock. Parent companies sometimes guarantee stock or bond issues of their subsidiary companies to make it easier for the subsidiary to raise money.

Other important descriptive expressions are used in relation to stocks. For example, the ownership interest of both common and preferred stock is called *equity*.

The stock's *par value* is the stated dollar value of that share as assigned by the company's charter. Par value of preferred stock is the dollar value on which dividends are figured, while for common stock, it is the value set for accounting purposes only, since it bears no relation to the market value of the common stock. Many companies today issue *no-par stock,* but they must give an arbitrary *stated value* (e.g., $10) per share on the balance sheet. Most state laws provide that the par value, whether it be $1 or $10 or more, must be fully paid when the stock is sold in order that the company's stock may be fully paid and nonassessable. In some states, no-par laws permit companies to issue stock with no par value, but with a stated or assigned value.

Authorized stock means the number of shares the corporation's charter allows the corporation to issue. Those shares that have not been issued, although authorized, are referred to as *unissued stock.* Often, more stock is authorized than is initially issued in order to allow future issuance with a minimum of difficulty. *Outstanding stock* refers to shares that have actually been issued and are held by persons other than the corporation itself.

If stock is issued always to persons other than the corporation and then is reacquired or bought back by the corporation, it is known as *treasury stock.* Treasury stock may be held in the corporation's treasury, reissued to shareholders, or permanently retired. Treasury stock is not entitled to receive dividends, nor may it vote. Once it is reissued, it is freed of these restrictions.

The price at which outstanding stock may be bought or sold from its owners is called the *market value*. If the market value for each share of stock becomes too high, the corporation may decide to have a *stock split* to make the shares more salable and marketable at a lower price. For example, a three-to-one split by a company with 1,000 shares outstanding would mean that after the split 3,000 shares would be outstanding. Each stockholder maintains the same interest in the corporation, but the number of shares he owns is now tripled. The total market value of the stock after a split should not increase simply by virtue of the split itself. Some stock split announcements are accompanied by news of a dividend increase, which may cause the market price to increase. A *reverse stock split* reduces the number of shares. In this case, stockholders may receive one new share for each two old shares.

Another type of ownership is a *voting trust certificate*. This certificate shows ownership interest in a voting trust, into which a group of stockholders deposit their shares and agree to have the trustees vote the shares. The purpose may be to pool, or concentrate, the voting strength of the group of stockholders over a sustained period. Usually, a voting trust is formed to provide a continuity of management over a period of time, either to get a corporation back on its feet financially or to obtain long-term financing that may require such continuity. These voting trust certificates, or certificates of beneficial interest, are sometimes listed on an exchange and are actively traded. At the termination of the trust, the underlying common or preferred stock is transferred to the current holder of the voting trust certificates.

The total of all outstanding common and preferred shares of a corporation is referred to as its *capital stock. Paid-in capital* refers to the dollar amount received by the corporation when it issued its capital stock. Of course, if a corporation has only common stock outstanding then its capital stock is the same as its common stock.

Bonds

The other major type of security is bonds, which are certificates[6] evidencing debts, or loans made by the bondholder (creditor) to the corporation. A *bond* is simply a form of an I O U to repay a loan at a future *maturity date*. Corporate bonds are generally issued in units of $1,000, although there are also $100 and $500 bonds. The principal is the amount (i.e., $1,000) to be repaid by the corporation to the bondholder and is shown on the face of the bond. Bond issuers may be a government or municipality as well as a corporation. *Baby bonds* are issued in denominations lower than the usual $1,000. For example, a $500 or $100 bond is called a baby bond.

A bond is secured when it is backed by security such as real property, machinery and equipment, or other suitable assets of the issuer. This security can be seized by the bondholder (creditor) if the terms of the bond indenture[7] —the legal contract between

---

6/ When a new bond is first issued, *temporary certificates,* which contain only two or three interest coupons, are often delivered. When the *definitive* bonds are issued, they are exchanged for the temporary certificates.

7/ The Bond Indenture Act of 1939, which contains provisions to safeguard bondholders, is described in Chapter 5, under the Securities Exchange Act of 1934.

corporation and bondholders—are not met. If the bond issuer does not pay the holder the stated rate of interest or repay the face amount of the bond at its maturity date, the bondholder may sue the corporation for defaulting. If the corporation becomes bankrupt, bondholders are paid before either preferred or common stockholders. Normally, as long as they receive their interest bondholders do not have any voice in management.

Interest is the amount the corporation must pay the bondholder for the use of the bondholder's money. The interest rate is usually expressed as a percentage of the face amount of the bond. It is affected, at the time the bond is issued, by two factors: (1) the supply and demand for money, and (2) the credit standing of the corporation.

The higher the interest rate and the more dependable the company, the more valuable the bond. Therefore, after the bond is issued and is being traded by the public, it may sell at a premium; that is, *above* its face amount. A bond with $1,000 face amount may be purchased for a premium at $1,060, while another with the same face amount may be purchased at a discount—at $980. Interest is normally paid semi-annually.

Types of bonds. Like stocks, bonds also vary according to the privileges they offer.

Convertible bonds can be converted into common stock or another security at a stated price and under stated conditions at the option of the holder. Such conversion privilege in a bond would have great value if the bond could be changed into common stock at a price below the current market value of the common stock. *Conversion parity* (or parity price) is the market price at which an equal exchange of value will result when the conversion privilege of a convertible bond or convertible preferred stock is exercised. Assume that a $1,000 bond is issued, convertible for 5 years into 50 shares of common stock. The conversion parity then will be $20. If the common stock rises above $20, the market value of the bonds will certainly be expected to rise at least proportionately. In practice, convertible bonds tend to reach a higher-than-proportionate market value in expectation of future profitable conversion possibilities.[8]

An investor in common stock would be concerned about possible *dilution* of his ownership if either bonds or preferred stocks could be converted into common stock at a price below the current market value. Similarly, stock purchase warrants, or outstanding options that permit their holders to buy new stock at a fixed price, would give rise to concern about the possible dilution of value to the common stockholders. Holders of convertible bonds are protected against any material change in the number of outstanding common shares, usually by automatic adjustment to the conversion ratio in the event of certain contingencies—e.g., payment of stock dividends.

Bonds may be either *secured* or *unsecured.* Secured bonds are backed up by a specific piece of property that the bondholder may take in the event of default. Unsecured bonds are not backed by specific property.

8/ Frequently, a convertible bond will be convertible into common stock at a conversion price. A conversion price of $20 means that a convertible bond could be converted into 50 shares of stock (1,000 divided by $20).

A *mortgage bond*[9] is secured by a mortgage lien on a specific corporation property, usually by real estate. A *first* mortgage bond has a claim to interest or assets that is superior or prior to the claim of some other bond such as a general mortgage or second mortgage bond. A general mortgage bond is backed by a blanket mortgage, not necessarily a first mortgage, on all of the assets of a corporation.

Mortgage bonds may be classified as either open-end, limited open-end, or closed-end. An *open-end bond* allows the corporation to issue additional bonds and usually requires that additional property be included under the mortgage. Prescribed earnings may also be required to keep the interest coverage ratio from falling. The interest coverage ratio is that of earnings to the amount of interest. *Limited open-end bonds* allow the corporation to issue a stated amount of additional bonds over a period of years in series. All bonds issued under the series would have the same claim on assets. *Closed-end bonds* prohibit the corporation from issuing additional bonds under the same mortgage. If issuance of additional bonds is permitted, they are junior to the original mortgage bonds.

A *collateral trust bond* is secured by collateral deposited with a trustee. The collateral is often the stock or bonds of companies controlled by the issuing company, but may be other securities. In the event of default, the bondholders may force the trustee to sell the collateral to satisfy the claims of the bondholders.

A *serial bond* is one of an issue whose portions mature in relatively small amounts at periodic stated intervals. For example, bonds with serial numbers 1 to 100 mature in 1970, those with numbers 101 to 200 in 1971, and so on.

A *sinking fund bond* requires, through a provision in the bond indenture, that the corporation gradually set aside by installment payments, usually to a trustee, an amount sufficient to repay the principal of the bonds at maturity, when the bonds are called or purchased on the open market. The arrangement for paying off the bonds by installment payments is known as *amortization*. At stated intervals, the company or its agent calls by lot the numbers of a stated percentage of the outstanding bonds and retires them from the proceeds of the sinking fund.

A *revenue bond's* interest and principal are payable only from the revenue or earnings of the issuing company. These bonds are frequently issued by railroads and municipalities to finance toll bridges, toll tunnels, and toll turnpikes. Revenue bondholders' interest receipts from bonds issued by a public authority (other than federal) are tax exempt—that is, exempt from the federal income tax.

An *income bond* is one on which interest is paid only when it has been earned and can be paid only from available income. It may be cumulative, so that the unpaid interest accumulates as a claim against the corporation when the bond is due. An income bond is also called an *adjustment bond*, because it is generally issued as the result of a corporate reorganization. Income bonds are rarely issued for public subscription. The purpose of an income bond is to furnish a corporation badly needed financial relief.

A *debenture* is a bond backed or secured only by the general credit of the issuing

9/ Mortgage bonds were used most frequently by railroads. They are sometimes used by public utility companies, and are infrequently used by industrial firms.

corporation. There is no specific mortgage or lien. Debenture bonds are issued extensively by industrial corporations. U.S. government bonds are also debentures. *Subordinated debentures* are those that in the event of default must await satisfaction of the claims of certain other parties whose claims have a higher priority, such as debenture holders or institutional lenders.

A *guaranteed bond* is guaranteed as to repayment of principal, interest, or both by a company other than the issuing company. A guaranteed stock, similarly, has its dividend guaranteed by a company other than the issuer.

A *refunding bond* is issued to permit reorganization or refinancing of the capital structure of a corporation. This type of bond often replaces an existing bond issue by retiring it. For example, assume that a company issued bonds that paid 6 percent interest, and some years later market interest rates were generally lower, say 3 percent. The company would then find it advantageous to repay the old bondholders with the proceeds of a new refunding issue (issued at 3 percent).

A *coupon bond* actually has coupons attached, and each coupon represents the interest payment due on a specific date. The coupons are presented for payment by the bearer; therefore, these are *bearer bonds*. Bearer bonds are easily negotiable, since the bearer—the person in physical possession—is considered the owner.

A *registered bond* differs from a bearer bond, which can be sold by the holder, in that the owner's name is recorded on the books of the issuing corporation or its agent. All transfers of ownership of registered bonds must be recorded. Interest payments are sent directly by check to the registered owner.

When a business is insolvent, a court may appoint a receiver to operate, reorganize, or liquidate the business. To help raise cash to get the company back on its feet, the receiver may obtain permission from the court to sell *receiver's certificates*. These certificates usually have first claim to any corporate earnings or assets.

Railroads and airlines often raise money to finance the purchase of movable equipment, such as locomotives or airplanes, by issuing a type of serial bond called *equipment trust certificates*. These certificates, sometimes called *rolling stock bonds*, mature at stated intervals, usually every six months. A trustee holds legal title to the equipment that backs issuance of the certificates. During the 15-year period, he receives from the railroad or airline payments that include dividends (such as interest), amortization of the principal amount, and expenses. The trustee would seize the equipment should the railroad or airline fail to make its scheduled payments.

Government and municipal bonds

Governments, federal and local, also issue bonds. These bonds are often referred to as *government* and *municipal bonds*. While a corporation borrows on its anticipated profits, governments borrow on their right to tax.

U.S. government bonds

United States government bonds are not secured, and bondholders have no guarantee other than an obligation to be repaid. Essentially, government bonds are debentures, backed by the general credit of the U.S. government and its agencies. Interest paid to U.S. government bondholders is fully subject to federal income tax, but is exempt from state income taxes. There are several types of governments.

Treasury bonds arc usually issued with a maturity in excess of 5 years and in $1,000 units. They are traded like other bonds. Their value is not constant, but varies with changes in the prime interest rate—the interest rate charged by banks on loans to their most financially stable customers. The financial section of local newspapers indicates their current market value.[10] They are usually callable by the Treasury at par at an option date several years prior to maturity. For example, the 4 1/8's, due May 15, 1989 to 1994, are callable at par in May, 1989, or on any interest payment date thereafter to maturity in May, 1994.[11]

Treasury notes are issued for shorter periods of time. Maturity dates are usually more than one year, but not more than five years from the issuance date.

Treasury certificates, issued by the Treasury Department, have maturities up to one year.

Treasury bills usually have a maturity of 90 days, 180 days, or 1 year. They are non-interest-bearing obligations sold and quoted on a discount basis. The 90- and 180-day bills are sold weekly by means of competitive bidding; the 1-year bills are sold at monthly auctions. Various bills, known as *tax anticipation bills,* mature on tax payment dates. Tax anticipation bills (or bonds) are U.S. government (or municipal) bonds issued with serialized maturity dates set in anticipation of the date when taxes will be paid by the purchaser. They are often purchased by companies to pay when due such government taxes as social security taxes. The maturity dates of tax anticipation notes generally fall on or about the dates such taxes are due to be paid by the companies.

Alphabet bonds or savings bonds, such as E and H, are unlike all other bonds, since they cannot be legally used as collateral. They are never traded on the open market, do not fluctuate in value, and are nonmarketable. Series E-bonds mature (as of June 1968) in 7 years, and return $100 for every $75 invested if held to maturity, which represents a compound interest rate of 4.25 percent per year. Such bonds may be redeemed at any time after two months from their issue date, but the redemption proceeds will include interest at a lesser rate of interest. The interest must be reported as taxable income when the bonds are redeemed at maturity by taxpayers who are on a cash basis. The maximum that may be purchased during a year by individuals is $20,000 face amount.

Series H-bonds mature in 10 years, are issued at par, and bear interest paid semi-annually by Treasury check mailed to the registered owner. Like E-bonds, they are issued only in registered form and are nontransferable. Their yield to maturity in 10 years usually is the same as the 7-year yield to maturity for E-bonds. The holder may redeem H-bonds 6 months after issuance and 1 month after notice, at par of $1,000.

10/ See p. 20 for sample quotations as shown in *The Wall Street Journal.*
11/ Since May, 1967, the Treasury has been selling Freedom Shares, which are bonds paying 5.00 percent when held to their 4½-year maturity date. These can be purchased only by a person who buys series E-bonds on the payroll savings or bond-a-month plan.

The maximum amount that may be purchased during a year by one individual is $30,000.

In addition to the U.S. government issues, there are *federal agency bonds.* These bonds are issued by federal agencies and are not government guaranteed. Examples are bonds of agencies, such as the Federal Home Loan Banks, Federal Land Banks, Federal National Mortgage Association, Bank for Cooperatives, and the Federal Intermediate Banks. These agencies in general are concerned with making funds available for residential and agricultural credit.[12]

Municipals

The local government bond is the municipal. The most important feature of municipals is that the interest paid to the holders of most municipal bonds is exempt from federal income tax.[13] Municipal bond investors are ordinarily people with large incomes who seek tax-free interest payments. Since municipals have satisfactorily paid both interest and principal, they enjoy a certain popularity with high-income investors. Municipals include bonds issued by states, counties, cities, towns, and nonfederal statutory authorities.

A municipal bond may be a *general* or a *limited* obligation bond. General obligations or unlimited tax bonds, also known as *full-faith-and-credit bonds,* are those whose payment is unconditionally guaranteed by the municipality, particularly one that has the power to levy taxes. The entire taxing power of the issuing municipality is pledged to the payment of such general obligations. Limited obligation (limited tax) municipal bonds, which are not supported by the full taxing powers of the issuer, include revenue and special assessment bonds.

Special assessment bonds are issued by a district, and are used to finance a public improvement within that district, such as a sewer or water system. The interest and principal on special assessment bonds are paid by revenues from taxes imposed on the residents of the district. In some cases, a municipality may guarantee payment of its district's special assessment bonds.

Interest and principal on *revenue bonds* are payable solely from the revenue earned or received from the financed project. These bonds are issued to finance the construction of income-producing public facilities, such as turnpikes, public utilities, airports, college dormitories, waterworks, bridges, and electric light and power facilities. Such bonds are usually issued by statutory authorities, such as the Port of New York Authority. When statutory authorities issue revenue bonds repayable out of earnings, they are not generally backed by the taxing power of the state(s) or the municipal

---

12/ Three agencies are involved in providing agricultural credit: the Federal Intermediate Credit Banks, Banks for Cooperatives, and the Federal Land Banks. Their outstanding issues at December 31, 1967, amounted to about $9.2 billion. Two agencies—the Federal Home Loan Banks and the Federal National Mortgage Association—are involved in channeling funds to residential mortgage markets. At December 31, 1967, outstanding issues amounted to about $9 billion.

13/ The 1819 case of *McCulloch* v. *Maryland* wherein Chief Justice Marshall stated that the power to tax is the power to destroy, established the precedent that the federal government would not tax interest of municipals and vice versa. Municipals are not exempt, however, from inheritance taxes or from the state income taxes of many states.

government(s) they operate under, unless special arrangements are made for such guarantees.

Obligations of states. Obligations of states normally are general obligation bonds. The state's ability to repay interest and principal is often measured by the following ratios.

1. Per capita debt, which is the total debt of the state divided by the population. It is of interest in considering whether the state is capable of supporting existing and additional debt.
2. The ratio of per capita debt to per capita income.
3. The percentage of state receipts required for debt service.

The state's ability to pay its debt, based on its ability to tax, particularly such taxes as income, corporate, sales, gas, tobacco, and liquor, is quite important, since most states (except New York) cannot be sued for failure to meet its commitments unless the state consents to the suit.

Obligations of cities and towns. Repayment of obligations of cities and towns is usually dependent on real property tax revenues of the municipality. Factors to consider in analyzing these bonds include:

1. The credit of the municipality as measured by its growth and industry diversification.
2. The competence of the municipal government.
3. The ratio of net debt per capita.
4. The percentage of debt to true value of real property under the tax jurisdiction.
5. Interest and debt retirement charges as a percentage of the budget.

In considering these factors, one must determine the amount of overlapping debt, which refers to the overlapping of two or more tax districts that have the power to levy taxes on property in their districts. For example, real estate may be taxed by both the city and county governments.

Obligations of statutory authorities. The ability of statutory authorities to meet payments on revenue bonds should be considered in the light of the project's nature and financial revenues, including:[14]

1. Sources of revenue.
2. Maturity provisions.
3. Application of revenues.
4. Protective covenants, including restrictions that relate to issuance of additional bonds.
5. Extent to which the facilities fill an economic need.
6. Competing facilities.

Municipalities may finance their needs by means other than bond issues, through issuance of *floating debt.* The floating debt is the nonfunded obligations of a state or municipality, including unpaid bills, tax anticipation notes, and bond anticipation notes. A local government receives most of its tax revenue once or twice a year. During

---

14/ Examples of statutory authorities are the Port of New York Authority and the Tennessee Valley Authority.

these periods of incoming receipts, it is *in funds,* but there may be other periods when it is short of cash. To meet its current bills, payroll, and so on, the local government may issue *tax anticipation notes,* which are usually paid off during the year of their issuance, or *bond anticipation notes,* which may be outstanding for several years. The most common short-term floating debts are the tax anticipation notes.

Information about municipals is available from the *Blue List,* which lists the current offerings of most municipal bond dealers.

Yield

Bond yield and stock yield are determined in the same manner. Yield means benefit. Just as a farmer measures his yield per acre in bushels or barrels, investors measure their yield in percentages. Municipal bonds are normally quoted on a yield basis. Assume that an investor purchases a 5 percent bond for $1,000. Its face value is $1,000, and assume that $1,000 is paid for the bond. It is selling neither at a *premium* —that is, above its face value—nor at a *discount*—that is, below its face value. Determining the yield is simple. Multiply .05 (5 percent) times the selling price of $1,000, or $50 to obtain the *nominal yield.* The *coupon rate* is 5 percent.

Bonds usually sell at a premium or at a discount. Then, the investor pays either more (premium) or less (discount) for the bond than its face value of $1,000. For example, an investor purchases a 5 percent bond whose face value is $1,000 at a discount, or below its face value. He pays only $800. It is still a 5 percent bond, and the annual interest will still be $50. But the cost to the investor has changed. The annual interest paid, $50, divided by the purchase price, $800, is the *current yield,*[15] or 6.25 percent. Note that the yield is greater than the coupon rate (of 5 percent). An investor buys a 5 percent bond with a face value of $1,000 at a premium, or above the face value. He pays $1,500 for the bond whose face value is only $1,000. The current yield is $50 divided by $1,500, or 3.33 percent. So if a bond is bought at a premium, the yield to the purchaser is less than the interest rate stated on the face of the bond.

However, the most important measure of bond yield is *yield to maturity.* Calculation of yield to maturity is similar to that of current yield, but goes one step further. The amount more or less that is actually paid, as compared to the face value, must be taken into consideration by the investor. Therefore, the current yield plus an adjustment for the premium or discount gives the *combined annual gain.* Yield to maturity is most accurately computed from bond tables, but it may be computed arithmetically, as shown in the following example.

On January 1, 1966, a $1,000, 4 percent bond, due January 1, 1986, is purchased for $800 (at a discount). The nominal yield is $40 per annum. The bond will appreciate $10 per year over the 20 years to maturity, since it will rise from $800 to $1,000, or $200 over 20 years. Therefore, the annual gain of $10[16] plus the nominal yield of $40 gives a combined annual gain of $50. The *average investment* in the bond consists

---

15/ Current yield = $\dfrac{\text{Annual interest amount}}{\text{Price of bond}}$.

16/ Or less the annual loss if the bond were purchased at a premium.

of the midpoint between $800 cost and $1,000 maturity value, which is $900. The yield to maturity is the percentage the combined annual gain bears to the average investment. Therefore, yield to maturity is $50 divided by $900, or 5.55 percent. Yield to maturity will be more than current yield on bonds purchased at a discount and less than current yield on bonds purchased at a premium.[17]

Bond quotations for corporate bonds, which include industrial, public utility, and railroad issues, are in percentages of the face amount of the bond. Thus, for bonds whose face amount is $1,000 a quotation of 105 means a price of $1,050; 95 means $950; 106¾ means $1,067.50. In other words, for a $1,000 face amount bond the market price equals 10 times the bond quotation. Fractions range from 1/8 to 7/8 in corporate bond quotations. A *point* as it pertains to bonds means 1 percentage point, or $10.

Bond quotations for government issues such as Treasury notes, bonds, and certificates are also quoted as a percentage of face amount. However, the decimal portion of the quotation represents fractions of 1/32ds. Thus, a Treasury bond quote of 98.16 means a market price of 985—that is, $980 plus 16/32 of $10; a quote of 99.8 means a market price of 992.50.

Treasury bills, however, are quoted in fractions representing 1/100th of a point. Bills are usually traded on a yield basis. Differences in bond yields are discussed in terms of *basis points,* which represent 1/100th of a percentage point. Thus, if a Treasury bill is offered at an asked yield of 4 percent and a corporate bond is offered at 4.48 percent (yield to maturity) the difference is 48 basis points.

Similar principles are applied to dividends from common stock. The par value has no real significance when we speak of common stock. It is the market value that is important. An investor owns a common stock, par value of $10, with a current market value of $50 per share. This stock has paid a dividend of $2 from earnings during the last 12 months. The current yield is $2 divided by $50, or 4 percent.

Preferred stock, like bonds, has a predetermined yield based on its par value. Since this return is constant,[18] it is often used to identify that particular stock. For example, a preferred stock that pays a dividend of $5 might be described as either: (*a*) par $100, 5 percent; or (*b*) $5, par $100. Although the preferred's par value is $100, its current market value may be only $75. Therefore, to determine the current yield divide the $5 by the $75 current market value, or 6.67 percent.

ADR's

There is in addition to stocks, bonds, governments, and municipals a fifth type of security. The *American Depository Receipt* (ADR) is simply a certificate issued by American banks to represent ownership of foreign securities. The non-United States

17/ Consider the various yields that apply to a 3.5 percent bond maturing in 10 years, quoted at 95. Nominal yield is $35 or 3.5 percent. Current yield is 3.68 percent. Yield to maturity is:

                  a) by formula . . . . .4.133 percent.
                  b) by bond tables . . . . .4.115 percent.

18/ Except in participating preferreds and preferreds that have passed their dividends and are in default.

corporation deposits shares of its stock in an overseas branch of a U.S. bank, which then issues an ADR. The ADR's rather than the actual foreign shares are traded. Owners of ADR's have all the rights and privileges of normal stockholders, but they cannot vote.

Priority of security holders

The order of priority by which security holders share in the earnings of a corporation after payment of interest to holders of bonds, is as follows.
1. After taxes are paid, dividends are paid on preferred stock.
2. Then, the amount not retained by the corporation for expansion is paid in the form of dividends to the common stockholders. (Participating preferred stockholders might also share in these distributions.)
3. The balance—retained earnings—is kept in the corporation for expansion. Retained earnings help to increase the value of the stock by building toward future earnings.

If a corporation becomes insolvent and enters bankruptcy proceedings, or is dissolved, the priority of distribution of assets is determined by the appropriate statute of the state of incorporation. Generally, bonds or debts (i.e., mortgage bonds) that are secured by liens are paid first; then, unsecured creditors are paid. After secured and unsecured creditors have been paid, the remaining assets are divided among the stockholders in proportion to the number of shares held by each. Preferred and common shareholders share alike, unless some preference is given to one class of stockholders.[19] Such preference usually would be found in the "Articles of Incorporation" or in the contract under which the shares are held.

Forms of ownership

The registration of ownership of stocks and bonds may be in either *registered* or *bearer* form; the names of the owners of securities issued in registered form are kept on record by the registrar. Interest payments or dividends and, at maturity date, the principal of bonds are sent by check directly to the registered owner.

Owners of bearer certificates possess the certificate and may cash in coupons to receive their interest[20] and, at maturity, the principal. The holder—that is, the person in possession of a bearer instrument—is presumed to be the owner.

Trading

Most bonds are traded over the counter, although some bonds are listed for trading on registered stock exchanges.

19/ Normally, the articles of incorporation provide for preferred stockholders to receive a stated amount (or par value) plus accrued dividends or dividends in default before common stockholders receive any share of the dissolution proceeds.

20/ Bonds may also be registered as to principal but not interest. Then, the principal is repaid to the holder of record. Interest is paid semiannually to whomever presents the coupon for payment.

Government, Agency and Miscellaneous Securities

Tuesday, October 15, 1968

Over-the-Counter Quotations: Source on request.
Decimals in bid-and-asked and bid change represent 32nds (101.1 means 101 1-32). a-Plus 1-64. b-Yield to call date. c-Certificates of indebtedness. d-Minus 1-64.

Treasury Bonds

			Bid	Asked	Bid Chg.	Yld.
3⅞s,	1968	Nov.	99.27	99.29	...	4.99
2½s,	1963-68	Dec.	99.16	99.18	...	5.19
4s,	1969	Feb.	99.14	99.16	d	5.45
2½s,	1964-69	June	98.13	98.17	— .1	4.78
4s,	1969	Oct.	98.24	98.28	...	5.22
2½s,	1964-69	Dec.	97.11	97.15	— .1	4.77
2½s,	1965-70	Mar.	96.23	96.27	— .2	4.84
4s,	1970	Feb.	98.9	98.13	— .2	5.25
4s,	1970	Aug.	97.19	97.23	— .3	5.32
2½s,	1966-71	Mar.	94.20	94.28	...	4.77
4s,	1971	Aug.	96.8	96.16	— .3	5.35
3⅞s,	1971	Nov.	95.19	95.27	— .3	5.36
4s,	1972	Feb.	95.18	95.26	— .4	5.39
2½s,	1967-72	June	91.28	92.4	— .4	4.87
4s,	1972	Aug.	95.4	95.12	— .3	5.35
2½s,	1967-72	Sept.	91.9	91.17	— .4	4.91
2½s,	1967-72	Dec.	90.28	91.4	— .6	4.88
4s,	1973	Aug.	94.8	94.16	— .2	5.31
4⅛s,	1973	Nov.	94.12	94.20	— .4	5.35
4⅛s,	1974	Feb.	94.8	94.16	— .2	5.33
4¼s,	1974	May	94.12	94.20	— .4	5.38
3⅞s,	1974	Nov.	92.24	93.0	— .4	5.23
4s,	1980	Feb.	86.16	87.0	— .8	5.56
3½s,	1980	Nov.	82.18	83.2	— .8	5.43
3¼s,	1978-83	June	77.16	78.0	— .8	5.45
3¼s,	1985	May	76.20	77.4	— .8	5.35
4¼s,	1975-85	May	85.4	85.20	— .10	5.59
3½s,	1990	Feb.	76.10	76.26	— .6	5.33
4¼s,	1987-92	Aug.	82.30	83.14	— .6	5.58
4s,	1988-93	Feb.	81.8	81.24	— .10	5.35
4⅛s,	1989-94	May	81.2	81.28	— .10	5.45
3s,	1995	Feb.	76.4	76.20	— .8	4.53
3½s,	1998	Nov.	76.10	76.26	— .6	5.02

U.S. Treas. Notes

Rate	Mat	Bid	Asked	Yld
5¼	11-68	99.31	100.1	4.75
5⅝	2-69	99.31	100.1	5.48
1½	4-69	98.16	98.24	4.29
5⅝	5-69	99.31	100.1	5.57
6	8-69	100.10	100.14	5.46
1½	10-69	97.2	97.10	4.40
1½	4-70	95.18	95.30	4.36
1½	10-70	94.8	94.12	4.54
5	11-70	98.28	99.0	5.52
5⅜	2-71	99.16	99.24	5.49
1½	4-71	92.16	92.30	4.57
5¼	5-71	99.11	99.19	5.42
1½	10-71	91.8	91.18	4.58
5⅜	11-71	99.15	99.23	5.48
4¾	2-72	97.18	97.26	5.48
1½	4-72	89.20	90.20	4.46
4¾	5-72	97.16	97.24	5.45
1½	10-72	88.8	89.8	4.50
1½	4-73	86.30	87.30	4.52
1½	10-73	85.26	86.26	4.50
5⅝	8-74	99.11	99.15	5.73
5¾	11-74	100.10	100.18	5.64
5¾	2-75	100.4	100.12	5.68
6	5-75	101.15	101.23	5.68

U.S. Treas. Bills

Mat	Bid Discount	Ask Discount	Mat	Bid Discount	Ask Discount
10-17	5.85	5.05	2-13	5.41	5.31
10-24	5.55	5.05	2-20	5.42	5.32
10-31	5.60	5.05	2-27	5.44	5.34
11- 7	5.17	4.97	2-28	5.42	5.31
11-14	5.18	4.98	3- 6	5.42	5.34
11-21	5.20	5.02	3-13	5.42	5.34
11-29	5.20	5.02	3-20	5.42	5.34
11-30	5.15	4.95	3-24	5.41	5.37
12- 5	5.18	5.05	3-27	5.43	5.35
12-12	5.17	5.04	3-31	5.43	5.33
12-19	5.18	5.06	4- 3	5.45	5.40
12-26	5.20	5.08	4-10	5.46	5.41
12-31	5.10	4.90	4-17	5.45	5.42
1- 2	5.34	5.27	4-22	5.46	5.42
1- 9	5.35	5.30	4-30	5.45	5.35
1-16	5.38	5.35	5-31	5.45	5.37
1-23	5.40	5.28	6-30	5.47	5.43
1-30	5.40	5.28	7-31	5.43	5.33
1-31	5.40	5.28	8-31	5.42	5.33
2- 6	5.41	5.31	9-30	5.36	5.32

Inter-Amer. Devel. Bk.

Rate	Mat	Bid	Asked	Yld
4¼	12-82	79.16	80.16	6.35
4½	4-84	80.0	82.0	6.34
4½	11-84	80.0	82.0	6.30
5.20	1-92	86.0	88.0	6.14
6½	11-92	98.16	100.0	6.50

Fed'l Home Loan Bk.

Rate	Mat	Bid	Asked	Yld
5.85	10-68	99.31	100.1	4.26
5⅝	11-68	99.29	100.1	5.21
5½	1-69	99.28	100.0	5.43
5.85	2-69	99.31	100.2	5.60
5.65	2-69	99.29	99.31	5.69
5⅜	3-69	99.24	100.0	5.36
6.25	4-69	100.5	100.7	5.68
6.00	5-69	100.1	100.3	5.76
6.30	6-69	100.10	100.12	5.72
5¾	7-69	99.31	100.1	5.69
6.00	9-69	100.2	100.10	5.65
6.00	2-70	100.8	100.16	5.61
6.00	3-70	100.8	10.16	5.63
6.00	4-70	100.6	100.14	5.70
5.80	5-70	99.27	99.29	5.86

Bank for Co-ops

Rate	Mat	Bid	Asked	Yld
5.90	11-68	99.31	100.1	5.10
6.20	12-68	100.1	100.3	5.32
6.20	1-69	100.1	100.3	5.64
6.00	2-69	100.0	100.2	5.71
5.55	4-69	99.27	99.29	5.75

Federal Land Bank

Rate	Mat	Bid	Asked	Yld
4⅛	2-72-67	94.16	95.16	5.62
4½	10-70-67	97.0	98.0	5.59
5½	10-68	99.30	100.0	5.36
5.95	12-68	100.0	100.4	5.16
4¾	1-69	99.16	99.24	5.67
4⅜	3-69	99.0	99.16	5.56
5.60	4-69	99.24	100.4	5.35
4¼	7-69	98.8	99.8	5.28
4⅝	7-69	98.20	99.20	5.13
6¼	9-69	100.10	100.18	5.61
4¼	10-69	97.28	98.28	5.41
5¾	1-70	99.24	100.8	5.53
5⅛	2-70	98.20	99.20	5.41
6.30	2-70	100.12	100.28	5.61
3½	4-70	96.16	97.16	5.31
6.20	4-70	100.12	100.24	5.67
5⅛	7-70	98.16	99.16	5.42
6.00	7-70	100.8	100.20	5.62
3½	5-71	94.24	95.24	5.31
6.00	10-71	99.28	100.0	6.00
5.70	2-72	99.4	99.16	5.86
3⅞	9-72	93.20	94.20	5.41
5⅞	10-72	99.24	100.24	5.66
4⅛	2-78-73	88.0	89.0	5.66
4½	2-74	93.16	94.16	5.71
4⅜	4-75	91.24	92.24	5.72
5	2-76	94.16	95.16	5.76
5⅜	7-76	97.16	98.16	5.61
5⅛	4-78	94.24	95.24	5.71
5	1-79	92.24	93.24	5.82

FIC Bank Debs.

Rate	Mat	Bid	Asked	Yld
5.75	11- 4	99.30	100.0	5.52
5.75	12- 2	99.30	100.0	5.55
5.95	1- 2	99.31	100.1	5.62
6.10	2- 3	100.0	100.2	5.72
6.45	3- 3	100.5	100.7	5.72
6.25	4- 1	100.4	100.6	5.72
5.95	5- 1	100.1	100.3	5.70
5.65	6- 2	99.27	99.2[illegible]	5.77
5⅝	7- 1	99.27	99.29	5.75

World Bank Bonds

Rate	Mat	Bid	Asked	Yld
3½	1969	98.24	99.24	3.55
5⅜	1969	99.8	100.8	4.85
5¾	1969	99.16	100.16	5.25
6⅛	1970	100.8	101.8	5.21
5.8u	1970	99.24	100.24	5.40
3½	1971	92.0	92.24	6.20
3	1972	91.0	92.0	5.40
4½	1973	92.0	93.0	6.10
3⅜	1975	84.16	85.16	6.05
3	1976	82.16	84.0	5.67
4½	1977	87.8	88.8	6.35
4¼	1978	84.0	85.0	6.36
4¼	1979	83.16	84.16	6.33
4¾	1980	87.16	88.16	6.11
3¼	1981	77.0	79.0	5.54
4½	1982	82.0	83.16	6.35
5	1985	85.0	86.16	6.34
4½	1990	77.16	79.0	6.31
5⅜	1991	87.0	88.16	6.34
5⅜	1992	87.0	88.16	6.32
5⅞	1993	91.0	93.0	6.44
6½	1994	100.0	101.16	6.38
6⅜	1994	98.0	98.12	6.51

FNMA Notes & Debs.

Rate	Mat	Bid	Asked	Yld
4⅜	4-69	99.10	99.18	5.30
4.65	5-69	99.10	99.14	5.66
6.10	6-69	100.4	100.8	5.69
5⅛	7-69	99.18	99.26	5.38
6	12-69	100.4	100.16	5.54
4⅝	4-70	98.4	98.20	5.60
6.60	6-70	100.28	101.12	5.71
4⅛	9-70	96.24	97.16	5.53
5¾	10-70	99.24	100.16	5.48
6	3-71	99.28	100.20	5.71
4⅛	8-71	95.0	96.0	5.68
5¾	9-71	99.12	99.24	5.84
4½	9-71	96.0	97.0	5.63
5⅛	2-72	97.8	98.8	5.71
4⅜	6-72	94.16	95.16	5.76
4¼	6-73	92.28	93.28	5.77
4½	2-77	90.16	91.16	5.80

Public Auth. Bonds

	Rate Mat.	Bid	Ask
AshdwnInDev	4¾s88	88	92
Cal Toll Brdg	3⅞s92	91	92
Camden InDv	4⅜s88	84	85
ChelanDistl	5s2013	98¼	99
Ches Br&T	5¾s2000	42	44
ChgoCalSky	3⅜s1995	53½	55½
ChgoOh Intl	4¾s1999	96¾	97¾
CityClintn Ia	4.20s91	86	89
ColumbiaStg	3⅞s03	80½	82
Delaw Tpk	4⅛s2002	93	95
DouglsCtyPU	4s2018	80½	81½
ElizRvT&B	4½s2000	101	102
Florida Tpk	4¾s2001	98½	100½
GrantCPU	2-3⅞-2005	78½	79½
GrantCPU	2-4⅞-2009	103½	104½
Gt New Orl	4.90-2006	91	92½
Illinois Toll	3¾s1995	85	86
Illinois Toll	4¾s1998	98½	100
Indiana Toll	3½s1994	78	80
JacksonvlExpw	4s92	84½	86
Jacksonvl Ex	4.10-03	84	85½
Kansas Tpke	3⅜s94	74½	76½
Kentucky Tpk	4¾-06	91	92½
KyTrnpike	4.85s2000	91½	93½
Lewisport Bldg	5s80	93	96
MackinacBldng	4s94	83	85½
Maine Turnpike	4s89	98	100
Md NE Expr	4⅛s02	98	99½
MassPortAut	4¾s98	104½	105¼
MassTurnpke	4-5s02	88	90
MassTurnpke	3.30-94	76	77½
N J Turnpke	3⅜s88	100	101½
N J Turnpke	3¼s85	90	91
N J T[illegible]ke	4¾s06	97	
	3.2[illegible]		

1 | Review questions

1. Common stock represents .... a corporation.
   1. a debt of
   2. an asset of
   ✓3. an ownership in
   4. the net worth of

2. A type of preferred stock on which dividends may exceed the specified rate is a ....
   1. cumulative preferred stock
   2. preferred stock with rights attached
   3. convertible preferred stock
   ✓4. participating preferred stock

3. Stock that has first claim on any earnings available for dividends is called .... stock.
   1. treasury
   2. common
   ✓3. preferred
   4. unissued

4. Sometimes, a corporation pays a dividend in shares of its stock rather than in cash because ....
   1. the dividend is not taxable to the shareholders, and such dividends may be used to capitalize surplus
   2. the corporation wishes to conserve cash for its operations
   3. one of the corporation's objectives is to achieve broader distribution of its shares
   ✓4. any of these

5. Bonds that are issued on the general credit of the issuer and are not secured are termed ....
   1. participating bonds
   2. consolidated mortgage bonds
   3. adjustment bonds
   ✓4. debenture bonds

6. A guaranteed corporate bond is one that is guaranteed as to principal and/or interest by ....
   1. the Securities and Exchange Commission
   2. the National Association of Securities Dealers, Inc.
   3. the New York Stock Exchange
   ✓4. someone other than the issuer

7. The callable or redemption feature of some preferred stocks provide that ....
   1. the holder receives a stipulated dividend and then shares in the earnings available for the common stockholders
   2. the holder has preference as to assets over the common stockholders in the event of liquidation
   ✓3. the company may call in the stock and redeem it at a specified price
   4. the holder has the right to convert the preferred stock into some other security issued by the corporation

8. A person appointed by written authorization to vote in the place of a stockholder is a ....
   ✓1. proxy
   2. right
   3. warrant
   4. indenture

9. The difference between U.S. Treasury bonds and U.S. Treasury notes is ....
   1. none
   2. bonds are issued as longer term obligations—more than five years.
   3. notes are more volatile
   4. both 2 and 3

10. For many reasons, general obligations of states and municipalities gener-

ally carry a lower interest rate than do corporate bonds. One reason is the theoretical safety of principal due to the issuers' power to tax. Another reason is ....

1. such bonds have never defaulted
2. investors feel they are doing a public service in buying them
3. interest earned by the holder of such bonds is not presently subject to federal income taxes
4. profits gained in the sale of such bonds are not subject to federal income taxes

11. Securities are issued by ....

1. partnerships
2., corporations
3. proprietorships
4. none of these

12. Not included in a corporation's capital structure is/are ....

1. bonds outstanding
2. common stock outstanding
3. preferred stock outstanding
4. authorized but unissued common stock

13. A charter from a state is necessary in order to form ....

1. corporations
2. proprietorships
3. partnerships
4. none of these

14. Dividends are ....

1. payments corporations are required to make to shareholders
2. distributions of debts
3. interest paid to shareholders on the basis of shares owned
4. pro rata distributions of profits among outstanding shares, usually paid in cash

15. Limited liability is characteristic of ....

1. proprietorships
2. partnerships
3. corporations
4. none of these

16. A corporation is usually managed by ....

1. shareholders and directors
2. executives and directors
3. shareholders and bondholders
4. shareholders and executives

17. Businesses can raise capital from two major sources: ....

1. equity and ownership
2., equity and debt
3., debt and loans
4. none of these

18. A loan that has been amortized has been ....

1. defaulted
2. paid off
3. altered as to interest charge
4. altered as to principal

19. A mortgage loan on a factory has as security ....

1. the general credit of the business
2. the factory itself
3. all assets of the business
4. none of these

20. An investor pays $5,000 for common stock of a corporation. If this corporation goes bankrupt, he can lose ....

1. no more than $5,000
2. more than $5,000

21. A bond with a face value of $10,000 is purchased for $9,500. At maturity, it will be redeemed at ....

1. $10,000
2. $9,500
3. $9,750
4. $10,000 plus interest

22. Dividends may be paid from ....

1. profits and earned surplus
2. profits and capital surplus
3. profits and reserves
4. current profits only

23. Treasury stock is ....
1. unissued stock
2. authorized stock
3. stock of another company held in the treasury
4. stock that has been issued and reacquired by the issuing company

24. Dividends may be paid in the form of ....
1. cash
2. stock
3. products
4. all of these

25. Dividends are declared by ....
1. management
2. the board of directors
3. the executives
4. the shareholders

26. The board of directors is elected by ....
1. the shareholders
2. the bondholders
3. the executives
4. the shareholders and bondholders

27. Treasury stock may be ....
1. held in the treasury
2. reissued to the public
3. retired
4. all of these

28. A person who buys 10 shares of General Corporation has .... General Corporation.
1. loaned money to
2. bought part of
3. neither loaned nor bought part of

29. A bond the issuing company can redeem at will is known as a ....
1. convertible bond
2. debenture bond
3. callable bond
4. none of these

30. When a company calls one of its bonds, it .... pays a premium to the bondholder.
1. never
2. generally
3. very seldom
4. always

31. When a bond is bought at a price greater than the face amount of the bond, it is said to have been purchased at ....
1. a discount
2. a premium
3. par
4. all of these
5. none of these

32. A conversion privilege in a bond may have value if the issuing company's common stock ....
1. increases in price
2. decreases in price
3. remains unchanged in price
4. none of these

33. The types of bonds generally exempt from federal income tax are ....
1. debentures
2. municipal bonds
3. equipment trust certificates
4. cumulative preferred stock

34. The interest and principal of .... are supported by the full taxing power of the governing unit that issues them.
1. general obligation bonds
2. special assessment bonds
3. revenue bonds
4. none of these

35. The *Blue List of Current Municipal Offerings* ....
1. lists the strongest municipal bonds currently offered
2. lists the current offerings of most municipal houses

3. lists illegal municipal bonds
4. none of these

36. Assessment bonds are payable from ....
    1. general tax levies
    2. revenue
    3. federal taxes
    4. assessments on the property owners who are directly or indirectly benefited by the bonds

37. Bonds used to finance the construction or acquisition of public works, such as electric light and power facilities and toll bridges, are called ....
    1. revenue bonds
    2. toll bonds
    3. public works bonds
    4. general obligations

38. Municipal bonds normally are quoted ....
    1. in dollars
    2. on a yield basis
    3. neither of these

39. Bonds whose interest and principal are generally payable only from revenues from specified property are ....
    1. tax bonds
    2. municipal bonds
    3. income bonds
    4. revenue bonds

40. Municipal bond investors usually are people ....
    1. of moderate means seeking diversified investments
    2. with large incomes seeking tax exemption
    3. small investors
    4. none of them

41. For the most part, municipal bonds have ....
    1. defaulted notoriously
    2. enjoyed a satisfactory payment record
    3. none of these

42. If a bond is bought at a premium, the yield to the purchaser is .... the stated interest rate on the face of the bond.
    1. higher than
    2. lower than
    3. the same as
    4. none of these

43. Federal income taxes need not be paid on interest received from ....
    1. municipal bonds
    2. corporate bonds
    3. series E savings bonds
    4. none of these

44. A call privilege can be exercised by the ....
    1. bondholders
    2. stockholders
    3. issuing company
    4. none of these

45. Dividends may exceed the specified rate on ....
    1. cumulative preferred stock
    2. preferred stock with rights attached
    3. convertible preferred stock
    4. participating preferred stock

46. The .... type of stock has first claim on any earnings available for dividends.
    1. treasury
    2. common
    3. preferred
    4. issued

47. Usually, back dividends on .... must be paid up before common stockholders may expect to receive cash dividends.
    1. preferred stock
    2. participating preferred stock
    3. cumulative preferred stock
    4. treasury stock

48. Mr. Stevens pays $90 for a 4.5 percent preferred stock with a par value

of $100. Dividends, if paid, would be .... per share.

1. $10
2. $5
√3. $4.50
4. $5.50

49. Guaranteed bonds are guaranteed by ....

1. the U.S. Treasury
2. the issuing company
√3. a company other than the issuing company
4. none of these

50. A bond secured by a piece of real estate is a .... bond.

√1. mortgage
2. debenture
3. collateral trust
4. serial

51. A corporation's profits are growing. In most circumstances, the corporation's .... would share most in these growing profits.

√1. common stock
2. preferred stock
3. participating preferred stock
4. bonds

52. A corporation that sells new securities to retire existing bonds is retiring its bonds through ....

1. a sinking fund
2. the convertible privilege
√3. refinancing
4. equity

53. Mr. Carlson has 100 shares of stock in a corporation. If this corporation offers a privilege subscription, Mr. Carlson would have .... rights.

1. 1
√2. 100
3. 10
4. 1,000

54. Precise details of the legal contract between the bondholder and the corporation are found in a document called the ....

1. bond certificate
√2. bond indenture
3. bond debenture
4. articles of co-partnership

55. A .... bond permits the issuer to gradually set aside money for its retirement.

1. callable
√2. sinking fund
3. serial
4. indenture

56. A bond of an issue whose parts mature at stated intervals is called a .... bond.

√1. serial
2. sinking fund
3. convertible
4. redeemed

57. If a corporation went bankrupt, ... would be paid first.

1. common stockholders
2. preferred stockholders
√3. bondholders
4. class B common stockholders

58. The current yield on a $100-par 5 percent bond selling at par is ....

1. $100
2. $10
√3. $5
4. $105

59. The .... type of bonds are usually paid by the issuer's check mailed to the bondholder.

√1. registered
2. coupon
3. both of these
4. neither of these

60. Bonds issued on the general credit of the issuer and not secured by any spe-

cific piece of property are called ....
bonds.

1. serial
2. mortgage
3. debenture ✓
4. collateral trust

61. A share of common stock sold for $300 before a stock split of 2 for 1. After the split, a share would cost about ....

1. $150 ✓
2. $400
3. $200
4. $100

62. Bonds that pay interest only when there is sufficient revenue are called .... bonds.

1. mortgage
2. income ✓
3. collateral trust
4. serial

63. A type of bond that has behind it some specific piece of property the bondholder can take and sell if the company fails to pay interest or principal is .... bond.

1. a secured ✓
2. an unsecured
3. a revenue
4. an income

64. If a corporation does not redeem its bonds at maturity, bondholders can ....

1. convert their bonds into common stock
2. do nothing
3. sue the corporation for defaulting ✓
4. none of these

65. A proxy is ....

1. management's representative at stockholders' meetings.
2. a person to whom a shareholder gives a power of attorney to permit him to vote the shareholder's stock at shareholders' meetings. ✓

3. oral authorization given by a shareholder to permit someone else to vote his stock for him at shareholders' meetings.
4. none of these.

66. A creditor could never force the owners of a .... to sell personal belongings to pay a business debt.

1. proprietorship
2. partnership
3. corporation ✓
4. any of these

67. The owners of a corporation are the holders of ....

1. authorized stock
2. bonds
3. stock outstanding ✓
4. unissued stock

68. Securities issued by a turnpike authority are likely to be classified as ....

1. common stock
2. certificates
3. municipal bonds ✓
4. none of these

69. The U.S. Government securities with the shortest maturity dates are ....

1. bills ✓
2. notes
3. treasury bonds
4. series E-bonds

70. Dividends on an issue of guaranteed stock are guaranteed by ....

1. the federal government
2. a warrant
3. a company other than the issuing company ✓
4. none of these

71. Certificates issued by American banks and trust companies against the deposit of foreign securities with the overseas branches of the banks, and of-

ten traded instead of the actual foreign shares, are called ....
1. certificates of registration
2. convertible securities
3. American Depository Receipts
4. mortgage bonds

72. Bonds issued on movable equipment, such as locomotives, are called ....
1. collateral trust bonds
2. equipment trust certificates
3. debentures
4. callable bonds

73. Guarantees on a guaranteed bond may extend to ....
1. interest
2. principal
3. both of these
4. neither of these

74. The type of bonds that can be retired by the issuer before maturity are ....
1. callable bonds
2. sinking fund bonds
3. serial bonds
4. convertible bonds

75. After a stock split, the total worth of an investor's stock is ....
1. about the same
2. greater
3. smaller
4. none of these

76. Mr. Brown owns 200 shares of Moss Corporation. Assume that in a privileged subscription 10 rights are required to buy 1 new share. Mr. Brown can buy .... new shares.
1. 2,000
2. 2
3. 20
4. 200

77. Among the issues of a particular company, ... is generally the riskiest or most volatile investment.
1. common stock
2. preferred stock
3. mortgage bonds
4. serial bonds

78. Miss White owns 51 shares of stock. If there were a 3-for-1 stock split, she would have a total of .... shares.
1. 51
2. 17
3. 153
4. none of these

79. Bonds that have as security other securities placed with a trustee are termed ....
1. security bonds
2. debenture bonds
3. equipment trust certificates
4. collateral trust bonds

80. On July 1, 1965, a $1,000, 3.5 percent bond that matures on June 30, 1985, is purchased for $800. The yield to maturity is ....
1. 3.5 percent
2. 4.0 percent
3. 4.5 percent
4. 5.0 percent

Refer to page 259 for correct answers.

2 | Financial statements

Any stockholder of a firm wants to keep informed about how his company is doing. Its income, expenditures, and general financial health are of interest to him. One way to keep informed is through the company's statement of financial condition, commonly referred to as the *balance sheet,* and its *statement of income.* These important documents should be read in relation to each other, since the information of both present the picture of a company's financial condition.

For example, Mr. Rich is an inventor who develops a new widget. He feels there will be substantial customer interest in widgets, and he now wants to begin manufacturing and selling. Mr. Rich starts the business, which he calls the Rich Company, with $4,000 on January 1, 1968. His *financial statement,* as of that date, would be:

RICH COMPANY
Balance Sheet
January 1, 1968

Assets		*Liabilities and Equity*	
Cash	$4,000	Liabilities	0
		Mr. Rich's equity	$4,000
		Total Liabilities	
Total Assets	$4,000	and Equity	$4,000

The *assets* of a company are everything the company owns, including amounts owed to the company by others. The *equity* represents the owner's interest or ownership. On January 1, 1968, Mr. Rich owned all the assets. The total of the left and the total of the right columns of a balance sheet are equal to each other; that is, they balance with the same total figure of $4,000. In other words, **assets equals liabilities plus proprietorship (equity).**

Mr. Rich soon uses the company's cash to buy machinery to start manufacturing, and he realizes that he needs more than just equipment to manufacture his widgets. He needs *working capital* for parts (raw materials) and to pay wages. So Mr. Rich goes to his bank, where he borrows $3,000 to be used as working capital. This loan is a *liability* since it represents money owed by the Rich Company.

Assets are the things *owned* by the company; liabilities are those things *owed* by the company. The balance sheet picture is now:

RICH COMPANY
Balance Sheet
February 15, 1968

Assets		Liabilities and Equity	
Cash	$3,000	Bank loan	$3,000
Equipment	4,000	Mr. Rich's equity	4,000
		Total Liabilities	
Total Assets	$7,000	and Equity	$7,000

Again, both columns balance with equal total figures. The bank loan resulted in an asset increase (cash) of $3,000 and a liability increase (bank loan) of the same amount.

Mr. Rich then uses $2,000 of his borrowed cash to buy materials for manufacturing widgets. The result of this transaction is simply a change on the asset side of the balance sheet, which reduces cash by $2,000 and establishes a new asset, *materials*, with an initial balance of $2,000.

Since Mr. Rich is spending much of his time selling widgets, he decides to hire a man to handle widget production. At the end of the month, in preparing his balance sheet Mr. Rich makes provisions for the wages that his new worker has earned but has not yet been paid. Since the worker has worked for 15 days and his monthly salary is $400, Mr. Rich provides for *wages payable* of $200 and reduces his own equity by the same amount. The situation is now as follows.

RICH COMPANY
Balance Sheet
February 28, 1968

Assets		Liabilities and Equity	
Cash	$1,000	Wages payable	$ 200
Materials	2,000	Bank loan	3,000
Equipment	4,000	Mr. Rich's equity	3,800
		Total Liabilities	
Total Assets	$7,000	and Equity	$7,000

Mr. Rich uses all his materials to manufacture 100 widgets, which he offers for sale to retail stores. Therefore, the materials asset is reduced to 0 and is offset by a new asset, *inventory*, of $2,000. He sells 40 widgets for $30 each—a total of $1,200—but he must wait for payment from his customers, even though he delivers the 40 widgets to them immediately. The sale of 40 widgets (40 percent of 100 widgets total) reduces inventory by $800 (40 percent of $2,000). A new asset, *accounts receivable* from customers is created with $1,200, and the $400 difference, which is the profit, reflects as an increase in Mr. Rich's equity. At this point, he has left in his inventory 60 widgets, which are valued at their cost of $20 each, total $1,200.

The balance sheet picture is now:

RICH COMPANY
Balance Sheet
February 28, 1968

Assets		Liabilities and Equity	
Cash	$1,000	Wages payable	$ 200
Accounts receivable	1,200	Bank loan	3,000
Inventory (60) widgets	1,200	Mr. Rich's equity	4,200
Equipment	4,000		
		Total Liabilities	
Total Assets	$7,400	and Equity	$7,400

What are some of the factors that changed since January 1, 1968?

1. **On the asset side:**
   a) The 40 widgets sold for the $1,200 now owed to the company by customers are reflected as accounts receivable.
   b) The raw materials were used up to make the widgets and are no longer reflected in the balance sheet. The unsold widgets are reflected as inventory, at their cost of $1,200.

2. **On the liabilities and equity side:**
   a) Mr. Rich owes his employee $200, which is reflected as wages payable of $200.
   b) Mr. Rich's equity decreased by $200 of wages payable and, as a result of the sale of 40 widgets, increased by $400. Thus, the present equity balance is $4,200.

Mr. Rich is so pleased with his profit that he discusses his progress with his accountant. His accountant is pleased too, but notices that Mr. Rich has not taken into consideration the wear and tear on his machinery. He explains that all buildings and equipment decrease in value due to wear and tear. This is called *depreciation*. Only land does not depreciate, because it is considered to have value for an indefinite period. However, any buildings on it decrease in value as the years pass. Mr. Rich and his accountant determine that his machinery will last about 80 months. Therefore, every month the machinery will depreciate 1/80 of its original value of $4,000.[1] The machin-

---

1/ Depreciation is the spreading of cost price less salvage value over the useful life of the asset. For Mr. Rich's machinery, it is assumed that there is no salvage value. There are several methods of determining depreciation, including straight line, declining balance, and sum of the years' digits.

ery will depreciate $50 each month. This depreciation reflects on the balance sheet as a deduction from the asset *equipment.* Because it is deducted from an asset, depreciation is called a *negative asset.* The depreciation reduces Mr. Rich's equity. Though depreciation is an expense, no cash is expended.

The financial picture of the Rich Company after the adjustment for depreciation is as follows.

RICH COMPANY
Balance Sheet
February 16, 1968

Assets			*Liabilities and Equity*	
Cash		$1,000	Wages payable . . . .$ 200	
Accounts Receivable		1,200	Bank loan 3,000	
Materials		0	Mr. Rich's equity 4,150	
Inventories		1,200		
Equipment at Cost $4,000				
Less Depreciation* 50		3,950		
			Total Liabilities	
Total Assets		$7,350	and Equity $7,350	

* The $50 represents 1 month's depreciation under the straight line method of determining depreciation.

Since an asset and Mr. Rich's equity were both reduced by $50, the total assets still equal total liabilities and equity.

Balance sheets

As we have seen, either each new financial factor reflects on both the *left* (assets) and the *right* (liabilities and equity) columns of a balance sheet, or any change on one side of the balance sheet is exactly counterbalanced by an equal opposite change on the *same* side. The balance sheet for any given day is like a snapshot of a particular company's financial position. By studying balance sheets over a period of time, it is possible to see how a company is progressing and whether or not its financial health is improving.

What we have seen with the small Rich Company is typical of how most companies start. As they grow larger, the fundamentals remain the same, but naturally there are many more financial factors that reflect on the balance sheet. The balance sheet of a larger manufacturing corporation (ABC Company) is more complicated, as is shown below.

The large corporation often divides its assets in several main categories.

1. *Current assets* include all cash and all items easily convertible to cash within the next 12 months.
2. *Fixed assets,* or *property, plant, and equipment* are highly illiquid and generally are

ABC COMPANY
Balance Sheet
December 31, 1968
(millions of dollars)

Assets

Current Assets:
Cash	$ 9.0	
Marketable securities at cost ($0 market value)	0.0	
Accounts and notes receivable	12.4	
Inventories at lower of average cost or market value	27.0	
Total Current Assets		$ 48.4

Investments:
Investment in subsidiary	4.7

Fixed Assets:
Building, machinery, and equipment	104.3	
Less: Accumulated depreciation	27.6	
	$ 76.7	
Land	19.4	
Total Fixed Assets		96.1

Other Assets:
Advances to officers	0.2	
Deposits with vendors	0.6	
Total Other Assets		0.8

Total Assets:		$150.0

Liabilities and Stockholders' Equity

Current Liabilities:
Accounts payable	$ 6.1	
Accrued liabilities	3.6	
Current maturity of long-term debt	1.0	
Federal income tax payable	9.0	
Other taxes payable	0.6	
Dividend payable	1.3	
Total Current Liabilities		$21.6

Reserves:
Reserve for contingencies	3.6

Long-Term Debt:
5% Sinking fund debentures due July 31, 1970	$27.0	
Less: Current maturities	1.0	
		26.0
Total Liabilities		$51.2

Stockholders' Equity (Capital):
5% cumulative preferred stock, par $100*	6.0	
Common stock, par $10†	15.0	
Capital surplus	9.6	
Earned surplus (retained earnings)	68.2	
Total Stockholders' Equity		98.8

Total Liabilities and Stockholders' Equity		$150.0

* $6 million in cumulative preferred stock divided by $100 par means that 60,000 shares are outstanding.
† $15 million in common stock divided by $10 par means that 1.5 million shares are outstanding.

not easily converted into cash. Examples are land, buildings, factories, and machinery.

3. *Investments* include long-term investments, such as stocks, bonds, and investments in subsidiaries or affiliates.

4. *Intangibles* include such items as goodwill, patents, trademarks, organization costs, leaseholds, and copyrights.

5. *Other assets* are not readily convertible to cash and do not fall into the other itemized categories.

The large corporation usually divides its **liabilities** and **stockholders' equity** into the following categories.

1. *Current liabilities* are the bills, debts, or obligations that are currently due for payment or will become due within the next 12 months.

2. *Reserves or reserves for contingencies* provide for unforeseen expenses. The company places a monetary amount on its books as a liability. Reserve for liability due to law suits is an example.

3. *Long-term debt* is any debt owed by the company and not payable within 12 months.

4. *Stockholders' equity* normally consists of the par (or stated value) of preferred and common stock issued and outstanding plus the earned surplus plus capital surplus. For ABC Company, this is $98.8 million.

Asset classifications

It is important to understand the various classifications of assets.

Current assets include cash, government securities, receivables, partly made goods (work in process), raw materials, prepayments of insurance or other expenses, marketable securities not held for investment, and inventories. All these items are either cash or can be converted easily into cash within the next 12 months. The sum of these items is total current assets.

1. *Cash* (on hand and in banks) includes bank deposits, cash in the company safe, and even petty cash.

2. *Marketable securities* include various short-term holdings, such as federal Treasury bonds, notes, and bills.

3. *Accounts receivable* are amounts owed to the company from trade accounts for goods and services sold, if they are collectible in the ordinary course of business within one year. Usually such accounts arise from the sale of goods on terms payable in 30, 60, or 90 days.

4. *Notes receivable* represent notes and acceptances received from trade customers or others. They are generally given in exchange for goods and services. If the company expects to collect the notes receivable in the ordinary course of business within one year, they are classified as current assets.

5. *Inventories* represent assets held primarily for sale (merchandise inventory) or manufacture into products for sale. A manufacturing company's inventory includes raw

materials, materials in the process of being manufactured, and finished goods. Inventories are usually shown in the balance sheet at the lower of their cost or market value. Most companies have in their finished goods inventory products that were manufactured at different times—e.g., 12 months ago or 3 months ago. The change in inventory from one period of time to another represents the quantity sold when adjusted for additions to the previous level. There are two basic ways of determining the quantity sold: (a) by conducting actual physical counts at different periods in time; (b) by bookkeeping records that keep a perpetual running inventory. The method of determining the value of the quantity sold has an important effect on both profits and assets. Profits are effected because the lower the cost of goods sold, the higher are profits. Assets are affected due to the valuation assigned to inventory in the current assets section of the balance sheet. The three most commonly used methods of inventory valuation are *FIFO, LIFO,* and *weighted average cost.*

a) FIFO, *first in, first out,* means that when sales are made from inventory the first goods sold are considered to be the oldest—that is, the first in. A firm that uses FIFO considers that current sales are from the oldest goods held. During a period of sharply rising prices, these old goods will have cost less than goods produced later, so the firm will earn a profit higher than will a firm that uses LIFO.

b) Under the LIFO, *last in, first out,* method, the goods sold are considered to be the newest—that is, the last in. In a period of rising prices, use of the LIFO method results in lower profits than would be realized by the FIFO method.

c) The *weighted average cost* inventory valuation method assumes that goods sold from inventory are expended at an average cost, which is affected by the number of units acquired at each price.

The following example will illustrate the three methods.

INVENTORY RECEIPTS

Date	Transaction	No. of Units	Cost Price	Total
1/1	Inventory on hand	200	$ 8	$1,600
1/10	Purchase	400	9	3,600
1/20	Purchase	300	10	3,000
1/31	Purchase	100	13	1,300
	Total	1,000		$9,500

Assume that during the month 700 units were issued or sold. This could be determined by a physical inventory, which shows an inventory balance of 300 units at month-end, or through bookkeeping records. The problem is to determine both the cost of the 700 units issued or sold and the value of the remaining inventory of 300 units.

The FIFO method states that the 700 units issued were the first 700 units obtained. These are:

```
1/1  ........................... 200 units at $ 8, total $1,600
1/10 ........................... 400 units at $ 9, total $3,600
1/20 ........................... 100 units at $10, total $1,000
```

Thus, under the FIFO method the cost of goods issued is $6,200, and the remaining inventory of 300 units has a value of $3,300 (100 units at $13 plus 200 units at $10).

The LIFO method states that the 700 units issued were the last 700 units obtained. These are:

```
1/31 ........................... 100 units at $13, total $1,300
1/20 ........................... 300 units at $10, total $3,000
1/10 ........................... 300 units at $ 9, total $2,700
```

Thus, under the LIFO method, the cost of the 700 units issued is $7,000, and the remaining inventory of 300 units has a value of $2,500 (200 units at $8 plus 100 units at $9).

The weighted average cost of inventory is determined by dividing the total inventory value ($9,500) by the number of units (1,000), or $9.50. Thus, the 700 units issued are valued at 700 times $9.50, or $6,650, and the remaining inventory is valued at 300 times $9.50, or $2,850.

Assume that the 700 units were sold at a sales price of $20 each, total $14,000. The cost of the units sold is deducted to determine gross profit on sales, as follows.

	FIFO	LIFO	Average Cost
Sales	$14,000	$14,000	$14,000
Cost of sales	6,200	7,000	6,650
Gross Profit on Sales	$ 7,800	$ 7,000	$ 7,350
Ending Inventory Value	$ 3,300	$ 2,500	$ 2,850

Thus, the effect on both profits and ending inventory of using different inventory valuation methods is apparent.

However, if the ending inventory of 300 units were sold for a total of $6,000, at the particular cost basis for each valuation method, additional gross profit on sales would be as follows.

```
FIFO .............................................. $2,700
LIFO .............................................. $3,500
Average cost ...................................... $3,150
```

These additional gross profits plus the gross profit on the earlier sale of 700 units equals $10,500. In other words, over an extended time period the total gross profit on sales will be the same for different valuation methods, even though profits will differ during interim fiscal periods. The ending inventory valuations on the balance sheet are normally shown at the lower of cost or market values. The three methods of valuing inventories relate to valuing their cost. Should the current market value be judged to be less than their cost, the cost basis would be written down or reduced to the applicable market value.

Investment in subsidiary represents an investment made by the parent (controlling) company in another corporation or business wholly owned or controlled by the parent. When the financial statement of the controlling company is combined with that of its subsidiary (termed consolidation), the financial statement of the controlling, or parent, company is more complete than when the actual cost of the investment is simply shown as investment in subsidiary.[2]

Fixed assets include property, plant (factory), and equipment. They are fixed tangible assets, such as buildings, machinery, automobiles, and equipment used by the business in the production of the goods and services it sells. Such assets are not intended to be converted into cash and are therefore categorized as fixed. They can, of course, be sold at their realizable value.

1. *Depreciation,* as we have seen in the Rich Company, reflects the spreading of cost over the estimated useful life of fixed assets used by the business for production of its goods and services. One fixed asset, land, does not depreciate.
2. *Depletion* refers to consumption of natural resources, which are part of a company's assets. Oil, gas, and mining companies have assets that deplete. Such assets are also known as wasting assets. The recording of depletion is a bookkeeping entry similar to depreciation and does not involve the expenditure of cash.
3. *Obsolescence* is the term that describes the loss of value of an asset due to lack of usefulness before it wears out. A TV set with an 8-inch screen is an excellent example of an inventory item whose value should be reduced due to obsolescence.

Intangible assets, such as trademarks, brand names, copyrights, patents, leaseholds, and goodwill, may appear on the balance sheet. *Goodwill* may represent the public's

---

2/ Normally, investments in subsidiaries are shown when a parent company owns 50 percent or more of the common stock of a subsidiary company. If less than 50 percent is owned, the ownership may be shown as investment in affiliates. There are three methods of accounting for investments in subsidiaries. The cost method carries the investment at cost, which is not adjusted for earnings of the subsidiary. Dividend receipts from the subsidiary are shown as dividend income by the parent. With the equity method, the asset—the original cost of the investment in the subsidiary—is increased by retained earnings of the subsidiary. The capital account, appraisal capital, or retained earnings of subsidiaries is increased by the same amount. The third method is *consolidation,* wherein financial statements of the parent company are prepared as though the parent and the subsidiary were a single entity.

interest in a product, the satisfaction of people who have used the product, or trade names. Goodwill normally originates when a corporation is sold for more than the amount at which its net assets are valued. The excess purchase price is then reflected on the new balance sheet as goodwill. Goodwill is the excess cost over net worth of the company purchased. When intangible assets do appear on the balance sheet, they are usually carried at a nominal value.

A *patent* is an exclusive right to a device or a process given to an individual or a company by the U.S. government. A patent's exclusivity is for 17 years. For example, the Ronson lighter some years ago was patented, and for many years there were no competitive imitations. After the patent expired, many companies introduced similar lighters.

A *trademark* is a drawing, design, picture, or other identifying means used by a company to distinguish its goods or services. A trademark does not have a legal life and may be used by a company for an indefinite period. *Brand names* may be protected by a trademark. A familiar trademark is the name Coca-Cola. The brand is simply a special name given by a company to one of its products in order to make it better known. Thus, Coca-Cola is a brand name that has been trademarked.

A *copyright* is registered at the Library of Congress of the United States, and is obtained by having a genuine publication that bears the appropriate copyright notice. The life of a copyright in the United States is 28 years plus the possibility of a 28-year renewal term. Things artistic in nature, such as books, works of art, music, and even a computer program, may be copyrighted.

Leaseholds may appear as an asset at a nominal value (e.g., $1) if the company is lessor of a property at a very favorable rental. A company that executed a 20-year lease of an office building 10 years ago could sublet its space at a much higher rental than the company pays. Leasehold improvements are physical improvements to leased property, such as a building.

Deferred charges or deferred costs represent expenditures for services or benefits that are allocable to the income of the future. Examples of such a deferred charge are bond issuance costs or research and development expenditures.

Another example is *organization expense,* which is the initial cost of establishing a company or new product. These assets are gradually reduced to zero over a period of years by amortization over their useful life.

Other Assets are assets that do not fall in any other category.

Liabilities

Current Liabilities are all a company's debts or obligations that are currently due or will become due and payable within the next 12 months.
1. *Accounts payable* are amounts payable to creditors for goods and services purchased by a company in the usual course of its business. These are distinguished from accrued liabilities, defined next.
2. *Accrued liabilities* are amounts that have been set aside to pay debts or bills that

will be due in the future. Examples include accrued interest on notes payable, accrued wages, and accrued interest.

3. *Current maturity of long-term debt* is the amount of such debt that will be due and payable within one year.

4. *Federal income and other taxes* include all accrued taxes.

5. *Dividends payable* include common and preferred stock dividends declared by the board of directors and, therefore, an obligation and liability until paid.

Reserves (for contingencies) are liabilities established by a charge to earned surplus to show that equity may decrease due to various contingencies. Examples include reserves for new factory and reserves for liability due to lawsuits. The effect of establishing such a reserve is to reduce the amount of earned surplus available for dividend distribution.

Long-term debt includes all debt (e.g., bonds) owed by the company that is not payable within the next 12 months. *Term loans* and loans from an insurance company or bank would fall within this category.

Capital

Stockholders' equity, owners' equity, book value, or *owner's capital* represents the net worth of a business. This is the excess of total assets over total liabilities. In a corporation, it is the par value of the preferred and common stock issued and outstanding, plus capital surplus, whose sum is also called capital stock, plus earned surplus.

1. *Capital surplus* is the amount in excess of par value or stated value paid by the stockholders into the corporation for their stock. For example, 1,000 shares of $10 par stock (total $10,000) are sold to the public, and the company receives $100 per share, total $100,000. Capital stock is credited $10,000, and capital surplus is credited $90,000. Thus, the capital initially contributed to a business by its owners is the sum of capital stock plus capital surplus. The American Institute of Certified Public Accountants (AICPA) prefers the term "capital contribution in excess of par value" to the more frequently used term "capital surplus."

2. *Earned surplus* is retained earnings or all the money, after dividends, that has been retained by the company since its inception. Also known as *retained income, retained earnings,* or *reinvested earnings,* it represents the amount of profit the company has plowed back into the business. Operating losses for a year would ordinarily be charged to earned surplus. The AICPA prefers use of the term "retained earnings."

The *capital structure* of a corporation is the stockholders' equity plus funded debt (normally bonds). Thus, the term "capitalization" or "capital structure" denotes the total dollar amount of all bonds and other funded debt, preferred stock, common stock, capital surplus, and earned surplus. The capital structure is the breakdown of the company's sources of capital into equity and funded debt. It is the sum of net worth (stockholders' equity, plus long-term debt). A conservative capital structure is one in which most or all of the capitalization is in the form of common stock, while an aggressive or speculative capital structure is one in which only a small portion of the capitalization is in common stock.

Funded debt (long-term debt) includes all outstanding bonds and notes that are payable after one year or longer; that is, it represents long-term indebtedness. *Term loans,* such as bank loans for long periods, may also be classified as funded debt. Short-term obligations—those that fall due within one year—are considered to be a current liability and are not part of funded debt.

Statement of income

The balance sheet (statement of financial condition) shows the financial health of the ABC Company at a particular date. In order to get an idea of the company's operations during the year or during a specific period of time, we must study the *statement of income* (profit and loss statement), which shows what income was received, the company's expenses and its net income (profit). A sample *statement of income* follows.

ABC COMPANY
Statement of Income
for Year Ended December 31, 1968
(millions of dollars)

Net sales (revenues)			$100.0
Cost of sales:			
Merchandise inventory, 1/1/68		$50.0	
Add: Merchandise purchases during year		25.0	
Merchandise available for sale		$75.0	
Deduct: Merchandise inventory, 12/31/68		25.0	
		$50.0	
Labor		10.0	
Manufacturing overhead		15.0	
Cost of goods sold			$75.0
Gross profit on sales			$25.0
Operating expenses:			
Selling expenses:			
Sales salaries	$1.0		
Advertising	2.0		
Depreciation of selling equipment	1.0		
Miscellaneous	1.0	$ 5.0	
General and administrative expenses:			
Officers and office salaries	$2.0		
Depreciation of office furniture	1.0		
Other expenses	2.0	5.0	10.0
Operating income (net profit from operations)			$15.0
Other income and expenses:			
Interest charges			1.3
Net Income before Taxes			$13.7
Provision for federal and state income taxes			6.6
Net Income after Taxes			$ 7.1

The statement of income must be viewed in the light of the use of revenue. The way in which net income is used for dividend payments and for plowing back earnings in the business is shown in the *retained earnings statement.*

ABC COMPANY
Retained Earnings Statement
for Year Ended December 31, 1968
(millions of dollars)

Retained earnings, January 1, 1968		$66.4
Net income per statement of income $7.1		
Deduct: Preferred stock dividends declared		
during year 0.3		
Earnings available for common stock $6.8		
Deduct: Common stock dividends declared		
during year 5.0		
Retained earnings for the year	1.8	
Retained Earnings, December 31, 1968	$68.2	

Sales is the total dollar value of goods and services sold during the year. *Cost of sales* (cost of goods sold) is the expense incurred in manufacturing, including raw materials, freight, rent, wages, and others. *Gross profits on sales* is the excess of income from sales over the cost of sales.

Operating expenses include expenditures for commissions, advertising, administration, and taxes such as excise and social security. Depreciation on buildings and equipment is also an operating expense. The inclusion of the depreciation expense reduces income by the actual amount of depreciation, even though depreciation is a bookkeeping entry and not a cash expenditure. *Operating income* (profit from operations) is the excess of income from sales over costs of doing business—that is, sales less cost of goods sold and operating expenses. An operating deficit would result if costs exceeded income.

Interest charges represent interest paid to bondholders or banks on borrowed capital. *Other income* is not shown on the ABC Company Statement of Income. Interest received on bank deposits and dividends from investments are examples of other income. *Provision for taxes on income* is an accrual for taxes to be paid during the next year on the current year's profits. Current (1/1/68) federal corporation tax is 22 percent on the first $25,000 of net income and 48 percent on income over $25,000. Otherwise, the corporate tax rate is not graduated as is the federal personal income tax. *Net profit, net income,* or *net earnings* is the company's profit remaining after all expenses and taxes have been paid. This is the most significant item on the income sheet and is known as "the bottom line."

From net income, dividends on preferred stock must be paid before any distribution is made to common stockholders. Should there be no current profit, dividends might possibly be declared by the board of directors from retained earnings.

Earnings available for common stock represent the balance of earnings for the year available for payment to common stockholders in the form of dividends or for retention in the business. The amount of net income that remains after payment of common stock dividends is called *retained earnings* or *earned surplus*. This amount is kept in the business and is plowed back for corporate expansion.

The preparation of financial statements is a complex task and is handled by expert accountants. The accounting profession has developed standards to routinize accounting methods. It is through the interpretation of these financial statements that most investors make their buy-and-sell decisions.

2 | Review questions

The items mentioned in questions 81 to 85 would normally be found:
1. in the asset section of the balance sheet
2. in the current liability section of the balance sheet
3. in the fixed liability section of the balance sheet
4. on the income statement

81. Raw materials and inventories ....

82. Sales and cost of sales ....

83. Mortgage bonds outstanding ....

84. Accounts payable ....

85. Land and equipment ....

86. Goodwill may represent ....
1. the public's interest in a product
2. the satisfaction of people who have used a product
3. trade names
✓4. all of these

87. When a company has a large amount of senior securities outstanding in relation to its stockholders' equity, the company is said to have high ....
1. credit standing
2. growth potential
3. leverage
4. all of these

88. Reserves for contingencies are ....
1. funds set aside for future expansion of a company
2. reserves set aside from earned surplus to show that equity may decrease because of various contingencies
3. reserves set aside from capital surplus for use in various contingencies
4. never employed by companies

89. Not included in a company's capitalization are ....
1. bonds
2. short-term loans
3. common stock and preferred stock
4. capital and earned surplus

90. Earnings retained in the business are called ....
✓1. retained earnings
2. net assets
3. capital surplus
4. none of these

91. Working capital usually is spent on ....
1. jewels for the boss's secretary
2. a new factory
3. land
✓4. raw materials or inventory

92. Funded debt does not include ....
1. equipment trust certificates
2. preferred stock
3. mortgage on equipment
4. debentures

93. A corporation has common and preferred stock outstanding, debentures, and earned and capital surplus. The corporation's capital structure includes ....
1. common and preferred stock outstanding and debentures
2. common and preferred stock outstanding, debentures, and earned surplus
3. common and preferred stock outstanding, debentures, and earned and capital surplus
4. none of these

94. It is not always possible to determine .... from a corporation balance sheet.

1. assets
2. liabilities
3. net income
4. cash

95. Company assets do not include ....

1. prepaid insurance
2. bonds
3. goodwill
4. accounts receivable

96. Ordinarily, ... do(es) not have amortization charges.

1. machines
2. cash
3. organization expense
4. buildings

97. .... is a current asset.

1. Capital stock
2. Accounts receivable
3. Goodwill
4. Land

98. Partly made goods are part of a company's ....

1. current liabilities
2. fixed assets
3. capital stock
4. current assets

99. A premium received from the sale of newly issued stock is shown as .... on the balance sheet.

1. earned surplus
2. common stock
3. capital surplus
4. sales

100. A 6 percent cumulative preferred stock par $100 sells at a discount. Its price could be ....

1. $600
2. $90
3. $110
4. $200

101. The issuing company sells 1,000 shares of common stock par $10 for $25. These shares are shown on the company's balance sheet, under common stock, at ....

1. $1,000
2. $10,000
3. $25,000
4. $35,000
5. $10,500

102. The capital initially contributed to a business by its owners is the sum of ....

1. stock and retained earnings
2. stock and capital surplus
3. retained earnings and capital surplus
4. earned surplus and capital stock

103. Shareholders' equity is represented on a balance sheet by ....

1. stock
2. capital surplus
3. retained earnings
4. all of these

104. Profits not distributed to shareholders are called ....

1. dividends
2. retained earnings
3. earned surplus
4. either 2 or 3

105. A company's profits after all expenses and taxes are paid is termed ....

1. net income
2. gross profit
3. operating profit
4. dividends

106. Capital surplus includes ....

1. reserves held for contingencies
2. profits retained in a business
3. the amount above stated value paid into a corporation by investors at the time of stock issuance
4. funded debt

107. .... is (are) not a liability.

1. Accounts payable
2. Five percent mortgage bonds
3. Prepaid insurance
4. Bonds

108. The liabilities of a business are ....

1. undistributed profits
2. the amounts the business owes others
3. the amounts owed to the business
4. capital surplus

109. Things a business owns and will generally turn into cash within a year are called ....

1. current assets
2. current liabilities
3. fixed assets
4. depreciation

110. Fixed assets include ....

1. cash
2. inventories
3. furniture
4. all of these

Refer to page 259 for correct answers.

3 | Analysis, economics, monetary and fiscal policy

In analyzing a specific security for investment purposes, various ratios and formulas are useful to determine its investment merits. Those that follow should prove sufficient for most practical considerations, and are the most commonly used tests employed by investment analysts. The balance sheet and statement of income provide the facts necessary for the computation of these ratios.

Liquidity, the ability of a company to pay its debts, is a factor of particular importance to both creditors and stockholders. Various credit ratios are used to measure liquidity and to test short-term solvency.

The *current ratio* or *working capital ratio* is the ratio of current assets to current liabilities. The formula is

$$\frac{\text{Current assets}}{\text{Current liabilities}}.$$

For ABC Company, this is $48.4 divided by $21.6, or 2.2. For every $1 of debt, the company has $2.2 of current assets.[1] The analyst should be concerned with the quality of the inventory and receivables that make up the current assets. The standard minimum for industrial firms is regarded as 2.0, or 2 to 1.[2] However, many companies have much higher ratios, and it is important to realize that even for a single company the ratio will fluctuate. A very sound company may have a lower ratio; the ratio for utilities and railroads is usually below 2 to 1. The current ratio varies from industry to industry, and within the same industry it varies seasonally. A common use of the current ratio of a company is for comparison with other companies in the same industry.

Working capital is found by subtracting current liabilities from current assets. For ABC Company, this is $48.4 less $21.6, or $26.8.[3] Working capital—money readily

---

1/ See p. 33.

2/ The theory that *any* company with a ratio of less than 2 to 1 has serious liquidity problems is no longer accepted.

3/ See p. 33.

available for use in the business—is used for such purposes as buying inventories or materials.

The *quick asset ratio,* or *acid test,* is the ratio of current assets, not including inventories, to current liabilities. Quick assets are current assets less inventories. Inventories are excluded in an attempt to refine the current ratio to a more accurate measure of liquidity. However, the acid test ratio still requires qualitative analysis of the receivables, which may or may not be worth their stated value.

The quick asset ratio is:

$$\frac{\text{Current assets less inventories}}{\text{Current liabilities}}$$

or

$$\frac{\text{Quick assets}}{\text{Current liabilities}}.$$

The acid test ratio for ABC is $48.4 less $27.0 divided by $21.6, or 1.0.[4] As a measure of liquidity, a favorable ratio is often considered 1.0 or 1 to 1; that is, for every dollar of current debt there is a dollar of assets, which can be turned quickly into cash. Nevertheless, many sound companies have lower ratios, and some companies with shaky financial structures have a higher ratio. Like the current ratio, the acid test will vary seasonally and from industry to industry. *Net quick assets* are found by subtracting total current liabilities from quick assets. For ABC, this is $48.4 less $27.0 less $21.6, which is slightly below zero.

Capitalization ratios test the financial strength of a corporation, and give comparisons of various elements in the capital structure to net worth. There are several important capitalization ratios. In all cases, the ratio relates the percentage of one part of the capital structure to the whole or total capital structure.

As we know, the total capital structure is the sum of bonds, preferred stock, common stock, capital surplus, and earned surplus. (For capitalization ratio purposes, it is common practice to eliminate the book value of intangible assets from net worth.)

For ABC Company, the capital structure is the sum of bonds ($26 million), preferred stock ($6 million), common stock ($15 million), capital surplus ($9.6 million), and earned surplus ($68.2 million), total $124.8 million. (ABC has no intangible assets.)

1. The *bond ratio* is the amount of bonds ($26 million) divided by the capital structure ($124.8 million), or 21 percent.
2. The *preferred stock ratio* is the preferred stock ($6 million) divided by the capital structure ($124.8 million), or 5 percent.
3. The *common stock ratio* is the common stock *and* surplus ($92.8 million) divided by the capital structure ($124.8 million), or 74 percent.

Note that the sum of the three ratios equals 100 percent. Normally, the bond ratio

4/ See p. 33.

for industrial companies should not exceed 33 1/3 percent of its capitalization, and at least half of the capitalization should be represented by common stock and surplus. The bond ratio for public utility and railroad companies should not exceed 50 percent of the capital structure. Too large a debt burden reduces the margin of safety to bondholders, increases fixed charges, decreases dividends available to stockholders, and in the event of a sudden recession could lead to a financial crisis.

A company that has bonds or preferred stock outstanding is said to be *trading on equity,* or *leveraged.* Leverage magnifies profits and losses to the common stockholders. If ABC Company earns more than 5 percent on the $6 million provided by preferred stockholders and more than 5 percent on the $26.0 million borrowed from the debenture holders, the excess accrues to the common stockholders. If the earnings on the $32 million were less than 5 percent, the shortage would be to the detriment of common stockholders.

Leverage is measured by the ratio of the funds supplied through debt and preferred stock ($32 million) to common stock equity (common stock plus surplus of $92.8 million). Thus, the leverage for ABC Company is $32 divided by $92.8, or about 34.5 percent. A public utility with a capitalization of 50 percent debt, 25 percent preferred, and 25 percent common and surplus would have a leverage of 3.0, or 300 percent.

Usually, the *break-even point* for a corporation is the point in amount of sales where total income exactly equals fixed and variable costs of operation. Another concept of break-even points is used in connection with leverage—the rate of return on total capitalization at which a shift of debt to equity or vice versa will not affect the return on common equity.

For ABC Company, the average interest on the preferred and outstanding debt is 5 percent. On the total capitalization of $124.8 million, 5 percent, or $6.24 million. must be earned in order that preferred dividends and bond interest may be paid while still returning 5 percent to the common stockholders on their investment, including surplus. At this point of earnings, a conversion of common stock to debt or vice versa will have no effect on the return on common equity.

Thus, as rate of earnings increases in the good year *by 5 percent* from the break-

EARNINGS

	Break-even	Poor		Good
Rate of earnings on total capitalization of $124.8 million	5.0%	0.0%		10.0%
Total earnings	$6,240,000	$ 0		$12,480,000
Preferred dividend and bond interest	(1,600,000)	(1,600,000)		(1,600,000)
Balance for Common	$4,640,000	($1,600,000)		$10,880,000
Return on common equity of $92,800,000	5.0%	(1.7%)		11.7%
Change in return on common by having leverage	0	(1.7%)	+	1.7%
Leverage	.345	.345		.345

even level, return on common equity increases above the 10 percent level by an amount equal to the leverage (.345) times the 5 percent increase, or an additional 1.7 percent. In the poor year, when rate of earnings decreases by 5 percent, return on common equity decreases below the 0 percent level by the leverage (.345) times 5 percent, or an additional 1.7 percent.

The simplified chart below will further clarify the effects of leverage. Assume that total capitalization is $250,000 common, $750,000 debt at 5 percent interest, total $1 million.

EARNINGS

	Break-even	Poor	Good
Rate of earnings on total capitalization	5%	0	15%
Total earnings	.$50,000	$0	$150,000
Debt service	37,500	37,500	37,500
Balance for Common	.$12,500	($37,500)	$112,500
Return on common equity	5%	(15%)	45%
Leverage	3.0	3.0	3.0

Thus, in the good year when rate of earnings increases from 5 to 15 percent, by 10 percent, the return on common equity increased to 15 percent plus the leverage (3.0) times the increase of 10 percent, or 45 percent. In the poor year, return on common equity decreases below the rate of 0 percent earnings by the leverage (3.0) times the 5 percent decrease from the break-even level. The following formula may be used to express the magnifying effect of leverage.

$$R = C + L(C - B).$$

R = rate of return on common equity.

C = rate of earnings on total capitalization.

L = leverage.

B = break-even percentage on debt, or average rate of interest (and preferred dividends) on outstanding debt.

It can readily be seen that when the overall rate of earnings on total capitalization (e.g., 15 percent) exceeds (is exceeded by) the average cost of debt service (e.g., 5 percent) the rate of return on common equity will be increased (decreased) from the overall rate by a multiple (the leverage, e.g., 3.0) of the difference.[5] The risk in

5/ Our definition of leverage is debt plus preferred divided by common plus surplus. Some authorities use a slightly different definition for a *leverage* factor, as follows: Total assets divided by common stock plus surplus. Thus, by this definition, leverage is the number of dollars in the business for each $1 of common stock equity.

leverage is insolvency in the case of failure to pay bond obligations in adverse times, or forced recapitalization in the case of failure to pay preferred dividends for a long period.

Other ratios are concerned with earnings, dividends, and efficiency of operations. The following are a few of the most important ones.

Earnings per share (EPS) of common stock is determined by dividing the earnings available for common stock (6.8 million), shown on the retained earnings statement, by the number of shares outstanding.[6] The number of shares of common stock outstanding is found in the stockholder's equity section of the balance sheet. The ABC Company has $15 million of common stock at $10 par, or 1.5 million shares,[7] so earnings per share are $4.53. The trend in EPS is of highest importance and significance to investors interested in income as well as in capital gains. Without increases in EPS, it is unlikely that dividends will increase or that the long-run trend of the market price of the stock will increase.

The *dividend payout ratio* is the ratio of dividends actually paid to common stockholders to net income available to common stockholders. For ABC Company, this is $5 divided by $6.8, or 74 percent. On the overall basis, for both preferred and common dividends, the ratio is $300,000 (preferred dividend) plus $5 million (common dividend) divided by $7.1 million, or 75 percent. The amount of net income retained in the business is one hundred percent less 75 percent, or 25 percent.

The *dividend per share of common stock* is simply the dividends paid on common stock divided by the number of shares outstanding. The ABC Company pays $5 million on 1.5 million common shares, or $3.33 per share.

The *dividend return (yield)* is the annual dividend per share divided by the market value (price) of the stock. If the dividend is $3 and the price if $50, the *return* or *yield* is 6 percent.

The *earnings per share of preferred stock* ratio is found by dividing the net income (available for preferred and common dividends) by the number of shares of preferred stock. The formula is

$$\frac{\text{Net income}}{\text{Number of shares of preferred stock}}.$$

For ABC Company, it is

$$\frac{\$7.1 \text{ million}}{60,000 \text{ shares}}$$

or $118 per share.

The *price-earnings ratio (p-e ratio)* is the ratio of market price of the stock to

6/ See p. 41.
7/ See p. 33.

earnings (net income) per share. It is a short way of saying that a stock is selling at so many times earnings. Some experts consider a good price-earnings ratio to be 10 times earnings; others use 15 or 20 times earnings as a yardstick. As we noted in figuring EPS above, the EPS for ABC Company are $4.53. If the market value of ABC common stock were $45.25, the p-e ratio would be 10, and if the market price were $90.50, the p-e ratio would be 20.[8]

Earnings on invested capital is another means of comparing the relative efficiency of similar companies. Another term sometimes used is "percent return on capital." The formula is:

$$\frac{\text{Net income plus fixed charges}}{\text{Capital structure}^9}.$$

For ABC Company, this is $8.4 million divided by $124.8 million, or 67 percent. This ratio is useful to compare with other companies in the same industry as well as for the company itself at successive intervals.

Some ratios are primarily concerned with sales. *Margin of profit* is equal to the operating income (profit) divided by net sales—in other words, the percentage earned in operating profit on every dollar of sales. For ABC Company, this is $15 divided by net sales of $100, or 15 percent. That is, after paying costs of operation the company has 15 cents left from each dollar of sales. From this amount, taxes, interest, and dividends must be paid. The ratio indicates the operating efficiency of the company.

The *operating ratio* is very important because it allows one to compare the operating efficiency of two similar companies and to compare the efficiency of one company to itself at periodic intervals. The formula is:

$$\frac{\text{Operating expenses}}{\text{Net sales}}.$$

For ABC Company, this is $85 divided by $100, or 85 percent. Note that the operating ratio plus the margin of profit equal 100 percent.

The *inventory turnover* is:

$$\frac{\text{Cost of goods sold}}{\text{Average inventory}}.$$

For ABC, this is $75 divided by $37.50,[10] or 2 times. In this case, the inventory is turned over only twice per year. This amount may then be compared with other firms in the industry to see whether it is favorable or unfavorable.

A low turnover may be due to: (1) poor merchandise, overbuying, a large stock of

8/ There is no correct price-earnings ratio. Through market forces of supply and demand, the p-e ratio may be 8, 15, or even 100.

9/ Excluding intangible assets.

10/ Average inventory is the sum of beginning inventory (50.0) and ending inventory (25.0) divided by 2.

old, unsalable merchandise; (2) an anticipated future increase in sales and so on. A higher turnover than the industry average may indicate superior merchandising, or it might indicate a real shortage of inventory for needed sales, or conservative pricing of closing inventories. A high turnover in and of itself is not necessarily desirable.

The *sales to net working capital ratio* is:

$$\frac{\text{Net sales}}{\text{Net working capital}}.$$

This ratio measures the efficiency of the use of working capital in a business. It is also a good means of comparing two companies with respect to the efficiency of use of working capital. For ABC Company, this is $100 divided by $26.8, or 3.4 times. Other ratios are used to evaluate the safety of investing in senior securities, such as preferred stock and bonds. *Interest coverage,* or fixed-charge coverage, is the number of times charges for long-term debts have been earned during the year. The formula is:

$$\frac{\text{Operating profit (before interest, taxes, and fixed charges)}}{\text{Annual interest charges (fixed charges)}[11]}.$$

The interest coverage for the ABC Company, from its statement of income, is $15 million divided by $1.3 million, or 11.4 times.[12] Coverages of 6 times or greater for an industrial company, 5 times for railroads, and 4 times for a public utility are regarded as adequate.

Preferred dividend coverage is:

$$\frac{\text{Net income}}{\text{Interest and preferred dividends}}.$$

For ABC, this is $7.1 divided by $1.6, or 4.4 times.

Investors may also be interested in the amount of assets available for distribution in the event that the corporation goes out of business. The *book value*[13] of a stock or bond issue is the value of the assets available for that issue, as stated on the books, after deducting all prior (senior) liabilities. It is generally expressed as so many dollars per share or so much per $1,000 bond. Normally, intangible assets such as goodwill are excluded in computing book value.

The total assets of ABC Company are $150 million. This amount less current liabilities and reserves of $25.2 million results in a net worth or book value of $124.8

11/ For *all* bond issues.

12/ If the corporation has more than one bond issue, the coverage on the senior issue is determined without consideration of the fixed charges for the junior issues. The junior issues' coverage would be determined by including their fixed charges plus the fixed charges of all equal or senior issues. A weakness of this method is that the senior issue could show good coverage when a junior issue is not covered at all. This method of computing interest coverage is called overall or cumulative. Another method, called prior deductions, would compute interest coverage on the junior of two issues, as follows: interest coverage equals (amount of revenue available for the junior issue after paying senior fixed charges) divided by (the junior fixed charges). This method is to be avoided.

13/ Also called net tangible asset value.

million. ABC Company has no intangible assets, so an adjustment is not required. The book value per $1,000 bond is determined by dividing $124.8 million by the number of bonds outstanding, 26,000,[14] or $4,800 per bond.

The book value[15] per share of preferred stock is determined by deducting from total assets all prior liabilities, including bonds and intangible assets, if any, which is $98.8 million divided by 60,000 shares, or $1,647 per share. Determination of the book value of common stock requires reduction of the net worth of $98.8 million by the amount of preferred stock outstanding, $6 million. The common book value is thus $92.8 million divided by 1.5 million shares, or $61.86 per share.

The *fixed asset to net worth ratio* is the ratio of fixed assets to net worth and is of special interest to long-term creditors. For ABC Company, this is fixed assets of $96.1 million divided by net worth of $98.8 million, or 97 percent. This ratio indicates the relative amount of owner-contributed capital that is invested in fixed assets. The higher this ratio, the less the protection is for creditors. A ratio of over 100 percent, though common for utilities and railroads, would be a mark of weakness for many industrial concerns.

A great amount of reliance is placed on the certification or accountant's opinion that accompanies a financial statement. The accountant's report expresses an *opinion*, not a guarantee, because the values of many items in financial statements cannot be precisely measured. Nevertheless, the opinion of an independent expert, with experience and skill in auditing and accounting, is very important to investors. The opinion usually affirms that (1) the statement has been prepared in accordance with generally accepted principles in accounting; (2) the statement presents fairly the financial condition at the end of the year and the results of operations during the period covered; and (3) the accounting principles followed are consistent with those of the preceding year.

The various tests we have discussed are employed and used regularly by investment analysts. Mutual funds have a staff of competent, well-trained specialists, who concentrate on this important function. This is one of the outstanding advantages of mutual funds for the average investor, who otherwise cannot afford the cost of availing himself of expert help.

Sources of information for analysis

The first step in analysis is to collect facts. Some of the sources of information available to the analyst include the following.

1. Prospectuses and registration statements filed at the SEC. The majority of large companies are required to register with the SEC and provide detailed financial data, which are available to the public. These two documents are supplemented by annual reports that most large companies must file at the SEC.

14/ The balance sheet shows $26 million in long-term bonds. $26 million divided by the face amount of $1,000 per bond means 26,000 bonds are outstanding.
15/ Also called net tangible asset value.

2. Financial newspapers.
   a) *Barron's* (weekly).
   b) *The Wall Street Journal.*
   c) *Commercial and Financial Chronicle.*
3. The ticker tape, which shows current purchases and sales on an exchange.
4. Newspapers, which contain remarks of corporate executives to the press, to the Society of Financial Analysts, or in public addresses.
5. Federal publications. The Federal Power Commission's annual statistical report offers substantial information about public utilities. The Interstate Commerce Commission publishes a vast amount of data about railroads, including an annual publication, *Statistics of Railways in the United States.*

   The Federal Reserve Board issues at nominal cost a monthly bulletin that contains a large amount of financial information about the state of the economy.

   State banking authorities issue data concerning banks, and state insurance departments issue data on insurance companies.
6. Annual, quarterly, and interim reports are a major source of information. Most reports contain as a minimum a condensed consolidated balance sheet and income statement.
7. Advisory and forecasting services provide information from the investor's point of view.
   a) Moody's Investors Service consists of five manuals published annually, including: industries, municipals and governments, transportation, public utilities, and banks and finance. Biweekly supplements update the manuals. A dividend record provides a continuing report of dividend payments and declarations.
   b) Standard & Poor's Corporation Service includes the *Standard Corporation Record* made up of six looseleaf alphabetical volumes revised monthly, with a daily news section. Various other surveys, trends, and statistical reports are also available from Standard & Poor's.
8. Annual stockholder meetings. Generally, a reasonable amount of important data is released at such meetings.
9. Periodicals.
   a) *Forbes*
   b) *Financial World*
   c) *Wiesenberger* (for mutual funds and closed-end funds)
   d) *Fundscope* (for mutual funds and closed-end funds)
10. Brokerage houses and banks periodically provide detailed research reports on particular companies.
11. Trade association journals contain useful information on developments in particular industries or sciences.
12. Short-term credit information is available from: Dun & Bradstreet, Inc., which publishes the *Reference Book* and analytical reports; the National Credit Office, which has financial statements for thousands of firms; and the Robert Morris Associates, which provides information to member banks.

The function of securities analysis is to use all available pertinent information, as discussed above, to appraise the investment characteristics of a security.

Investment characteristics

The basic characteristics of an investment are safety, rate of return, marketability, tax status, and growth potential.

In considering *safety,* one must consider both dollar safety and purchasing power safety. Thus, though a government bond has the highest degree of dollar safety it affords virtually no protection against inflation. Two methods of increasing the degree of safety in equity investing are dollar cost averaging and formula purchase plans.

Dollar cost averaging calls for a fixed number of dollars to be invested in a specific security at regular fixed intervals (e.g., monthly) during a period of time. Consider the following example.

Investment Number	Investment Amount	Price per Share	Shares Purchased
1	$100	$10.00	10
2	$100	$ 8.00	12.5
3	$100	$ 5.00	20
4	$100	$ 4.00	25
5	$100	$ 2.00	50
6	$100	$ 4.00	25
7	$100	$ 5.00	20
8	$100	$ 8.00	12.5
9	$100	$10.00	10
Totals	$900	$56.00	185.0

The average price paid for the shares is $56 divided by 9 investments, or $6.22. The average cost of the shares purchased is $900 divided by 185 shares, or $4.86. The 185 shares purchased are worth at the current $10 price per share a total of $1,850. Thus, the profit is $950.

Dollar cost averaging does what the name implies—averages the cost of the investments. In the above case, sale of the securities at any price above the average cost of $4.86 would yield a profit.

Investors may also seek to lessen the risks of investing by such means as *formula plans* of several types. The constant dollar method is a formula used by some investors for establishing the timing of their purchases and sales of stock.

The constant dollar method requires periodic review of the value of the stock portfolio (e.g., monthly). For example, an investor has a diversified portfolio of securities valued at $75,000 at current market prices. Each month, when he reviews his portfolio, he either sells or buys in sufficient amounts to maintain the market value at $75,000.

This method forces the investor to sell as prices rise, and to buy when prices fall. However, during an extended bull market, the method is disadvantageous, since the investor will accumulate cash as prices continue to rise.

Discussion of various other formula plans, such as constant ratio, variable ratio and percentage methods may be found in Lucile Tomlinson's *Practical Formulas for Successful Investing,* published by Funk & Wagnalls, and George Leffler's *The Stock Market* published by Ronald Press.

The *rate of return* desired is a definite influence in selecting investments. Bonds, mortgage loans, and preferreds have a fixed rate of return. Common stocks and real estate do not.

The *marketability* of a security is its third characteristic. The market for a stock may be broad—that is, the stock is widely held and traded in large volume—or the market may be the converse—that is, narrow. The market price of a stock may tend to fluctuate within a narrow range; then, it is considered stable. Or the price may fluctuate widely, as do glamor stocks.

The *tax status* of an investment is important because it is the return or gain after taxes that is relevant to an investor. Tax-exempts, capital gains, and the 85 percent dividend credit to corporations are all factors.

Growth potential is the last and perhaps, for many investors, the most important investment criteria. Various factors relating to growth potential are discussed later in this chapter.

Government bond analysis

Federal government issues fall into three categories: (1) the direct debt, (2) the guaranteed obligations of federal agencies, and (3) nonguaranteed obligations of the federal agencies.

The investment merit of government bonds depends entirely on the willingness of the government to pay interest and principal, since there is no question of the government's ability to pay. Nevertheless, two risks of any debt ownership apply to governments as well as any other bonds. These are the risk of price fluctuation due to changes in interest rates, and the risk of loss of purchasing power due to inflation.

The direct debt is an actual obligation of the federal government. Included are Treasury bills, certificates, notes, and bonds, as well as series E and H savings bonds. The interest on these obligations is fully subject to the federal income tax but not to state income tax. The principal of the issues is subject to both federal estate and gift and state inheritance taxes, but is exempt from state property taxes.

Guaranteed obligations of federal agencies include only the Federal Housing Administration debentures issued in exchange for assignments of insured mortgage loans that have been foreclosed. The Commodity Credit Corporation is also authorized to issue directly guaranteed obligations. The federal government, in effect, is fully responsible for the bonds of: The International Bank for Reconstruction and Development (World Bank), Public Housing Administration, and New Housing Authority.[16] The Treasury also is fully responsible for Veteran's Administration Guaranteed Mortgages and Federal Housing Administration Guaranteed Mortgages.

There is strong presumption but not an actual guarantee of the obligations issued by five federal agencies, including:

1. The Federal Land Banks, which make loans to owner/operators of farms.
2. The Federal Intermediate Credit Banks, which accept at a discount agricultural loans made by banks and agricultural credit companies.
3. The Federal Loan Banks, which extend credit chiefly to member savings and loan associations.
4. Banks for Cooperatives, which make loans to eligible cooperative associations.
5. The Federal National Mortgage Association (also called Fannie Mae), which is chiefly engaged in buying FHA-insured and VA-guaranteed loans from the lending institutions.

About 50 percent of the direct debt of the federal government is held by individuals and commercial banks and Federal Reserve banks. The remaining 50 percent is widely distributed.

State and municipal bond analysis was discussed in Chapter 1. The following points will amplify the preceding discussion. State bonds, often categorized as municipals, have a legal status different than the bonds of cities, counties, townships, school districts, and others, in that suit may not be brought against a state without its consent, but may be brought against the other political subdivisions.

The ability and willingness of state and municipal governments to pay both interest and principal is important, because defaults and repudiations of debt have occurred in the past. One should consider their ability to pay fixed charges based upon their expected revenues. One should also consider the ratio of all debt, including overlapping debt, as explained in Chapter 1, to the *actual* value of property in the tax district as well as the assessed value. In addition, the *legality* of the debt issue should be ascertained.

As previously mentioned, interest payments on all debts of state and local governments are currently exempt from federal income taxes. However, capital gains on the sale of these securities are not exempt and are taxed like any other capital gain. Municipals are subject to federal estate and gift taxes. Interest payments may or may not be subject to state income tax. Municipals may or may not be subject to state personal property taxes.

The equivalent value of a tax-exempt municipal to a normal bond may be computed by the following formula:

$$\frac{1}{1 - \text{Tax rate}} \times \text{Tax exempt yield} = \text{Equivalent value}.$$

Thus, a taxpayer in the 75 percent income tax bracket would receive, after taxes, the

16/ Interest receipts from Public Housing Authority issues are exempt from the U.S. federal income tax.

same amount from a 3.5 percent municipal as he would from a 14 percent corporate bond:

$$\frac{1}{1 - .75} \times .035 = .14$$

As a result, the yield on high-grade municipals is usually less than that on government bonds.

New municipals are usually sold by the issuers to underwriters on a competitive, sealed-bid basis, and then are reoffered to the public. Commercial banks are permitted by federal law to act as underwriters on general obligations, but not on pure revenue issues. Municipal securities are not required to be registered with the Securities and Exchange Commission. Generally, trading in municipals takes place in the over-the-counter market.

Corporate bond analysis

The capacity of the obligor to pay interest and principal when due is paramount. The chief indications of such capacity include the following.

Credit of the obligor is the most important factor. A high credit rating allows the obligor to borrow to pay interest, if necessary. Several measurements of credit of obligors are as follows.

1. Earnings coverage of interest charges, which is

$$\frac{\text{Profits (before income tax)}}{\text{Fixed charges}},$$

should be for stable industries two times or more, for volatile industries three times or more. For industries sensitive to the business cycle, adequate coverage under recession conditions should be considered.

2. The factor of safety is the percentage by which earnings before tax may decline until they fail to cover fixed charges. For example:

> Earnings before tax = $3,000,000
> Fixed charges   = $1,000,000
> Factor of safety   = 66 2/3%

3. The trend of earnings for the future is quite important, as is consideration of their vulnerability to cyclical declines in business activity.
4. If both senior (e.g., debenture) and junior (e.g., subordinated debentures) are outstanding, one must consider: for junior issues, coverage of combined senior and junior charges; for senior issues, coverage of senior charges only.
5. Cash flow coverage of debt service must be considered. Since in a recession capital spending can be stopped, depreciation cash flow can be used to pay charges and principal.

6. Miscellaneous credit factors include: cash and liquid investment; ownership of securities that can be pledged for borrowing; and large-scale expenditures for research and other areas, which can be cut back, if necessary.

Protective provisions of bond issues, over and above the credit of the obligor, are important to determine. Some provisions include:

1. A mortgage on physical property.
2. A pledge of securities under a collateral trust agreement.
3. A preference over others through subordination of other indebtedness.
4. Priority in the event of future reorganization due to failure to meet interest charges or maturities.

Bond Ratings provide an excellent guide to investors. Widespread use is made of the rating investment services' ratings of publicly owned bonds. Such ratings, however, do not take the place of analysis. Because ratings are widely followed, they influence bond yields and prices. The value of a rating system is limited by the number of tests used, and because historical rather than future performance is analyzed.

Bonds are rated by at least two major firms—Moody's, and Standard & Poor's, who specialize in furnishing investors with statistical services. Their bond ratings are as follows.

Moody's		Standard & Poor's
Aaa	prime grade	AAA
Aa	very high grade	AA
A	high grade	A
Baa	medium grade	BBB
Ba	lower medium	BB
B	speculative	B
Ccc, Cc	very speculative	CCC, CC
C	income bonds in default	C
Ddd, Dd, D	default	DDD, DD, D

Real estate mortgage bonds are another form of investment bonds. They entail possible servicing problems as well as limited marketability. They are chiefly held by institutions, such as banks, savings and loans, and insurance companies. Such bonds are often amortized by periodic repayments of principal and interest over the life of loan. Real estate mortgage bonds may be collateralized by the following types of property: (1) residential (homes, apartments); (2) commercial (offices, stores, shopping centers); (3) industrial (factories); and (4) eleemosynary (churches).

Some factors in analyzing mortgages include: (1) value of the pledged property and terms of the mortgage; (2) income of the property and the obligor (borrower); (3) whether the loan is insured or guaranteed; (4) willingness of the borrower to meet his obligations.

Many home mortgages are insured by the Federal Housing Administration. If the borrower defaults, the mortgage holder forecloses and exchanges the title for debentures in an amount slightly exceeding the unpaid balance of the loan, on which interest[17] and principal are guaranteed by the U.S. Treasury. The Veterans Administration also guarantees mortgages for up to 60 percent of the appraised value, maximum $7,500, for loans to qualified borrowers. In the event of default, the VA pays its liabilities in cash rather than in debentures.

The major holders of real estate mortgage loans are savings and loan associations, life insurance companies, and mutual savings and commercial banks. The excellent safety record of loans on owner-occupied dwellings has given them a high investment standing with institutions.

Preferred stock

The ability of the issuer to meet regular dividend payments is a key question in analyzing preferred stocks. The usual methods of bond and stock analysis are applicable to this hybrid, which has characteristics of both. In addition, several points to investigate in a preferred issue are as follows.

1. If a dividend is passed, do the preferred stockholders have the contingent right to vote? Some charters provide that the preferred stockholders in such cases may have exclusive or majority voting rights until dividend arrears have been paid up. Statutes in some states give preferred stockholders the right to vote on questions that affect the status of the corporation's property as a whole. Most state statutes allow voting on amendments to the certificate of incorporation, which modify the rights of the preferred holders.
2. Do the bylaws or certificate of incorporation give preferred shares preference in the distribution of assets on dissolution?
3. Are the dividends cumulative; that is, do dividends not paid during a year accumulate and have to be paid at a later date, before dividends can be paid on the common stock?
4. Is the preferred participating? Is it convertible into common stock?
5. Are there other provisions to protect the preferred holder? For example, is payment of common dividends prohibited unless, x (e.g., 2) years of preferred dividends have been set aside as a reserve? Is consent of the preferred stockholder required before new bonds or stock with preferential rights may be issued?
6. Is the preferred callable? What is the call price in relation to the present and anticipated future market price?

Though preferred has little appeal to the issuer from the tax point of view, it has great appeal to the corporate investor. Bond interest received is fully taxable to the corporate stockholder, but only 15 percent of the preferred dividends received are currently taxable to corporate investors.

In computing dividend coverage ratios for preferred issues, it is important to consider earnings after tax to all fixed charges of issues senior to and ranking with the preferred issue. One should not simply consider the preferred dividends alone.

17/ The interest rates are set twice a year and approximate the market yield on long-term Treasury bonds.

Common stock analysis

The aim of bond analysis is to determine the debtor's ability to pay and willingness to pay interest and principal. The aim of stock analysis is to determine probable future values per share. Factors to be analyzed include the following.

The *earnings per share* record is probably the single most important ratio. A stable growth of profits may indicate that this trend is likely to be maintained in the future in the absence of developments that cause a change. The probable trend of earnings per share may be made by estimates of: sales volume, selling prices, costs, diversification into new fields, and adjustments for nonrecurring items.

Price-earnings ratio, whose relative importance changes as economic conditions and investor attitudes change, reflects chiefly five factors.

1. *Trend of earnings per share*. If it is upward, future dividend increases and increases in value of stock may be anticipated. Expected future profit growth in effect is discounted or adjusted for by a high price-earnings multiple.
2. *The quality of reported earnings* is affected by the accounting practices used by the corporation. For example, the larger the depreciation allowance, the greater the ability to finance future expansion. Research and development outlays lead to future increases in sales. Inventory accounting and nonrecurring items affect earnings. The use of the FIFO method of inventory valuation causes higher profits in periods of rising prices that disappear if prices stabilize.
3. Expected dividend increases may cause a higher multiple due to both low- and high-income-tax-bracket investor preference. Low-bracket investors prefer a larger yield; high-bracket investors look forward to anticipated capital gains.
4. *Investor and institutional demand* for a stock or particular class of securities causes price (earnings) ratios to rise.
5. The *quality of management* is weighed heavily by institutional and professional investors.

Industrial securities

Industrial securities include all corporate enterprises except financial, public utility, and railroads. Major classes include the following:

1. Mining, petroleum, and other extractive enterprises, which are dependent on limited amounts of natural resources.
2. Manufacturers of industrial materials, such as metals and chemicals.
3. Manufacturers of producer durable goods and military equipment.
4. Manufacturers of consumer nondurable goods, including textiles, foods, and tobacco.
5. Manufacturers of consumer durable goods and building materials.
6. Wholesale and retail outlets.
7. Service industries, such as air transport and bus lines, that may have public utility characteristics.

Many firms fall into more than one category. This is increasingly true in 1968 as the urge to merge has hit corporations, resulting in the so-called conglomerates.

Securities analysis is based upon an assumption that a persistent study of facts improves one's chances of choosing securities that will advance in price and of avoiding those that will decline. The first step in *fundamental* security analysis is to collect the facts. Both statistical data and public opinion or psychology are important tools for the analyst's consideration. Some of the major facts that should be known involve three principal considerations—those of the economy, specific industries, and those of a particular company.

Factors to consider concerning the economy are:

1. What are general business conditions? Is the economy moving forward or regressing?
2. What are the promising industries; what is their future? The trick is to avoid future horse-and-buggy industries and to avoid industries that may face problems such as excess production.

In industry analysis, one must identify and study the dominant influences that affect earnings and value. These vary from industry to industry and time to time. For example, factors to consider in several industries include the following.

1. *Oil stocks:* (a) location of crude reserves, (b) proportion of crude requirements produced by the company, (c) political risks inherent in foreign reserves.
2. *Autos:* (a) cyclical fluctuations in demand, (b) adaptability to changing public taste.
3. *Chemicals and drugs:* (a) new product development, (b) price competition, (c) research program.
4. *Retail stocks:* (a) adaptability to changing public buying habits and population trends, (b) ability to compete with discount houses.
5. *Tobaccos:* (a) adaptability of products to consumer health concern.

Industry factors include:

1. The long-term trend of the industry compared to general business conditions.
2. Domestic and foreign competition within the industry and from other products or services.
3. Prospective technological changes and their impact on earnings.
4. Labor (wage) factors.
5. Sensitivity of the industry to business fluctuations.

There are six principal factors to consider in the particular company.

1. *Prospective earnings* are of primary importance, since securities prices tend to reflect future earning power rather than current or past performance. Three important items to consider in estimating future earnings are sales prospects, selling prices, and costs.
   a) *Sales prospects* depend mainly on: the company's position in the industry, the outlook for the industry, competition, and development of new products.
   b) If *selling prices* can be raised without adversely affecting demand, profit margins go up. Adverse factors that lower prices include: competition, antitrust law prosecution, technological changes, marketing policies, and tariff changes.

c) In estimating *costs,* one must consider changes in: raw material prices, technological processes, wage rates (percentage of wages to total costs and the labor union situation), taxes, price levels (rising prices with FIFO inventory valuation lowers cost and increases profits), sales volume (quantity or volume transactions tend to allow cost savings per unit through quantity buying, etc.).

2. *Cash flow* is net profit plus depreciation and depletion less capital expenditures (for asset acquisition). The amount by which cash flow exceeds net profit means money available for: new productive assets; repayment of debts; and replacement of assets.

3. The *working capital position* indicates the ability to meet current debts. A large inventory could be dangerous if, for example, styles change and the inventory becomes difficult to eliminate.

4. *Accounting peculiarities* may over- or understate earnings relative to other companies. Earnings are relatively understated when costs of developing new products are expensed. Earnings are relatively overstated when companies capitalize the cost of developing new products.

5. Several *capital structure* factors should be checked, including:
   a) Possible dilution due to outstanding convertibles, or stock option plans.
   b) Coverage of senior interest and dividend costs.
   c) Whether liabilities of subsidiaries are consolidated into the parent's balance sheet.

6. *Dividend prospects* are important, since a rising trend in cash dividends seems to enhance the growth image of a stock.
   Other factors that should be checked include the following.

1. In extraction industries, the amount of proven reserves is very important.

2. Will any new patent or processes provide largely royalty income?

3. Changes and peculiarities in accounting practices must be investigated. For example, after World War II airlines were unable to obtain new aircraft. The expiration of depreciation on old planes on hand resulted in higher and nonrecurring profits.

4. New laws may affect profits. For example, the auto safety regulations will affect the auto industry. Can such costs be passed on to consumers without reducing demand?

5. Antitrust or other litigation can be very costly and should be investigated.

Financial securities

Financial securities include stocks of banks, insurance companies, finance companies, and investment companies.

Bank stocks

The assets of banks consist mainly of loans and securities. The most important factors in analysis are the quality of assets and cost of funds. Assets may be understated, hidden assets such as common stocks may not be shown on the balance sheet, and real estate may be shown considerably below its true market value.

Banks usually derive their earnings mainly from interest on loans and investments, and to a minor extent from fees and charges for services. Ratios commonly used in analyzing bank stocks are:

1. Net operating earnings per share (excluding capital gains and losses) after taxes.
2. Market price as a percent of net operating earnings.
3. Market price as a percent of book value.
4. Dividends as a percent of net operating earnings.
5. Earning assets per share.
6. Capital as a percent of deposits and/or risk deposits.
7. Ratio of time to total deposits.
8. Book value per share.

Regulation of bank stocks. Approximately 33 percent of commercial banks (e.g., those that accept demand deposits) operate under national charters issued by the Comptroller of the Currency. Such banks must have the word "national" in their name. The remaining 67 percent of commercial banks are chartered by the states and are regulated by state banking departments. All national banks are required to be members of the Federal Reserve System; state banks may apply for membership. Banks holding about 85 percent of all commercial bank deposits are members of the Federal Reserve System. All members are subject to the regulations of the Federal Reserve Board (FRB). About 97 percent of bank deposits are insured by the Federal Deposit Insurance Corporation (FDIC). The FDIC insures bank deposit accounts up to $15,000 and collects an annual assessment from banks to build up an insurance fund.

Some of the significant factors involved in the investment merits of a bank security include the following:

1. Growth in deposits in the long run is likely to parallel growth in earnings and profits.
2. Banks in areas that are expanding considerably are to be favored.
3. Banks in nonexpanding areas that can gradually take over a growing percentage of area deposits (e.g., through aggressive branch banking) are also to be favored.

The experience and ability of bank management is crucial, because banks operate on very high leverage since liabilities (deposits) are often 10 to 12 times capital. Thus, several bad loans could have a serious effect on a bank's financial structure.

Insurance stocks

Earnings are generally from two sources: (1) investment earnings on stockholder equity and excess interest on policy reserves, and (2) underwriting gains from other insurance operations. Insurance companies may be divided into two major groups: (1) fire (property) and casualty companies, and (2) life companies.

Life insurance companies include both stockholder-owned companies and mutual companies that, theoretically, are owned by the policyholders. Life insurance companies collect premiums on life and health contracts from which they pay policy claims, operating expenses, and commissions, and set aside and invest legal reserves to meet future claims. The amount of such legal reserves is required by law. Life premiums are computed to recognize four elements: (1) mortality and other benefit costs; (2) operating expenses, including sales commissions; (3) the rate of interest the insurance company assumes it will earn on investments; and (4) profit.

There are only two basic types of policies, those that provide death protection only, with no savings (term), and those that combine death protection with savings through cash surrender values (ordinary life, 20- or 30-year payment life, and endowments). The importance of the assumed rate of earnings on investment of the savings portion of the second type of policy is to be particularly noted. If actual experience were exactly equal to the assumptions used in calculating premiums, insurance companies would earn only the specific profits assumed in the computed rate. Since mortality rates have declined due to increasing life expectancy, since costs have either not increased or have even been reduced through both the use of computers and the sales of higher policy denominations, and since investment yields have exceeded assumed rates, profits in excess of those assumed in the premium computation have in many instances been realized.

The asset side of an average life insurance company balance sheet is composed predominantly of investments. The liability side is predominantly reserves. Usually, only about 9 to 11 percent of total assets are represented by capital and surplus funds. Thus, life insurance companies' leverage is similar to that of commercial banks.

The federal tax status of life insurance companies is unique and favorable, although considerably increased taxation was imposed on many life companies as a result of the Life Insurance Company Tax Act of 1959. In general, taxable investment income plus 50 percent of the excess of operating gain over taxable investment income is taxed at corporate rates, the other 50 percent of the excess is taxed only to the extent that it is distributed or made available to stockholders. Long-term capital gains are taxed at 25 percent.

Life insurance analysis is complicated by the extremely high cost of writing new business, which normally exceeds the entire full first-year premiums. Analysts generally adjust earnings to compensate for the surplus investment in new business by an increase based on the type of new business written. In analysis, earnings also may be adjusted for amounts allocated to reserves in excess of statutory requirements.

Life insurance stocks have been cyclical in nature and may be regarded as a growth industry. The relative amount of consumers' savings directed toward this medium has declined as mutual funds and savings and loans have grown. Many life insurance companies are meeting the threat of mutual fund competition by buying or starting their own mutual funds or by writing variable annuities.

Fire (property) and casualty stock insurance companies have expanded rapidly in terms of the gross income they receive from premiums. About 75 percent of total business is written by stock, as opposed to mutual companies.

The profitability of such companies depends partially on the types of risks underwritten. Some of the various lines written include: straight fire, extended coverage, allied fire lines, home multiple peril, commercial multiple peril, ocean and inland marine, accident and health, group accident and health, workmen's compensation, bodily injury liability, property damage liability, auto collision, bodily and property damage, auto fire and theft, fidelity, surety, glass, burglary and theft, boiler and machinery, credit and livestock.

The asset side of fire and casualty companies is predominantly their investments, including roughly equal amounts of bonds and stocks. The liabilities are mainly short-term reserves for claims and premiums that have been collected in advance.[18] Stockholders' equity may approximate 40 to 50 percent of total assets.

The income statement of fire and casualty companies is divided into net under-writing gain or loss and net investment income. Unrealized profits or losses in asset values do not reflect in the statement of income but are reflected in surplus. Under-writing gains are overstated, as previously mentioned, because all costs of writing new business are charged to current operations, even though the premium income is prorated over the life of the contract. Some companies do not even show realized capital gains and losses in the income accounts, but reflect them as adjustments to surplus.

General factors of interest to investors include: kinds (lines) of insurance written, capability of management, extent of hidden reserves through conservative accounting, relation of book value and liquidating value to the market price of common shares, adjusted net operating earnings per share, and the trends within the company and the industry. Most life and fire and casualty stocks are traded over the counter, although several are traded on exchanges.

Factors in insurance company analysis include: rate of growth of the company, types of policies outstanding, the trend of interest rates, the trend of mortality, taxa-tion, method of computing reserves (some are more conservative than others), policy lapse ratio, and percentage of participating and nonparticipating policies.

Most states have insurance departments that enforce state laws regulating both types of insurance companies. Regulations usually pertain to: calculations of values of policy reserves and loss reserves, claims paid and unpaid, investments of assets and valuation of securities, accounting procedures, reporting to state insurance depart-ments, and commissions paid to representatives. Fire and casualty rate charges are also regulated.

Financial companies stocks

Financial companies include installment finance, business finance, savings and loan companies, and personal loan companies. Factors in financial companies analysis in-clude: quality of assets, cost of funds, rate of growth, and tax considerations.

Investment company stocks

Investment companies stocks include closed-end funds and mutual funds. Factors in analyzing closed-end funds include: (*a*) investment record; and (*b*) ratio of market

---

18/ Conservative accounting practiced by fire and casualty companies overstates these amounts by failing to prorate costs of writing new business over the life of the policies.

price to net asset value. Mutual fund factors include: (*a*) investment record; and (*b*) suitability of portfolio for the investor's objectives. These securities are discussed in much more detail in Chapter 4.

Public utility securities

The various types of public utilities include: electric light and power, gas, telephone, telegraph, water, and transit companies. Railroads are also public utilities but are separately classified for analysis because of regulation and economic factors.

Distinctive features, as compared to other corporations, are the following.

1. The utility generally must obtain a *franchise* from the local government; the franchise is a contract between the utility corporation and the local government.
2. The franchise is usually exclusive, giving the utility a legal monopoly to serve a specified area.
3. Rates charged, financing, and other aspects of operation are subject to regulation in the public interest.
4. Utilities enjoy special legal privileges, such as the use of public streets and the ability to acquire property by right of eminent domain.

The main provisions of franchises include the following.

1. The kind of service to be performed may be a single service, such as supplying electricity, or multiple services, such as both gas and electricity.
2. The duration of the franchise may be either indeterminate, perpetual, or limited.
3. The franchise may be exclusive or nonexclusive although the present tendency is to avoid duplication and wasteful competition by refusing to grant more than one franchise for a given service in a given area.
4. Franchises are usually limited to serving a specified geographic area.

Rates and charges at one time were established in the franchise, but now are generally regulated by state or local authorities. Under judicial precedents, utility rates are generally established at levels that give a reasonable return on the capital invested and also provide the public with service at rates that customers can afford.

In the Hope Natural Gas case, the U.S. Supreme Court decided in 1944 that

rates which enable the company to operate successfully, to maintain its financial integrity, to attract capital, and to compensate its investors for the risk assumed certainly cannot be condemned as invalid, even though they might produce only a meager return on the so-called *fair value* rate base. From the investor or company point of view, it is important that there be enough revenue not only for operating expenses but also for the capital costs of the business. These include services on the debt and dividends on the stock ... by that standard, the return of the equity owner should be commensurate with returns on investment in other enterprises having corresponding risks. The return, moreover, should be sufficient to assure confidence in the financial integrity of the enterprise, so as to maintain its credit and attract capital.

Prior to this decision, the fair value of utility property on which rates were based was the present-day cost of reproduction less depreciation, regardless of original cost. Today, the original cost valuation method prevails.

Regulatory authority

The Federal Power Commission has power to regulate natural gas transmission companies; the Federal Communications Commission regulates interstate telephone, telegraph, and radio industries; the Interstate Commerce Commission has jurisdiction over interstate commerce conducted by railroads, oil pipeline, express, and sleeping-car companies; and the Securities and Exchange Commission regulates public utility holding companies.

However, state commissions have wide power of regulation over companies that operate within a single state, often including franchises, rates and services, security issues, and accounts and reports. The attitude of the state commissions is particularly important in that the courts seem disinclined to overrule their rate decisions. Generally, if the earnings of a public utility yield substantially more than 6 percent on the prudent or fair value of its investment, either federal, state, or local authorities will either order a rate investigation or immediately order a reduction in rates.

Some of the factors involved in public utility investment analysis are the following.

1. The rate of growth in the demand for service in the area served as measured by population, employment, industry, and living-standard trends is very important. Competition from other sources must be considered.

2. Franchise continuation and possible rate changes by the regulating authority must be considered.

3. The load factor—the actual average output (average load) in a given period divided by what would have been produced at the maximum demand for its services (peak load)—is indicative in that the higher the load factor, other things being equal, the more profitable the operation, since plant capacity is idle a smaller percentage of the time.

4. The state of plant and equipment is important in terms of both adequacy for future expansion and its age. Since newer equipment is generally more efficent than older, the larger the proportion of the plant that is comparatively new, the lower will be the company's operating costs. General guidelines include the following.

   a) The investment in plant and equipment of an electric, gas, or telephone company should not exceed five times the annual operating revenues.

   b) Utilities should have a retirement reserve of over 15 percent to cover replacement of plant and equipment.

5. Regulatory authorities seek to maintain a reasonable balance between bond and stock capitalization. The SEC has restricted dividend payments of a subsidiary company to its parent holding company as follows.

   a) If common stock equity is less than 20 percent of total capitalization, dividend payments are limited to 50 percent of available earnings.

   b) If common equity is less than 25 percent, dividends are restricted to 75 percent. The SEC favors a capital structure of 50 percent debt, 20 to 25 percent preferred stock, and 25 to 30 percent common stock.

6. Analysis of the earning power of utilities must consider that earnings substantially above a fair return rate on the fair value of property are vulnerable, and that earnings below such level may allow for future rate increases.

In addition to rate regulation, basic economic factors that affect earnings are the demand for services as measured by business conditions; employment; and the cost of providing services as measured by wages, fuel costs, and taxes. Generally, acceptable earnings of double fixed interest charges apply to gas and electric utilities. Utilities (electric, gas, telephone, and water) usually are favored by institutional and some individual investors because they have enjoyed stable, steady growth, because they pay out in dividends a relatively high percentage—70 to 80 percent—of earnings, and because they entail relatively low risk.[19]

Railroad securities

The Interstate Commerce Commission (ICC) and state commissions have regulatory power over railroads. The ICC has the power to:

1. Fix freight and passenger rates on its own initiative or the petition of users or competitors.
2. Pass on the issuance of new securities.
3. Regulate accounting.
4. Pass on proposed mergers, consolidations, and leases.
5. Regulate other phases of railroad activity.

A *merger* is the absorption of one or more existing corporations by another existing corporation. Therefore, mergers differ from consolidations in that the absorbing corporation is not a newly formed corporation.

In a *consolidation,* two or more companies, by agreement and under legislative authority, become united into a new corporation. The new corporation takes over both companies' property, rights, privileges, contracts, and franchises, and assumes their liabilities and other obligations. Generally, stockholders of the consolidating companies exchange their shares for stock of the consolidated company and become stockholders of the new company.

Recapitalization involves a major rearrangement of the capital stock. This may occur by means of stock splits, stock dividends, retirement of shares, changes in the par value of the stock, or reclassifications by means of exchange of common stock for preferred, or preferred for common.

Refinancing refers to the substituting of one security for another in a company's capital structure. For example, bonds may be called and replaced with others that pay a lower rate of interest. Issues of preferred may be replaced in a similar manner. The refinancing of senior securities may affect the value of common stock.

Reorganization occurs in a bankrupt company. When a corporation defaults on its debt, the firm is seldom liquidated. Instead, the courts arrange for the corporate

19/ The relative decline of importance and earnings of transit (e.g., bus and streetcar) companies indicates the importance of analyzing potential competition to public utilities.

properties to be temporarily placed in the possession of a *trustee in bankruptcy* while the corporation is reorganized. The intent behind reorganization is to have the bankrupt corporation emerge with a sturdy capital structure that reflects the real value of its properties and earning power, even if this means that old stockholders are dropped out entirely and old bondholders must become stockholders.

Railroads have suffered from difficulties with labor unions as well as intensive competition from other carriers. The majority of most railroads' operating income is from freight (about 85 percent) rather than from passenger traffic (7 percent). The density of traffic is an important factor in railroad revenues. Density is the revenue ton-miles carried per mile of line per year.

The generally accepted minimum level for a profitable operation for a mainline is 1 million ton-miles per year. Railroad expenses primarily involve:

1. Train and station labor, and supplies and fuel (about 50 percent of total operating expenses).
2. Maintenance of ways and structures (about 14 percent of total operating expenses).
3. Maintenance of equipment (about 23 percent).
4. Cost of obtaining traffic (about 4 percent).

Many ratios are used in analyzing railroad securities, including the following.

1. Operating ratio—operating expenses divided by operating revenues.
2. Maintenance ratio—maintenance expenses and depreciation divided by operating revenues.
3. Transportation ratio—transportation expenses divided by operating revenues.
4. Average tons per loaded freight car ratio.
5. Freight cars per freight train ratio.
6. Train miles per train hours (speed).
7. Ton-miles per train hour.

An unusual feature of railroad financial statements, which are subject to ICC regulation, is that income taxes are deducted before computing operating income. Thus, fixed charge coverage tends to be understated.

The railroad industry faces the need to adapt itself to the changing economic and technological factors, and the analyst must attempt to measure the success, or lack thereof, in making such adaptions. Since 1956, trucks, oil pipelines, and inland waterway transportation have increased their number of ton-miles carried by a greater proportion than have the railroads.

Real estate

Real estate investment may be either as equity in the form of direct ownership or as debt in the form of real estate mortgages or bonds secured by real estate.

Direct investment in real estate can be in: land, owner-occupied houses, income-producing houses and apartments, farms, mines, oil wells, industrial property, hotels, motels, golf courses, and parking lots. Analysis of such investment is a field in itself, apart from securities analysis. Real estate generally is much less liquid than securities investment, but it is not subject to fluctuating stock market values. Real estate management must either be performed by the owner or delegated to professionals. The caliber of the professional management and the economic and social factors in the environment of the property are important.

Classification of securities

We have discussed securities on the basis of their fundamental characteristics according to their industry or business. In addition, according to the volatility of their market price securities may be classified as either cyclical, defensive, or growth stocks. Three other common classifications are blue chip, income, and special situation.

Cyclical industries are those that do well in periods of prosperity and poorly in readjustment periods. Security values of corporations in such industries generally fluctuate widely—more widely than those of other industries. Examples of cyclical industries include steels, railroads, automobiles, and machinery. During periods of prosperity, people are buying new cars at a rapid rate; consequently, the automobile industry prospers. However, in difficult times people are not so willing to commit themselves to the purchase of a new automobile; thus, the automobile industry will face rapidly declining business.

Defensive industries, which are often called belly industries, are the more stable ones that are subject neither to sharp rises nor sharp declines in business. They include such industries as food, utilities, and tobacco. When times are difficult, people still must eat and most continue to smoke cigarettes. One can see that periods of unusual prosperity and periods of readjustment do not have so great an effect on these industries as on the cyclical industries. *Income stocks*—that is, stocks that have paid regular annual dividends for an extended period of time—are typical of defensive issues. Many electric companies are excellent examples of income stocks.

Growth industries are those with prospects of future growth and expansion greater than that of the general economy. *Growth stocks* in these industries generally pay out a smaller percentage of earnings in the form of dividends, since they are usually plowing back much of their earnings into new products, new developments, new processes, research, and so on. Among these industries are electronics, missiles, chemicals, and drugs. Characteristics of a growth stock include:

1. An above-average rate of earnings on invested capital over a period of years, and the likelihood of a continuation of such earnings rate.
2. A high rate of retained earnings.
3. Emphasis on research, development of new products, effective merchandising methods, good cost control, favorable employee relations, and good management training programs, as well as management depth.
4. Excellent opportunities for future growth in sales and earnings.

The generally accepted definition of a *blue chip* security is stock of a company that has a national reputation and a wide acceptance of its product or service. That company is likely to make money and pay dividends in bad times as well as in good times. Blue chips represent the highest grades of income and growth stocks.

When some special development or occurrence is expected to materially affect the market value of a corporation stock, apart and independent of market conditions, the stock of that corporation can be considered a *special situation*. A new patent, changes in management personnel, recapitalization, refinancing, reorganization, merger, or consolidation may be developments that can make a company a special situation.

Stock values

Stocks are said to have intrinsic value, intrinsic worth, investment value, or real value. Since the stock market is an auction market, there is little relationship between book value or par value and the market value of stocks. There is no recognized standard for measuring the investment value of stock, although many experts feel that stock prices should be capitalized on the basis of earnings. Some use an average price-earnings ratio of 10 to 1, others 15 to 1, and in recent years some ratios have soared much higher. The number of times earnings that the market price of a stock will command is also highly dependent on the future expectation of both the particular stock, its industry, and the economy. No real agreement exists among investment analysts on what price-earnings ratio is reasonable. The consensus appears to be that market prices reflect psychological reactions to future prospects and rather subjective judgments. Some of the more important factors that seem to reflect in high price-earnings ratios include the same elements found in a growth stock.

1. The prospect of future growth of earnings per share.
2. A stable earnings growth pattern, with minimum amounts of fluctuation from projected rates of increase.
3. Strong corporate emphasis on research and development and frequent introduction of new products, and high-caliber management.

In reality, a stock is worth only what it will bring in the market.

Interpreting the facts

The second step in analysis is to interpret the facts. This interpretation should be directed toward estimating future earnings. Estimated future earnings should be multiplied by an assumed or typical price-earnings ratio to predict future market values of the security. By comparing this estimate with current market value, one can decide whether the security is over- or underpriced. For example, an analyst predicts estimated future earnings of a stock will be $3 per share. The stock has consistently traded at 15 times earnings. Thus, the future market value of the stock may be estimated at $45 per share. Based on the present market value, the net result of the analysis will be a decision to do one of four things: (1) buy, (2) don't buy, (3) sell, or (4) hold. Obviously, analysis must be a continuing process, and it is essential that an investor be in a position to continually receive relevant information about all securities in his portfolio.

In the final analysis, the analyst weighs the *risks* of each investment against the possibilities of gain, and attempts to buy and sell at the most opportune moments. This weighing of risks and possible gains will enable one to choose between such issues as blue chips, special situations, growth stocks, or income (defensive) stocks.

Economics

Every analyst must keep abreast of changing economic conditions, including the basic direction of the economy and its relation to the field of money and banking. *Economics* is the study of how men choose to use scarce or limited productive resources (land, labor, machinery, etc.) to produce various commodities (such as wheat, beef, etc.), and distribute these resources to various members of society for their consumption. Economics involves prices, wages, interest rates, stocks, bonds, banks, credit, taxes, and private and governmental expenditure patterns.

If the economy is operating at full employment, then the production of one commodity (e.g., butter) must be reduced in order to produce more of something else (e.g., guns). Also, assuming full employment, if the government decides to reduce everyone's taxes, then individuals will have a sudden surplus of funds. This extra money would be partially saved, but the extra amount actually spent on goods and services in a situation of full employment would result in higher prices. This increase in price due to a greater availability of money without a proportionate increase in the output of goods or productivity is known as *inflation.*

Deflation, on the other hand, is expressed by falling prices. If there were general unemployment and people were spending all their money on food, clothing, and shelter, there would be a general reduction in the prices of other goods and services to attract customers. *Depression* (e.g., 1929) is an aggravated and extreme case of deflation. Depression can be characterized by widespread unemployment, falling prices, numerous bankruptcies, and so on. A *recession* (e.g., 1957) is a much less severe type of depression. A recession can be characterized by a general reduction of business activity accompanied by lower profits and unemployment.

Federal Reserve System

The monetary policy of the Federal Reserve System, administered by the Board of Governors, has a great deal of influence on the economy in the following ways.

1. The *discount rate* is set by the Federal Reserve banks. This is the rate each Federal Reserve bank charges member banks in its district to borrow reserve funds by rediscounting commercial papers or by obtaining advances based on the bank's promissory note secured by government securities or eligible commercial or agricultural paper. If the discount rate is raised, banks generally follow suit and money becomes tight. In December, 1967, discount rates were 4.5 percent. The rate charged by commercial banks to their best customers is called the *prime* rate. In December, 1967, the prime rate was 6 percent. Since brokerage firms borrow the money used to finance margin purchases from commercial banks, any changes in the prime rate or supply of money can have a direct effect on the securities mar-

kets. Such loans to brokers are usually *call loans* and may be called by the bank for repayment according to whatever agreements were arranged.

2. *Legal reserve requirements* are set by the Federal Reserve. Member banks must keep a portion (usually one sixth or one seventh) of their clients' deposits as deposits with the Federal Reserve. By increasing the reserve requirement, the Federal Reserve can reduce the supply of money.[20] Reserve requirements as of June, 1968, for reserve city banks are 17 percent of net demand deposits (12½ percent for large country banks) and 3 percent of savings deposits.[21] The Federal Reserve has discretion to vary the required percentage for demand deposits between 10 and 22 percent, and for savings deposits between 3 and 10 percent.

3. Through *open market operations,* the Federal Reserve further controls the supply of money. By selling or by buying government bonds in the open market, the Federal Reserve authorities can either reduce or increase the supply of money.

4. The Board of Governors is also responsible for establishing margin requirements. Margin is the amount of cash that an investor who buys securities on credit must initially pay. Through regulation **T**, the Federal Reserve establishes margin requirements for loans made by brokers and dealers, and through regulation **U** credit extended by banks on stock purchases. In June, 1968, both margin requirements were 80 percent for equity securities and 60 percent for convertible bonds. Regulation **G**, effective March 11, 1968, regulates credit extended by persons other than banks, brokers, and dealers—that is, by other lenders—for the purpose of purchasing or carrying registered equity securities. In June, 1968, margin requirements set by regulation **G** were identical to regulations **T** and **U**.

Ideally, the economy should follow a steady pattern of growth hampered by neither inflation nor depression, and it is socially desirable that there be relatively little unemployment. The government attempts to keep the economy moving forward in such a manner through the use of both monetary and fiscal measures.

20/ An increase in the reserve requirement at a time when *no excess reserves* are in the banking system will cause banks to contract their loans. Assume that the reserve requirement is increased from 15 to 20 percent for demand deposits. Assume the following situation for all member banks before the increase in reserve requirements.

		Required Reserves
Demand deposits ....$100 billion	15% reserve req.	$15.0 billion
Time deposits ....$150 billion	4% reserve req.	$ 6.0 billion
Loans and investments ....$290 billion	...	...
Total required reserves		$21.0 billion

The change in reserve requirements means an increase in required reserves on demand deposits and total required reserves of $5 billion. Banks must increase their deposits at the Federal Reserve by this amount. If bank assets were fully committed in loans and investments, and there were no excess reserves, then $5 billion of loans must be reduced or investments sold. Thus, presuming that the Federal Reserve will either rediscount, make advances, or buy securities, a reduction of $5 billion will suffice.

If the Federal Reserve will lend $5 billion to the banks, no reduction will be necessary. If the Federal Reserve will not rediscount, make advances, or buy securities, a reduction of loans and investments in the banking system of closer to $25 billion will take place due to a multiplier effect.

21/ An increase in reserve requirements from 16.5 to 17 percent (and from 12 to 12.5 percent) took place in late 1967, after the pound sterling devaluation. The effect of the 0.5 percent increase was to increase by $550 million the affected banks' required deposits at the Federal Reserve.

Monetary measures used by the government largely relate to those methods employed by the Federal Reserve. *Fiscal measures* relate to government spending and taxation policies. If without increasing taxes the government spends billions, raised by borrowing, on Great Society, urban renewal, park, and welfare programs, the result in periods of unemployment will probably be increased business activity.

An individual cannot spend more money than he has. However, the government can spend as much as it likes and has in many years spent considerably more than its income. This is known as deficit spending. Such spending, when financed by borrowing without increasing taxes, tends to stimulate the economy, and to the extent that rampant inflation does not result it is beneficial. However, inflation will occur if such deficit spending occurs in periods of full employment, and it is particularly harmful to people who have fixed incomes from pensions and to creditors and others.[22]

One result of government spending policies is that billions of dollars have been spent overseas on foreign aid, by our armed forces, and by tourists. Even though U.S. exports to foreigners substantially exceed imports from abroad, these sources have put a surplus of dollars in foreign hands. The result is that some foreign central banks (France, notably) have converted some of their dollars into gold.

The *balance of payments* is the difference between the amount of money the United States spends abroad and what it receives. A negative balance occurs when spending exceeds receipts.

The following is a summary of the receipts and payments of the United States during 1966.

Receipts (billions of dollars)

Exports of goods and services including investment income	$43.0
Foreign investments in the U.S.	2.5
Total Receipts	$45.5

Payments (billions of dollars)

Imports of goods and services	$37.9
Remittances and pensions	1.0
U.S. government aid grants and capital flow	3.4
Private capital flow, including direct investments	4.1
Miscellaneous	0.4
Total Payments	$46.8
Net Deficit	$1.3

Though there is no direct correlation between surplus or deficits in the balance of

22/ From 1958 through 1967, United States deficits have totaled $27.5 billion.

payments and the U.S. gold stock, continued deficits mean more and more dollars are in the hands of foreigners. Those that ultimately come to rest in foreign central banks may be exchanged for U.S. gold at the rate of $35 per ounce. During the period from the end of 1957 to June 30, 1967, the U.S. gold stock declined from $22.8 billion to $13.1 billion. As a result, in January, 1968, President Lyndon Johnson instituted mandatory controls on direct foreign investment by business, including regulations requiring a certain amount of required profit repatriation of business firms. The Federal Reserve Board was also given authority to introduce mandatory controls on U.S. bank lending and remittances abroad.

These actions supplement the Interest Equalization Tax of 1964, which is a tax on the amount of certain foreign securities purchased by U.S. citizens or residents. Since large amounts of capital were raised in the United States by foreign issues due to relatively lower interest rates, the tax, which is presumably temporary, is to equalize the cost of borrowing in the United States to the cost of borrowing abroad. The interest equalization tax applies to such certain purchases made after July 18, 1963.

The money market

Analysts must be aware of the way the money market functions, as changes in interest rate levels cause changes in the market prices of debt securities. The money market specializes in short-term U.S. government securities and prime short-term commercial or financial paper. The *money market* is characterized by the short-term nature of its activity as opposed to the *capital markets,* which are for long-term funds.

Money market instruments are close substitutes for cash and for each other, and are a principal medium of temporary investment by banks, businesses, and financial institutions. In addition to short term U.S. government securities, other money market media include: negotiable time certificates of deposit, federal funds, banker's acceptances, commercial paper, and call loans.

Certificates of deposit (CD's) are negotiable or non negotiable certificates given by a commercial bank in exchange for a time deposit. Regulation Q of the Federal Reserve Board prescribes the maximum rate of interest that may be paid by member banks on time and savings deposits made in the United States. The maximum rate is 6.25 percent for certificates of deposit that are $100,000 or more and are for a minimum duration of 180 days, and 5 percent for time deposits of less than $100,000 for at least 90 days. (The maximum rate is 4 percent for passbook savings deposits and time deposits of a duration less than 90 days.)[2][3]

Federal funds are another name for the deposit balances of member banks at the Federal Reserve bank. Since some banks may have more on deposit than is required,

---

23/ These are the maximum rates in June, 1968. Maximum rates are subject to change. The maximum rate that may be paid on certificates of deposit (CD's) of $100,000 or more of shorter duration than 180 days is:

    30-59 days—5½%
    60-89 days—5¾%
    90-179 days—6%

and other banks may be deficient, trading in federal funds takes place. The interest rate charged for lending federal funds usually will not exceed the discount rate. Transactions take place through federal funds houses. Daily volume of transactions is estimated at $1 to 4 billion. Federal funds are also used extensively for other purposes, including large transactions in government issues. Settlement of transactions between a buyer and seller may be done on a same-day basis with federal funds.

A *banker's acceptance* begins as a draft drawn by, let us say, an exporter against his customer, ordering him to pay a specified sum either at sight or after a specified period of time for goods that have been purchased. When the customer takes possession of the goods, he simultaneously endorses the draft with the word "accepted" and his signature. With this endorsement, the draft becomes an acceptance. The exporter may find it difficult to sell or discount the acceptance if the customer is not well known. Therefore, arrangements are often made for drafts to be drawn against the customer's bank. When such a draft is accepted by the customer's bank, it is known as a banker's acceptance. These acceptances are then traded through banker's acceptances houses.

Commercial paper consists of short-term promissory notes of business firms, which are sold by commercial paper houses to their customers.

Call loans are bank loans to brokers or dealers against listed or government securities as collateral. The proceeds of these loans are used by brokers to finance customers' margin accounts and by dealers to carry securities they are distributing.

The following article, reprinted from *The Wall Street Journal,* August 18, 1968, shows various money market quotations at that date.

MONEY RATES

New York—Bankers acceptance rates for 1 to 90 days, 6% to 5 7/8%; 90 to 180 days, 5 7/8% to 5¾%.

Federal funds in an open market: Day's high 6¼%; low 4%. Closing bid none; offered 4%.

Call money lent brokers on Stock Exchange collateral by New York City banks, 6 1/8% to 6½%; by banks outside New York City, 6% to 6½%.

Call money lent on Governments to dealers by New York City banks, 6 3/8% to 6 7/8%; to brokers by New York City banks, 6 1/8% to 6½%; to brokers by banks outside New York City, 6% to 6½%.

Commercial paper placed directly by a major finance company was as follows: 30 to 270 days, 5¾%.

Commercial paper sold through dealers, 30 to 270 days, 5 7/8% to 6 1/8%.

Certificates of deposit: Rates paid at New York City banks, 30 days to 59 days, 5½%; 60 to 119 days, 5 5/8%; 120 to 269 days, 5¾%; 270 to 360 days, 5 5/8%.

On July 31, 1967, the *Federal Reserve Bulletin* reported the following money market rates and approximate amount of issues outstanding. (Capital market issues, such as corporate bonds, government bonds, and municipals, are included for comparison. The Federal Reserve discount rates and commercial bank prime rate are also included.)

	Rates	Value Outstanding (Billions)
Moody's Corporate Bonds rated Baa	.6.26%	...
Call loans to brokers	.?	$ 3.6***
Moody's Corporate Bonds rated Aaa	.5.58%	...
Commercial bank prime rate	.5.50%	...
Standard & Poor's Preferreds	.5.34%	...
Certificates of deposit	.5.0 to 5.5%	$19.1
Treasury notes and bonds (3 to 5 years)	.5.17%	****
Treasury notes and certificates (9 to 12 months)	.4.98%	$54.7
Prime commercial paper* (4 to 6 months)	.4.92%	$16.1*****
Treasury bills yield (9 to 12 months)	.4.90%	******
Government long-term bonds	.4.86%	$97.4
Treasury bills (6 months)	.4.72%	$58.5
Finance company paper (3 to 6 months)	.4.70%	*******
Prime banker's acceptances** (3 to 6 months)	.4.58%	$ 4.1
Municipal bonds rated Baa	.4.43%	...
Treasury bills (3 months)	.4.20%	******
Nonnegotiable savings bonds	.4.15%	$51.2
Federal Reserve discount rates	.4.0%	...
Municipal bonds rated Aaa	.3.86%	...
Federal funds rate	.3.79%	...
Standard & Poor's 500 Common Stock Dividend yield	.3.15%	...

* On June 30, 1967, in billions of dollars.
** Averages of bid and asked prices.
*** On December 30, 1966.
**** Value outstanding is included in Treasury notes and certificates.
***** Includes finance company paper and commercial paper.
****** Value outstanding is included in Treasury bills (6 months).
******* See prime commercial paper.

Technical analysis

Most of the foregoing discussion pertains to the *fundamental* values of a security. The fundamental analyst looks at both qualitative factors of a company, which include its management capability, labor relations, and so on, and quantitative factors, such as financial ratios, sales, earnings and cost trends, and others.

Another method of analysis, which may be used in conjunction with the fundamental approach, is technical analysis.[24] The technical analyst is concerned with the condition of the market, usually graphically displayed by charts, and with various trading factors, including the following.

24/ Technical analysis is sometimes used exclusively without any consideration of fundamental values. This occurs when market traders buy and sell solely on technical market factors without regard to the securities' underlying fundamental values.

1. The *short interest* is borrowed stock that has been sold. The seller expects the price of the stock to decrease. If the price does decrease, he will buy in the stock sold short and deliver this stock to the broker from whom he originally borrowed. Short sellers eventually must buy, and a large short interest thus is generally regarded as a favorable technical point.

2. The *floating supply* of stock is stock in brokers' hands. A large floating stock is considered a menace to the market and is a weak technical indicator.

3. When the amount of *loans to brokers* has increased substantially, the technical position is weak, because it indicates that buyers are not paying cash but are buying heavily on margin.

4. The *volume of sales*—that is, the number of shares traded—is an important indicator of the technical position of the market. A rising market with high volume is obviously more encouraging and significant than a rise occurring on low volume. A rising market is termed a *bull,* and a falling market is called a *bear.* Individuals who predict a rise are called bulls, and those who predict a decline are bears.

5. The volume of *odd-lot* purchases and sales is also used to indicate the technical market position. One theory says that if odd-lot buying is heavy, the market will fall. This theory presumes that the small (odd-lot) investor is usually wrong.

6. Other technical factors include the short-range price level of the market (as measured by the Dow Jones or other average or index) and current events that affect investor psychology.

An investor may combine fundamental and technical analysis in the following way. First he decides that a particular security is worth buying on the basis of its fundamentals. He then *times* his purchase, that is, he decides when to buy based on technical factors.

Stock averages and indexes

Important statistical tools of the analyst to measure the state of the economy and the condition of the stock market include *indexes* and *averages.*

An *index* is a statistical yardstick expressed in terms of percentage of a base year or years. For example, the Federal Reserve Board's Industrial Production Index is based on 1957 to 1959 as 100. In June, 1967, the index stood at 155, which meant that industrial production that month was 55 percent higher than in the base period.

Another example is the Standard & Poor's 500 Stock Index, which is based on the market prices of 425 industrials, 25 railroads, and 50 utilities. The Standard & Poor's Index is computed by multiplying the price of each share by the number of shares of the issue. The sum of these total market values for the stocks covered is then expressed as a percentage of the average market value during the years 1942 to 1943. The percentage figure is then divided by 10, and the quotient is the index. Five companies of the 425 in the Standard & Poor's 425 Index comprise 30.7 percent of the weight of the index. These five companies are General Motors, IBM, Du Pont, Standard Oil of New Jersey, and American Telephone and Telegraph.

The National Quotation Bureau (NQB) publishes an index based on the sum of the bid prices of 35 industrial issues traded in the over-the-counter market. None of the issues used in the index are listed or traded on any stock exchange.

During 1966, the New York Stock Exchange began publishing a price index that covers every listed common stock on the NYSE. The price indexes are based on the aggregate market value of NYSE common stocks adjusted to eliminate the effects of capitalization changes, new listings, and delistings. The aggregate market value, which is the sum of the individual stock values times the number of shares listed, is the expressed value relative to the base period market value of 50 on December 31, 1965. The New York Stock Exchange common stock price indexes include composite, industrial, transportation, utility, and finance.

An *average* is normally computed by dividing the arithmetic sum of a group of numbers by the number of items involved. For example, a simple average of 50 leading stocks is obtained by totaling the prices of all and dividing by 50. An index is not an average. The Dow Jones Industrial Average of 30 leading industrial stocks is often used as an indicator of activity on the New York Stock Exchange.[25] Other averages include the Dow Jones Utility Average (15 stocks), Rail Average (20 stocks), Bond Average (40 railroads, 10 public utilities, and 10 industrials), the 65 Stock Average and Municipal Bond Yield Average (20 stocks).

The Dow Jones Industrial Average is often criticized because it covers only 30 stocks. However, at December 31, 1965, these 30 stocks accounted for 32.7 percent of the total market value of the 1,254 listed common stocks. The Dow Jones Averages, as popularly quoted, do not reflect reinvestment of dividends.

THE DOW JONES AVERAGES

Year-End	Industrials	Utilities	Rails
1967	905	128	233
1966	786	136	203
1965	969	152	247
1964	874	155	205
1963	763	139	179
1962	652	129	141
1961	731	129	144
1960	616	100	131
1959	679	88	154
1958	584	91	158

25/ The Dow Jones Average is a weighted rather than a simple average. The Dow Jones Industrial Average, for example, is a number higher than the numerical average of prices of the 30 stocks that compose it because of the use of a divisor. The numerical sum of the market prices of the 30 stocks is divided by a figure adjusted for each stock split of any of the component 30 stocks. An example will illustrate the need for such an adjusted divisor. Assume 3 stocks compose the average, A, B, and C. The market prices are: A, $30; B, $20; and C, $10. The total, $60, divided by 3 is the average, $20. If stock A splits 2 for 1, let us assume its market price drops to $15. The sum of the three market prices drops to $45, and the average to $15. This is obviously incorrect. By adjusting the divisor from 3 to 2.25, the discrepancy is corrected, since $45, the market price sum divided by 2.25 equals $20, the correct average. The actual divisor used in the Dow Jones Industrial Average was 2.163 at January 5, 1968.

The New York Times averages of stock prices are based on the average of the high prices, the low prices, and the closing prices of 25 railroads, 25 industrials, and the 50 stocks combined. Bond averages for industrials, rails, utilities, and a composite group of the three types are also published by *The Times*.

If it is used by the buyers of common stocks, the technical approach attempts to guess which way the general market, or particular stocks, will move on the basis of statistics related to their trends in the recent past. One of the oldest technical approaches is the Dow Theory.

The Dow Theory is an interesting approach to economic forecasting through analysis of the price levels of securities. It holds that the stock market is a barometer of business. The purpose of the theory is to forecast business cycles—that is, the large movements of depression and prosperity. The theory, as modified since the death of its originator in 1902, holds that the stock market at any given time is composed of three movements analogous to the tide, a wave, and a ripple, as follows.

1. The major trend (tide), lasting from 1 to 6 years.
2. The intermediate or secondary movement (wave), lasting from several weeks to a few months.
3. The short swings (ripple), which are day-to-day fluctuations.

Some of the principles underlying the Dow Theory are as follows.

In a bull market—that is, when the major trend (tide) is upward—the peak and trough of each intermediate swing (wave) will be higher than the previous peak or trough.

bull market

In a bear market, each wave's peak and trough will be lower than the one before it.

bear market

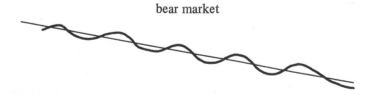

When a peak fails to exceed the preceding peak and the next trough fails to equal the preceding trough, the tide has changed. At point A in the chart below, a peak failed to exceed the preceding peak; at point B, a trough breakthrough or penetration of the support level occurred.

When the primary tide is downward, each subsequent trough will reach new lows and each peak will fall short of the level reached by the previous one. At point A below, a trough exceeded the previous trough, and the next successive peak at B exceeded the previous peak. Point C, through which the breakthrough occurred, is known as a *resistance level.*

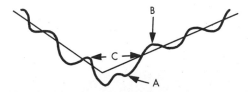

A true indication of a change in the tide is not given until any apparent change in the industrials is confirmed by similar penetrations or breakthroughs in the rail average.

One must note that even among experts there is disagreement on when secondary wave breakthroughs occur, and that the Dow Theory predictions are not always true. The Dow theorist will realize that a change in the tide has occurred only at some date after the event, when it has been confirmed.

Tape readers

Another type of technical market analysis is performed by the *tape reader,* who watches the hour-to-hour fluctuations in prices as they are reported on the ticker tape. The tape reader trades in and out of securities on a very short-run basis—e.g., often within one day—and tries to take small profits on each transaction. His theory is that news events that affect stock prices are available to traders well before they reach the general public through the newspapers, and they reflect in stock price movements as revealed on the ticker tape. Several factors that influence tape readers are resistance points, double or triple tops and bottoms, and influences of various similar stocks on one another.

A *resistance level* is the price level where heavy selling or buying pressure is encountered. Thus, a recent peak or low of a stock may be regarded as a resistance level. Tape readers are concerned with very short-term price movements—e.g., the ripples.

bullish

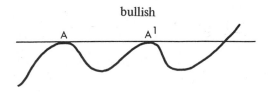

In the above chart, the stock reached point A, then fell, reached point A¹ again and fell. Point A¹ is a resistance level, and when a penetration occurs on the third try it is regarded as a very bullish signal. Had the stock failed to penetrate, after a double top at A and A¹, it would be regarded as a bearish signal.

bearish

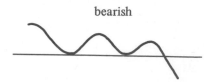

Similarly, if a double bottom is reached and the stock then penetrates the resistance level, it is bearish. If it approaches the level of the double bottom but does not penetrate, it is bullish.

Volume, or the number of shares being traded, is also of significance to the tape reader, who is interested in knowing whether a stock is being accumulated or distributed. If the stock shows higher volume at the higher prices and smaller volume at lower prices, it is an indication of accumulation. If the high volume occurs at the lower prices, it may be a sign of distribution with weakness in the stock to follow.

Chart traders

Chart traders tend to their charts, just as tape readers watch their tapes. Sometimes, the patterns that stock prices make do reveal interesting information about the supply and demand for the stock. For example, consider the following chart. This

triangle indicates that the volume declined and price range of trading narrowed. When the volume is low, a sudden revival of supply or demand is likely to cause either a sharp fall or rise.

Another indicator used by chart traders is the *head and shoulders,* as shown below.

head and shoulders top   head and shoulders bottom

The head and shoulders top—that is, a rise and a fall, a peak and a fall followed by a rise but not so high as the peak and a fall—is believed to indicate a further decline. The head and shoulders bottom is believed to indicate a future rise.

Various other formations regarded as significant by chartists include double tops or bottoms, complexes, broadenings, gaps, and shakeouts. The chartist is not so active a trader as the tape reader.

The foregoing discussion might be categorized in Dow Theory terminology by considering tape readers as ripple traders, chartists as wave traders, and advocates of formula plans as tide investors. It can easily be seen that the job of a securities analyst is a highly interesting and challenging one. It is in the best interests of every registered representative to have a basic understanding of the analyst's activities.

3 | Review questions

Assume that a company's financial statements are as follows:

Current assets	$100	Current liabilities	$ 50	
Fixed assets	$100	Bonds	$ 30	
		Common stock	$ 20	
		Retained earnings	$ 20	
		Capital surplus	$ 80	
Total Assets	$200	Total Liabilities and Equity	$200	

Sales	$500
Cost of sales	$400
Gross profit on sales	$100
Operating expenses	$ 20
Operating profit	$ 80
Interest charges	$ 2
Net income before tax	$ 78
Provision for tax	$ 38
Net income	$ 40

Based on the above information, answer questions, 111 to 118.

111. The current ratio is ....
1. 1 to 1
2. 2 to 1
3. 3 to 1
4. None of these

112. Working capital is ....
1. $100
2. $200
3. $50
4. None of these

113. The bond ratio is ....
1. 20 percent
2. 30 percent
3. 40 percent
4. 60 percent

114. The margin of profit is ....
1. 12 percent
2. 14 percent
3. 16 percent
4. 18 percent

115. Interest coverage before interest and taxes is ....
1. 10 times
2. 20 times
3. 30 times
4. 40 times

116. The net worth is ....
1. $100
2. $120
3. $140
4. $200

117. If only 10 shares of common stock of this company are outstanding, the earnings per share are ....
1. $4
2. $40
3. $400
4. none of these

118. If the dividend payout ratio for this company is 80 percent, ... must be paid in common stock dividends.
1. $400
2. $16
3. $32
4. $40

119. An approach to stock analysis that is distinguished from fundamental analysis is ....
1. company
2. qualitative
3. technical
4. industry
5. none of these

120. A technical analyst is most concerned with ....
1. a company's income statement
2. the price history of a company's stock
3. what a company produces
4. a company's balance sheet

121. The Dow Jones Average indicates ....
1. what stocks to buy or sell
2. the trend of the market as measured by prices of a specific group of stocks.
3. what the average price of stocks will be in the future
4. none of these

122. The Federal Reserve does not affect the economy through ....
1. discount rate
2. fiscal policies
3. legal reserve requirements
4. open market operations

123. A person who is willing to take a relatively large risk with his capital in the hope of receiving a greater-than-average profit is called ....
1. an investor
2. a trader
3. a proprietor
4. a speculator

124. The highest grade income and growth stocks are called ....
1. speculative issues
2. sure things
3. blue chips
4. special situations

125. A common stock that is expected to go up in price after certain corporate events take place is sometimes referred to as ....
1. speculative issue
2. special situation
3. growth stock
4. none of these

126. When two companies join and form a third company, they are said to have ....
1. consolidated
2. reorganized
3. merged
4. none of these

127. The bond ratings ranked in order of relative safety are ....
1. D-C-A
2. AAA-D-C
3. AAA-BB-B

128. An income stock may be described as ....
1. stock on which regular annual dividends have been paid for an extended period of time
2. stock of a company that puts most of its profits back into the business
3. stock of a company undergoing reorganization
4. none of these

129. A company that has been unable to meet its debts can undergo reorganization under the supervision of ....
1. its stockholders
2. the SEC
3. the courts
4. none of these

130. The information that a securities analyst uses is ....
1. statistical data only
2. data containing the opinion of others
3. both of these
4. neither of these

131. A fundamental securities analyst would be most influenced by ....
1. charts of a stock's price fluctuations
2. a company's balance sheet and income statement
3. the volume of shares traded on a given day
4. the short interest

132. The first step in a fundamental analysis is usually to examine the facts concerning ....
1. general business conditions
2. the company itself
3. industry conditions
4. a chart of the company's part stock price movements

133. Margin of profit is ....
1. the dollar amount of profit earned during the fiscal year
2. the percent earned on every sales dollar
3. earnings in excess of net income
4. profits retained in the business

134. Working capital is ....
1. the excess of current assets over current liabilities
2. the excess of assets over liabilities
3. capital raised by selling bonds
4. none of these

135. Current ratio is the ratio of ....
1. current assets to current liabilities
2. assets to liabilities

3. fixed assets to debt
4. common stock to capital structure

136. The traditional standard minimum current ratio is ....
1. 1 to 1
2. 2 to 1
3. 3 to 1
4. none of these

137. .... is not a test of the adequacy of a company's working capital.
1. Acid test
2. Current ratio
3. Ratio of equity to funded debt
4. Working capital ratio

138. A company with a profit margin of 20 percent ....
1. makes an operating profit of 20 cents on every sales dollar
2. makes a profit of 20 percent on all expenses
3. makes a profit of 80 cents on every sales dollar
4. none of these

139. Deficit spending by the government to stimulate the economy would be considered ....
1. a monetary policy measure
2. a fiscal policy measure
3. a Federal Reserve Board control
4. all of these

140. The Dow Theory is used by its advocates ....
1. to predict the price movement of a particular stock
2. to predict business cycles
3. both 1 and 2
4. none of these

Refer to page 259 for correct answers.

4 | Mutual funds and
Investment Company Act of 1940

Mutual funds

A basic advantage of the mutual fund is that investors who combine their moneys gain full-time professional investment management. In pooling investments, each individual investor has a stake in the whole fund. The relatively large resources available to the investors' fund allow the spread of risks over a large number of investments that the investors probably could not afford individually. So a mutual fund provides diversification.

The mutual fund can afford to employ full-time analysts who are professionals in selecting investment securities. Thus, the mutual fund provides professional selection that most individuals probably could not hope to match. It is thought, too, that some mutual funds attract the highest caliber of professional investment management that even relatively large investors could not obtain.

The job of securities analyst for a mutual fund is a continuing task. Selection of desirable securities is followed by continuous supervision of the investment portfolio. This is accomplished by replacing with stronger ones those securities that show signs of weakening.

Thus, three main advantages of a mutual fund are *diversification, selection,* and *professional supervision and management.* Since these services are performed for a fund or pool of thousands of investors, the cost to each investor is only a small pro rata percentage of the total cost.

Mutual funds are another name for *open-end investment companies.*[1] Their operations are regulated by the Investment Company Act of 1940 (the '40 Act), a federal law that also regulates a second type of management company called the *closed-end investment company.* The important difference between an open-end and a closed-end

---

1/ Most open-end and closed-end companies are literally mutual operations. Historically, however, only open-end companies are referred to as mutual funds.

company is in the way shares are bought and sold.[2] The buyer of open-end shares pays the net asset value per share plus a sales charge.[3] *The sales charge, according to the '40 Act, must be neither unconscionable nor grossly excessive.* The sales charge depends on the amount of an investor's purchase and the rate set by the individual fund, and it is shown in the fund's prospectus.

If one is interested in buying shares in an open-end fund, new shares normally are available.[4] Generally, purchases are made from a securities broker-dealer who obtains newly issued shares from the fund underwriter. Also, when the investor needs cash, or for any other reason wants to sell, the fund normally redeems the shares at the current net asset value per share.[5] This redemption feature of open-end investment companies is unique. Naturally, the amount realized by the investor may be more or less than his cost, depending on the market value of the underlying portfolio securities at the time of redemption. Shares may be sold back to the fund underwriter through a local dealer, or tendered directly to the fund or its custodian bank. The specific redemption procedures and provisions are outlined in details in the fund's prospectus.

In a closed-end fund, the buyer pays the market price, which may be at a premium (above) or at a discount (below) in terms of the net asset value per share. He will also pay brokerage commissions and odd-lot fees as they apply. When the investor sells, he takes his chances on whether the selling price will be above or below the net asset value per share, which will depend on the current supply and demand, because closed-end funds have a fixed number of shares outstanding. After the initial sale, the company no longer issues shares, nor will it redeem them.[6] Thus, after issuance the shares are traded over the counter or on an exchange.

Historically, the first funds were closed-end investment companies, starting in Belgium over a hundred years ago. The idea spread to England, Scotland, and eventually to the United States. The first mutual fund (open-end investment company) that offered shares to the general public was formed in 1924 and still operates today as one of the largest in the country. The number of open-end management companies that are members of the Investment Company Institute increased from 68 in 1940 to 182 in 1966.[7]

Of the 26 closed-end funds listed in the 1967 edition of *Investment Companies*, by Arthur Wiesenberger, 21 traded at a 1966 year-end discount from net asset value, ranging from 6 to 51 percent. Four funds sold at premiums ranging from 9 to 18 percent, and one fund traded at net asset value.

The following chart summarizes the differences between open-end (mutual) and closed-end funds.

2/ The principal technical difference is that open-end funds always stand ready to redeem their shares as hereafter described. Also, but not necessarily, open-end companies make continuous offering of their shares.

3/ Except in the few no-load funds, which make no sales charge.

4/ A currently effective registration statement is required.

5/ In a few cases, usually no-load funds, a redemption fee of 1 or 2 percent is deducted from the net asset value per share.

6/ Some closed-end funds buy their shares on the open market, at a discount.

7/ During the 1940 to end of 1967 period, the assets of mutual fund members of the Investment Company Institute increased from $0.5 billion to $44.7 billion.

A COMPARISON OF OPEN-END AND
CLOSED-END INVESTMENT COMPANIES

	Open-End	*Closed-End*
Number of shares outstanding . . .	Constantly changing	Fixed
Public offering of new shares	Continuous	One-time basis*
Outstanding shares redeemed by issuer	Yes	No
Redemption price	Net asset value per share; in a few funds, NAV less redemption fee	Not redeemable by issuer
Where shares are bought or sold	In most cases, through an investment dealer from the fund underwriter	Over the counter or on an exchange
From whom shares are purchased or to whom shares may be sold	Purchased from an underwriter through a dealer; sold or redeemed similarly	Purchased from another stockholder or from inventory of a dealer; sold as common stock is sold
Relation of purchase price to net asset value	Purchase price is public offering price, which is net asset value plus a sales charge, if applicable; net asset value determined by value of securities in portfolio	No precise relationship; purchase price determined by supply and demand; thus, price may exceed net asset value if trading at a *premium,* or be less than net asset value if trading at a *discount*
Buying or selling	Sales charge normally included in public offering price; usually no redemption charge; amount of sales charge and redemption charge, if any, clearly stated in fund prospectus	For both purchases and sales there is normally the equivalent of a stock exchange commission if transaction is handled on an agency basis; for transactions on a principal basis, there would be an appropriate markup or markdown.

* A closed end company may make more than one public offering but if so, it will not be continuous. Each will be a single offering of a fixed number of shares.

The *capital structure* or *capitalization* of a mutual fund is generally simple. All shares of stock issued by registered management companies must be voting stock, which must have equal voting rights with all other outstanding voting stock. Mutual funds are prohibited by the '40 Act from issuing preferred shares or debt of any kind.

Some mutual funds provide for limited borrowing from banks when judged desirable to further their investment objectives. The few mutual funds that borrow are known as leveraged funds. Such borrowing may not exceed 33 percent of net assets. The '40 Act provides that funds may borrow money as long as there is at least 300 percent collateral asset coverage.[8]

Prior to the Depression (1929), most investment companies were closed end. Closed-end funds often have complex capital structures, including preferred stock, warrants, or bonds, in addition to their common shares.

Funds are characterized by their investment portfolio as well as their investment objectives. A fund may have as its investment objective current income, capital appreciation, or both income and appreciation. Descriptions of the various types of categories of funds follow.

Categories of funds

The *bond fund* invests only in bonds. A bond fund's objectives are income and stability of capital. Either objective may be primary with the other secondary. The *municipal bond fund* is not an open-end fund and can be purchased in underwriting or over the counter. Its portfolio consists predominantly of tax-exempt securities.

The *bond and preferred stock fund* invests only in senior securities. It could have all bonds or all preferred; however, it will normally be invested in both types of securities. This fund's objective also is income.

The *balanced fund* at all times keeps some of its money in common stocks and the rest in cash and senior securities—that is, bonds and preferred stock. The percentage of each type of investment will generally vary as economic conditions change. The prospectus of the fund will state whether the fund varies the portion of its portfolio in stocks or whether a constant percentage is kept in junior and senior issues. A balanced fund's objective normally is stability and conservation of capital.

The *common stock fund* invests only in common stocks, except for cash and short-term government issues. The investment objective may be growth, or growth with income, or both income and growth. However, many diversified common stock funds may vary the portion of assets invested in common stocks.

A *diversified common stock fund* invests at least 75 percent of its total assets in such a way that not more than 5 percent of its total assets are in any one company, and not more than 10 percent of the outstanding voting stock of any particular company is owned. The other 25 percent of assets could be invested all in one company or diversified, as the fund management chooses. There are more funds in this category than any other.

A *nondiversified fund* includes all other funds and is not required to diversify its investments to the same degree. An Internal Revenue Code provision for favorable

8/ If a fund borrows up to one third of net assets, net assets remain unchanged because the increase in total assets is offset by the loan liability. Thus, the net assets would be 3 times (300 percent) the amount borrowed.

taxation is that not more than 25 percent of the assets of a nondiversified company may be invested in any one company; 50 percent of the assets must be invested so that not more than 5 percent of the fund's assets are in any single company; and not more than 10 percent of the voting securities of any single company are owned by the fund.

Tax-free exchange (swap) funds usually are diversified common stock funds. These funds were formed between 1960 and the first part of 1967 to exchange fund shares for portfolio securities offered by investors. Investors were able to obtain the greater diversification of a fund without incurring immediate capital gains tax liabilities on the securities offered in exchange. No additional funds of this type can be created unless new legislation is enacted by Congress.

Specialized funds, although they may be diversified, confine their activities to certain industries or groups of industries, state or regions of the country, or foreign countries. Examples include electronic or TV funds and funds that invest primarily in Florida or California. Most of the Canadian and international funds that exist were originally incorporated in Canada as NRO (nonresident-owned) companies. Before enactment of the Revenue Act of 1962, such funds offered U.S. citizen investors some tax advantage because of their ability to retain and reinvest net income and capital gains. Now, however, to minimize the funds' taxes they must distribute capital gains and dividends. Most NRO companies have now changed their domicile to the United States.

A *special situations fund* invests or seeks to invest in a company when management thinks that some special development that has occurred or is expected to occur will cause an increase in the value of the stock apart from general market conditions. Normally, funds interested in special situations are also common stock funds.

An *income fund* has an investment objective of maximizing current income. Investments normally would be in bonds or preferred stocks that currently yield more than common stocks.

The following chart shows the relative importance in terms of size of the various types of U.S. funds categorized by their portfolios.

Type of Fund	Total Net Assets 12/31/66	% of Total
Diversified common stock	$25,059,400,000	69.0%
Balanced	7,112,000,000	19.6
Specialized	1,445,300,000	4.0
Income	1,361,800,000	3.8
Tax-free (swap)	927,800,000	2.6
Bond and preferred stock	229,900,000	0.6
Canadian and international	158,400,000	0.4
Total	$36,294,600,000	100.0%

Within the general category of funds, or management companies, there are two additional broad classifications. The *restricted management type fund,* as defined in the fund's charter and bylaws, places on management such restrictions as a prohibition against borrowing and never investing more than 5 percent of assets in any one stock. A *fully managed fund* is another type. Some funds cannot be classified in terms of their portfolios; they may in certain circumstances be wholly invested in common stocks, at other times in both senior and junior securities, and still at other times wholly in senior securities. When management is given the right to invest any proportion of assets in the different types of securities, at the sole discretion of management to choose the proportions, the fund is known as fully managed.

There are various other fund types, but those described are the most important. Generally, the name of each type describes its particular quality or objective. Now, let us look at the structure of a mutual fund.

Mutual fund structure

Most funds are corporations, and as such issue common stock shares with equal rights concerning dividends, voting, and so on. However, in a few cases funds have been established as trusts. The initial size of a fund must be at least $100,000. Mutual funds are created or established by their sponsors. Funds usually register with the SEC under the provisions of the Investment Company Act of 1940. Naturally, the registration statement (and the prospectus) must disclose all matters of fundamental policy. Companies with more than 100 shareholders that are in the investment business or offer their shares to the public must register.

As in all corporations, there is a board of directors. Funds that are established as trusts have a board of trustees. Annually at the stockholders' meeting, the directors are elected by the shareholders. The directors appoint the fund officers who carry out the day-to-day activities, and together they are responsible for the fund.

The fund's officers may arrange an *investment advisory agreement* (or management contract) with a management company; the contract must be approved by the fund's shareholders and a majority of independent members of the board of directors. The investment managers make all investment decisions within the limits established by the prospectus. The fact that the management company is hired to supervise the investments of the fund does not in any way relieve the officers and directors from their responsibility for the decisions made. The investment advisory agreement must be approved annually either by a majority vote of the fund's shareholders or by a majority of the independent, nonaffiliated fund directors. All voting at stockholders' meetings is done in person or by signed proxy; each share has one vote.

As stated above, most mutual funds elect to have the actual job of the portfolio management contracted to an investment management company. When we refer to management in mutual fund companies, we refer to the investment adviser who manages the portfolio.

For this service, the fund pays a management fee to the management company or investment adviser. The fee is generally not more than 0.5 percent of the fund's average net assets over the year. The average management fee for all funds is less than this amount, since many funds pay a lower rate of management fee as the size of the fund's net assets increases. In 1967, the average fee was 37/100 of 1 percent.

Mutual fund financial statements must be certified by an independent accounting firm, whose selection must be annually authorized or ratified by stockholders. Financial reports must be issued at least semiannually.[9] The annual reports must be audited by an independent public accountant.

Mutual funds—sources of possible gains

Shareholders of mutual funds may receive dividends from the fund's interest and net investment income and capital gains distributions if during the year stocks are sold for more than their cost. Besides dividends and capital gains—two possible sources of fluctuating income—there is also the possibility of unrealized appreciation, which is the increase in market value of the fund's portfolio compared to the original cost of the investments that the fund made. Taxable income to shareholders is not generated until such unrealized appreciation becomes realized through the sale of portfolio securities.

Dividends are paid from net investment income. Net investment income includes dividends from equity securities held in the fund portfolio and interest paid on debt securities held by the fund less the fund's operating expenses. Dividends are normally taxable to the shareholder as are any dividends paid by a corporation. In Chapter 10, "Internal Revenue Code," the tax situations of both the fund and its shareholders are more fully discussed. Dividends may be accepted in cash or reinvested. Some funds allow dividends to be reinvested at net asset value per share without a sales charge.

Distributions of capital or capital gains distributions are payments made to fund shareholders from net gains on sales of portfolio securities. When available, capital gains distributions are normally declared annually and are considered a return of capital that should be reinvested to keep the investment intact. It should be noted that these payments, as well as dividends, are taxable to the shareholder even though they are reinvested. Whether distributions are reinvested or taken in cash has no effect on their taxability to shareholders. When capital gains distributions are reinvested, the transaction is at the net asset value per share without a sales charge. The '40 Act provides that if dividends are paid from any source other than current income or accumulated undistributed income, and if capital gains are paid from any source other than such gains, an explicit written statement of such source must be sent to shareholders.

9/ Pursuant to the '40 Act, semiannual and annual reports must contain the following: (*a*) a balance sheet, including the number of shares outstanding; (*b*) a list of the values of securities owned; (*c*) statement of income; (*d*) statement of surplus; (*e*) statement of remuneration paid to all directors, members of an advisory board, officers, and affiliated persons; (*f*) statement of the aggregate amount of portfolio purchases and sales; (*g*) statement of the changes in net assets; (*h*) net asset value at the beginning and at the end of the three preceding years, and dividends and capital gains paid during the three years. In general, segregation must be made of items amounting to 5 percent or more of the category reported.

Mutual fund distribution

Most funds enter into a contract with an *underwriter,* often called *sponsor* (or distributor), to market its shares to the public.[10] The underwriter buys shares at the net asset value per share from the fund to fill orders that have been received by the underwriter. The underwriter does not hold shares in inventory. The underwriter sells the shares to investment dealers who have placed orders for them at the offering price less the dealer's concession or commission. In some cases, the underwriter sells shares at net asset value to a plan company, which sells to the dealer who transacts business with the public. The public pays the public offering price, which includes the net asset value plus the *load,* or commissions, for the dealer and underwriter. The '40 Act provides that the principal underwriter must not sell open-end investment company shares to the public at any price other than the public offering price described in the fund's prospectus. Thus, special deals, rebates, or kickbacks are prohibited by law.

The dealer receives part of the commission for handling the promotion and sale of shares, including the establishment and continued training and supervision of a sales organization. The underwriter receives part for meeting the expenses of preparing sales literature used by dealers and for general sales service.

The following chart outlines the typical distribution process for fund shares. The

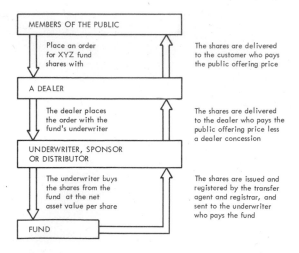

offering price (asked price) of mutual fund shares is the *net asset value* (NAV) per share and the load or sales commission. The net asset value is the assets of the fund less its liabilities divided by the number of shares outstanding. To determine the offering price, the following formula is used:

$$\frac{\text{Net asset value}}{(100\% - \% \text{ of sales load})} = \text{Offering price.}$$

10/ An exception occurs in the case of no-load funds—that is, funds that have no sales organization to provide information and service to clients. These funds often sell directly to the public without the services of underwriters and broker-dealers.

Therefore, if the sales load is 8.5 percent, and the net asset value per share is $5, then:

$$\text{Offering price (O.P.)} = \frac{\$5}{(100\% - 8.5\%)} = \frac{\$5}{91.5\%} = \$5.46.$$

Since the sales load is always a percentage of the offering price, the answer may be checked as follows:

O.P. × Charge % = Load
$5.46 × .085 = $0.46 (the sales charge)
O.P. − Load = NAV
$5.46 − 0.46 = $5.00 (the net asset value).

The *bid price* is the same as net asset value per share. (A redemption fee would be subtracted from the NAV for those few funds with such a charge.) The *redemption price* is the net asset value (minus, in a few funds, a redemption charge). The sales load is divided between the underwriter and the dealer. Normally, the underwriter retains approximately 20 percent of the load, and the dealer receives 80 percent as his concession. Thus, if the sales charge is 8 percent the underwriter normally retains about 1.6 percent and the dealer receives a concession of 6.4 percent.

Understanding the net asset value per share is very important. Most funds obtain market quotations for all securities held by the fund at 1 p.m. and again at 3:30 p.m. on all days on which the New York Stock Exchange is open. After considering other assets and liabilities, the net asset value per share is computed by dividing net assets by the number of shares outstanding. Normally, net asset value per share is computed two times per day. The net asset value per share computed as of 1 p.m. is effective for orders placed with the underwriter between 2 p.m. and 4:30 p.m. that day. The net asset value per share computed as of 3:30 p.m. is effective from 4:30 p.m. that day until 2 p.m. the next day the New York Stock Exchange is open. Both the SEC and the NASD regulate the pricing of mutual fund shares.

Mutual fund financial statements

Assume that a mutual fund balance sheet is as follows.

```
Assets:
    Securities, at market value ....................$90,000,000
    Cash in Bank ................................ 10,000,000
    Receivables ................................. 10,000,000

        Total Asset Value ......................       $110,000,000
    Liabilities ....................................        10,000,000

        Net Asset Value ........................       $100,000,000
```

The *total asset value* is the sum of the fund's assets—that is, cash, securities, and receivables. The *net asset value,* or total net assets, of the fund is $100 million, which is total assets less liabilities. If the fund has outstanding 10 million shares, the *net asset value per share* (bid price) is $10. If the sales charge is 8.5 percent, then the offering price is $10.93.

A mutual fund *statement of income* may appear as follows.

Income:
  Dividends $100,000
  Interest ....$ 25,000

        Total Investment Income $125,000
Expenses:
  Management fees ....$ 20,000
  Other expenses ....$ 5,000

        Total Expenses .... $ 25,000

        Net Investment Income $100,000

Dividends are paid from net investment income. The Investment Company Act of 1940 prohibits payment of dividends from any other source unless the fund discloses such source.

Another financial statement included in mutual fund reports is the *statement of realized and unrealized gains or losses for the year.* It may appear as follows:

Net realized gain on investments ....$ 200,000

Increase in net unrealized appreciation
    of investments $19,988,000

Capital gains are declared and paid from the net realized gains. The increase in unrealized appreciation is, of course, reflected in the increased net asset value per share of the fund. Unrealized appreciation represents the increase in market value of securities still in the fund's portfolio above the original cost paid by the fund.

The mutual fund *statement of changes in net assets* for the year may appear as follows.

STATEMENT OF CHANGES IN NET ASSETS

Net Assets, January 1, 1968 .... $ 70,000,000
Investment income:
  Net investment income ....$ 100,000
    Less: Dividend paid ....$ 98,000

Undistributed income .... $ 2,000
Realized and unrealized gains and losses:
  Net realized gains ....$ 200,000
    Less: Capital gains distributions paid ....$ 190,000

Undistributed net gains .... $ 10,000
Increase in net unrealized appreciation
    of investments ....   ' $ 19,988,000
Capital stock issued and repurchased:
  Received on issue of 3,857,232 new shares $30,000,000
    Less: Paid on redemptions of 2,436,217 shares ..$20,000,000

Net increase .... $ 10,000,000

    Net Assets, December 31, 1968 .... $100,000,000

The statement of changes in net assets summarizes the fund's activities. The net assets, $100 million, are the same as the balance sheet figure; the net investment income, $100,000, is obtained from the income statement. Realized gains, $200,000, increase in net unrealized appreciation, $19.988 million, and the change in capital stock, $10 million, complete the financial picture.

Redemption or sale of open-end fund shares

By definition, open-end fund shares are redeemable securities. Under the terms of the Investment Company Act of 1940, a fund must make payment for shares tendered to the fund or to its designated agent within seven days.[11] In practice, most funds redeem shares, without charge, at the next prevailing net asset value per share on any business day after the redemption order is received. Details of redemption procedures are given in the fund prospectus, and NASD member underwriters must redeem shares as indicated in their fund prospectus. Though shares are redeemed at net asset value, the amount realized by the investor may, of course, be more or less than his cost depending on the net asset value at the time of redemption.

The continual issuance of new shares and the repurchase or redemption of old shares have no effect on shareholders who are neither buying nor selling, because all transactions are at net asset value.[12] An example will best clarify this.

Assume that three persons (A, B, and C) form their own mutual fund by investing $50,000 each. At inception of the fund, before any investments are made, selection of the first net asset value per share (NAV) is arbitrary. Let us say it is $10.

The initial situation is:

Shareholder	Invest- ment	Number of Shares Purchased at $10
A	$ 50,000	5,000
B	$ 50,000	5,000
C	$ 50,000	5,000
Total	$150,000	15,000

Fund management invests the $150,000, and at some future date when the value of all the investments is determined the shareholders are pleased to find that the current market value of the portfolio is $180,000. Dividing by the shares outstanding, 15,000, they determine the current NAV has increased to $12.

Elated with his profit, Mr. B decides to sell his 5,000 shares, for which he is paid the current NAV, $12, total $60,000. The status of the fund before and after Mr. B's redemption is:

11/ Except when: (a) the New York Stock Exchange is closed other than for normal weekends and holidays, (b) an emergency exists, (c) it is not reasonably practicable to determine the net asset value, (d) the SEC declares such periods.

12/ As the assets under management increase, expenses per dollar of assets managed tend to reduce. Therefore, increased sales are of some possible benefit to existing shareholders.

Fund before Redemption

Portfolio value $180,000
Shares outstanding 15,000
NAV per share ....$ 12

Fund after Redemption

Portfolio value $120,000
Shares outstanding ....$ 10,000
NAV per share ....$ 12

Thus, the interest of the remaining shareholders, Mr. A and Mr. C, is unchanged by Mr. B's redemption. They still have 5,000 shares each, total value $120,000. Similarly, a purchase by a new shareholder would not effect the remaining shareholders.

Fund purchases and services

Mutual funds offer several different methods for purchasing securities, as well as certain services to investors.

Methods of purchasing mutual funds. Fund shares are usually purchased in *dollar amounts;* that is, the investor buys $1,000 worth of XYZ Fund shares. The precise number of shares and fractional shares bought is determined by dividing the public offering price (asked price) into the dollar amount of the investment. A fixed number of shares—e.g., 200—may also be purchased. These would be purchased at the public offering price (asked price), which includes the sales charge.

Quantity purchases and the letter of intent. Most underwriters reduce their sales charges when quantity purchases, ranging from $5,000 to $25,000 and up, are made. For any given fund, the details will appear in the prospectus. The purchase need not be a single lump-sum purchase to qualify for the reduced sales charge if the investor signs a *letter of intent,* signifying his intent to purchase the required dollar amount within a period not to exceed 13 months.[13] Rules issued pursuant to the Investment Company Act require the public offering price to be maintained, except that the sale at net asset value is allowed to periodic payment plans, employees of the investment adviser or underwriter, or tax-exempt organizations if such sales are authorized in the prospectus.

To qualify for a reduced sales charge on a lump-sum quantity purchase or through use of the letter of intent, the purchaser must be: (*a*) an individual; (*b*) an individual, his spouse, and children under the age of 21; or (*c*) a trustee or other fiduciary of a single trust estate, or single fiduciary account, or a pension or profit-sharing plan qualified under Section 401 of the Internal Revenue Code.[14] This means that investment clubs or other groups of individuals *cannot* band together for the purpose of obtaining reduced sales charges on purchases of investment company shares.

Accumulation plans. Regular purchases of fund shares can be made either through an informal or level charge plan or by means of a contractual plan.

13/ A rule issued under the '40 Act prohibits periods longer than 13 months.
14/ This is required by the '40 Act and rules issued thereunder.

Many funds permit investors to start a level charge or *voluntary (open) account.* They require an initial purchase, usually of a stated minimum amount, and an indication of the investor's wish to invest monthly or at some fixed interval at least a minimum stated annual amount. The exact amount of the required initial investment and of the allowable subsequent minimum periodic investment will be stated in the prospectus. Under these plans, a specific dollar amount (e.g., $500) is invested in fund shares at the current public offering price (asked price).

Plan companies and many underwriters and distributors offer *periodic payment plans, contractual, penalty, prepaid charge, or front-end load plans.* Under these contractual plans, an investor normally makes investments of a fixed dollar amount at regular periodic intervals, usually monthly, for a fixed number of years (10 years, 12½, 15, or 20).[15] The assets of such plan companies are invested in fund shares. The plans are separate legal entities, and are categorized by the '40 Act as *unit investment trusts* or *periodic payment plans.* The investor receives a plan certificate and confirmation slips detailing the shares that accumulate in his account. Details are given in the plan prospectus, which together with the fund's share prospectus must be given to prospective investors. The plan prospectus must contain the statement, "This prospectus is valid only when accompanied by the current fund prospectus."

The Investment Company Act of 1940 limits contractual plan sales charges to a maximum of 9 percent of the total investment and allows up to 50 percent of the first year's payments to be deducted for sales charges. The concentration of sales charges in the first year and the resulting likelihood that a plan discontinued during the first year or two will show a loss account for the terms "penalty," "prepaid charge," or "front-end load," which are given in these plans.

The term "contractual" may be easily misunderstood, since the investor under such a plan has no contractual obligation to make payments or to complete his intended investment. The plan company (sponsor) and custodian, however, have a contractual obligation to the investor to allow him all the features and privileges explained in the plan prospectus. Some of these plan features, which often are not available through voluntary plans, are the following.

1. After a specific number of monthly payment units have been made in a monthly payment plan (e.g., 13 or 18) and immediately in fully paid or single payment plans, *partial redemption or liquidation may be effected up to 90 percent of the market value* of the shareholder's shares either in cash or by a share withdrawal. *Future replacement of the dollar amount or shares withdrawn may be made without a sales charge.* Should investors redeem a portion of their mutual funds other than through a contractual plan, the amounts redeemed may not be replaced without payment of the applicable sales charge. The importance of this privilege to a contractual plan investor over a period of years can be quite significant.

2. Possible tax benefits in some contractual plans treated as associations taxable as a corporation occur wherein *some or all of the distributed or reinvested dividends are treated as a return of capital rather than ordinary income.* To the extent that a

---

15/ State laws preclude the offering of contractual plans in California, Illinois, and Wisconsin.

planholder receives a return of capital rather than ordinary dividend income he incurs no current taxation and postpones any tax liabilities on such income. Since the return of capital lowers his cost basis for his shares if he ultimately sells the shares, he will pay at favorable capital gain tax rates rather than ordinary income rates. Should he die without selling the shares, no income taxation would have occurred.

3. *The right to name, through a declaration of trust or statement of beneficiary, beneficiaries who would receive the plan* in the event of the planholder's death is important because it may avoid probate. Probate costs generally range from 2 percent to as high as 20 percent, and shares that must go through the process of probate may be tied up for periods of several months to several years.

4. Optional *low-cost group plan completion insurance protection,* which completes the plan if the planholder dies before completing his scheduled investments, is advantageous to many people in financial planning. The insurance coverage is for the difference between investments actually made, e.g., $1,000, and the total face amount of the plan, e.g., $18,000. In the event of an insured planholder's death, the insurance company pays the amount necessary, e.g., $17,000, to the fund custodian bank to complete the plan.[16]

5. A *guaranteed charge structure* that is not subject to increase is an advantage. Voluntary account investors have found that sales charges, custodian charges, or both may be increased for future investments.

6. *Dividend (and capital gain distribution) reinvestment without sales charge* can amount to significant savings.

7. *Guaranteed bank custodianship* for a fixed period of years without any change in charges not provided for in the initial plan prospectus protects investors from rising costs of this service.

8. *Letters of intent* and *automatic withdrawal accounts* are explained in other parts of this chapter.

9. Perhaps the most important feature of the monthly investment unit or systematic type of contractual plan is that *it is a plan*. It represents a carefully determined method for investing wherein a fixed number of dollars are planned for investment in accordance with the planholder's personal financial situation. Because planholders know at the commencement of their plan that early termination will probably result in a loss, they have an incentive, from the beginning, to continue regular investments.

10. In many cases, particularly in the larger plan denominations, the *sales charge for the completed plan is less* than if an equivalent amount were invested at the same intervals in a voluntary or open type of account.

Single payment or fully paid plans, as well as systematic investments, are available through contractual plans. Fully paid plans allow a single lump-sum investment, usually $1,000 or more, and may provide all of the above-mentioned features, except group life insurance and the discipline of a monthly plan. Level charges, e.g., 8.5 percent, are deducted from fully paid investments. Single payment plans may also provide letters of

16/ Plan completion insurance protection is not available in Missouri, North Carolina, South Carolina, and Texas.

intent and allow for subsequent lump-sum investments into the same account under rights of accumulation.

Some contractual plan sponsors also provide for reduced sales charges based on the accumulated value of shareholder's purchases over a period of years. When the value of existing holdings of an investor (or the face amount he has invested) plus the amount being currently invested reach a breakpoint level, e.g., $25,000, a reduced sales charge is applied to the current investment. This feature is termed "rights of accumulation."

Automatic dividend reinvestment. Automatic reinvestment of all dividends and distributions payable to the account of the shareholder to purchase additional shares is a service provided by most underwriters. Some companies permit reinvestment of income dividends at net asset value, others at offering price. Capital gains distributions are reinvested at net asset value. Most funds require the reinvestment of capital gains distributions if income is to be reinvested, but nearly all encourage reinvestment of capital gains distributions in any circumstances. Some companies declare capital gains distributions in shares and require an affirmative action by the shareholder to obtain cash.

Withdrawal plans. Several funds and plan companies have arranged for *systematic withdrawals* or for the planned partial or complete exhaustion of an account over a period of years. To illustrate, an investor with a starting balance of $30,000 in fund shares might choose to withdraw $150 per month. Depending on the amount of investment income earned, payment of this amount may require taking capital—that is, redeeming shares—to maintain the level of payment. A fund investor with a systematic withdrawal plan may receive either: (*a*) the proceeds from the periodic liquidation of a specified number of shares, or (*b*) a fixed dollar amount obtained by selling a varying number of shares.

Conversion privileges. When a single management organization has more than one fund, each with a different investment objective, it is often possible to exchange shares in one fund for shares in another fund at net asset value without paying the usual sales charge. Investors should consider possible capital gains tax liabilities before exercising such conversion privileges.

Fund custodian

The fund custodian is usually a national bank or trust company retained by the fund to hold the cash and securities of the fund. It may also perform a number of essential clerical-type services for the fund and its shareholders. These services may include: (*a*) *transfer agent* of the fund, (*b*) *registrar* of the fund shares, (*c*) dividend disbursing agent of the fund, (*d*) receipt of investor payments and investment of these payments in fund shares, (*e*) custodian of individual owners' fund shares, (*f*) bookkeeping functions, and (*g*) mailing of certificates of ownership to fund investors.

It is very important to understand the limited role of the custodian. The custodian does not perform any management, supervisory, or investment functions. The custodian takes no part in the sale or distribution of the fund shares and affords no protection against possible decline in the value of fund shares. The fund prospectus gives the name of the custodian and its functions.

Management fees, custodial fees and operating costs

One of the normal operating expenses, which include such costs as taxes, legal fees, auditing fees, cost of annual and quarterly reports, and cost of declaring and paying dividends, is the fund *management fee.* The amount of this fee on an annual basis will vary from one fund to another but is, on the average, *about 0.5 percent of the fund assets,* subject in some instances to sliding scale reductions as assets increase.[17]

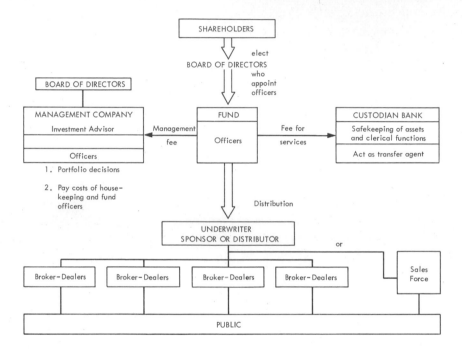

In total, operating expenses, including management fees, are normally less than 1 percent of the average net assets of the investment company. Thus, the expense ratio of a mutual fund is found by dividing total operating expenses by average net assets. The expense ratio varies from fund to fund. The general range is from about 0.5 percent to 3 percent.

The holder of a contractual plan normally pays a nominal administrative service fee, which is deducted from each investment by the custodian. The administrative fee is retained by the custodian. In addition, an annual custodian fee of about $6 for various services performed by the custodian may be deducted from the dividends credited to the investor's account, as well as a delegated duties fee of $1.50 or $2 per year. Nominal custodial charges of various types may also be charged to investors in voluntary accumulation plans, or in some cases the fund itself pays the charges to the custodian.

17/ The actual average, as reported in congressional hearings during 1967, is 37/100 of 1 percent.

Nominal one-time service charges may also be applied for such services as reregistering an account or assignment of the account. The chart on page 106 describes the relationship between the fund and other parties.

It is important to measure a fund's management in terms of its objectives. Each fund sets forth its objectives in its prospectus, such as: "long-term growth of principal and reasonable income through investment in high-grade common stocks." Other funds' objectives may read: "income yield as high as is consistent with reasonable risk, capital growth a secondary consideration"; "conservative long-term growth of income and capital"; "current income consistent with possible growth of capital." The objectives help classify the funds, as follows.

1. Conservation-of-principal funds (or stability of capital) are usually balanced funds or bond funds, which invest in those securities that react least to changing economic conditions.

2. Income funds place emphasis on income with varying degrees of risk, depending on the fund's objectives.

3. Growth funds emphasize appreciation or growth of capital. Again, the degree of risk depends on the company's objectives.

Investment Company Act

The Investment Company Act of 1940, also known as the '40 Act, was passed by Congress in an attempt to protect investors by requiring many sound procedures and forbidding unsound ones such as lack of adequate information to investors and self-dealing by investment managers. The '40 Act authorized Securities and Exchange Commission (SEC) regulation of a number of matters concerning the operation of investment companies.

The '40 Act categorizes investment companies,[18] which are issuers engaged primarily in the business of investing, reinvesting, owning, holding, or trading in securities, or who hold themselves out to be so engaged,[19] as one of three types.

Face amount certificate companies issue a certificate that contains a promise to pay a specified amount to the investor on a specified date; the amount is based on a fixed rate of return. These certificates are usually offered on an *installment plan purchase method.* Such certificates are usually backed by real estate or mortgages. They no longer represent a significant part of the overall investment company industry.

Unit investment trusts issue redeemable securities, each of which has a specified interest in specified securities. *Periodic payment plans or contractual plans* are in this category. They are organized under trust indentures and have no board of directors. In practice, there are two types: (*a*) a fixed trust, which issues shares of beneficial interest

---

18/ Assets of registered investment companies increased from an approximated $2.5 billion in 1941 to over $44 billion at the end of 1965.

19/ An investment company is presumed to be one engaged in the business of investing, reinvesting, owning, holding, or trading in securities, which owns or proposes to acquire securities that have a value exceeding 40 percent of such issuer's total assets. The determining factor is whether the issuer is actually engaged in investing and holds investment-type securities that account for more than 40 percent of the company's assets, and has more than 100 shareholders.

in a fixed portfolio; and (*b*) the trust that holds the mutual fund shares purchased by planholders of contractual plans.

Management companies, which include mutual funds, are the third and by far the largest category. These managements have the broadest discretion in the selection of securities for the portfolio. This category includes both *closed- and open-end management companies.* The distinguishing feature is that open-end companies issue redeemable securities.

Management companies are further divided into diversified and nondiversified companies. Generally speaking, *diversified* companies must have at least 75 percent of their assets invested so that: (*a*) not more than 5 percent of its assets are invested in any one corporation, and (*b*) not more than 10 percent of the voting securities of any single corporation are owned. Any other management company that is not a diversified company is a *nondiversified* company. Most mutual funds and the majority of closed-end funds are registered with the SEC as diversified companies.

The main provisions of the Investment Company Act are as follows.

Investment companies must register with the SEC through the prescribed registration statements, including all information and documents required under the Securities Act of 1933 and Securities Exchange Act of 1934. Otherwise, investment companies are prohibited from use of the U.S. mail or other forms of interstate commerce.

Directors, who are responsible for the activities of a mutual fund, are normally appointed by management and subsequently elected by shareholders. Not more than 60 percent of the directors of a registered investment company may be employees or affiliates of the investment adviser, or officers or employees of such registered company. Conversely, at least 40 percent of the directors of the fund must be persons independent of and not affiliated with the investment company and adviser.

A majority of the board of directors of a registered investment company may *not* consist of any single category of the following:

1. Officers, directors, or employees of the fund's regular broker.
2. The principal underwriter of the registered investment company or persons affiliated with such principal underwriter.
3. Investment bankers or affiliates of investment bankers.
4. Officers or directors of any one bank.

Any exception to the affiliation requirements above occurs in: (1) an open-end investment company that (2) imposes no sales charge, (3) pays a management fee of 1 percent per year or less, (4) charges a premium on issuance of securities or a discount on redemption of such securities of not more than 2 percent, and (5) has only one class of stock outstanding, each share having equal voting rights with every other share. If all these requirements are met, all members of the board of directors, except one, may be affiliated persons of the investment adviser.

Officers, directors, and other insiders are closely limited in their dealings with the fund. A mutual fund may not purchase the securities of any company if one or more of the officers or directors of the fund or its investment adviser owns more than 0.5 percent of the securities of that company, or if together such officers and directors own more than 5 percent of the securities. Officers, directors, and large stockholders of closed-end investment companies must report their transactions in the company to the SEC.

The sales load on periodic payment plans (contractual plans) may not exceed 9 percent over the life of the plan, and no more than 50 percent may be deducted as sales load from the first 12 payments. The 9 percent limitation is applicable to single payment certificates as well. The mutual fund shares underlying a periodic payment plan must be redeemable, and all payments into such plans must be deposited with a trustee or custodian.

Sales charges for investment company shares (as opposed to periodic plans) may be neither unconscionable nor grossly excessive.

Shareholders must initially approve and periodically reapprove management contracts (the approval may be by a majority of unaffiliated directors), selection of independent auditors, and changes in company policy on investment objectives. Such investment advisory (management) and underwriting contracts must be in writing. They usually are initially effective for two years, and thereafter must be specifically approved annually by a majority vote of shareholders or a majority of unaffiliated directors. Both contracts are automatically terminated in the event of assignment, and are cancelable on 60 days' notice by fund directors or stockholders. In addition, the terms of both contracts must be approved by a majority of the independent members of the investment company's board of directors.

A majority vote of shareholders is also required to change any of the stated or fundamental policies of the investment company, including:

1. Changing to open-end from closed-end.
2. Changing to nondiversified from diversified company.
3. Borrowing money.
4. Making loans.
5. Underwriting securities of others.
6. Purchasing or selling real estate or commodities.

Securities and cash owned by the company must normally be deposited with a custodian bank or, in certain cases, with a stock exchange firm, or otherwise be kept safe as the SEC may require. All officers and employees of the registered management company who have access to securities or funds must be bonded. No officer or director of the company, adviser, or underwriter may be protected against full liability of their actions by any escape clauses.

The SEC has general supervision over the accounting methods, semiannual and annual reports to stockholders, use of proxies, selling methods, prospectuses, and so on. Proxy statements are required to list details of the company's contract with its investment adviser as well as the relationships that exist between the adviser and fund officials.

A fund may not trade on margin or sell short without prior shareholders' approval or in contravention of any SEC rules. In open-end companies, borrowings from banks must have 300 percent collateral asset coverage; mutual funds (open-end companies) may issue only common stock. Closed-end companies may have senior securities and/or borrow money from banks, subject to various asset coverage collateral requirements.

Every registered investment company must file with the SEC the periodic reports that are sent to shareholders. These reports include financial statements that have been certified by independent public accountants, besides other required information. They are filed both semiannually, and annually; however, only the annual report must be certified by independent auditors or public accountants. Shareholders must receive financial reports at least semiannually.

It is established that in principal transactions between dealers and customers in shares of open-end investment company shares the current public opening price be maintained. Rebates or kickbacks are not allowed.

It should be understood that registration of a fund under the Investment Act of 1940 does not involve any federal or state agency supervision of the management of a fund or of the investment practices or policies of the fund.

Registered open- and closed-end investment companies are prohibited from issuing shares for (a) services, and (b) property other than cash or securities (not securities of the registered investment company itself), except as a dividend or distribution to its security holders or in connection with a reorganization.

No registered management company may lend money or property to any person unless the company's registration statement expressly permits such loans, and even then if the borrower is under common control with the company.

The underwriter of registered open-end companies, registered unit trusts, and registered face amount certificate companies and the companies must file with the SEC all sales literature relating to the sale of their securities within 10 days of use.

Investment companies that are required to file registration statements under both the '40 Act and the '33 Act may cross-file copies of the required documents.

The SEC is empowered to prescribe the format and order of items in the prospectuses of periodic payment plan and face amount certificate companies.

All registered unit investment trusts (which includes periodic payment plans) must have a custodian or trustee with an aggregate capital, surplus and retained earnings of at least $500,000. The custodian or trustee may not resign unless either the trust has been completed or liquidated or a successor trustee has been appointed and has accepted.

An enormous amount of books and records must be maintained by registered investment companies. The following must be permanently retained for the first two years in an easily accessible place.
1. Journals for:
   a) Purchases and sales of securities.
   b) Receipts and deliveries of securities.
   c) Receipts and disbursements of cash, including all other debits and credits.
2. Ledgers that reflect asset, liability, reserve, capital, income, and expense accounts, including separate ledger accounts for:
   a) Securities in transfer.
   b) Securities in physical possession.

c) Securities borrowed or loaned.

d) Monies borrowed or loaned and the collateral.

e) Dividends and interest received.

f) Dividends receivable and interest accrued.

g) Each portfolio security.

h) Each broker-dealer, bank, or other person through whom portfolio transactions are effected.

i) Each shareholder of record.

j) Each portfolio security, showing the location of all securities owned (long) and short.

3. Corporate charters, certificates of corporation or trust agreements, by-laws, and minute books.

Other records that must be preserved for six years, the first two in an easily accessible place, include:

1. Record of each brokerage order or other portfolio purchase.

2. Record of all puts, calls, spreads and straddles, and other options.

3. Trial balances (at least monthly).

4. Record of how and why all brokerage orders were placed or allocated.

5. Record of who authorized purchase or sale of portfolio securities.

6. Record of all advisory advice received from the investment adviser.

7. Copies of vouchers, confirmations, and other data.

It is unlawful for any person to destroy, mutilate, or alter any record whose preservation is required. It is unlawful to make any untrue statement of or omit any material fact in any document filed with the SEC, or to cause another person to violate the act.

The SEC may bring suit against officers or directors of a registered investment company, members of an advisory board or investment adviser, or the principal underwriter of an open-end fund or face amount certificate company for gross misconduct or gross abuse of trust. Any person convicted of larceny or embezzlement in connection with a registered investment company, willfully violating any portion of the '40 Act or its rules and regulations, making untrue statements of a material fact, or omitting to state any material fact may be fined not more than $10,000 or imprisoned not more than 2 years, or both.

The SEC is empowered to make such investigations as it deems necessary to determine whether a violation of the act has taken place. Witnesses and records may be subpoenaed, and attendance may be forced through the courts. A witness may not refuse to testify before the commission on the grounds of self-incrimination, but if the witness claims this privilege he cannot be prosecuted for his testimony except on the grounds of perjury. Any person aggrieved by an order of the SEC may obtain a review in the U.S. Court of Appeals within any circuit wherein such person resides or has his principal place of business, or in the U.S. Court of Appeals for the District of Columbia.

Violations of the act are subject to the jurisdiction of U.S. district courts for both civil and criminal actions.

All information filed with the SEC pursuant to the act is available to the public, unless its disclosure is deemed neither necessary nor in the public interest or for the protection of investors.

The SEC is required to submit an annual report to Congress concerning its work and recommendations.

Any contract made in violation of the act is voidable.

Any person who within 10 years has been convicted of a felony or misdemeanor arising from the sale of securities or from his own actions, or any person who is enjoined from the securities business, is ineligible to be an officer, director, member of an advisory board, or investment adviser of a registered investment company.

Affiliated persons,[20] promoters of, or principal underwriters for a registered investment company in most cases are prohibited from buying or selling securities from or to the company, and from borrowing money or other property from the company.

Clearly, the '40 Act gives the SEC the powers to strictly regulate investment companies in the public interest and for the protection of investors.

20/ An affiliated person of another person is one who, among other things, directly or indirectly owns, controls, or has voting power involving 5 percent or more of the outstanding voting stock of the other person.

4 | Review questions

141. The primary advantages of mutual fund investing include ....
1. professional management
2. diversification
3. selection
4. all of these

Answer questions 142 to 145 by choosing the number of the phrase that best describes the term mentioned.
1. invests in high yield securities
2. invests in certain industries or regions
3. invests only in junior securities
4. invests wherever management thinks best

142. Fully managed fund ....

143. Specialized fund ....

144. Common stock fund ....

145. Income fund ....

146. Fund shareholders may receive payments from a fund in the form of ....
1. dividends
2. capital gains distributions
3. both 1 and 2
4. none of these

147. A fund's capital gains distributions are paid from the fund's ....
1. net realized profits
2. net investment income
3. unrealized appreciation
4. none of these

148. A fund investor ....
1. takes his capital gains distributions in cash
2. accepts his capital gains distributions in additional fund shares
3. either 1 or 2
4. none of these

149. A mutual fund shareholder may redeem his shares ....
1. at any time
2. on any business day
3. only when there is another buyer for them
4. once per month

150. Most open-end companies redeem their shares at the per share ....
1. net asset value
2. net asset value minus a redemption charge
3. public offering price
4. net asset value plus 8.5 percent

151. A mutual fund investor may receive a discount by making purchases in ....
1. round lots
2. large dollar amounts
3. neither of these
4. both 1 and 2

152. A breakpoint is ....
1. the maximum sales charge permitted on a purchase of fund shares
2. the dollar amount at which a quality discount is obtained on a purchase of fund shares
3. the maximum dollar amount an individual should invest in fund shares
4. none of these

153. To receive a quantity discount on a purchase of fund shares, an investor ....
1. must make a single, lump-sum investment
2. may total the amounts of separate purchases within 13 months or make a single, lump-sum investment
3. must ask for it
4. none of these

154. The time limit for making separate purchases of fund shares, to qualify for a quantity discount is ....

1. 24 months
2. 12 months
3. 13 months
4. 18 months
5. 6 months

155. An investor's pledge that he will purchase enough fund shares within the time limit to qualify for a quantity discount is known as ....

1. a best effort
2. a limit order
3. a letter of intent
4. right of accumulation

156. Investment company shares traded at a discount or at a premium are ....

1. open-end shares
2. closed-end shares
3. common stock funds
4. balanced funds

157. Investment company shares with the greater liquidity are ....

1. open-end shares
2. closed-end shares
3. both of these
4. neither of these

158. Under the Investment Company Act of 1940, an individual who redeems his shares must be paid within ....

1. seven days
2. seven business days
3. three business days
4. none of these

159. Generally investors who redeem fund shares are paid at ....

1. the next published bid price
2. the bid price published a week later
3. the public offering price
4. none of these

160. All management companies ....

1. provide their investors with some diversification or portfolio
2. are classified as diversified companies under the Investment Company Act of 1940
3. neither of these
4. all of these

161. Any management company not classified as a diversified company under the Investment Company Act of 1940 is known as a ....

1. nondiversified company
2. closed-end company
3. balanced company
4. none of these

162. A balanced fund is a ....

1. leverage company
2. fund that invests in bonds, preferred stocks, and common stocks
3. bad investment
4. fund that invests only in common stocks

163. A fund that invests in a diversified group of common stocks within a particular industry or geographical area is a ....

1. diversified common stock fund
2. specialized common stock fund
3. balanced fund
4. income fund

164. A fund that invests in a wide cross section of common stocks is a ....

1. diversified common stock fund
2. balanced fund
3. nondiversified balanced fund
4. none of these

165. Most investment companies are ....

1. balanced funds
2. diversified common stock funds
3. income funds
4. bond and preferred stock funds

166. A specialized common stock fund may invest its assets according to ....
1. type of industry
2. geographical area
3. either 1 or 2
4. none of these

167. A fund that invests in the common stocks of electronics companies is a ....
1. specialized common stock fund
2. diversified common stock fund
3. balanced fund
4. all of these

168. A fund whose portfolio consists entirely of a diversified group of Kentucky common stocks is a ....
1. diversified common stock fund
2. specialized common stock fund
3. balanced fund
4. income fund

169. A balanced fund ....
1. must maintain an equal balance of bonds, preferred stocks, and common stocks in its portfolio
2. may vary the proportions of various classes of securities in its portfolio, according to management's judgment of market conditions
3. either 1 or 2, depending on policy stated in fund's prospectus
4. none of these

170. A fund may invest for the purpose of ....
1. current income
2. capital appreciation
3. both for capital appreciation and for income
4. any of these

171. A fund that invests primarily in high-yielding securities is ....
1. a growth fund
2. an income fund
3. a "special situations fund"
4. all of these

172. A fund that seeks capital appreciation attempts to purchase for its portfolio ....
1. high-yielding securities
2. growth securities
3. bonds
4. none of these

173. A special situations fund follows a relatively ....
1. conservative investment policy
2. aggressive investment policy
3. neither of these

174. Shares of an open-end company normally may be purchased ....
1. at any time
2. only when another shareholder wants to sell his shares
3. only when they are traded on an exchange
4. none of these

175. Investment companies in existence today generally issue ....
1. bonds
2. preferred stock
3. common stock
4. none of these

176. Investment companies that issue fixed-income securities or have bank loans in addition to common stock are known as ....
1. balanced funds
2. leverage companies
3. stock funds
4. specialized funds

177. The number of shares an open-end company has outstanding is ....
1. fixed
2. continuously changing
3. the same as a closed-end fund

178. The dividends and interest a fund receives are known as the fund's ....
1. realized capital gains
2. net investment income

3. total investment income
4. none of these

179. The managers of the XYZ Fund are permitted to handle the fund's portfolio in whatever way they think best. The fund is considered a ....
1. balanced fund
2. fully managed fund
3. income fund
4. none of these

180. A fund is managed by its ....
1. sponsor
2. underwriter
3. directors and officers
4. sales organization

181. The managers of a fund ....
1. make all investment decisions completely as they wish
2. make all investment decisions within the limitations set forth in the fund's prospectus
3. make no investment decisions
4. none of these

182. Generally a fund's officers ....
1. perform their own investment research
2. contract an investment advisory organization to perform research
3. are not concerned with the fund's operations
4. none of these

183. Under the Investment Company Act of 1940 a mutual fund may .... make no dividend payment from any source other than its accumulated net undistributed income.
1. in any circumstances
2. without disclosing to its shareholders the source of payment
3. neither of these

184. The type of investment company that promises the return of a stated sum of money to the investor is the ....
1. management company
2. periodic payment plan company
3. stock fund
4. face amount certificate company

185. The face amount of a face amount certificate is the ....
1. total amount paid by the investor
2. amount promised to the investor on maturity of the certificate
3. neither of these

186. The sales charge on contractual plan purchases is known as a ....
1. front-end load
2. level charge
3. bargain
4. letter of intent

187. The sales charge on a periodic payment plan may never be ....
1. unfair
2. more than 9 percent of the total amount of the purchases for the first year
3. more than 9 percent of the total amount of the plan
4. more than 5 percent of the total amount of the plan
5. more than 12 percent of the total amount of the plan

188. Contractual plan sales charges for the first 12 monthly payments may ....
1. not be more than 50 percent
2. not be more than 9 percent
3. not be more than 75 percent
4. none of these

189. The phrase "penalty plan" refers to a ....
1. contractual plan
2. voluntary plan
3. automatic withdrawal plan
4. systematic withdrawal plan

190. Plan completion insurance is paid if the planholder ....

1. is financially unable to continue making payments on his plan
2. dies before completing the payments on his plan
3. both 1 and 2
4. neither 1 nor 2

191. If a contractual planholder with plan completion life insurance dies before completing the payments on his plan, the insurance company pays into his account ....

1. a fixed dollar amount
2. the total amount of the plan
3. the total amount of the unpaid payments on the plan
4. the face amount of his plan

192. When a contractual planholder with plan completion life insurance dies, the insurance company makes payment ....

1. into the custodian bank
2. directly to the planholder's beneficiaries
3. either 1 or 2

193. The SEC reviews ....

1. prospectuses published by investment companies
2. reports sent to fund shareholders
3. both 1 and 2
4. none of these

194. The SEC .... annual independent audits of financial statements in reports sent to fund shareholders.

1. encourages
2. requires
3. forbids

195. The Investment Company Act of 1940 does not ....

1. regulate investment practices within the investment company industry
2. provide for the supervision of business judgment in the management of a company's portfolio

3. both 1 and 2
4. none of these

196. The Investment Company Act of 1940 ....

1. defines an investment company for legal purposes
2. provides the investor with a guarantee against loss
3. provides for tax treatment of funds
4. all of these

197. Before the Crash of 1929, most investment companies were ....

1. open-end management companies
2. closed-end management companies
3. neither of these

198. When selling a contractual plan, a salesman ....

1. must use both the plan prospectus and the fund prospectus
2. must use only a fund prospectus
3. must use only a plan prospectus
4. need not use any prospectus

199. A plan prospectus does not ....

1. give detailed information regarding the fund that underlies the plan
2. describe the types of plans offered by the plan company
3. give a detailed breakdown of the sales charges for all plans offered
4. have any importance

200. A plan prospectus must include ....

1. the underlying fund's statement of investments
2. a statement that "this prospectus is valid only when accompanied by the current (name) fund prospectus"
3. neither of these

201. The general public usually purchases fund shares ....

1. directly from the fund
2. from the fund's distributor

3. from a securities dealer
4. from the underwriter

202. The .... plan is designed to encourage the investor to make regular payments of a fixed dollar amount for a specified number of years.
1. voluntary
2. systematic withdrawal
3. monthly investment
4. contractual

203. An investor who is permitted to exchange shares of one fund for shares of another is said to have a ....
1. transfer statement
2. conversion privilege
3. bonus
4. none of these

204. A conversion privilege applies to ....
1. all funds
2. funds under the same sponsorship
3. neither of these

205. If a fund's officers contract an investment management organization to advise on investment decisions, ... has (have) the final responsibility for all of the fund's investment decisions.
1. the sponsor
2. the directors and officers
3. the investment management organization
4. none of these

206. A fund's portfolio is managed by ....
1. the sponsor
2. the investment adviser
3. the custodian
4. none of these

207. A fund's custodian ....
1. holds in safekeeping the fund's cash and securities
2. supervises the determining of portfolio policies
3. both 1 and 2
4. neither 1 nor 2

208. Most investment companies register with the SEC under ....
1. the Investment Company Act of 1940
2. the Federal Reserve Act
3. neither of these

Use the following data for answering question 209.

Income:
Cash Dividends $600,000
Interest 50,000
Expenses 10,000

209. Net investment income equals ....
1. $540,000
2. $660,000
3. $640,000
4. none of these

210. The income dividend a fund shareholder receives is paid from ....
1. net realized capital gains
2. net investment income
3. total investment income
4. all of these

211. A plan whereby mutual fund dividend payments are automatically accepted in additional fund shares is referred to as ....
1. an automatic dividend reinvestment plan
2. an accumulation plan
3. a voluntary open account
4. a contractual plan

212. The ABC Fund currently owns XYZ common stock with a market value greater than its original cost. This security has ....
1. unrealized appreciation
2. unrealized depreciation
3. realized appreciation
4. none of these

213. Mutual funds are ....
1. closed end
2. open end

214. Unrealized depreciation becomes realized ....
1. when any security is sold
2. when the security that shows unrealized depreciation is sold
3. at the end of the fiscal year
4. when growth securities are bought for the portfolio

215. The ABC Fund realized profits of $100,000 and losses of $10,000 for the year ending December 31, 1961. The fund's .... amounted to $90,000 for the year.
1. net investment income
2. unrealized appreciation
3. net realized gains
4. none of these

216. Voluntary plans are offered by ....
1. mutual funds
2. periodic payment plan companies
3. the New York Stock Exchange
4. none of these

217. Contractual plans are offered by ....
1. Mutual funds
2. periodic payment plan companies
3. the New York Stock Exchange
4. none of these

218. When used in connection with investment companies, an open account is a ....
1. contractual plan
2. voluntary plan
3. none of these

219. The sales charge on voluntary open account purchases is known as a ....
1. front-end load
2. level charge
3. neither of these

220. The investor with a .... is able to withdraw from his plan after one year with the least risk of loss.
1. voluntary open account
2. contractual plan
3. both of these

221. An open-account holder may liquidate his holdings ....
1. only when he has invested a specific sum of money
2. only after a certain number of years have passed
3. whenever he wishes
4. none of these

222. The fund investor with a systematic withdrawal plan may ....
1. receive the proceeds from the periodic liquidation of a specified number of shares
2. receive a fixed dollar amount for each withdrawal
3. either 1 or 2
4. none of these

223. Under the Investment Company Act of 1940, the periodic payment plan company or contractual plan company is classified as a ....
1. management company
2. unit investment trust
3. face amount certificate company
4. none of these

224. The periodic payment planholder makes investments of ....
1. any amount he wishes
2. a fixed dollar amount, or multiples of it
3. neither of these

225. The price a mutual fund shareholder generally pays when he purchases fund shares is ....
1. the net asset value per share
2. the public offering price
3. both of these
4. neither of these

226. The market value of a fund's investments plus its cash and receivables equals the fund's ....

1. total asset value
2. net asset value

Use the following data for answering questions 227 to 229.

Assets:
Securities $150,000
Cash in bank   30,000
Receivables   10,000
Liabilities . . . . $ 10,000
Number of shares
   outstanding   18,000

227. The total asset value is . . . .
1. $190,000
2. $200,000
3. $150,000
4. $180,000

228. The net asset value is . . . .
1. $190,000
2. $200,000
3. $150,000
4. $180,000

229. The . . . . is $10.
1. net asset value
2. net asset value per share
3. public offering price
4. none of these

230. A fund's net asset value per share is ordinarily computed . . . .
1. once a day
2. twice a day
3. twice a week
4. monthly

231. The sales charge on a fund share is generally computed as a percentage of . . . .
1. the public offering price
2. the net asset value per share
3. neither of these

232. The issuing and pricing of open-end shares is regulated by . . . .
1. the SEC
2. the NASD
3. both 1 and 2
4. neither 1 or 2

233. Most mutual funds are . . . .
1. leverage companies
2. not leverage companies

234. The type of management company that has outstanding a fixed number of shares is known as . . . .
1. a closed-end company
2. an open-end company
3. neither of these

235. Mutual funds are . . . .
1. closed-end management companies
2. open-end management companies
3. neither of these

236. New shares are continuously issued by . . . .
1. closed-end management companies
2. open-end management companies
3. neither of these

237. Closed-end shares are purchased . . . .
1. through a sales organization
2. over the counter and on securities exchanges
3. neither of these

238. A mutual fund normally invests its assets in . . . .
1. a single corporate security
2. a diversified group of securities
3. a closed-end investment company
4. foreign securities

239. A periodic payment plan invests its assets in . . . .
1. a diversified group of government and corporate securities
2. a closed-end investment company
3. an open-end investment company
4. neither of these

240. A mutual fund issues . . . .
1. shares
2. contractual plans
3. neither of these

Refer to pages 259-60 for correct answers.

5 | Securities Act of 1933
Securities Exchange Act of 1934
Other security laws

Mutual funds, possibly more than any other investment medium, are regulated by federal laws to practically the smallest details in order to protect the individual investors. There are three main laws: Securities Act of 1933; Securities Exchange Act of 1934; and Investment Company Act of 1940, which, as noted in Chapter 4, is the most important in terms of mutual funds because it touches on *all* facets of mutual fund operation. Now, let us look into the important provisions of each of these other two laws.

Securities Act of 1933

The Securities Act of 1933, also known as the '33 Act or Truth in Securities Act, provides among other things that most securities offered to the public by an issuing company (new issues) or by any person in a control relationship to such a company must be registered with the Securities and Exchange Commission (SEC). Since open-end investment companies continually offer their shares to the public, this act applies to mutual funds. The expressed purpose of the '33 Act is: "To provide *full and fair disclosure* of the character of newly issued securities . . . and to *prevent frauds* in the sale thereof."

Again, then, the registration provisions relate to *newly issued* securities or securities in the hands of persons in control, not to those already in the hands of the public.

"Full and fair disclosure" of relevant information is required in a *prospectus.* A prospectus is a summary of the registration statement filed with the Securities and Exchange Commission.[1] All issuers of registered securities, including open-end investment companies, must furnish each prospective customer for a new issue with a prospectus. Among the information contained in the prospectus is a statement:

1. Of the company's investment objective and policies.

1/ Misleading statements or omissions of material facts from the registration statement subject the signers of the registration statement to criminal penalties of up to 5 years imprisonment or fines up to $5,000 as well as civil suits.

2. Of the inherent risk involved in purchasing fund shares.
3. That the fund gives the investor no assurance that its investment objectives will be attained.
4. That the amount an investor will be paid when he liquidates his shares may be more or less than the original cost, depending on the market value of the fund's portfolio.
5. Of the investments owned by the fund, including number of shares held, cost price, and current market value.
6. Of the policy of the fund regarding (a) borrowing money, (b) issuing senior securities, (c) underwriting securities, (d) concentrating investments in a particular industry, (e) purchasing real estate or commodities, (f) making loans, (g) turning over its portfolio.
7. Showing names and addresses of affiliated persons.
8. Of the sales load expressed as a percentage of the public offering price, and any redemption or repurchase charge and other redemption provisions.
9. Of assets and liabilities, statement of changes in net assets, and a price makeup that shows how the offering price is determined.
10. Of financial information both for the fund as a whole and on a per-share basis.

The registration of newly issued securities under the '33 Act can become effective 20 days after the registration statement is filed with the SEC. Typically, with necessary amendments and processing delays the registration statement more normally becomes effective about 60 days after the first filing. *The Securities Act of '33* pertains to new issues and secondary distributions by controlling stockholders. The *Securities Exchange Act of 1934* requires *registration* for the listing of a security on an exchange and for certain over-the-counter securities.

Registration information for an issue to be listed on an exchange is filed with a national securities exchange, with a copy to the SEC. When the exchange authorities certify to the SEC that the security has been approved for listing by the exchange, the registration becomes effective 30 days after receipt of such certification by the SEC.

Securities traded in the over-the-counter market must be registered (if they meet stockholder member requirements and amount of asset requirements) by filing registration statements directly with the SEC. Such registrations normally become effective within 60 days after such filing.

The information that must be provided in the registration statement is essentially similar for both '33 and '34 Act registrations and includes the following.

1. Type of business.
2. Capital and financial structure.
3. The terms, position, rights, and privileges of the different classes of securities outstanding.
4. The terms on which the company's securities are to be, and during the preceding three years have been, offered to the public.
5. A listing of the directors, officers, and underwriters, and each security holder of

more than 10 percent of any class of any equity security, their remuneration, and their interests in the securities of, and their material contracts with, the issuer and any person who directly or indirectly controls or is controlled by, or is under direct or indirect common control with, the issuer.

6. Remuneration paid to the three highest paid officers who receive $30,000 per year or more, and all directors.
7. Bonus and profit-sharing arrangements.
8. Management and service contracts.
9. Stock options existing or to be created.
10. Material contracts made within two years prior to filing of the registration statement, or to be executed after the filing, including every material patent or contract for a material patent.
11. Balance sheets and profit and loss statements for not more than the three preceding fiscal years, certified by independent public accountants.
12. Any further financial statements required by the SEC.
13. Copies, as the SEC may require, of articles of incorporation, bylaws, trust indentures, underwriting arrangements, and material contracts.

Finally, the Securities Act was designed to *prevent fraud* in the sale of securities.

The '33 Act *exempts* from registration requirements securities of the U.S. government, states, and territories, and political subdivisions thereof, securities subject to the Interstate Commerce Act, security issues sold only on an intrastate basis, private placements sold to a limited number of investors, and securities issued by nonprofit organizations. The act also exempts from registration *regulation A* offerings when the entire issue is less than $300,000. A simplified prospectus, known as an *offering circular,* [24] must be given to prospective purchasers of securities issued under regulation A.

Although the SEC requires registration and reviews prospectuses, it does not approve or disapprove of any security. Its purpose in reviewing a prospectus is to be sure the potential investor is given full opportunity to examine the important details concerning any new security offered to him. In order to advise everyone that the SEC is not passing judgment, the following statement or *disclaimer* must appear in heavy type on every prospectus: **"These securities have not been approved or disapproved by the Securities and Exchange Commission, nor has the commission passed upon the accuracy or adequacy of this prospectus. Any representation to the contrary is a criminal offense."**

Red herring is trade jargon for a preliminary prospectus, and is so called because certain information is printed in red around the border of the first page. Based on the preliminary prospectus, or red herring, investment dealers solicit from prospective investors an indication of interest. This indication of interest simply means that when the final prospectus is available, and the offering is actually made, the prospective client has indicated his interest in purchasing some of the new issue.

A *stop order* suspending the effectiveness of a registration statement may be made by the SEC, after opportunity for a hearing is given, if it appears that the registration statement is inaccurate. The period between the filing date and the date the registration statement becomes effective (which must be at least 20 days) is called the *cooling off* period.

Unless a registration statement is in effect, it is unlawful to sell or to make delivery of a security through the instruments of interstate commerce, including the U.S. mails. If additional information is needed from the issuer, the SEC asks for it by issuing a *deficiency letter* (called by the SEC a letter of comment). The additions or changes requested in the deficiency letter are supplied in an amended registration statement.

Securities Exchange Act of 1934

The Securities Exchange Act of 1934 is the law passed by Congress to establish and maintain *fair and honest markets* for the buying and selling of securities. From this law came the Securities and Exchange Commission (SEC), and from the 1938 Maloney amendment to this act there developed the National Association of Securities Dealers (NASD). The main provisions of the '34 Act are as follows.

All stock exchanges must register with, unless exempted by the SEC, and be regulated by the SEC. Also, securities listed on such exchanges must be registered. The Exchange Act forbids trading on an exchange in any security, except exempt securities, unless the security is registered on at least one national securities exchange.

Management corporations, or sponsors, which also act as principal underwriter and distributor of fund shares, must register as a broker-dealer with the SEC. All brokers and dealers who deal in the over-the-counter market, in interstate and foreign commerce, and through the U.S. mails must be registered with the SEC. Broker-dealers who deal solely intrastate (within one state) need not register. Otherwise, every broker-dealer must file an application for registration in duplicate on a special form called BD. Such registration becomes effective *30 days after filing,* unless revoked or denied by the SEC. Registration with the SEC is required as a prerequisite to membership in the NASD. The initial and periodic fees payable to the SEC by a registered broker or dealer who is not an NASD member are described later in this chapter.

To control the amount of the nation's credit made available to the securities markets. the Board of Governors of the Federal Reserve System, *through the '34 Act,* was given the right to set margin requirements for listed securities and to prohibit loans for the purpose of purchasing unlisted securities. Note that the Board of Governors sets margin requirements, but was given the authority to do so by the '34 Act. This is discussed in more detail later in this chapter.

The Securities and Exchange Commission (SEC) was established to provide for control of the trading of securities on exchanges and in the over-the-counter market in order to prevent inequitable and unfair practices. The Securities and Exchange Commission is the official federal governing agency in charge of regulating the securities business, and is responsible for the enforcement of the various securities laws. The SEC reviews both prospectuses and reports to shareholders of investment companies. The SEC Commission consists of five persons appointed by the President of the United

States, for five-year terms. The commission is charged with *responsibility for administering the following acts.*

1. *The Securities Act of 1933.* The primary purpose is to provide "full and fair disclosure of the character of securities sold in inter-state commerce, and to prohibit fraudulent acts and practices in the sale of securities, to prohibit misrepresentation of facts." This purpose is accomplished by the requirement to register with the SEC "newly issued" securities or those being sold by a person "in control."

2. *The Securities Exchange Act of 1934.* The primary purpose is to require the registration of National Securities Exchanges and broker-dealers (through the Maloney Act Amendment in 1938) that do business in interstate commerce.

3. *The Public Utility Holding Company Act of 1935.* The purpose of this act is to eliminate abuses connected with the operations of holding companies involving electric and gas operating companies and natural gas pipeline companies. A holding company, by definition, owns or controls 10 percent or more of the outstanding voting securities of an electric or gas public utility company. Under the act, all public holding companies that have electric or gas subsidiaries in more than one state are required to register with the SEC. Holding company structures are regulated by the SEC. Registered holding companies must receive SEC approval before issuing securities. Holding company borrowing from subsidiaries is prohibited by the act.

4. *The Trust Indenture Act of 1939.* This act requires that indentures securing publicly offered debt securities be qualified with the SEC. A trust indenture (deed of trust) is a contractual agreement between a corporation that issues bonds, debentures, or other debt securities and a trustee or trustees who represent the investors who purchased such debt. Under a trust indenture, the trustee represents the bondholders and deals with the issuing corporation on their behalf. The act requires that in carrying out his duties the trustee use the same degree of care and skill a "prudent man" would use in the conduct of his own affairs. The act applies to those trust indentures under which more than $1 million in securities may be outstanding at any one time. The act requires the trust indenture to include the following:

    a) Appointment of a corporate trustee that is financially responsible, with a minimum combined capital and surplus of $150,000, and is free from conflicting interests with the bondholders.

    b) Specification of the action the trustee will take if the issuing corporation fails to live up to the terms of the indenture.

    c) Provision for the trustees to submit annual reports to the bondholders.

    Under the act, the trustee is charged with various duties, including:

    a) Authenticating the bonds, but not in any way guaranteeing principal or interest.

    b) Seeing that interest and taxes are paid when due, and in the event of default notifying the bondholders within 90 days.

    c) Seeing that sinking fund and collateral covenants of the indenture are complied with.

d) Submitting annual reports to the bondholders.

The trustee can be sued for negligence if conditions warrant, and under the act exculpatory clauses, which eliminate all liability of a trustee, are outlawed. Securities issued under an indenture subject to the act must also be registered under the Securities Act of 1933.

5. *The Investment Advisers Act of 1940.* This act regulates and requires registration of individuals or firms who receive compensation for giving investment advice to others. The act requires that registered investment advisers:

a) Disclose the nature of any personal interest in transactions recommended to clients.

b) Do not enter into profit-sharing arrangements with clients.

c) Are not allowed to assign investment advisory contracts without the client's consent.

d) Who engage in fraudulent or deceitful activities in connection with client affairs are committing an unlawful practice.

Several exceptions to the requirement that investment advisers register under the act include:

a) Advisers with fewer than 15 clients during the previous 12 months who do not represent to the general public that they are investment advisers.

b) Advisers who have only investment or insurance companies as clients.

c) Advisers who furnish advice only to residents of the state in which the adviser maintains his principal place of business, and who do not give advice concerning securities listed on a national securities exchange or securities accorded unlisted trading privileges on such exchanges.

Other exemptions from the act include: newspapers, banks, government securities houses, magazines of general circulation, broker-dealers who give incidental and gratuitous advice, and individuals such as attorneys, accountants, engineers, and teachers who give purely incidental advice. The SEC may deny registration as an investment adviser for reasons similar to those for denying broker-dealer registration, and it may revoke registrations for violations of the act.

6. *The Investment Company Act of 1940.* The '40 Act provides for the registration and regulation of companies primarily engaged in the business of investing, reinvesting, owning, holding, or trading in securities.

The 1934 Securities Exchange Act, in addition to charging the SEC with responsibilities for these 6 acts, provides definitions of an exchange, facility, member, broker, dealer, bank, director, issuer, person, security, equity security, exempted security, buy, sell, listed, officers, short sale, and others.

Restrictions are placed on borrowing by members, brokers, and dealers, and on the hypothecation (lending) of securities carried for customers' accounts.

The Net Capital or *20 to 1 Rule* specifies that a registered broker-dealer must not permit his aggregate indebtedness to exceed *20 times* (2,000 percent) his net capital. This rule is also enforced by the NASD for its members. Minimum capital of $5,000 or $2,500 is also required pursuant to a rule adoped by the SEC. Financial reports are required. Every broker-dealer must file annual reports of financial condition with the SEC on a special form called X-17-A-5. These reports show details of assets, liabilities, net worth, and so on.

Certain acts considered to be manipulative, fraudulent or deceptive are prohibited either in the over-the-counter market or on an exchange. These include:

1. *Manipulation,* which is artificially causing the price of a security to rise or fall.
2. *Wash sales,* which are the purchase and sale of the same security by the same person at about the same time to give the appearance of activity.
3. Inducing purchases or sales by making false or misleading statements.
4. *Churning,* which is causing a customer to buy or sell excessively and not in his best interests.
5. *Matched orders,* when two individuals act together to buy and sell as in wash sales.
6. Rumor or false information spreading.
7. Any untrue statement of a material fact and any omission of a material fact necessary in order that a statement not be misleading, if the statement or omission is made with knowledge or reasonable grounds to believe that it is untrue or misleading.
8. Representations by a broker or dealer that registration with the SEC or failure of the SEC to deny or revoke such registration indicates that the commission has passed on or approved the financial standing, business, or conduct of the broker or dealer, or the merits of any security.
9. Failure of a broker or dealer to give a customer, before completion of a transaction (normally time of payment or delivery), *written confirmation* that shows (*a*) whether he is acting as a dealer, a broker for the customer or another party, or both, and (*b*) when he acts as a broker, the name of the person from whom the security was bought (for the customer who is a buyer) or to whom the security was sold (for the customer who is a seller), the date and time of such transaction (or an indication that such information will be furnished on request), and the source or amount of any commission or other remuneration to be received in connection with the transaction.
10. Failure of the broker or dealer to make written disclosure of control or common control with the issuer of a security he buys from or sells to a customer.
11. Failure to disclose to a customer the broker's or dealer's participation in an underwriting.
12. Discretionary transactions for a client's account that are excessive in size or frequency in view of the financial resources and character of such account.
13. Failure to properly record details of discretionary transactions.
14. Representations to a customer by a broker or dealer participating in an underwriting that sales are *at the market* or at a price related to the market price, unless such broker or dealer has reasonable grounds to believe that a market exists other than that made, created, or controlled by him or any person for whom he is acting or with whom he is associated in the underwriting, or by whom he is controlled or whom he controls or with whom he is under common control.

15. Failure to state clearly the assumptions under which financial statements are prepared when such statements purport to give effect to the receipt and use of the proceeds of the sale of securities.

16. Violation of any of the many rules concerning a broker's or dealer's unauthorized pledging (hypothecation) of his customer's securities.

Transactions brought about by false or misleading statements of material facts, or by the omission of facts, are *fraud*, and constitute a criminal offense.

Registration of national securities associations is permitted under the Securities Exchange Act of 1934. This led to the Maloney Act and the creation of the National Association of Securities Dealers.

Trading by directors, officers, and principal stockholders (insiders) is regulated. The law requires that every person who is directly or indirectly the beneficial owner of more than 10 percent of any class of any registered equity security, other than an exempted security, or who is the director or an officer of the issuer of such security must file a statement with the exchange and with the SEC of the amount of all equity securities of which he is the beneficial owner. Any changes in ownership must be reported within 10 days of the close of the calendar month in which they occurred. These provisions were adopted as measures for control of unfair practices by corporate insiders. This section permits recovery by the corporation or other stockholders of short-term (within six months) insider profits, and it prohibits short sales and sales against the box by such individuals.

Periodic reporting to the SEC by issuers of registered securities is required. Those registered with an exchange must file with the exchange copies of the information given to the SEC. Information that must be furnished includes the following.

1. Annual reports within 120 days after the close of the fiscal year, containing certified financial statements and various other pertinent information.
2. A report within 10 days after the end of any month during which:
   a) Changes in control occur.
   b) Any significant amount of assets are disposed of or acquired.
   c) Any extraordinary legal proceedings are entered into.
   d) Changes occur in the rights of any security holder.
   e) There is a significant increase or decrease in securities outstanding.
   f) A default occurs on senior securities.
   g) Any significant stock options are granted.
   h) A material revaluation of assets occurs.
   i) A proxy submission is made.
   j) Any other materially important events occur.
3. Semiannual reports of operating results in certain circumstances.

Proxy statements and solicitations are required to be detailed and truthful, and must disclose all pertinent information concerning the matter to be decided on, as well as provide space for the shareholder to vote yes or no on each issue. When the management of a registered security solicits proxies for an annual meeting at which directors will be elected, the proxy statement must be accompanied or preceded by an annual report, including financial statements, for the last two (one for investment companies) fiscal years.

It is unlawful for any broker-dealer to represent that any government agency has passed upon the investment merits of any security.

One of the more important provisions of the Exchange Act is that the SEC may adopt rules and regulations designed "(a) to *promote just and equitable principles of trade;* (b) to provide safeguards against *unreasonable profits* or *unreasonable rates* of commissions or other charges; (c) in general to *protect investors* and the public interest; and (d) to remove impediments to and perfect the mechanism of a free and open market." Pursuant to this statutory authority, the SEC has adopted the following rules.

1. Every nonmember (non-NASD) broker or dealer[2] and associated person (any employee whose functions are other than clerical or ministerial):

   a) Shall observe *high standards* of commercial honor and *just and equitable* principles of trade in the conduct of his business.

   b) Shall have *reasonable grounds* for believing that *recommendations* to customers to buy, sell, or exchange securities are *suitable* for the customer on the basis of information furnished by the customer after reasonable inquiry concerning the customer's investment objectives, financial situation, and needs, and any other information known by the broker, dealer, or associated person.

   c) Shall not exercise any discretionary power for a customer unless the customer has given prior written authorization and has indicated his reasons for such authorization.

2. Every nonmember broker or dealer shall:

   a) Exercise diligent supervision over all the securities activities of all his associated persons, and every associated person shall be subject to the supervision of a qualified supervisor designated by such broker or dealer.

   b) Establish and maintain written procedures, with a copy of such procedures in each business office, in order to comply with the below-listed supervisory requirements.

      (1) The review and written approval of a designated supervisor is required for: the opening of each new customer account; securities transactions of associated persons; all correspondence pertaining to the solicitation or execution of such transactions; handling of customer complaints; delegation of discretionary authority by customers, and of each discretionary transaction effected in such discretionary accounts.

      (2) The frequent examination of all customer accounts is required to detect and prevent irregularities or abuses.

      (3) When more than one supervisor has been appointed, the broker or dealer

2/ Nonmembers who are members of a national securities exchange may be exempt from these rules in certain cases.

must designate those qualified persons who will supervise the supervisors and inspect each business office to insure that the written procedures are enforced.

The *keeping of certain records* by brokers and dealers who are registered with the SEC is required. One important provision requires brokers and dealers to maintain in their files the personnel records for each registered representative.

Required books and records that must be preserved for a period of not less than six years, the first two in an easily accessible place, are as follows.

1. Blotters, or other records of original entry, containing an itemized daily record of all purchases and sales of securities, all receipts and deliveries of securities—including certificate numbers—all receipts and disbursements of cash, and all other debits and credits. Such records shall show the account for which each transaction was effected, the name and amount of securities, the unit and aggregate purchase or sale price if any, the trade date, and the name or other designation of the person from whom purchased or received or to whom the securities were sold or delivered.

2. Ledgers, reflecting all assets and liabilities, income, expense, and capital accounts.

3. Ledger accounts, itemizing separately each cash and margin account of every customer, and of the number, all purchases, sales, receipts, and deliveries of securities for such account, and all other debits and credits to such account.

4. A Securities ledger, reflecting separately for each security, as of the clearance dates, all long or short positions carried by the dealer, and showing:
   a) The location of all securities long.
   b) The offsetting position to all securities short.
   c) In all cases the name or designation of the account in which the security is carried.

5. A record for every new customer account and for any customer to whom recommendations are made that shows the customer's name, his date of birth, address, nationality, and tax identification or social security number. In addition, the record must bear the signatures of the customer, the representative, and his supervisor. The record must further show the customer's occupation, marital status, investment objectives, and other information concerning the customer's financial situation and needs. Such items of information (except for name, address, and social security number) need not be contained in the customer's record if, after reasonable inquiry, the customer declines to furnish the information and a statement to that effect is included in the record.

Records that must be kept for a period of not less than three years, the first two years in an easily accessible place, are the following.

1. Ledgers, showing securities in transfer, dividends and interest received, securities borrowed or loaned, moneys borrowed or loaned and the pertinent collateral, and securities failed to receive or failed to deliver.

2. A memorandum of each brokerage order, and of any other instruction given or received for the purchase or sale of securities, whether executed or unexecuted, to show: the terms and conditions of the order or instructions, and of any modification or cancellation thereof; the account; whether the account is discretionary; the

time of entry; the price at which executed; and, to the extent feasible, the time of execution or cancellation.

3. A memo of each purchase or sale of securities for the account of the broker or dealer, showing the price and time of execution.

4. Copies of confirmations of all purchases and sales, and copies of notices of all other debits and credits for securities, cash, and other items.

5. A record in respect of each cash and margin account, showing the name and address of the beneficial owner and, for margin accounts, the signature of such owner.

6. A record of all puts, calls, spreads, straddles, and other operations in which the broker has any direct or indirect interest, or which such broker has guaranteed or granted. Such record will show an identification of the security and the number of units involved.

7. All checkbooks, bank statements, canceled checks, and cash reconciliations.

8. All bills receivable or payable, paid or unpaid, relating to the business of a member, broker or dealer, as such.

9. Originals of all communications received and copies of all communications sent by a member, broker or dealer (including interoffice memoranda and communications), relating to his business as such.

10. All trial balances, computations of aggregate indebtedness, and net capital (and working papers in connection therewith), all of which must be prepared at least once a month, as well as financial statements, branch office reconciliations, and internal audit working papers relating to the business of a member, broker or dealer, as such.

11. All guarantees of accounts, and all powers of attorney and other evidence of the granting of any discretionary authority given in respect of any account, and copies of resolutions empowering an agent to act on behalf of a corporation.

12. All written agreements entered into by a member, broker or dealer, relating to his business as such, including agreements with respect to any account.

Every broker must maintain, until at least three years after the associated persons have terminated employment, a questionnaire or application for employment executed by each associated person of each member, broker or dealer. The questionnaire or application must be approved in writing by an authorized representative of the member, broker or dealer, and must contain at least the following information with respect to the person.

1. His name, address, social security number, and the starting date of his employment or other association with the member, broker or dealer.

2. His date of birth.

3. The educational institutions attended by him and whether or not he graduated therefrom.

4. A complete, consecutive statement of all his business connections for at least the preceding 10 years, including his reason for leaving such prior employment, and whether the employment was part-time or full-time.

5. A record of any denial of membership or registration, and of any disciplinary action taken, or sanction imposed on him by any federal or state agency, or by any national securities exchange or national securities association, including any finding that he was a cause of any disciplinary action or had violated any law.

6. A record of any denial, suspension, expulsion, or revocation of membership or registration of any member, broker or dealer, with which he was associated in any capacity when such action was taken.

7. A record of any permanent or temporary injunction entered against him or any member, broker or dealer, with which he was associated in any capacity at the time such injunction was entered.

8. A record of any arrests, indictments, or convictions for any felony or any misdemeanor, except minor traffic offenses, of which he has been the subject.

9. A record of any other name or names by which he has been known or which he has used.

However, if an associated person has been registered as a representative of a member, broker or dealer, with, or his employment has been approved by, the National Association of Securities Dealers, Inc., or the American Stock Exchange, the Boston Stock Exchange, the Midwest Stock Exchange, the New York Stock Exchange, the Pacific Coast Stock Exchange, or the Philadelphia-Baltimore Stock Exchange, then retention of a full, correct, and complete copy of any and all applications for such registration or approval is deemed to satisfy requirements 1 to 9. The term "associated person" means a partner, officer, director, salesman, trader, manager, or any employee who handles funds or securities, or solicits transactions or accounts for a member, broker or dealer.

These rules do not require that a member of a national securities exchange make or keep such records of transactions cleared for such member by another member as are customarily made and kept by the clearing member.

The rules concerning record keeping do not require that a member of a national securities exchange or a registered broker or dealer make or keep such records reflecting the sale of United States tax savings notes, United States defense savings stamps, or United States defense savings bonds, series E, F, and G.

Such records are not required with respect to any cash transaction of $100,000 or less involving only subscription rights or warrants that by their terms expire within 90 days after the issuance thereof.

Every member, broker, and dealer must preserve for a period of not less than six years after the closing of any customer's account any account cards or records that relate to the terms and conditions with respect to the opening and maintenance of such account.

Every member, broker and dealer, must preserve during the life of the enterprise and of any successor enterprise all partnership articles or, in the case of a corporation, all articles of incorporation or charter, minute books, and stock certificate books.

After a record or other document has been preserved for two years, a photograph of it on film may be substituted during the balance of the required time.

If a person who has been subject to these rules ceases to transact a business in securities, that person must, for the remainder of the periods of time specified in this rule, continue to preserve the records he had preserved pursuant to this rule.

The main provisions of the '34 Act are those that require the registration of national securities exchanges and broker-dealers with the SEC. Most of the other provisions give teeth to the law.

Through the Securities Exchange Act of 1934, the Federal Reserve Board was given the responsibility of determining margin requirements. Regulations T and U establish these requirements.

Federal Reserve Board *regulation T* limits *broker-dealers* in the amount of credit they can make available to finance the purchase and sale of securities.

When a customer buys a stock, he may either pay cash or buy on margin. Buying on margin means that the customer pays part of the cost in cash and borrows the balance of the purchase price from his broker. Margin is the percentage of the total purchase price that the customer pays in cash. The balance is an interest-bearing loan made to customers by firms that are members of an organized securities exchange. Initial margin requirements are established pursuant to regulation T, and have varied from a low of 40 percent to a high of 100 percent. At May 30, 1968, required margin was set at 80 percent for equities and 60 percent for debt issues convertible into equities.

The term "special cash account" is used in regulation T to describe customer transactions that are effected with the understanding that they will be settled promptly (within two or three days). Regulation T allows seven full business days after the trade date. If the purchaser has not paid for the securities within that time, the broker-dealer will cancel or otherwise liquidate the transaction.

There are a few exceptions to this requirement. When the amount owed is less than $100, the broker-dealer may, at his option, disregard regulation T. When the amount is over $100, the broker-dealer may apply to the NASD or appropriate committee of a national securities exchange for an extension of time, which will be granted if exceptional circumstances warrant.[3]

If a transaction is canceled due to failure to make payment within the proper period of time, the client's account must then be *frozen* for 90 calendar days. When an account is frozen, the customer may make purchases only if the full purchase price is deposited in the account before completion of the transaction. The requirement to freeze the account may be disregarded in two instances.

1. Whenever a sale is made without prior payment for the securities being sold, if full payment is received before seven full business days have elapsed and the proceeds of the sale have not been withdrawn on or before the day on which such payment is received.

2. Whenever delivery of the securities purchased is being made to another broker-dealer who furnishes the delivering broker with a written statement that the secu-

3/ Other exceptions to the seven-day rule include extensions for securities that are unissued at the time of purchase, and purchases made on the understanding that payment is to be made on delivery of the securities.

rities are being accepted for a special cash account of the customer in which there are sufficient funds to make full cash payment for the securities.

Regulation T prohibits a broker-dealer from arranging or granting loans for customers for the purpose of buying securities by using unlisted[4] securities as collateral. In other words, the regulation allows broker-dealers to extend credit on securities that are registered (listed) on a national securities exchange. Thus, broker-dealers may not grant or arrange loans for the purpose of buying mutual funds.

Regulation T prohibits a broker-dealer from arranging loans with other third parties in contravention of the requirements that apply to loans by brokerage firms.

Regulation T prohibits a broker-dealer from giving credit to or arranging credit for a customer with respect to any transaction in any security that was part of a new issue in which the broker-dealer participated as a selling group member within 30 days prior to such transaction.

Federal Reserve *regulation U* establishes requirements that *banks* must follow in lending money to brokers or the public where securities are pledged as collateral. The regulation gives banks an advantage over broker-dealers, who are controlled under regulation T, in that a bank can loan money with unlisted securities as collateral, whereas a broker-dealer may loan money only on registered (listed) securities. Regulation U relates to bank loans made against collateral of stock for the purpose of buying listed securities.[5] Such loans may not exceed the maximum loan value of the stock used as collateral. At June 10, 1968, the maximum loan value of any equity, listed or unlisted, was 20 percent of its current market value. In other words, 80 percent margin was required for equities. For debt convertible into equity, 60 percent margin was required. Regulation U does not apply to loans made outside the states of the United States and the District of Columbia.

In summary, regulation T establishes margin requirements for loans made by broker-dealers to clients and prohibits broker-dealers from granting credit on unlisted securities, including mutual funds. On the other hand, regulation U establishes margin requirements for loans made by banks.[6]

1964 amendments

The Securities Acts Amendments of 1964 effected a sweeping extension of the authority of the Securities and Exchange Commission. By the new law, many securities traded over the counter are subjected for the first time to registration requirements and disclosure provisions that have applied since 1934 to securities traded on a national exchange. This control was accomplished by extending the registration, periodic reporting, proxy solicitation, and insider reporting and trading provisions of the Ex-

4/ To be acceptable as collateral, the securities must be registered on a national securities exchange.

5/ Mutual fund shares are treated as listed securities for the purposes of regulation U.

6/ Regulation G, effective early in 1968, requires other (nonbank, nonbroker-dealers) lenders to register with the Federal Reserve System, and imposes maximum loan values for loans made for the purpose of carrying registered equity securities and debt convertible into such equities.

change Act to a substantial number of securities not listed on organized securities exchanges. When fully operative, it is estimated that the new law will require registration by about 3,500 companies (including certain banks) not presently covered by the Securities Exchange Act of 1934.

The 1964 amendments provide that companies who transact business in interstate commerce and have over $1 million in assets are required to register each class of equity security held by at least 500 shareholders. This requirement to register over-the-counter securities under the '34 Act is of great importance in that the registration requirement does far more than is superficially apparent. Once a stock is registered, the issuer becomes subject to several other forms of SEC supervision: periodic reports are required, the rules for proxy solicitation become applicable, and the corporation's officers, directors, and stockholders are subject to restrictions on insider trading. Registration may be terminated 90 days after certification to the SEC that the number of stockholders of a particular class of stock has declined to less than 300 persons.

The following types of securities are exempted from the 1964 amendments requiring SEC registration of certain over-the-counter securities.

1. Securities listed and registered on a national securities exchange (already required to register under the '34 Act).
2. Securities issued by a registered investment company (already must register under the '40 Act).
3. Securities of savings and loans institutions, other than stock representing nonwithdrawal capital.
4. Securities of certain nonprofit organizations operated exclusively for religious, educational, fraternal, charitable, or benevolent purposes.
5. Securities of certain agricultural marketing cooperatives, nonprofit mutuals, or cooperative organizations that supply a commodity or service primarily to members.
6. Direct obligations issued or guaranteed by the United States, a state, or political subdivision thereof.
7. Insurance companies' securities when:
    a) The state of incorporation regulates or requires the filing of annual reports and the solicitation of proxies in accordance with the requirements of the National Association of Insurance Commissioners.
    b) Insider trading is subject to regulation similar to that of the '34 Act.
8. Bank securities regulated by the Federal Reserve, Controller of the Currency, or Federal Deposit Insurance Corporation.

Securities issued by state banks that are neither members of the Federal Reserve System nor insured by the Federal Deposit Insurance Corporation are regulated by the SEC and are subject to the 1964 amendments.

The SEC is empowered to exempt all or part of issues from registration, periodic reporting, proxy solicitation provisions, and insider reporting if such exemption is not inconsistent with the public interest and the protection of investors. Certain foreign securities have thus been exempted when ownership by less than 300 U.S. residents is involved, or when reports to the SEC are made in a satisfactory format. The SEC has also exempted interests or participations in employee stock purchases or bonuses, profit-sharing, retirement, pension, incentive, savings, thrift, or similar plans if the interest or participation is nontransferable except in the event of death or mental incompetency. In addition, any security is exempted if issued solely to fund such plans.

The '64 amendments facilitate or provide the following.

Proxy statement rules are extended to O-T-C registered securities.

Insider trading rules are extended to O-T-C registered securities.

The NASD is empowered to require that members meet certain standards of financial responsibility. A minimum capital rule for broker-dealers, including NASD members, became effective December 1, 1965. It requires that broker-dealers have and maintain net capital of at least $5,000.

In certain cases, the minimum net capital is reduced to $2,500. These are: when a member broker-dealer deals exclusively in mutual fund shares and/or share accounts of insured savings and loan associations, except for the sale of other securities for a customer's account to obtain funds for immediate reinvestment in mutual funds, or as a broker or dealer transacting business as a sole proprietor. A broker-dealer who elects the $2,500 minimum must promptly transmit all funds and deliver all securities received in connection with his activities as a broker-dealer, and may not otherwise hold funds or securities for customers, or owe money or securities to customers. Minimum capital must be maintained, and the broker-dealer may not allow aggregate indebtedness to exceed 2,000 percent (20 times) its net capital. Candidates for the NASD principals examination should thoroughly study the computation of minimum net capital requirements, including the definition of aggregate indebtedness. This information is contained in the *NASD Manual* reprint, available from the NASD.

The NASD is also given a statutory basis for rules requiring that partners, officers, or supervisory employees associated with or employed by a member firm meet certain standards relating to experience and training.

The 1964 amendments enlarge the disciplinary powers given to both the SEC and the NASD. Whereas in the past disciplinary action could be taken only by naming a firm in the action, under the new law both the SEC and the NASD may now proceed against individuals without naming a firm or member. The law provides a basis for the NASD to amend its bylaws in order to appropriately discipline "persons associated with members" for rule violations. The sanctions that may be imposed on broker-dealers were expanded to include censure and suspension of registration for up to 12 months. The new law allows the SEC to use three sanctions in disciplinary actions against individuals.

1. Censure the individual.
2. Independently bar the individual from association with a broker-dealer firm.
3. Suspend the individual from association with a broker-dealer firm for a period not to exceed 12 months.

The 40-day period during which a prospective purchaser of a newly registered issue must be furnished a prospectus is extended to 90 days when the issuer has never before issued any security under an effective registration statement.

A statutory basis is given for the NASD to adopt rules in the area of price quotations.

Authority is given to the SEC to summarily suspend trading of any over-the-counter registered security for a period not exceeding 10 days.

Registration as broker-dealer with SEC. Broker-dealers who operate entirely in intrastate commerce (within a given state) are not required to register with the SEC. However, most broker-dealers do operate in interstate commerce by virtue of using the U.S. mail, which causes them to be within the interstate commerce classification. Any broker-dealer who is registered with the SEC is automatically considered to fall within federal jurisdiction.

In order to register with the SEC, as a broker-dealer (BD), the following is required.

1. Form BD in duplicate.
2. Financial statements in duplicate.
3. List of securities in which the applicant has an interest.
4. A notarized oath that the information submitted is correct, to the best of knowledge and belief of the applicant.

The SEC may permit the registration to become effective or, after notice and an opportunity for a hearing are given, deny or suspend registration. Grounds for so denying or suspending registration as well as for censuring a registered broker or dealer or associated person include any of the following.

1. False or misleading statements or omissions with regard to any material fact in any application for registration or report filed with the SEC, or any proceeding before the SEC.
2. Conviction within 10 years preceding the filing of the application or any time thereafter of any felony or misdemeanor that the SEC finds:
   a) Involves the purchase or sale of a security.
   b) Arises out of the conduct of business of a broker, dealer, or investment adviser.
   c) Involves embezzlement, fraudulent conversion, or misappropriation of funds or securities.
   d) Involves mail fraud or fraud by wire, radio, or TV.
3. Order, judgment, or decree of any competent court, enjoining the broker-dealer from acting as an investment adviser, underwriter, broker, dealer, or employee of a bank, investment company, or insurance company.
4. Willful aiding, abetting, or inducing of violations of any provisions of the securities acts (1933, 1934, company act of 1940 or advisers act of 1940), including failure to reasonably supervise.

The SEC requires SEC registered broker-dealers who are not members of a national securities exchange (e.g., not NASD members) to meet certain qualification standards. Any person who has not been continuously associated with such non-NASD member broker-dealers since July 1, 1963, must pass a general securities examination (SECO)[7] by July 1, 1966. All associated persons must pass the SECO examination if they are

7/ SECO (SEC-only) refers to the examination, forms, fees, and so on that are required to be filed by the brokers or dealers who are registered with the SEC and who are not members of a registered national securities association (the NASD).

engaged in sales trading, research or investment advice, public relations, advertising, training or hiring of sales representatives, and so on. In addition, the broker-dealer firm must report to the SEC personal histories of all associated persons on form *SECO-2* or *SECO-2F* (for foreign associates).

Fees that must be paid to the SEC by registered non-NASD member brokers or dealers in general include:

1. Initial fee payable as described on Form SECO-5 (at May 30, 1968, this fee is $150).

2. An initial fee to register each associated person as prescribed by Form SECO-2 (at May 30, 1968, this fee is $25 for each associated person). No fee is payable for foreign associated persons who do not transact business with U.S. citizens or residents. However, Form SECO-2F (foreign) must be filed for each such associated person. In addition to the initial fee to register associated persons, examination fees are also payable.

3. Annual assessment fees as provided on form SECO-4, on or before June 1 of each year. The annual assessment fee is composed of three elements: (*a*) a base fee (at May 30, 1968, $100); (*b*) a fee for associated persons (at May 30, 1968, $5 for each such associated person, excluding foreign associates); and (*c*) an office fee for each office of the broker or dealer (at May 30, 1968, $30 for each office). The combined total of the base fee and associated person fee is limited to $15,000 for a single year.

None of the above fees are paid by a broker or dealer who applies for membership in the NASD within 45 days of his becoming registered with the SEC (provided, of course, that he becomes an NASD member). In general, brokers or dealers who are members of the NASD are also exempt from the SECO fees, as are members of a national securities exchange who carry no accounts for customers and whose business is entirely or almost entirely on national securities exchanges. Such members of exchanges must file Form SECO-4, even though no fees may be payable.

Summary

The Securities Act of 1933 obtains full disclosure by requiring, for new issues and security sales by persons in control, registration with the SEC and delivery to buyers of a summary of the registration information in the form of a prospectus.

The Securities Exchange Act of 1934, as amended, requires broker-dealers in securities to register with the SEC. Securities listed on a national securities exchange must also be registered with the SEC. In addition, relatively widely held, large companies must register, even though the securities are not listed on a national securities exchange. Registration with the SEC brings the issuer under controls for periodic reporting, proxy disclosures, insider trading, and full-disclosure requirements. Additionally, controls are instituted to protect investors from fraudulent, manipulative, and deceptive practices, as well as to ensure the orderly functioning of the securities markets.

5 | Review questions

241. The .... provides that certain securities offered to the public must be registered with the SEC.
1. '34 Act
2. Federal Reserve Act
3. Investment Trust Act
4. '33 Act

242. The SEC examination for registered representatives is required for persons associated with ....
1. NASD firms
2. non-NASD firms
3. both 1 and 2

243. The SEC ....
1. reviews investment company prospectuses
2. approves investment company securities
3. passes on the accuracy of statements in investment company prospectuses
4. none of these

244. In its prospectus a mutual fund must include ....
1. the statement, **"These securities have not been approved or disapproved by the Securities and Exchange Commission, nor has the commission passed upon the accuracy or adequacy of this prospectus. Any representation to the contrary is a criminal offense."**
2. the company's investment objectives and policies
3. a statement explaining the inherent risk involved in purchasing fund shares
4. all of the above

245. A fund must state in its prospectus ....
1. that the company gives the investor no assurance that its investment objectives will be attained

2. that SEC supervision does not involve supervision of a fund's investment decision
3. that the amount an investor will be paid when he liquidates his shares may be more or less than their original cost, depending on the market value of the fund's portfolio
4. all of these

246. The statement of investments included in a fund's prospectus must show ....
1. portfolio changes made during the fiscal year
2. the securities owned by the fund on a particular date
3. both 1 and 2
4. none of these

247. From a fund's statement of investments you are able to learn ....
1. how many shares of a security are owned by the fund
2. what the fund originally paid for a security
3. what the market value of a particular security in the portfolio is on a particular date
4. all of these

248. A fund must include in its prospectus ....
1. a statement of assets and liabilities
2. a statement of investments
3. a price makeup sheet
4. all of these

249. In its prospectus, a fund gives financial information ....
1. only for the fund as a total
2. only on a per-share basis

3. both for the fund as a total and on a per-share basis
4. none of these

250. Purchasers of securities issued under regulation A must be given a copy of ....
1. the registration statement
2. the offering circular
3. the red herring
4. all of these

251. Provisions of the Securities Act of 1933 are violated by ....
1. false or misleading information on a registration statement
2. the sale of nonexempt securities unless a registration statement is in effect
3. the sale of nonexempt securities to a customer who has not been shown a prospectus
4. all of these

252. Calculation of a fund's redemption price and the fund's redemption provisions must be included in the fund's ....
1. registration statement
2. prospectus
3. both 1 and 2
4. neither of these

253. Excessive activity in a customer's account, especially an account in which the broker or dealer has been given discretionary powers, is termed ....
1. fixing
2. pegging
3. churning
4. free-riding

254. The Securities Exchange Act of 1934 makes it a criminal offense for a broker or dealer to ....
1. perform any action that constitutes a fraud against the public

2. make false or misleading statements intended to induce the purchase or sale of a security
3. withhold information that may influence a customer's decision to purchase or to sell a security
4. all of these

255. The Securities Exchange Act of 1934 makes illegal the use of manipulative devices in the securities transactions ....
1. on securities exchanges
2. in the over-the-counter market
3. both of these
4. neither of these

256. The Securities Exchange Act of 1934 requires that all brokers and dealers who are not specifically exempted from registration must register with the ....
1. Federal Reserve Board
2. National Association of Securities Dealers
3. Securities and Exchange Commission
4. Civil Aeronautics Board

257. The Securities Exchange Act of 1934 defines a broker or dealer operating in interstate commerce as one who ....
1. transacts business in only one state
2. transacts business only on an exchange
3. uses the U.S. mails or other instrumentalities of interstate commerce
4. none of these

258. The Securities Exchange Act of 1934 requires that all brokers and dealers must register with the SEC except those who transact business ....
1. only on an exchange or only in intrastate commerce
2. only in the over-the-counter market or only in interstate commerce
3. both of these
4. none of these

259. Brokers and dealers registered with the Securities and Exchange Commission must file periodic reports of financial condition. These reports must be filed ....

1. semiannually
2. every two years
3. annually
4. quarterly

260. According to a rule of the Securities and Exchange Commission, no broker or dealer may permit the ratio of his aggregate indebtedness to his net capital to exceed ....

1. 2 to 1
2. 20 to 1
3. 10 to 1
4. 5 to 1
5. 100 to 1

261. Regulation T of the Federal Reserve Board relates to ....

1. the extension of credit to customers by brokers and dealers
2. the extension of credit to brokers and dealers by banks
3. the sale of tea by brokers
4. none of these

262. The special cash account referred to in regulation T is an account in which the customer is expected to pay ....

1. in cash rather than by check
2. before completion of any transaction
3. promptly, after completion of a transaction
4. none of these

263. Regulation T provides that in normal circumstances a customer who makes a purchase transaction in a special cash account must make payment within ....

1. 15 calendar days
2. seven full business days

3. seven calendar days
4. a reasonable time

264. Regulation T requires that a customer who makes a purchase transaction in a special cash account must make payment within a specified period of time. If the customer does not pay within the time period specified in regulation T, the broker or dealer who made the transaction must ....

1. file a report with the SEC
2. close the account and refuse to accept any future orders from the customer
3. either cancel the transaction or apply for an extension of the time allowed for payment
4. none of these

265. If a customer who makes a purchase transaction through a special cash account can show good cause for his failure to pay within the period of time specified in regulation T, the broker or dealer may apply for an extension of time. Application for an extension must be made to ....

1. the Federal Reserve Board
2. the Securities and Exchange Commission
3. the National Association of Securities Dealers or any national securities exchange
4. none of these

266. The provisions of regulation T with regard to special cash accounts may be disregarded by a broker or dealer in handling any transaction when the amount of money owed by a customer on a purchase transaction in a special cash account is ....

1. $500 or less
2. $100 or less
3. $300 or less
4. $15,000 or less

267. If a customer who makes a purchase transaction through a special cash

account fails to pay within the period specified by regulation T and the transaction is canceled, the customer's account will be frozen for a period of ....

1. 30 days
2. six months
3. 90 days
4. 36 days

268. When a customer's account is frozen, the customer ....

1. can make no transactions in the account in any circumstances
2. can make purchase transactions only if the full purchase price is deposited in the account before completion of the transaction
3. can make sales but cannot make purchases in the account in any circumstances
4. is judged incompetent

Refer to page 260 for correct answers.

269. Regulation U of the Federal Reserve Board relates to ....

1. extension of credit to brokers and dealers by banks
2. extension of credit to customers by brokers and dealers
3. credit granted by banks to finance submarine manufacturing
4. all of these

270. With certain specified exceptions, new issues of securities must be registered with the Securities and Exchange Commission before they may be offered for sale to the public. The registration of new securities issues is required by ....

1. the Investment Advisers Act of 1940
2. the Securities Act of 1934
3. the Securities Act of 1933
4. regulation T

6 | SEC Statement of Policy and state laws

The SEC Statement of Policy

Though not actually a law, the SEC policy statement established those standards the SEC considered to be set forth in the Securities Act of 1933, the Securities Exchange Act of 1934, and the Investment Company Act of 1940. The policy relates to sales literature, which includes any communication, whether in writing, by radio, or by television, used by an issuer, underwriter, or dealer to induce the purchase of shares of an investment company.

To the extent they are transmitted to shareholders and do not contain an express offer, reports of issuers are not deemed to be sales literature within the meaning of this definition, but they still must conform to the Statement of Policy. Communications between issuers, underwriters, and dealers are included in this definition of sales literature only if such communications are passed on either orally or in writing, or are shown to prospective investors or designed to be employed in either written or oral form in the sale of securities.

For the purpose of interpreting the Statement of Policy, a piece of sales literature is deemed materially misleading if such sales literature (1) includes an untrue statement of a material fact, or (2) omits a material fact necessary in order that, considering the circumstances of its use, a statement not be misleading.

The Statement of Policy relates to sales literature, advertising, and sales practices the SEC considers misleading. Among those practices, clarified by the Statement of Policy, are the following.

It is misleading and a violation of the Statement of Policy to represent or imply a percentage return to investors in a mutual fund unless based upon current or historical figures that relate, among other things:

1. Dividends from net investment income paid (not capital gains) during a fiscal year to the average monthly offering price for such fiscal year, provided that if any year prior to the most recent fiscal period is shown, the rate of return for all subsequent fiscal years, similarly calculated, shall also be stated.

2. Dividends paid from net investment income during the 12 months ended not earlier than the close of the calendar month immediately preceding the date of publication relating to the current offering price at date of publication.

In either case, the basis of the calculation shall be shown, and adjustment made for capital gain distributions and any other factor necessary to make the presentation not misleading. Net investment income shall include net accrued undivided earnings contained in the price of the capital shares.

A statement that the return is based upon dividends paid during the period shown and is not indicative of future results, and a statement of the change in net asset value or the percentage change thereof during the period shown must be included. Following are two examples of how rates of return on investment company shares may properly be stated.

CASE 1
Historical Basis

Dividends from income for fiscal 1967 . . . .$ 1
Average monthly offering price for fiscal 1967 . . . . .$20
Rate of return ($1 divided by $20) 5%

CASE 2
Current Basis

Dividends from income during last 12 calendar
  months (July 1, 1966 to July 1, 1967) $0.80
Offering price, July 15, 1967 . . . . $19.20
Capital gain distribution, December 1966 . . . .+$ 0.50

Adjusted offering price (19.20+/.50) $19.70
Rate of return (0.80 divided by 19.70) 4.06%

Safety of capital cannot be represented without explaining that market risks are inherent in the investment plan.

It is misleading to imply that the government or the federal or state *authorities* are involved with supervision of fund management or its investment policies.

It is misleading to represent the *custodian of securities* as having any supervision over management except in its role as safeguarder of securities and cash owned by stockholders.

Redemption must be explained in terms of the changing value of shares, depending on the market value of the portfolio at the time of redemption. In other words, it must be stated that the redemption value may be more or less than the investor's cost, depending on the market value at the time of redemption.

Comparisons generally cannot be made if they imply that the fund has the same degree of safety as other forms of investment (i.e., bonds or bank) or that government protection of other forms of investment applies to mutual funds.

Comparisons with a market index or other security can be made only if all pertinent information is pointed out to make the comparisons clear and fair, including the material differences or similarities between the subjects of comparison, and if the purpose of the comparison is stated. Any comparisons of one investment company with another investment company not under the same management or sponsorship must be filed with the NASD for clearance before use.

Performance charts and tables cannot be misleading in any way and must be in the prescribed format explained in the Statement of Policy. Any illustrations of investment performance must give effect to the *highest* sales charges currently asked. Definite limitations are placed on the *period of time* performance studies may show. These periods are: (1) the life of the fund, (2) the life of the contractual plan, (3) the most recent 10-year period, or longer period if shown in multiples of 5 years. Such charts must not represent or appear to represent that the company's past performance will be repeated in the future.

Management claims cannot be exaggerated in regard to ability or competency.

Sales charges must be clearly spelled out. If sales charges are not mentioned in a piece of sales literature, reference must be made to the prospectus for such charges and other information.

Industry performance against company performance cannot be made if unfair implications would result from such comparisons.

Reprints of published articles or documents on investments cannot be used unless they satisfy the conditions of the Statement of Policy.

It cannot be stated that investment companies are operated as nonprofit organizations or are similar to cooperatives.

It is misleading to say that investment company shares generally have been selected by *fiduciaries*.

The investment of a fixed sum of money in the same security at regular intervals regardless of fluctuations in the price of the security is called *dollar cost averaging*. It is misleading to discuss or portray the principles of dollar cost averaging, or cost averaging, or to discuss or portray any periodic payment plan or continuous investment plan without making clear that:

1. The investor will incur a loss under such a plan if he discontinues the plan when the market value of his accumulated shares is less than his costs.
2. The investor is placing his funds primarily in securities subject to market fluctuations, and that the method involves continuous investment in such shares at regular intervals regardless of price levels.
3. The investor must take into account his financial ability to continue such plan through periods of low price levels, and there is no guarantee against loss in a declining market.

Only the term dollar *cost* averaging or *cost* averaging may be used. The terms "averaging the dollar" or "dollar averaging" are prohibited.

In any sales literature designed to encourage investors to switch from one investment company to another, or from one class of security to another class in an investment company, it is misleading to omit the substance of the following statement in a separate paragraph in body-size type:

Switching from the securities of one investment company to another, or from one class of security of an investment company to another, involves a sales charge on each such transaction, for details of which see the prospectus. The prospective purchaser should measure these costs against the claimed advantage of the switch.

Since by their nature *withdrawal plans* carry the risk of exhausting invested capital, any discussion of plans or any presentation to the public should be handled with care. It must be pointed out that withdrawals normally represent both income and return of principal, and involve depletion of principal to the extent that withdrawals exceed income dividends.

The withdrawal period exhibited must be either 10 years or the life of the fund, whichever is less. Sales material showing a pay-in or holding period with a subsequent withdrawal period may not be used. The results of a withdrawal plan initiated at the beginning of the last year covered by the full table must also be shown in a prescribed format.

Contractual plan companies must use specific formats in presenting their performance. Use of any other format could be misleading. Such tables must be prepared on the basis of assumed investments, involving the largest sales charge and the smallest permissible monthly payment. Summaries of such charts must include: (1) total payments, (2) total dividends reinvested, (3) total investment cost, (4) total capital gains reinvested, and (5) total liquidating value.

It is misleading to represent or imply that investment companies in general are direct sources of *new capital* to industry, or that a particular investment company is such a source, unless the extent of such investments is disclosed.

It is misleading to *combine into any one amount* distributions from net investment income and distributions from any other source (e.g., capital gains), or to represent or imply an assurance that an investor will receive a stable, continuous, dependable, or liberal return, or that he will receive any specified rate or rates of return. Dividends and capital gain distributions must be shown under separate headings.

It is misleading to represent or imply an assurance that an investor's capital will increase, or that purchase of investment company shares involves a preservation of original capital and a protection against loss in value. When discussing accumulation of capital, preservation of capital, accumulation of an estate, protection against loss of purchasing power, diversification of investments, financial independence, or profit possibilities, explanation of the *market risks* inherently involved in the investment is required.

The SEC has delegated to the NASD the administration of the Statement of Policy, which governs standards for sales literature *prepared by dealers* to describe the shares of investment companies. Sales literature prepared by sponsors and underwriters is, of course, filed directly with the SEC and need not be resubmitted by dealers to the NASD.

Literature relating in general terms to investment companies may be used with the public before a prospectus is given. This may be done only if the dealer has not yet decided which particular securities will be offered. If the intent of the dealer is to offer a particular security, a prospectus must be sent with such general literature. Such general literature or advertising must be both accurate and applicable to all investment companies.

All NASD members must file with the NASD all sales literature prepared by or for them, including all: newspaper, radio, or television advertising or scripts; postal cards; form letters; and individually typed sales letters that repeat the same central idea. These must be filed by the member firm with the NASD within three days after first use. Dealers need not file with the NASD material prepared by sponsors or underwriters of investment company shares, nor do dealers who are NASD members have to file any literature directly with the Securities and Exchange Commission.

In advance of use or publication, NASD members may submit any sales material concerning investment company shares, together with a request for comment on whether such material seems to meet the Statement of Policy requirements. When advance comment is requested, a revised copy for final check must be filed prior to publication, and the finished piece still must be submitted within three days after first use or publication.

Dealer-only material that would violate the Statement of Policy if used as sales literature must be marked at the top of the first page as follows.

Not for use with members of public. This memorandum is prepared by (name of dealer) for dealer information only and may not be reproduced or shown to members of the public, nor used orally or in written form as sales literature. Use with members of the public will be considered a violation of the Statement of Policy of the Securities and Exchange Commission.

Dealer-only material must be distributed in single copies only, on the basis of one copy to any dealer office, including branch offices. Additional copies may not be supplied by an underwriter or its wholesale representative to a dealer or any of its registered representatives, either voluntarily or on request.

Sales literature that relates directly or indirectly to the securities of a particular investment company or companies that are subject to the prospectus requirements must be accompanied or preceded by such a prospectus. Advertising, such as in newspapers, that is in this category is limited to what may be said in so-called *tombstone advertisements*. Such ads are limited to stating:

1. The name of the issuer of the security.
2. The full title of the security and the amount being offered.
3. For an investment company registered under the Investment Company Act of 1940, the company's classification and subclassification under that act, whether it is a balanced, specialized, bond, preferred stock, or common stock fund, and whether in the selection of investments emphasis is placed on income or growth characteristics.
4. The price of the security.
5. The name and address of the dealer from whom a prospectus may be obtained. The effect of the tombstone ad requirement is that it cannot contain any sales message.

State laws

Blue-sky laws refer to the state laws that regulate the offering and sale of securities within state boundaries. Blue-sky laws derive their name from regulations adopted to prevent the offering of "speculative schemes which have no more basis than so many feet of blue sky."[1] Although these regulations vary considerably from one state to another, they have the common goal of protecting both investors and firms from unscrupulous operators and of preventing fraudulent sales of securities.

State laws place restrictions on the investments that may be made by trustees or guardians. In some states, trustees are limited to investments that are on the *legal list* of that state, unless the trust instrument specifically gives the trustee freedom from this restriction by granting him broader investment powers. In other states, the trustee may invest in a security if it is one that would be bought by a "prudent man" of discretion and intelligence, who is seeking a reasonable income and preservation of capital—hence, the *prudent man rule*.

In recent years, approximately 40 states have adopted some variation of the prudent man rule, which permits trustees to invest all or part of the assets in securities not on a so-called legal list. The prudent man rule in most of these states permits trustees to invest in mutual funds. However, some states designate classes and groups of securities—the legal list—that may legally be purchased by a trustee who operates in that state.

The provisions of blue-sky laws in 49 states (Delaware and the District of Columbia have no blue-sky laws) vary greatly. Basically, the laws are concerned with:
1. Registration of nonexempt securities to be sold.
2. Registration or licensing of broker-dealers.
3. Antifraud or protection of investor provisions designed to prevent, expose, and penalize fraud.
4. Registration or licensing of investment advisers.

Federal statutes are designed to not interfere in any way with the operation of state blue-sky laws, since each state has police power, delegated by the U.S. Constitution, that it may exercise for the protection of its people.

The first blue-sky law was enacted in Kansas in 1911. Since then, and particularly since 1956, substantial progress has been made in promoting uniformity among state securities laws. The Uniform Securities Act, a model law approved and recommended by the National Conference of Commissioners on Uniform State Laws in 1956, has several sections.
1. Section 1 prohibits fraudulent practices in connection with the sale or purchase of securities, or furnishing of investment advice; the provisions are similar to those of the Securities Exchange Act of 1934.
2. Section 2 requires the registration of broker-dealers, agents, and investment ad-

---

1/ *Hall* v. *Geiger Jones Co.,* 242 U.S. 539, 550 (1917).

visers, and prohibits fraudulent actions by them. Fees for registration are prescribed, and in many cases surety bonds must be posted.

3. Section 3 provides for the registration of nonexempt securities. Three types of registration are provided.

   a) Registration by notification. This method is generally applicable to companies that have a five-year or more record of operation or have been previously registered. A registration statement must be filed.

   b) Registration by coordination. This method applies when the offering is also registered with the SEC under the '33 Act. Usually, the issuer simply files with the state authority the same information that is filed with the SEC.

   c) Registration by qualification. This method is the most complex in that the issuer must file data similar to that required if a filing were also being made with the SEC.

   Fees are prescribed for registering with the state authority. Generally, the following types of securities are exempt from registration, though they are not exempt from the antifraud requirements.

   a) Securities listed on a national securities exchange.

   b) Exempt securities (government issues).

   c) Securities regulated by banking, insurance, or other government authorities, such as the Interstate Commerce Commission.

   d) Securities issued by nonprofit organizations.

   Each state requires broker-dealer registration with a designated agency of the state government. A broker who is licensed in one state is not automatically entitled to do business in other states. It is very important to remember that registration with the SEC, the NASD, or an exchange is not enough; state registration requirements also must be met. Information about state securities laws may be obtained by contacting the proper state authority, usually called the securities commission or commissioner of corporations or finance. The state securities authority normally is located in the city that is the state capital.

4. Section 4 contains provisions to implement the first three sections for violations of the act.

   Though approximately one third of the states have adopted all or parts of the Uniform Securities Act, state laws still vary widely in their provisions.

   All federal and state security laws are both criminal and civil in nature; that is, they impose civil liabilities and criminal penalties for their violation. A criminal action is brought by the state (the people) against the violator, and the penalty is fine or imprisonment. A civil action is brought by one individual against another to impose monetary liability for damage caused by the violation, or by a federal or state agency for an injunction against a violation.

Gifts to minors

Since a minor may not have securities registered in his own name, such gifts are usually made either through an irrevocable trust or through a custodian registration under either the Uniform Gift to Minors Act or the Model Law. All states except two, Alaska and Georgia, have adopted the Uniform Act.

Gifts of securities may be made to minors through properly designed trusts. Such trusts may remove the securities from the donor's ownership, and the income from the securities would be available to the trust. Through either the Model Law or the Uniform Act, securities may be given to a minor by merely registering the securities in the name of a qualified adult as custodian. The income is taxed to the child, who has a $600 exemption and a $100 dividend exclusion.

Custodianship under the Uniform Gift to Minors Act permits an adult to be named as manager of certain of the child's property, even though the child himself continues to be the legal owner. Securities owned under the provisions of the act are normally registered, "Lawrence Rosen, as Custodian for Stacey Andrea Rosen (the minor) under the Kentucky (name of the state in which the minor, donor, or custodian resides) Uniform Gift to Minors Act."

Since minors generally cannot make binding contracts, except for necessities, a broker-dealer would not be able to hold the minor to his bargain. Hence, broker-dealers will not knowingly execute an order for a minor.

The powers of the custodian include: (1) holding the securities, (2) managing the investment, and (3) accepting or reinvesting income or dividends. The custodianship ends when the child reaches age 21.

Should the minor die before reaching age 21, the accumulated investment passes to his estate. Should the custodian die before the minor reaches age 21, a successor custodian, normally the child's legal guardian, is appointed. If there is no guardian, a court appoints the successor.

Normally, income from securities held under the act is taxable to the minor in his lower tax bracket, and is not taxed to the parent. However, if custodianship income is used for the child's support—such support is the legal obligation of the parent—then it is taxable to the parent.

If the donor of the securities to the minor is not the custodian, and the custodian dies, the securities are not part of the custodian's estate, nor are they subject to federal estate taxation. The donor is subject to payment of federal gift taxes only if the gifts exceed allowable exclusions and exemptions. These rules are intricate and tax counsel should be consulted. However, the general procedure is as follows.

1. There is an annual gift exclusion of $3,000 ($6,000 if the donor is married, and both he and his wife join in the gift and are U.S. citizens) for gifts to any one person. This means that every year the donor may give up to $3,000 each ($6,000 if his wife is also a U.S. citizen) to any number of other persons without filing a gift tax return. If he gives over $3,000 (or $6,000, if applicable) to any one person in one year, the excess over this amount is a taxable gift, and the donor must file a return reporting all such excess amounts (taxable gifts) made during that year. The gift tax return is due at the same time as the income tax return, ordinarily on or before April 15 of the following year.

2. Even when taxable gifts are reported on a gift tax return, as described above, no tax is payable until the donor has used up his entire lifetime exemption of $30,000 of taxable gifts ($60,000 if his wife is also a U.S. citizen). This $30,000 ($60,000) exemption is a lifetime exemption, not an annual exemption. Taxable gifts (amounts in excess of the annual exclusion) are cumulated from one year to the next. From the time when the lifetime exclusion is used up, tax must be paid on the excess.

Under the act, gifts may be registered in neither joint custodianship nor joint ownership by minors.

6 | Review questions

271. The SEC Statement of Policy considers investment company literature materially misleading if such literature ....
   1. is interesting
   2. includes an untrue statement of a material fact
   3. omits to state a material fact necessary to make the literature not misleading
   4. both 2 and 3

272. With regard to the custodian bank, ... may be stated in investment company sales literature.
   1. that the custodian protects the investor's account against loss
   2. that the custodian supervises the fund's investment decisions
   3. the specific functions of the custodian
   4. none of these

273. The Statement of Policy on investment company sales literature requires ....
   1. an explanation, when discussing redemption features of open-end shares, that the redemption price may be more or less than the price paid for the shares, depending on market conditions
   2. that investment company shares be compared with government bonds, insurance companies, and savings accounts to imply similarity
   3. both 1 and 2
   4. neither 1 nor 2

274. The Statement of Policy on investment company sales literature forbids ....
   1. any extravagant claims regarding management ability
   2. any implication that investment company shares are generally selected for investment by fiduciary groups
   3. any implication that investment companies are nonprofit organizations
   4. all of the above

275. The phrase(s) .... may be used in reference to a plan for continuous and regular investment in investment company shares, regardless of the price level.
   1. dollar averaging or averaging the dollar
   2. dollar cost averaging
   3. cost averaging
   4. both 2 and 3

276. When dollar cost averaging or any periodic payment plan is discussed, ... must be made clear to the investor.
   1. that the investor will incur a loss if he discontinues the plan when the market value of his shares is less than their cost
   2. that these securities are subject to market fluctuations, and this method involves continuous and regular investment in such shares, regardless of price levels
   3. that the investor must consider his financial ability to continue such a plan through periods of low price levels, and that there is no guarantee against loss in a declining market
   4. all of the above

277. The Statement of Policy ....
   1. forbids dealers from recommending that investors switch securities of one fund for those of another or one class of securities for another
   2. requires that when a dealer recommends switching securities of one fund for those of another or one class of securities for another it be made clear that such switching involves additional sales charges on each transaction
   3. neither of these

278. A dealer who offers a variety of investment company shares ....

1. must always use a prospectus along with any other sales literature and advertising he uses
2. need not use a prospectus when he uses literature and advertising that refers in general terms to investment company shares and their characteristics as a medium for investment
3. need not ever use a prospectus along with other sales literature and advertising

279. The SEC states that whether or not a communication or advertisement requires concurrent or prior delivery of a prospectus depends on ....

1. the nature of the material
2. the intent of the sender
3. both 1 and 2
4. none of the above

280. If the intent of the sender of a piece of investment company literature is to obtain purchasers for a particular security, the sender ....

1. must include a prospectus along with this literature
2. need not also use a prospectus
3. neither of these

281. In order to qualify as "general and institutional literature and advertising," the literature must be ....

1. accurate
2. applicable to investment companies in general
3. both 1 and 2
4. none of these

282. Some state laws permitting gifts of securities to minors require that an adult be registered as ....

1. custodian
2. agent
3. principal
4. none of these

283. The term "prudent man rule" refers to a type of state law that governs ....

1. investments made by nonprofit corporations
2. investments made by investment companies
3. investments made by trustees
4. investments made by banks

284. The standards that govern sales literature used in offering open-end investment company shares to the public are explained in ....

1. Statement of Policy
2. Rules of Fair Practice
3. Better Business Bureau
4. none of these

285. Investment company sales literature covered by the Statement of Policy generally includes ....

1. reports from issuers and sales letters
2. newspaper, radio, and television advertising
3. all of the above
4. none of these

286. Dealers need not file .... with the NASD.

1. sales material prepared by sponsors or underwriters of investment company securities
2. sales material prepared by the dealer regarding an investment company security
3. any sales literature regarding investment company securities
4. both 1 and 2

287. Investment company sales literature is ....

1. always subject to the Statement of Policy
2. not subject to the Statement of Policy if it is prepared by a dealer
3. neither of these

288. Salesmen of investment company securities ....
1. may use sales literature that complies with the Statement of Policy
2. may not use sales literature that is materially misleading
3. both 1 and 2
4. none of these

289. Sales literature about investment company securities is considered materially misleading if it ....
1. includes an untrue statement of fact
2. omits to state a material fact necessary in order to clarify a statement
3. both 1 and 2
4. none of these

290. When computing rates of return on investment company shares, ... must be included in the calculation.
1. current offering price and total income dividends paid
2. change in asset value during the period
3. a statement that the return is not indicative of future results
4. all of the above

291. The Statement of Policy on investment company sales literature makes it violative to ....
1. combine under one heading distributions from income and those from capital or other sources
2. assure an investor that he will receive a regular return on his investment if past results appear to support this statement

3. both 1 and 2
4. neither 1 nor 2

292. The Statement of Policy forbids ....
1. any reference to government regulation or registration of any investment company
2. any mention of government regulation or registration without explaining that this does not involve supervision or management activities
3. neither 1 nor 2

293. State laws governing the sale of securities are known as ....
1. blue laws
2. blue-sky laws
3. laws of supply and demand
4. none of these

294. State laws governing the sale of securities generally contain provisions that make illegal ....
1. the transfer of securities
2. the hypothecation of securities
3. fraudulent sales of securities
4. all of these

295. A broker-dealer registered with the SEC, the NASD, or a national securities exchange ....
1. need not comply with the registration requirements of the state in which he does business
2. must also comply with the registration requirements of the state in which he does business

Refer to page 260 for correct answers.

7 | Investment banking

Remember the small Rich Company, which manufactured widgets? As this company expands, it may find a need for raising additional capital to foster its expansion, or Mr. Rich may find himself with such a big company that he thinks he may not be able to find someone with enough money to buy the company from him, should he want to sell. For expansion, capital is needed for the company; for sale, capital is needed to purchase Mr. Rich's controlling interest.

In either case, the problem is one of raising capital. One method of raising capital is through *investment bankers.* Investment bankers do not, as the name erroneously implies, accept deposits or checking accounts.

An investment banker, or *underwriter,* is a principal who acts as the middleman between the issuer—the corporation issuing new securities—and the public. Usually, one or more investment bankers buy a new issue of stocks or bonds outright from a corporation. The buying group forms an underwriting syndicate or underwriting group to buy the issue. The underwriters plus others who may join them in a selling group then sell the issue as principals to the public and institutions.

Thus, underwriting is a method by which a corporation raises capital by the sale of its own securities. The managing underwriter is the firm that negotiates with a prospective issuer of securities. Details concerning the underwriting are spelled out in a contract, known as the *underwriting agreement,* between the managing underwriter and the issuer. The managing underwriter often gathers a group of other investment bankers into a syndicate to assist in underwriting (purchasing and then reselling) the issue.

An offering of securities never before issued is known as a *primary* distribution. A *secondary* distribution refers to the sale of a large block of securities that have already been the subject of a primary distribution, that is, stock that had previously been issued. In this case, an investment banking firm purchases a large block of securities owned by one or a few investors and then redistributes the securities to the public. The securities offered in a secondary are often listed on an exchange. The secondary avoids the price fluctuation or drop that may result from a sudden sale of a large block of securities on an exchange.

A new issue may be sold without an underwriter—that is, by the organizers or by the corporation itself. This method is often used by small corporations. A rights offering may be made directly to existing shareholders, or a new issue may be sold to an institutional investor through a private sale or placement; that is, a corporation may raise capital through direct sale of securities to a financial institution, such as an insurance company, without using the services of an underwriter.[1] Or the services of the underwriter may be used in making the private placement.

A new issue may be sold through a public offering underwritten by an investment banker. Terms of the underwriting agreement between the issuer and the underwriters are arranged either by private negotiation or by competitive bids. Before agreeing to handle an underwriting, the investment banker will conduct a careful study of the corporation and the industry in order to determine the investment merits of the proposed new issue.

An investment banker is particularly useful as an adviser to corporations. Some questions that should be considered by an issuer of securities and on which an investment banker's advice may be useful include the following.

1. Should additional capital be raised by equity or debt?
2. Should the equity issued be common or preferred stock?
3. Should the debt be raised by issuing bonds or by bank loans?
4. Should the issue be offered to the public or privately placed, and through what marketing or distribution method?
5. Should the issue contain special features such as participation in earnings, convertibility, and callable clause?
6. Is an issue likely to be accepted in view of the present condition of the investment market?
7. Perhaps most important, what public offering price should be established for equity issues?

At the same time, investors look to the underwriters for assurances that the issuer has been accurate and open in its projections for the future.

Formation of the underwriting group

Because an underwriter may be unable financially or unwilling from a business point of view to take an entire issue, often more than one investment banker is involved in underwriting a securities issue. For this purpose, the managing underwriter customarily forms a *selling syndicate* (or underwriting group). A syndicate is a joint venture, a temporary form of organization created by the managing underwriter for the specific purpose of carrying through a particular transaction, and dissolved on completion of the transaction. In terms of liability, most syndicates are of limited liability, in

---

1/ When rights are issued to shareholders, allowing them to subscribe to new stock, the provisions of the issue are usually registered with the SEC. During the period between filing of the registration statement at the SEC and the date it is declared effective, the rights or the new shares may be traded on a when, as, and if-issued basis. If the issuance does not take place, all this trading is canceled.

which a participant is responsible for buying only the amount of securities equal to his agreed participation. The detailed arrangements, responsibilities, and liabilities of each syndicate member will be spelled out in a series of contracts known as the *Agreement Among Underwriters*. Each member of the syndicate underwrites a specific amount of the issue.

During the period when the underwriting group or syndicate is being formed, the manager may arrange for a *selling group,* composed of NASD members, through whom the distribution or public offering is to be made.[2] A member of the selling group assumes no financial responsibility comparable to that of the underwriter; that is, he is not obligated beyond selling the specific number of units of the issue that are allotted to him and that he commits himself to sell. Usually, a selling group member is not required to purchase any portion of his allotment that remains unsold, though he may be penalized for failing to sell his allotment.

The Securities Act of 1933 sets forth in detail the registration and prospectus requirements that must be observed. There is a minimum 20-day waiting period, called the *cooling period,* between the date of filing the registration statement with the SEC and the date the registration can become effective and the securities offered to the public. Orders may not be accepted until the effective date of registration. During this period, a preliminary prospectus may be circulated to potential investors for informational purposes. Red herring,[3] the term used for the preliminary prospectus, derives its name from the legend printed in red across its top to indicate that it is not the final prospectus. The *red herring* is an incomplete prospectus that lacks such information as the price of the offering. The prospectus is a booklet required by the Securities Act of 1933. It is a short summary of the registration statement and makes full disclosure of all material facts of the new issue. Large interstate new issues may not be publicly offered without a prospectus.

Near the end of the 20-day cooling period, the underwriters will call a *due diligence meeting,* where the underwriters, officers of the corporation issuing the securities, and members of their legal and accounting staffs will review the current status of the corporation and discuss the registration statement and prospectus. This meeting serves as a means of maintaining proper supervision over offerings to the public. The meeting also allows the underwriters to determine that all representations the issuer makes about its financial standing and proposed use of money are accurate and true.

During the cooling period, or before, the underwriters qualify the issue for sale in the desired states. In states whose securities laws require registration of new issues before sale, it is necessary to legally qualify, or *blue sky,* the issue so that there will be

---

2/ The NASD Committee on Underwriting Arrangements reviews new issues and advises members of the reasonableness and fairness of the underwriting spread.

3/ Potential investor indications of interest are solicited with the red herring prospectus. These indications of interest allow the managing underwriter to estimate demand for the issue and assist him in making allocations to the syndicate. As soon as the registration is effective, prospectuses are distributed and the securities are offered for sale to potential purchasers. Prospectuses must be given to all potential purchasers, before a sale is made, for a minimum period of 40 days after the effective date. Prospectuses must be given for 90 days if it is the first issuance of the company's securities under an effective registration statement.

no delays when the cooling period has expired and the security is to be offered to the public.

The compensation underwriters receive—the *underwriting spread*—is the difference between the public offering price and the price the investment banking group pays to the issuer. The amount of the spread, or underwriting discount, is not all profit to the underwriters, since the underwriters' expenses and sales costs must be deducted. Expenses, sales costs, and other allowable charges are described in the prospectus.

On the effective date of the underwriting, usually the day of receipt (or the day after) of registration from the SEC, the issuers are paid and the selling group and underwriters begin to offer the issue to the public. The final step in the underwriting procedure is the underwriter's payment to the issuing corporation of the agreed-on amount for the securities.

Hot issues are new issues in great popular demand. Once the initial public offering has been made, the newly issued securities trade in the market at a price higher than the underwriting price. Stringent NASD regulations exist to protect investors from underwriters' withholding of the securities being underwritten. (These regulations are discussed in Chapter 9.)

For a variety of reasons, however, a new issue may not attract widespread investor interest. It may then be necessary to *stabilize the price* during the distribution period. This means that the underwriters may make purchases in the market to prevent the market price from falling below the public offering price of the issue.

There are several basic types of underwritings—firm, best efforts, all-or-none, and standby. If the underwriters make a *firm commitment,* they are acting as dealers; that is, they agree to buy the entire issue. Thus, the issuer is guaranteed receipt of the full amount of the issue. If they are acting under the *best efforts agreement,* the underwriters are agents for the issuer, and there is no commitment to purchase any of the securities being distributed. The arrangement may also be on an *all-or-none* basis. Then, no sales are final unless the entire issue is sold. If the entire issue is not sold, all purchasers receive full refunds. A *standby* underwriting means that the underwriters agree to purchase and distribute any portion of an issue not purchased by stockholders who have been issued stock rights.

An underwriting may be arranged in two basic ways—by negotiation or competitive bidding. Public utility, railroad, and certain other types of securities are sold to underwriters on a *competitive bidding* basis. When competitive bidding is used, various investment bankers are invited to submit sealed bids. The lowest bid in terms of the underwriting spread receives the issue. The major difference between the two procedures, thus, is the manner of determining the sales price of the new shares. In a *negotiated* underwriting, the price is determined, as the name implies, by negotiation between the issuer and the underwriter. Most industrial stock underwritings are arranged through negotiation.

7 | Review questions

296. If the SEC finds that the information is incomplete or inaccurate on a registration statement submitted under the Securities Act of 1933, the SEC may ....

1. apply to the NASD for an extension
2. refuse to permit the registration to become effective
3. issue a subpoena
4. none of these

297. The document that must be delivered to buyers of securities registered under the Securities Act of 1933 is ....

1. the annual report
2. the financial statement
3. the prospectus
4. the registration statement

298. The purchase of a new issue of securities from an issuer with a view to reselling the securities to the public is called ....

1. underwriting
2. speculating
3. buying
4. refinancing

299. Investment bankers customarily ....

1. buy securities from an issuer and sell them to the public
2. distribute large blocks of securities held by a few persons or a single owner
3. buy and distribute securities of federal and state governments and of municipalities
4. all of these

300. Investment bankers usually help their customers to obtain ....

1. short-term capital
2. long-term capital
3. neither of these

301. The compensation received by the underwriters of an issue of securities is called the ....

1. differential
2. commission
3. markup
4. underwriting spread

302. An underwriter may enter into an agreement to underwrite an issue of securities by ....

1. private placement or secondary distribution
2. private negotiation
3. competitive bidding
4. private negotiation or competitive bidding

303. A .... joins in a distribution of a securities issue and is committed to purchase only the securities that are allotted to him at the time of the offering.

1. specialist
2. dealer
3. selling group member
4. selling syndicate member

304. One who negotiates with a prospective issuer of securities and after the terms of the offering have been agreed on either buys the issue at a specified price or sells it on behalf of the issuer is called ....

1. an underwriter
2. a selling group member
3. a broker
4. a trader

305. The direct sale of an issue of securities to one or more institutional in-

vestors, without utilizing the services of an underwriter, is called ....

1. private negotiation
2. competitive bidding
3. secondary distribution
4. private placement

306. The term .... refers to a group of underwriters engaged in underwriting an issue.

1. buying syndicate
2. selling syndicate
3. purchase group
4. all of these

307. The underwriter—usually the one who formed the underwriting group—who negotiates with the issuer is called ....

1. a selling group member
2. a managing underwriter
3. a specialist
4. none of these

308. A type of underwriting in which the underwriters agree to purchase an entire issue of securities from an issuer at a specified price with a view to reselling the issue to the public is called ....

1. best efforts
2. standby underwriting
3. private placement
4. a firm commitment

309. The term .... refers to an underwriting in which the underwriters agree to purchase and distribute any portion of an issue not purchased by stockholders who have been issued stock rights.

1. standby underwriting
2. best efforts
3. private negotiation
4. a firm commitment

310. A meeting held prior to an underwriting, where representatives of the issuing company meet with the underwriters and selling group members to

answer questions about the new issue and to declare their intention to disseminate information about the new issue honestly and accurately is called ....

1. an indication of interest meeting
2. a due diligence meeting
3. an Agreement Among Underwriters
4. none of these

311. During distribution of a new issue, the members of the selling group place orders for the purchase and sale of the securities at the public offering price, thus preventing the market price of the securities from falling below the public offering price. This form of price manipulation has been given SEC approval and is called ....

1. pegging
2. free riding
3. churning
4. stabilization

312. The term .... is used to describe an arrangement whereby an underwriting group agrees to act as agent for the issuer of a new issue of securities, and to attempt to distribute the issue to the public.

1. standby underwriting
2. due diligence
3. firm commitment
4. best efforts

313. In firm and standby underwriting, the members of the .... make a legal financial commitment to an issuer to purchase all or a specified portion of a new issue of securities.

1. selling group
2. selling syndicate
3. NASD
4. exchange

314. In a process called .... an investment banking company may purchase large blocks of securities owned by

one or a few large investors, and then redistribute the securities to the public.

1. primary distribution
2. standby underwriting
3. private placement
4. secondary distribution

315. Selling syndicate members and selling group members engaged in the underwriting and distribution of a new issue of securities registered under the Securities Act of 1933 may not accept or confirm orders from the public prior to ....

1. receiving a statement that the SEC has approved the securities
2. the effective date of registration
3. receiving a statement that the NASD has approved the securities
4. none of these

Refer to page 260 for correct answers.

8 | The over-the-counter market and registered stock exchanges

The over-the-counter market

The over-the-counter market is an informally organized market that consists of broker-dealer houses throughout the country. It is in the over-the-counter market that primary underwritings take place.

Both the number of securities traded and the dollar volume of securities traded in the over-the-counter market are greater than on all national securities exchanges combined. While only about 3,000 securities are listed on exchanges, it is estimated that approximately 40,000 are traded over the counter.

The over-the-counter market is largest because:

1. Government, municipal, and most corporate bonds trade principally in the over-the-counter market.
2. New issues (primary distributions) are first available in the over-the-counter market.
3. One can buy and sell large blocks of securities in the over-the-counter market without affecting the price on the exchange, and redistributions of a very large block of stock can usually be accomplished more effectively in the over-the-counter market.
4. Any transaction not made on an exchange is said to have been effected in the over-the-counter market.
5. Mutual fund shares are traded in the over-the-counter market.
6. Most bank and insurance stocks are traded in the over-the-counter market.
7. All securities not actually listed on any stock exchange are traded in the over-the-counter market.

Broker-dealers

A *broker* does not sell or buy from his own inventory. He operates as an *agent*, selling for the account and risk of others, and he receives a commission for his services.

A *dealer* is an individual or firm acting as a *principal* rather than as an agent. A dealer buys for his own account and sells to his customer from his own inventory. The dealer's gross profit is derived from marking up the prices of securities he sells to prices higher than those he paid. The NASD requires that dealers' transactions with customers be at prices reasonably related to the market, and that brokers obtain the best price possible for their customers and charge fair commissions.

The same individual or firm can function as a broker-dealer—that is, either as a broker (agent, with no inventory) or as a dealer (principal, with his own inventory)—at different times. However, he must always disclose to the customer the capacity he is acting in.[1] Most over-the-counter business is transacted by broker-dealers who are registered as such with the SEC and who are members of the National Association of Securities Dealers.

Trading in the over-the-counter market

Prices are established by individual negotiation between buyers or their brokers and other brokers or dealers. The over-the-counter market is, thus, a *negotiated market.*

For example: Mr. Buyer in Louisville, Kentucky, wants to buy 100 shares of Stay-Well Insurance Company, which is traded exclusively in the over-the-counter market. Mr. Buyer calls his broker and asks for a price quotation. The broker checks the market by referring to the pink sheets issued by the National Quotation Bureau, Inc. The pink sheets show that a brokerage firm in Chicago is currently making a market in Stay-Well Insurance, and is quoting it at 20 bid 20¾ asked. The broker informs Mr. Buyer that Stay-Well can probably be purchased for about 20¾. If this price is agreeable to Mr. Buyer, he may give the broker an order to buy Stay-Well at 20¾ or better—that is, at a lower price if it is possible.

At this point, the Louisville broker would call or wire the Chicago broker. The conversation might be similar to the following:

> Louisville broker: What is your market in Stay-Well Insurance?
> Chicago broker: 20 bid and 20¾ asked.
> Louisville broker: What is the size of your market?
> Chicago broker: 300 shares either way [sell or buy].
> Louisville broker: I will pay 20¼ for 100.
> Chicago broker: I will sell 100 at 20½.
> Louisville broker: I will take 100 at 20½.
> Chicago broker: I have sold you 100 shares of Stay-Well Insurance Common at 20½.

In actual practice, the Louisville broker might have checked the quotations of several dealers before making an offer. Since various brokers may be willing to sell a particular security at various prices, a broker who wants to buy a security for a customer will check the market by telephoning several brokers who he believes are making a market in that security.

In the example, the Louisville broker acted as an agent for Mr. Buyer, and will

---

1/ These rules are further explained in Chapter 9, NASD Rules of Fair Practice, Section 4, pp. 202 to 3.

charge a fair commission for his services. The Chicago broker acted as a dealer or principal for his own account. The Louisville broker might also have purchased the shares for his own account and then as a dealer sold them with a markup to Mr. Buyer. After the telephone conversation, the share certificate of Stay-Well Insurance must be delivered to the Louisville broker and cash settlement made to the Chicago dealer.[2]

Making a market

A dealer who stands ready either to buy a security at the bid price or sell at the asked price is said to *make a market*. His activity is similar to that of a specialist on an exchange. The shares he has on hand are known as his *inventory*, or his position in the security. Of course, the dealer's profit is the difference between the price he paid and the price he receives.

When a dealer quotes his market prices, the prices are normally firm. *Firm prices* are offers to sell or buy at a price for a brief moment or a specified period of time. A firm price quotation is binding on the dealer. If a dealer quotes a price of 28 to 29 firm, he is prepared to buy at 28 and sell at 29. This is the actual market. Unless a dealer specifies to the contrary, the prices he quotes are firm at that moment for the usual trading units (e.g., 100 shares or 5 bonds of the security). However, the size of the market a dealer is making may be determined by inquiry to be larger than a normal trading unit.

Sometimes, in giving a quote a dealer may indicate that it is not firm but subject to checking or confirmation. A *subject price* quotation means the price is subject to confirmation, and the dealer is not willing to immediately consummate a transaction. The term "indicated" or "workout" market is essentially the same as a subject market. It is the range of prices at which it is believed a security can be bought or sold within a reasonable period of time.

Examples of firm quotations are: "The market is 26 to 26¼." "We can trade it 26 to 26¼." Examples of subject quotations are: "It is quoted 26 to 26¼." "Last I looked, it was about 26 to 26¼."

For a fee, the dealer who is making a market in the over-the-counter market may publish his bid and offer (bid and asked prices) in the *pink sheets* issued daily by the National Quotation Bureau, Inc., a privately owned publishing company. The prices quoted in the pink sheets are wholesale prices between dealers, and are approximate, not definite. Brokers use the pink sheets primarily to determine which brokerage houses are making a market in a specific security. The pink sheets (nickname for the National Daily Quotation Sheets) also facilitate business for broker-dealers. A broker who wants to sell a particular security can so indicate by placing the notation *"Bid Wanted"* (BW) by the name of that security. A broker who wants to buy may state *"Offer Wanted"* (OW).

2/ In a regular-way transaction, delivery must be made on the fifth full business day following the trade date—the date the transaction took place. On or before the first full business day following the trade date, written confirmations normally must be exchanged.

Entries in the pink sheets may appear as follows.

(Name of Security)	(Dealer)	(Telephone)	(Bid)	(Asked)
Acme Electric Corp. Com	Goodbody & Co NY	212 WH3 4680	OW	
	Lapham & Co NY	212 WH3 1975	8½	9
	May & Gannon Inc Boston	212 CA6 2610	8 5/8	9

Through the National Daily Quotation Sheets, quotations are published on about 10,000 stocks and 2,000 corporate and municipal bonds (on yellow sheets). The sheets are printed regionally in New York (pink sheets), Chicago (green sheets) and San Francisco (white sheets). Monthly summaries of the National Daily Quotation Sheets are also printed in book form.

Since the pink sheets are distributed primarily to broker-dealers, the National Quotations Committees of the NASD compile bid and asked quotations on the most actively traded securities (about 1,400) for release to local newspapers and the public. However, these are wholesale or nominal quotations that represent a sampling of the prices at which dealers will buy or sell from one another, and are not the prices at which the dealer will deal with the public. The qualifications to enable a company to have its securities included in the NASD quotations are described in Chapter 9, NASD.

Over-the-counter quotations from *The Wall Street Journal* are shown on page 169. These include such securities as industrial and utility stocks, insurance stocks, bank stocks, corporation bonds, and public authority bonds. In addition, there are separate quotations for government securities (page 170) and mutual funds (page 169), both traded over the counter. Quotations for over-the-counter securities are under the headings "Bid," "Asked," and "Bid Change." However, these headings do not represent actual transactions. They represent the prices at which dealers are willing to buy or sell from one another, and do not include retail markups, markdowns, or commissions.

As previously mentioned, these prices are supplied to newspapers by the National Quotation Committee of the NASD. Before 1966, these prices were average or approximate prices at which the public could expect to do business. Currently, the prices are the approximate wholesale prices at which dealers will buy or sell from one another. The newspaper quotes are based upon information taken by sample from a few broker-dealers in various parts of the country.

Mutual funds quotations, page 169, show the bid and asked prices. The mutual fund bid prices reflect the actual net asset value per share—the price at which the fund will redeem outstanding shares—and the offering price includes the sales charge. This is the price a purchaser must pay for newly issued shares.

Types of orders

Several types of orders may be given to a broker-dealer. A *market order* is to be executed as soon as possible, at the best possible price. A *limit order* is to be executed

Over-the-Counter Markets

Tuesday, October 15, 1968

These quotations, supplied by the National Association of Securities Dealers, are bids and offers quoted by over-the-counter dealers to each other as of approximately 3 p.m. (Eastern time). The quotations do not include retail markup, markdown or commission, and do not represent actual transactions.

Additional quotations are included in a weekly over-the-counter list published each Monday on this page.

A

Stock & Div.	Bid	Asked	Bid Chg.
A A I Corp	16	18	+ ½
Academic Prs	28¾	29¼	— ¼
Acme Elec .16	16½	17	+ ¼
Acme Industs	7½	8¼	— ½
AcmeVisbl .50	44½	45½	— ½
Acushnet .50g	36	37	.....
Adams Russel	27½	82½	.....
Add W Pub .10	16¼	16¾	— ⅜
Adley Corp	9¼	10	+ ¼
Advance Ross	14¾	15¼	.....
Aero Systems	26½	27	.....
AffiltdHosp .40	30¾	31¾	.....
A G Foods Inc	56	57½	— ½
Air California	15¼	16	+ 1½
Air Industries	17¾	18½	— ¼
Airborn Frght	14	14¾	.....
Ala TenNG .80	13½	14	— ¼
Albertsons .36	16½	17	.....
Alco Standard	35	36	.....
AlconLab .40a	57½	59½	.....
Alden Electrn	8¼	8⅝	.....
Alico Land Dv	17½	18¼	+ 1¼
Alleg Beverag	13½	13⅝	+ ⅜
AllegPepsi .40	17	17½	.....
AlliedAero Ind	10¼	10¾	.....
Allied Equit	12¼	12¾	.....
Allied Prod wt	12	13	.....
Allied Thr 1½	40	41½	.....
Allyn Bac .40g	22¾	23¾	+ 1¼
AloeCrem Lab	6¼	6¾	— ⅛
Alphanumr In	59	61	— ½
Alpine Geophy	26½	28½	.....
AmAutoVd .20	15⅝	16⅛	+ ⅛
AmBuldM .20	23½	25	.....
AmDis Tel .40	38¼	39	— ½
Am Elect Lab	22½	23½	— ¼
AmExpres .80	73½	...	...

Stock & Div.		
Contl Comp		
Contin Scr		
Contrafund		
Conwed Cp		
Cooper Labo		
Corenco C		
CorneliusC		
Cornet Strs		
Corporate E		
CrdthrftF 1.4		
Crescent Tec		
Crompton 1.4		
CrossComp		
Cyber Tronic		
Cypress Con		
DallasArm .5		
Dalto Electror		
DamonCre .50		
Danly Mch .50		
Dasa Corperat		
Data Design L		
Data Products		
Datronic Rent		
Davis Food Sv		
DaytonCp .60c		
DaytonMal 1a		
D C Inter .60		
Dean Foods		
DecoratrIn .20		
Defense Elect		
Dearborn Cm		
Delhi Aust Ltd		
Delhi Tayl Oil		
DeLuxeCk .80		
Denv ... .60		

Bank Stocks

Stock & Div.	Bid	Asked	Bid Chg.
AmBT Pa 1.52	33	35	+ ½
AmFletch 2.24	60½	61½	+ 3½
Am Nat Chic 1	66½	68	+ ½
AmSvLoan .15	18¾	19¾	+ 1
ArizonBk 1.12	27¾	28¾	.....
Bk AmSF 2.20	82¼	82¾	+ 1½
BankCalif 1.80	49	49½	+ 1½
Bk ofDela 1.60	38½	40½	.....
Bank of NY 3	104	106	— 2
Bk of NY pf 4	107	110	.....
Bk ofSacra .60	23	24	.....

Public Auth. Bonds

	Rate Mat.	Bid	Ask
AshdwnInDev	4¾s88	88	92
Cal Toll Brdg	3⅞s92	90½	92
Camden InDv	4⅜s88	84	85
ChelanDistl	5s2013	97¾	98¾
Ches Br&T	5¾s2000	41½	43½
ChgoCalSky	3⅜s1995	52	55
ChgoOh Intl	4¾s1999	96¼	97¼
CityClintn Ia	4.20s91	86	89
ColumbiaStg	3⅞s03	80½	82
Delaw Tpk	4½s2002	92	95
DouglsCtyPU	4s2018	80	81
ElizRvT&B	4½s2000	100½	101½
Florida Tpk	4¾s2001	98	100
GrantCPU	2-3⅞s-2005	78	79½
GrantCPU	2-4⅞s-2009	103½	104½
Gt New Orl	4.90-2006	90	92
Illinoi Toll	3¾s1995	85	86
Illinois Toll	4¾s1998	98	100

Insurance Stocks

Stock & Div.	Bid	Asked	Bid Chg.
Alex Hamiltn	10¼	10⅝	+ ⅛
All Amer Life	19¼	19¾	+ ⅜
AllCity Ins .10	12	12¾	.....
Allied Life Ins	6½	7	— ⅛
All Amer LF	11¼	11¾	— ⅛
AmBkrAs .10	18	18¾	.....
AmCapTex 5i	3⅛	3½	.....
AmerFam 15i	34½	36	+ ½
AmFidelity Lf	10⅞	11⅜	.....
Amr. Founders	(z)	(z)	(z)
AmFndtn .05d	5¾	6¾	+ ¼
AmerGenrl .40	26⅜	26⅞	+ ⅛
AmrGn pf 1.80	35½	36	.....
AmHeritg .15d	14¼	14⅝	+ ¼
Am Incm Life	19¾	20¼	— ¼
Am Life Comp	5⅝	6	.....
AmNatl Ins	15¾		

Corporation Bonds

	Rate Mat.	Bid	Ask
AmTel&Tel	4⅞s1994	78	80
AmTel&Tel	5⅛s2001	84½	86½
Duke Power	4½s92	78½	80½
FirstNatCityBk	4s90	114¼	115¼
F M C w deb	3⅛s81	154	159
Food Fair db	5½s75	81	84
Fruehauf cv db	4s76	135	140
Home Oil cv	5½s84	148	153
Lowenst Deb	4⅞s 81	74	78
Mid Am PL	6½s80	90	94
Mitsui w deb	6⅜s78	95	101
Molybdenum	5½s76	82	86
Nowst Nitro Gl	6s79	68	

Mutual Funds

Monday, October 14, 1968

Price ranges for investment companies, as supplied by the National Association of Securities Dealers:

	Bid	Asked	Bid Chg
Aberdeen	3.33	3.64	— .01
Adviser Fd	9.20	10.05	+ .01
Affiliated	9.62	10.40	+ .03
All Am Fd	1.35	1.48	.....
Amcap Fd	6.61	7.22	+ .03
Am Bus Sh	3.87	4.18	+ .02
AmDiv Inv	12.15	13.28	— .03
Am Grwth	7.63	8.29	+ .02
AmInv (v)	(z)	(z)	
Am Mutual	10.92	11.93	+ .07
AmNat Gw	3.72	4.07	+ .01
Anchor Group			
Cap Fnd	10.38	11.38	.....
Div Grw	15.74	17.25	+ .01
Div Inv	10.66	11.68	— .01
Fund Inv	12.09	13.25	+ .01
Assoc Fnd	1.71	1.87	— .01
Axe-Houghton:			
Fund A	9.49	10.32	+ .03
Fund B	11.16	12.13	+ .05
Stock Fd	8.92	9.75	+ .01
Axe Scie	7.79	8.47	+ .02
Babson (v)	8.88	8.88	+ .02
Blue Ridge	14.38	15.72	— .01

	Bid	Asked	Bid Chg
ShTr Bos	14.98	16.37	— .06
Chem Fd	19.78	21.63	+ .06
Colonial Funds:			
Colonial	14.72	16.09	+ .03
Equity	5.96	6.51	+ .05
Growth	8.55	9.34	— .03
Com Stock	6.20	6.74	+ .04
Commonwealth Funds:			
Capital	23.73	25.93	...
Income	11.91	13.02	+ .04
Investm	11.21	12.25	+ .02
StockFd	11.78	12.78	.....
Commonwealth Trust:			
A & B	1.81	1.96	.....
C & D	2.00	2.16	.....
Comp Cap	10.74	11.74	+ .04
Comp BdSt	12.27	13.34	+ .02
Composit	x11.83	11.86	+ .01
Concrd (v)	23.34	23.34	— .02
Consol Inv	14.25	14.62	+ .13
Consmr In	5.68	6.21	.....
Convert Sc	12.61	13.58	— .01
Corp Ledrs	17.22	18.85	— .01
Coutry Cap	14.31	15.47	.....

	Bid	Asked	Bid Chg
Ivst Fund	16.36	17.88	+ .02
IvyFnd (v)	28.89	28.89	+ .14
Johnst (v)	23.03	23.03	— .03
Keystone Custodian Funds:			
Cust B 1	21.27	22.21	.....
Cust B 2	22.67	24.73	— .08
Disct B 4	10.34	11.28	+ .02
Cust K 1	9.66	10.54	+ .01
Cust K 2	7.64	8.35	— .01
Cust S 1	23.17	25.28	+ .04
Cust S 2	12.53	13.67	.....
Cust S 3	9.87	10.77	— .01
Cust S 4	7.13	7.79	+ .01
Polaris	6.30	6.90	+ .04
Knickr Fd	8.64	9.46	+ .03
Knickr Gth	13.80	15.12	+ .02
Lex Inc Tr	11.42	12.48	+ .03
Lex Resch	17.51	19.14	+ .02
Liberty Fd	8.17	8.93	+ .03
LifeIns Inv	8.43	9.21	+ .02
Life & Grw	5.57	6.08	+ .01
Loomis Sayles Funds (v) :			
Canadn	40.52	40.52	.....
Cap Dev	14.31	14.31	+ .05

	Bid	Asked	Bid Chg
Nafn Wide	11.37	12.31	+ .04
N E A Mut	12.04	12.29	+ .04
Neuwr (v)	30.05	30.05	+ .14
New Eng	11.79	12.75	+ .01
New Horiz	31.67	31.67	+ .04
Newton Fd	16.86	18.43	.....
New World	16.03	17.52	+ .06
Noeast (v)	17.76	17.76	.....
Oceang Fd	10.15	11.09	+ .04
Omega Fd	9.87	10.05	.....
O Neil Fnd	22.49	23.93	+ .04
100 Fund	18.22	19.91	+ .06
1 Will (v)	17.71	17.71	— .02
Oppenhm	9.29	10.15	— .01
Penn MutF	22.18	22.18	+ .16
Pen Sq (v)	9.89	9.89	(z)
Phila Fund	16.13	17.68	+ .01
Pilgrim Fd	11.87	12.97	+ .02
Pilot Fund	9.27	10.13	+ .04
Pine St (v)	12.68	12.68	+ .06
Pioneer Fd	(z)	(z)	
Planned In	15.16	16.57	+ .07
PriceG (v)	26.16	26.16	+ .04
Pro Fund	10.52	11.19	— .01

Government, Agency and Miscellaneous Securities

Tuesday, October 15, 1968

Over-the-Counter Quotations: Source on request.
Decimals in bid-and-asked and bid change represent
32nds (101.1 means 101 1-32). a-Plus 1-64. b-Yield to call
date. c-Certificates of indebtedness. d-Minus 1-64.

Treasury Bonds

				Bid	Asked	Bid Chg.	Yld.
3⅞s,	1968	Nov.	....	99.27	99.29	...	4.99
2½s,	1963-68	Dec.	....	99.16	99.18	...	5.19
4s,	1969	Feb.	....	99.14	99.16	d	5.45
2½s,	1964-69	June	....	98.13	98.17	— .1	4.73
4s,	1969	Oct.	....	98.24	98.28	...	5.22
2½s,	1964-69	Dec.	....	97.11	97.15	— .1	4.77
2½s,	1965-70	Mar.	....	96.23	96.27	— .2	4.84
4s,	1970	Feb.	....	98.9	98.13	— .2	5.25
4s,	1970	Aug.	....	97.19	97.23	— .3	5.20
2½s,	1966-71	Mar.	....				
4s,	1971	Aug.					

U.S. Treas. Notes

Rate	Mat	Bid	Asked	Yld
5¼	11-68	99.31	100.1	4.75
5⅝	2-69	99.31	100.1	5.48
1½	4-69	98.16	98.24	4.29
5⅝	5-69	99.31	100.1	5.57
6	8-69	100.10	100.14	5.66

U.S. Treas. Bills

Mat	Bid Discount	Ask	Mat	Bid Discount	Ask
10-17	5.85	5.05	2-13	5.41	5.31
10-24	5.55	5.05	2-20	5.42	5.32
10-31	5.60	5.05	2-27	5.44	5.34
11- 7	5.17				

Federal Land Bank

Rate	Mat	Bid	Asked	Yld
4⅛	2-72-67	94.16	95.16	5.62
4½	10-70-67	97.0	98.0	5.59
5½	10-68	99.30	100.0	5.36
5.95	12-68	100.0	100.4	5.16
4¾	1-69	99.16	99.24	5.67
	3-69	99.0	99.16	5.54

FNMA Notes & Debs.

Rate	Mat	Bid	Asked	Yld
4⅜	4-69	99.10	99.18	5.30
4.65	5-69	99.10	99.14	5.66
6.10	6-69	100.4	100.8	5.69
5⅛	7-69	99.18	99.26	5.38
6	12-69	100.4	100.16	5.54
4⅝	4-70	98.4	98.20	5.60
6.60	6-70	100.28	101.12	5.71

World Bank Bonds

Rate	Mat	Bid	Asked	Yld
3½	1969	98.24	99.24	3.55
5⅜	1969	99.8	100.8	4.85
5¾	1969	99.16	100.16	5.25
6⅛	1970	100.8	101.8	5.21
5.80	1970	99.24	100.24	5.40

Inter-Amer. Devel. Bk.

Rate	Mat	Bid	Asked	Yld
4¼	12-82	79.16	80.16	6.35
4½	4-84	80.0	82.0	6.24
4½	11-84	80.0	80.0	
5.20				

Bank for Co-ops

Rate	Mat	Bid	Asked	Yld
5.90	11-68	99.31	100.1	5.10
6.20	12-68	100.1	100.3	5.32
6.20	1-69	100.1	100.3	5.64
6.00	2-69	100.0	100.2	5.71
5.55	4-69	99.27	99.29	5.75

FIC Bank Debs.

Rate	Mat	Bid	Asked	Yld
5.75	11- 4	99.30	100.0	5.52
5.75	12- 2	99.30	100.0	5.55
5.95	1- 2	99.31	100.1	5.62
6.10	2- 2	100.0	100.2	5.72

Fed'l Home Loan Bk.

Rate	Mat	Bid	Asked	Yld
5.85	10-68	99.31	100.1	4.26
5⅝	11-68	99.29	100.1	5.21
5½	1-69	99.28	100.0	5.43
5.85	2-69	99.31	100.2	5.60
5.65	2-69	99.29	99.31	5.69
5⅝	3-69	99.24	100.0	5.36
6.25	4-69	100.5	100.7	5.68
6.00	5-69	100.1	100.3	5.76
6.30	6-69	100.10	100.12	5.72
5¾	7-69	99.31	100.1	5.69
6.00	9-69	100.2	100.10	5.65
6.00	2-70	100.8	100.16	5.61
6.00	3-70	100.8	10.16	5.63
6.00	4-70	100.6	100.14	5.70
5.80	5-70	99.27	99.29	5.86

only at a stated price or better for a specified period of time, which may be a day, a week or a month.[3] *Good 'til canceled* (GTC), or *open* orders remain in force until the customer instructs that they be canceled. GTC orders must be confirmed at least every six months on the last business day of April and October. *Fill or kill* (FOK) orders are *immediate or cancel* orders. The order must be executed at once at the specified price, or it is to be canceled.

A *stop order* is an order to buy or sell at a specified price, and becomes a market order as soon as the price of the stock reaches, or sells through, the price specified by the buyer or seller. A stop order may be used in an effort to protect a paper profit, or in an attempt to limit a possible loss to a certain amount. Since it becomes a market order when the stop price is reached, there is no certainty that it will be executed at that price. If a stock rises to a certain price, stop orders to buy may be used by those who have sold short.[4] In addition, all sale orders are either long or short sales.

Delivery or clearing of transactions

Transactions in stocks and bonds demand a clear understanding of the time when

3/ Orders are generally considered to be day orders unless otherwise specified.

4/ Another type of order is the stop-loss-limit. In this case, when the specified price is reached the order becomes a limit order to buy or sell at a certain price or better.

delivery of securities and payment is required. NASD and Stock Exchange rules normally require settlement to be made in one of the following ways.

1. *Cash transactions* require settlement on the day of the contracts.[5] In other words, delivery of the stock or bond certificate is made to the buyer and cash payment is made to the seller on the trade date—the day the contract is made.

2. *Regular-way* transactions require settlement by 12:30 p.m. on the *fifth full business day* following the day of trade.[6] Regular-way transactions are the most frequently used, as the name implies.

3. A *delayed delivery* requires settlement to be made between the third and the seventh day following the day of trade.

4. *Seller's option* transactions require settlement in not less than 5 days or more than 60 calendar days, as specified in the contract.[7]

Most over-the-counter broker-dealers are members of the National Association of Securities Dealers, which numbered 3,659 investment firms at June 30, 1967. There were at that time 90,525 registered representatives.

Since an NASD firm may not give a discount, concession, or commission to any nonmember, any firm dealing in the over-the-counter market is substantially handicapped if it is not an NASD member. Notable exceptions to this include several large mutual fund distribution organizations that have their own sales forces who sell only the particular funds distributed by their organization.[8] Such organizations may not sell or offer any other mutual funds whose sponsor or distributor is an NASD member. Nor may NASD members sell a mutual fund whose sponsor or distributor is not a member.

In practice, most members of Stock Exchange firms that deal with the public are also NASD members. Thus, a stock exchange firm conducts business both on the exchange and in the over-the-counter market.

Stock exchanges

The other main areas of trading—buying and selling securities—are the stock exchanges. A stock exchange is a central meeting place where member brokers may buy and sell securities for their clients in an *auction market*. The exchanges provide the facilities for securities trading in order that sellers and buyers may meet through brokers. In this way, the forces of supply and demand interact through auction bidding to set the prices at which transactions take place. Most companies who list their securities for trading on a registered securities exchange seek greater liquidity and marketability for their issues, although there is no guarantee that listing on an exchange will provide these desired characteristics.

Of the several stock exchanges, the *New York Stock Exchange* (NYSE) is the

---

5/ The settlement date is the date on which delivery and cash payment must be made.
6/ Until early 1968, settlement was required on the fourth full business day.
7/ Further details are explained in Chapter 9, NASD.
8/ These firms are registered with the SEC and their representatives, and principals are subject to the previously explained examination and personal requirements.

largest. Others include the *American Stock Exchange* (ASE) and regional exchanges such as the *Midwest Exchange* and the *Pacific Coast Exchange.*[9] The NYSE and ASE are located in New York City. Approximately 85 percent of the members of each are members of both exchanges. Many members of the two biggest exchanges are also members of one or more regional exchanges.

The New York Stock Exchange accounts for the majority of dollar value and percent of shares traded on all United States exchanges. The American Stock Exchange accounts for more dollar and share volume than all the regional exchanges combined.[10]

Most stock exchanges, including all that are significant in terms of volume, must register with the SEC, which has supervisory functions with respect to their rules and practices, as well as authority to suspend or expel exchange members who violate the Securities Exchange Act of 1934. This act requires that all securities traded on an exchange be registered with the SEC, unless a special exemption applies. In addition to such federal and self-regulation, the exchanges are also subject to state regulation.

No security can be *listed* on either the New York or American Exchange unless its issuer files an application for registration with both the exchange and the SEC. Each exchange has certain minimum requirements that must be met before a security may be traded (listed) on the exchange. To be listed on the NYSE, a corporation must have, among other requirements: a minimum of 2,000 stockholders, including at least 1,700 round-lot holders; a minimum of $1.2 million annual profit after taxes; and minimum net tangible assets of $10 million.[11]

Unlisted securities are never traded on the NYSE. The listing agreement between a company and the NYSE provides that the public will receive timely disclosure of earnings statements, dividend notices, and other information that would influence or affect the value of securities or decisions of investors.[12] The listing application allows the exchange to determine the suitability of the applicant for trading and also provides the public with information to aid its analysis of the merits of the security. Many securities are listed dually on several exchanges, but a security is never traded on both the New York and American Exchanges.

Unlisted trading occurs when securities of unlisted companies are traded on the floor of the exchange. No unlisted trading has taken place on the NYSE since 1910.

9/ In mid-1966, there were 16 exchanges in the United States, of which 13 were registered with the SEC and 3 exempted from registration as national securities exchanges.

10/ During 1966, the dollar value of the trading on all registered exchanges was $123 billion, of which 80.1 percent was transacted on the NYSE and 11.5 percent on the American. Of 32 billion shares traded, 69.2 percent was on the NYSE and 22.9 percent on the American Stock Exchange.

11/ Other requirements include: (a) $12 million of aggregate market value of the common stock, and (b) at least $2 million of annual, before-tax earnings under competitive conditions. In addition, there must be some degree of national interest in the company. Only common stock with voting rights may be listed on the NYSE.

12/ ASE listing requirements at February 1, 1968 were: (a) a minimum of 900 stockholders, including at least 600 round-lot holders; (b) pretax earnings of at least $500,000 and aftertax net of at least $300,000 in the latest fiscal year; (c) reasonable prospects of maintaining this level of earnings; (d) net tangible assets of at least $3 million; (e) a minimum of $2 million aggregate market value for the publicly traded shares; (f) public distribution of at least 300,000 shares; and (g) a minimum market price for the company's shares of at least $5 for a reasonable period of time before filing of the listing application.

However, on the ASE and regional exchanges unlisted trading does take place in substantial volume.[13]

If the exchange feels that continued trading in a security is inadvisable because of a decline in (*a*) the number of shareholders, (*b*) market value of the outstanding securities, or (*c*) earnings, the exchange may delist the issue.

At the end of 1966, the total market value of all securities listed on the NYSE was $611 billion. Approximately $483 billion of this amount was represented by stocks (98 percent were common stocks), and $128 billion by bonds (73 percent were U.S. government and New York City issues).

Approximately 1.5 million publicly and privately owned corporations file income tax returns. Of these, approximately 40,000 are quoted in the over-the-counter market. Of these 40,000, about 7,500 have sufficiently widespread ownership to be considered publicly owned, and 2,500 are listed or traded on national or regional stock exchanges. About 1,300 of these have common stock issues that are listed on the NYSE. At the end of 1966, 1,665 stocks (common and preferred) and 1,272 bonds were listed and traded on the NYSE. Approximately 1,100 stocks and 100 bonds were traded on the American Exchange.

Since the NYSE dominates the trading on organized exchanges, we will confine our discussion to its organization and practices. In order to transact business on the floor of the New York Stock Exchange, a person must own a *seat,* of which there are 1,366. Seats may be thought of as membership. During 1967, the cost of a seat rose to $450,000. The term seat originates from the days when members of the exchange transacted their business while seated in chairs. Only individuals may own seats. Each applicant must be at least 21 years of age, an American citizen, be sponsored by at least two exchange members, pass a test administered by the exchange, and be of good character and repute. Although the seat or membership is held by an individual, he may be associated with others in a corporation or partnership.

In addition to members of the NYSE, several thousand allied members comprise the partners or voting stockholders of member firms and corporations. Allied members, though not allowed on the floor of the exchange, are subject to the same rules and regulations as members. Employees of NYSE member firms who are engaged in offering securities to the public or in trading securities must first be approved as a registered employee.

In addition to being 21 years of age and of good character and repute, the prospective registered employee must work on a full-time basis and pass an examination for either standard (full) registration or limited registration. Full registration allows the employee to handle all types of securities transactions. Limited registration restricts the employee's activities to mutual fund shares and the Monthly Investment Plan (described later in this chapter). Six months' experience is required for full registration,

---

13/ An exchange may apply to the SEC for permission to allow unlisted trading in an issue. Such permission will not normally be granted unless the issuer is registered with the SEC and listed on at least one national securities exchange.

three months for limited registration, and eight months for full registration after a limited registration. Study outlines for registration exams are available from the New York Stock Exchange, Publications Division, 11 Wall Street, New York, N.Y., and the American Stock Exchange, 86 Trinity Place, New York, N.Y.

The New York Stock Exchange policy and regulations governing the conduct of members and allied members are established by a board of governors, which consists of 33 members, including the chairman of the board, the president of the exchange, and representatives from in and outside the New York metropolitan area.[14]

The board is primarily engaged in determining policy. An advisory committee of governors has wide disciplinary powers over members of the exchange for violations of the exchange constitution, its rules, resolutions of the board, or for conduct inconsistent with just and equitable principles of trade.

Types of exchange members

There are several types of floor members—those who actually buy and sell stocks on the exchange—including: the floor trader, commission broker, specialist, floor broker, and odd-lot dealer.[15]

A *floor trader* is a member who buys and sells for his own account. A floor trader has the advantage of being able to trade for his own account as a dealer without paying commissions, and has direct access to the floor of the exchange to observe the technical nature and trend of the market.

A *commission broker,* the most numerous type of floor member, is one who represents the public in buying securities by acting as an agent. Commission houses that obtain a substantial part of their business from distant areas over closed wires are also known as wire houses.

The *specialist* trades in only a few issues assigned to a particular post on the floor of the exchange. He assumes two main responsibilities.

1. To maintain an orderly market. The specialist must be prepared to buy or sell for his own account (make the market), to a reasonable extent, when there is a temporary disparity between supply and demand. In this case, he acts as a dealer.

2. To act as a broker's broker. For example, a commission broker on the exchange floor may receive a limit order—that is, an order to buy or sell at a specific price or

---

14/ The composition of the board is as follows.
    a) One member of the exchange, who is elected chairman.
    b) One president of the exchange, who may not be a member of the exchange.
    c) Thirteen members of the exchange who live and work in New York City; not less than seven must be in firms that do business directly with the public, and not less than ten must spend a substantial portion of their time on the exchange.
    d) Six members or allied members of the exchange who live and work in New York City, and are partners or stockholders in firms that do business directly with the public.
    e) Nine members or allied members who live and work outside New York City, and are partners or stockholders in firms that do business directly with the public.
    f) Three public members who are elected by the other governors and who are not engaged in the securities business.
15/ The floor is the large room in which securities are bought and sold.

better. It may be to buy at $50 a stock that is at that time selling at $60. He cannot wait at the particular stock trading post until the price reaches the specified level. So he leaves the order with the specialist, who enters the order in the specialist's confidential book to be executed when the market reaches the price called for in that order. In this case, the specialist acts as a broker.

Because of his more-or-less inside position, the specialist must give preference to orders he is handling as a broker over any purchase for his own account. His activities are closely supervised and regulated by the exchange.

The *floor broker,* known as a two-dollar broker, is a subagent and acts for the commission broker when the commission broker is too busy to execute all his orders himself. At one time, floor brokers charged a standard fee of two dollars. Though fees have increased, the name persists.

The *odd-lot dealer* is a special type of floor member. Most orders are for round lots; that is, for 100 shares or multiples thereof. Orders for less than 100 shares are handled by the odd-lot dealer, who must accept all odd-lot buy and sell orders brought to him. The price at which an odd-lot dealer buys and sells is based on the *next* round-lot transaction that takes place after he receives his odd-lot order. Since odd-lot sales are not permitted on the floor of the exchange, the odd-lot dealer buys in round lots and breaks up the round lots into smaller units for his clients, who are always other exchange members. An odd-lot dealer never deals directly with the public. Most odd-lot business is handled through two member firms who specialize in this activity. The usual *differential* between the odd-lot price and the round-lot price is 25 cents (¼) on stocks selling at $55 or more a share, and 12.5 cents (1/8) for stocks selling at less than $55. If the most recent round-lot price were $57, then the odd-lot dealer would sell at 57¼ or buy at 56¾—a difference of ¼. If the last round-lot price were $37, then the odd-lot dealer would sell at 37 1/8 or buy at 36 7/8—a difference of 1/8.

A typical transaction

Now, let us examine a rather typical transaction on the floor of the exchange—an order to buy 100 shares (round lot) of ABC Co., given by a customer to the registered representative of a member firm in Louisville, Kentucky. This is a market order, which means an order to buy as soon as possible at the best price possible. The market order is telephoned by direct wire, or is teletyped to the firm's New York office. The New York office telephones the order to its clerk on the floor of the exchange. The firm's clerk at the exchange summons his broker, who personally receives the order to buy 100 shares of ABC. The broker goes to the *post,* a horseshoe-shaped booth where the specialist in ABC is stationed, and he determines the price, which is 57 to a quarter. This means the specialist has (1) an order to sell 100 shares at 57¼ and (2) an order to buy at least 100 shares at 57.

Since the broker has a market order—that is, to buy immediately at the best price possible, he may bid 57 1/8 in a loud voice to determine if other brokers want to sell at that price. If they do, he executes the order with them; if not, he may return to the specialist and execute the order at 57¼. Both the buying and selling brokers record the transaction by telephone to their respective offices. At the same time, notation of the transaction is recorded and sent to the ticker tape department.

Ticker tape

The ticker tape prints the name of the stock, the number of shares sold, and the price paid. All reporting on the tape is of round-lot transactions. Odd-lot sales are not made on the exchange floor, so they do not appear on ticker tapes.

The ticker is the instrument that prints the prices and the volume of security transactions. This information is then sent throughout the United States within minutes after each trade on the floor of the New York Stock Exchange.

Sales of 100 shares of a stock, in which the unit of trading is 100 shares, will be printed with no quantity indicated. For example, a sale of 100 shares of U.S. Steel, whose symbol is X, at 56, will be printed X56. Unless otherwise specified, all stocks printed on the tape are common stocks. Sales of 200 or more shares of a stock, in which the unit of trading is 100 shares, will be indicated by printing the number of shares sold in hundreds followed by the letter s, and then the price. Thus, a sale of 200 shares of U.S. Steel at 56 will be printed X2s 56. When 1,000 shares or more are sold, the quantity will be printed in full as: X1000s 56.

Bond trading

Bond trading on an exchange is carried out not on the floor but in separate bond rooms. Any member of the exchange may deal in bonds, but he usually refers such orders to a member who is stationed in the bond room.

The unit of trading in bonds on the NYSE is one $1,000 bond. The bond ticker tape records the number of bonds, the bonds' ticker symbol, and the price.

Bonds are traded in two ways—active and cabinet. In the *active crowd,* bonds are traded by oral bids and offers. In the *cabinet crowd,* the order to buy or sell is entered on a card, which is then filed in a cabinet with other bids and offers for that particular bond. The cards are filed in order of both price and time of receipt. When the high bid reaches the low asked, a sale takes place and is executed by an exchange employee.

Bond quotations are in percentages of principal in $1,000 amounts. A bid of 100 means 100 percent of $1,000, or $1,000; a bid of 104 means 104 percent of $1,000, or $1,040; and a bid of 97 means 97 percent of $1,000 or $970.

Corporate bonds are quoted in fractions of 1/8; government bonds, which are not traded on exchanges, are quoted in fractions of 1/32. So a government bond at 103.16 would be 103 16/32, or 1035. A corporate bond bid of 103¼ represents $1,032.50. Corporate bond issues are normally quoted *"and interest,"* which means that added to the sale price will be an additional sum equal to the accrued interest from the last interest payment date to the date of settlement.

Other types of trading

Hedging is the practice of counterbalancing sale or purchase of one security by making a purchase or a sale of another. Some forms of hedging are arbitrage, puts and calls, selling against the box, and short sales.

Arbitrage is a technique employed to take advantage of differences in stock prices on different exchanges or in different countries. The practice of an arbitrageur is to purchase in one market and immediately sell in another at a higher price. His profit is the difference in prices, less expenses. Arbitrage helps to keep the price of a stock uniform on various exchanges.

A *call option* is an option to buy shares of stock. If the option is exercised, the owner of the option calls in the stock and buys at the agreed price established by the call option. When the market value of a security is expected to rise, call options are popular.

A *put option* is an option to sell shares of stock. If the option is exercised, the owner of the option puts or sells the stock at the price stated in the put option contract. These are advantageously used when it is anticipated that the market price will fall.

Selling against the box is a method used by an investor to protect a paper profit by selling short and borrowing the shares to make delivery rather than surrendering his own shares from his safety deposit box.

If an investor owns 100 shares of ABC stock, which has advanced in price, he can protect his profit by selling against the box as follows. He sells 100 shares short, borrowing 100 shares to make delivery. He retains in his safety deposit box the 100 shares he already owns. If ABC declines, the profit on his short sale is exactly offset by the loss in the market value of the stock he owns, which is still in the box. If ABC advances, the loss on his short sale is exactly offset by the profit in the market value of the stock he has retained. He can close out the short sale by buying 100 shares to return to the person from whom he borrowed, or he can send the lender the 100 shares he owns.

A *short sale* is a hedging method whereby a person who believes a stock will decline sells shares of it, even though he does not own any. For example, an investor instructs his broker to sell short 100 shares of ABC. The broker borrows the stock in order to deliver 100 shares to the buyer. The money value of the shares borrowed is deposited by the broker with the lender. Sooner or later, the investor must cover his short sale by buying the same amount of stock he borrowed and must return to the lender the number of shares borrowed.

According to a rule of the SEC, no short sale of a security on a national securities exchange may be made at a price lower than the price that security last sold at on that exchange. Additionally, a short sale may be made at the same price as the last sale only if that price (the last sale) is higher than the one that preceded it. For example, if the last sale were made at $50, and the one preceding it at $49½, a short sale could be made at $50.

If it is possible to buy—*short covering*—at a lower price than the stock was sold short, the profit is the difference between the two prices, less commissions and taxes. If the stock price goes up, then there will be a loss.

A *spread* is an option that combines in one contract both a put and a call at different prices. For example, it may give the bearer of the contract the right to sell 100 shares of XYZ stock to Mr. Option Giver at $60 per share, or to buy from him at $70.

A *straddle* is an option that gives the bearer the right to both buy from and sell to the maker a specified number of shares at a fixed price for a limited period of time.

With a *discretionary order,* the customer specifies the stock or the commodity to be bought or sold, and the amount. His agent is free to act at his discretion on the time and price.

Seller's options are special transactions on the stock exchange that give the seller the right to deliver the stock or bond at any time within a specified period, ranging from not less than 5 business days to not more than 60 days.

Terms in the markets

Some terms that relate to the securities markets, both on exchanges and over the counter, are the following.

Give-ups refer to giving brokerage commissions, and they originate two different ways. A member of the exchange on the floor may act for a second member by executing an order for him with a third member. The first tells the third member that he is acting on behalf of the second member, and he instructs that all or a portion of the brokerage be given to the second member. The second way that give-ups may originate is in the following situation. An investor has an account with ABC Company, but is in a town where they have no office. He goes to another member firm, and informs them he has an account with ABC Company and would like to buy some stock. After verifying his account, the firm may execute his order and tell the broker who sells the stock that the firm is acting on behalf of ABC Company. They give up the name of ABC Company to the selling broker, or the firm may simply wire the order to ABC Company, who will execute it. In both cases, the investor pays only the regular commission.

A *long position* in a stock means that one has ownership of that stock. Being long 100 General Motors means that the investor owns 100 shares of GM. A person who sells stock he owns would be *selling long*.

A *short position* is the opposite of a long position. Being short 100 General Motors means that the investor does not own any shares of GM, and that he has sold and is obligated to deliver 100 shares of GM. He is said to be *selling short*.

Watered stock describes stock that has been issued without the company's receiving an equivalent value in cash, services, or property. Its value has been diluted, or watered.

The term originates from the shady practice formerly followed by some western cattle dealers. Cattle on the way to the cattle markets were first fed salt, then given substantial quantities of water to increase their weight just before delivery to the scales of cattle dealers.

Boiler room is a term to describe high-pressure telephone peddling of stocks of dubious value. A typical boiler room is simply a room lined with desks or cubicles, each with a salesman and a telephone. The salesmen call what are known as sucker lists.

MIP or *Monthly Investment Plan* is a pay-as-you-go method of buying New York Stock Exchange listed shares for as little as $40 every 3 months, or up to a maximum of $1,000 per month. Under the MIP, an investor buys stock by the dollar's worth. If the price advances, he gets fewer shares, and if it declines he gets more shares. He may discontinue purchases at any time without penalty. The only charge for purchases and sales is the usual commission for buying and selling, plus the regular odd-lot dealer differential. The commission ranges for each purchase and sale are from 6 percent on small transactions to slightly below 1.5 percent on larger transactions.

A *wash sale* is a fake sale in which no real change in ownership takes place. For example, a speculator places a matched order with two brokers, selling a given amount of stock through one broker and buying it through another. The primary purpose of wash sales is to establish a fictitious price, either to create a profit opportunity or to establish a loss, generally for tax purposes. Wash sales are illegal and are barred by the stock exchanges.

Quotations of various prices in the daily newspaper fall into several major categories. It is important to know these categories, and how to read the financial news to obtain desired information. Most newspapers carry daily quotations. The two main categories are stock exchange quotations and over-the-counter securities quotations. Most newspapers carry the transactions of the New York Stock Exchange, the American Stock Exchange, and often a number of other leading regional exchanges. Of these, the New York Stock Exchange is by far the largest in number of issues listed and in volume of business done. See the New York Stock Exchange quotations on page 180.

The tabulation *Most Active Stocks* (page 181) is a complete record of the significant facts about the previous day's trading in the few stocks that accounted for a large proportion of the day's volume. Like bonds, stocks are referred to in terms of *points*. For bonds, a point means 1 percent of par face amount, usually $10. In stocks, a point means $1. For example, a stock selling at 25 points is selling at $25. Usually, stock prices are referred to in dollars. Changes in the price are quoted in points (e.g., General Motors is up a point today).

Stocks selling at $1 or more per share are quoted in fractional points. These are fractions from 1/8 to 7/8; each 1/8 is equal to 12 1/2 cents. Although these fractions are in terms of 8ths, one sees such fractions as 1/4. This is simply 2/8 reduced to 1/4. The fractions most frequently seen are: 1/8, 1/4, 3/8, 1/2, 5/8, 3/4, and 7/8. The market price of active stocks usually fluctuates between 1/8 and 1/4. Stocks selling below $1 per share are quoted in smaller fractions, but this is uncommon.

Refer again to page 180, and note that before the abbreviated name for each

New York Stock Exchange Transactions

Tuesday, October 15, 1968

A-B-C

—1968— High	Low	Stocks Div.	Sales in 100s	Open	High	Low	Close	Net Chg.
22¼	15½	Abacus .52t	x6	20½	20⅞	20½	20½	− ⅛
66⅞	41⅞	Abbott Lab 1	139	65½	65¾	65¼	65¼	.....
48	28	Abex Cp 1.60	46	47¾	47¾	47¼	47½	− ⅜
68⅜	39½	ACF Ind 2.20	172	53⅜	54⅛	53¼	53⅝	+ ⅝
48⅝	36	Acme Mkt 2b	54	45½	45¾	45	45½	+ ⅛
19⅜	16	AdamEx .18h	12	19	19⅛	19	19	− ¼
30⅝	17⅝	Ad Millis .20	100	18¾	19	18⅛	18¼	− ¾
91⅞	52	Address 1.40	96	87⅛	88	87⅛	87½	+ ⅛
25⅛	16½	Admiral	50	20¼	20⅜	20	20	− ¼
60⅜	46⅛	AetnaLif&C 1	443	58½	58½	57⅝	57⅞	+ ⅞
44	31	Air Prod .20b	82	42	42	40¾	41⅝	− ¾
123½	104½	Air Pd pf4.75	1	120	120	120	120	−1½
36⅞	28½	AirRedtn 1.50	185	32¼	32¼	31⅝	32	.....
14⅜	8⅛	AJ Industries	95	11⅞	12⅛	11⅝	11⅞	− ¼
22	17⅜	Ala Gas .96	27	19¼	19¼	19	19¼	.....
47½	32	Alberto C .20	28	42⅜	42⅜	41¾	42⅛	− ¼
27⅜	21¼	AlcanAlum 1	94	25¼	25⅜	25	25⅜	+ ⅜
23⅛	12¼	Alleg Cp .10e	70	22⅛	22¼	21⅞	22	− ⅛
72¾	48¾	AllegLud 2.40	101	54	55⅜	53¾	55	+1
76⅜	58	AllegLud pf 3	2	66	66	66	66	.....
25⅜	20¾	AllegPw 1.28	62	23⅜	23⅞	23⅛	23⅝	+ ½
48⅜	24¾	AllenInd 1.40	13	48¼	48⅝	48¼	48⅝	+ ⅝
43	34	AlliedCh 1.90	462	35⅝	35¾	35⅜	35¾	+ ⅛
38¾	24½	Allied Kid 1	16	36½	37	36½	37	+ ½
28⅜	23⅝	Alld Main .40	41	26⅝	27⅜	26⅜	27⅜	+ ½
25¾	23⅝	AlliedMill .75	50	25⅞	27	25⅞	27	+1½
63¾	33⅜	Allied Pd .60	66	34⅝	35	34⅛	35	+ ⅜
51¼	35⅝	AlliedStr 1.40	15	47	47	46¾	46¾	− ¼
70	63	AlliedSt pf 4	z30	68⅛	68⅛	68⅛	68⅛	−1¾
22	16	AlliedSup .60	57	19¾	20	19¾	19⅞	+ ⅛
38⅛	24	Allis Chal .50	126	27⅞	28⅜	27⅝	27⅝	− ¼
25⅝	12	Alpha P Cem	55	23¼	23⅜	22½	22½	− ¾
20⅞	10⅝	Alside .20	374	17⅜	17⅜	16¾	16¾	− ½
81½	62½	Alcoa 1.80	205	72⅝	73¼	72	72	− ⅞
64	41⅝	AMBAC .60	33	59¾	60	59½	59⅞	+ ⅝
45¼	28½	AmrcEs 1.20	3	36⅛	36½	36⅛	36½	+ ½
65¾	56¼	AmrEs pf2.60	10	58	58½	58	58½	+ ¾
94⅜	75	Amerada 3	141	85¼	86½	85	86¼	+1
39	29¼	AAirFiltr .80	89	34	34⅞	33¾	34⅞	+1⅛
33⅞	24	Am Airlin .80	316	30⅛	30⅝	30	30¼	.....
34½	21	Am Baker 1	76	32⅞	33	32⅝	32⅝	.....
33	20¼	AmBk Note 1	6	31	31	30½	31	− ¼
65	53	AmBkN pf 3	z10	63½	63½	63½	63½	+1
74¾	43¾	AmBdcst 1.60	85	70⅝	70⅝	70	70	−1
54½	45⅞	Am Can 2.20	77	50¾	51	50½	50½	.....
32¾	28¾	ACan pf 1.75	1	30⅝	30⅝	30⅝	30⅝	.....
26⅛	14¼	Am Cem .60	72	22	22¼	21⅝	21¾	− ¼
47	35	A Chain 1.60	18	42	42¼	40¾	40¾	−1
22	16⅜	AmCons 1.05t	3	19¼	19¼	19	19	.....
35½	25	Ceco Cp .80	21	32	32¼	31⅝	31⅝	− ⅝
70	50½	CelaneseCp 2	90	68⅜	68⅞	68	68	− ⅜
75½	66½	Celan pfA4.50	3	71¼	71¼	70¾	70¾	.....
59⅞	41¼	Cenco Ins .30	102	51⅝	53	51⅜	53	+1¾
55⅜	31	Cen Aguir .40	8	45¼	45¼	44½	44½	.....
28⅞	12¼	CenFdry .30r	220	28⅞	31	28¼	30¾	+2¼
30⅝	25¾	Cen Hud 1.48	23	27½	27¾	27⅜	27¾	+ ½
27⅞	21⅞	CentIllLt 1.24	22	23⅞	23⅞	23⅝	23⅞	.....
84½	71	C IllLt pf4.50	z60	75⅜	75⅝	75⅜	75⅝	+ ½
24	19¼	CenIllPS 1.12	46	21¾	22	21¾	21⅞	− ¼
27	25¼	CentLaEl .88	8	26¼	26¼	26	26	.....
20½	18¼	CenMPw 1.08	16	20¼	20¼	20	20	.....
48	39⅛	Cent SW 1.70	26	40½	40½	40⅛	40½	+ ⅛
25¼	19	Cent Soya .80	97	23⅛	23⅜	23	23⅛	+ ⅛
50¾	37½	Cerro 1.60b	190	39⅞	40	39⅝	39⅝	.....
40⅜	15¾	Cert-teed .80	54	34½	34¾	34⅛	34½	+ ¼
40	17¼	Cert-ted pf.90	9	34	34⅜	34	34	+ ⅛
66	40¼	CessnaA 1.40	35	54	54¼	53½	53⅝	− ¾
21¼	14¾	CFI Stl .80	145	20½	21⅛	20⅜	21⅛	+ ⅞
20⅜	5⅞	Chadbn Goth	227	18⅝	19⅛	18⅜	18⅝	+ ¼
32¾	26⅛	ChampS 1.20	56	32½	32¾	31⅞	32⅜	− ⅜
56⅜	32½	ChmpNtl 1.60	44	54⅜	54¾	54	54	+ ⅛
55⅞	47⅞	ChartNY 1.70	42	53¼	54	53⅛	54	+ ⅜
87½	61½	ChaseBk 2.40	36	84	84½	84	84⅜	+ ⅝
29	14¾	Checker Mot	7	27⅞	28¼	27¾	28	− ⅛
56½	38⅛	Chemetn 1.80	13	43	43	42¾	43	+ ¼
18⅝	11¾	Chemway .20	59	16¾	16⅞	16½	16⅞	.....
46¼	32	Ches Va 1.60	23	45½	45¾	45	45	− ½
75	60¼	Ches Ohio 4	23	73	73⅜	73	73¼	+ ⅜
48½	34⅛	Chesebro .84	21	41	41¼	40½	40¾	− ¼
15	11½	ChicEast Ill	19	14⅞	15	14⅝	14⅝	− ¼
69	32	ChiMil StP P	24	54½	54⅞	54½	54⅝	− ⅜
97	69⅜	ChMSPP pf 5	2	82	82	82	82	− ¾
38	24¼	Chi Music 1	23	34	34	33⅝	33⅝	− ⅜
48	34½	ChiPneu 1.80	35	44⅛	45½	44⅛	45⅛	+1
29⅞	17⅝	Chi RI Pac	3	24¾	24¾	24½	24½	− ½
27	15¼	ChRIP ct UP	1	24¼	24¼	24¼	24¼	.....
27⅝	15⅝	ChRIP ctNW	8	24	24¼	24	24	− ¼
72	44¾	ChiTitleTr 2	49	70¼	70⅝	70	70⅝	+ ⅛
24⅞	14⅞	ChockFull .60	128	18	18	17⅝	17⅝	− ¾
45	26½	ChrisCraft 1a	62	36⅞	37⅜	36¾	37⅛	+ ½
44¾	31	CCft cvpf.10r	9	36⅝	36⅝	36⅜	36⅜	.....
23	18¼	CCft prpf 1	2	19⅞	19⅞	19⅞	19⅞	− ¼
59½	30⅞	Chromall .66	159	59	59	58	58	−1⅛
40⅝	39⅝	Chromall wi	8	40	40	40	40	− ½
70⅝	48	Chrysler 2	252	69¼	69½	68⅝	68¾	− ¼
29⅛	24⅞	CinnGE 1.40	88	26⅞	28⅜	26⅞	28⅛	+1½
72½	65	Cin GE pf 4	z180	67¾	68	67¾	68	+ ¼
61	38¾	Cin Mill 1.20a	17	53¾	53¾	53⅜	53½	− ¼
60	31⅝	CITFin 1.80	479	57⅞	58½	57⅜	57⅜	− ½
148⅞	100¾	CIT F pf5.50	6	145	145	145	145	+3¾
65½	43¼	Cities Svc 2	277	60⅝	61⅛	60	60	− ⅛
117	81¾	CitS cvpf2.25	1	107	107	107	107	−1
65	37¾	City Inv .30b	168	58⅞	58⅞	57¼	57¾	−1⅛

New York Stock Exchange Bonds

Monday, October 14, 1968

—1968— High	Low	Bonds	Sales in $1,000	High	Low	Close	Net Chg.
140	99¾	CollinsR cv4⅞s87	11	106	106	106	+ ⅛
90½	83	ColoFuel cv4⅞s77	28	90	88¾	89	.....
90½	83	Col Gas 5⅛s85	6	87⅜	87⅜	87⅜	+4⅜
89½	81½	Col Gas 5s82	1	85	85	85	+ ½
86⅝	77½	Col Gas 4⅞s83	7	83⅛	83	83⅛	.....
83½	75	Col Gas 4⅜s83	16	81½	81¼	81¼	− ¼
78½	72½	Col Gas 3⅞s81	12	77	77	77	.....
176½	101½	Col Pict cv4¾s87	86	170	164	170	+6¾
91	74¾	ComlSolv cv4½s91	85	76½	75¼	76½	+ ½
79½	75	Comw Ed 3s77	10	78½	78⅜	78⅜	− ⅝
59	53	Com Ed 2¾s99	1	54	54	54	− ½
109⅝	84	ComwOil cv4¼s92	10	104	103½	103½	− ½
89	80	Con Edis 5s87	2	83⅛	83⅛	83⅛	+ ⅛
87	76	Con Edis 4¾s91	5	78½	78½	78½	− ½
82½	73¼	Con Edis 4⅝s93	5	76	76	76	.....
82¾	74	Con Edis 4⅝s91	4	80½	80½	80½	.....
77	69	Con Edis 4s88	27	70	69⅞	70	+1
73½	68½	Con Edis 3⅜s82	5	71	71	71	− ¼
88½	84¾	Con Edis 3s72	8	87⅝	87½	87½	.....
70	63⅛	Con Edis 2¾s82	10	66	66	66	+1⅜
85½	77	GMot Acc 4⅝s83	20	79⅛	79	79	.....
84½	76	GMot Acc 4⅝s86	3	79⅞	79⅞	79⅞	− ⅛
82½	76	GMot Acc 4s79	22	77⅜	77⅛	77⅛	−1⅜
84¾	79¾	GMot Acc 3⅝s75	10	82⅛	82⅛	82⅛	+ ½
92	87⅝	GMot Acc 3½s72	13	90⅜	90⅛	90⅛	− ¼
99⅝	94½	GMot Acc 3s69	31	97 17-32	97½	97 17-32	+1-32
100	92¾	Gen Tel El 6¼s91	7	96¼	96¼	96¼	.....
111½	99¾	GenTel El cv5s92	74	108¾	107½	108¾	− ⅛
104¾	91	GenTel El cv4s90	25	97	96½	96⅞	+ ¼
193	105	G Time cv4¾s79	7	176	176	176	+1
114	82	GiddLew cv4⅝s87	2	96⅛	96⅛	96⅛	.....
75⅝	68¾	Glen Alden 6s88	889	71	70½	70½	− ⅝
126	105½	GordonJwy cv5s88	7	123	123	123	.....
94⅞	80½	Grace Co cv4¼s90	12	93	92¼	92½	+ ⅜
105¼	81¾	GranCStl cv4⅝s94	115	94½	93	94½	+1⅜
160	109¾	Grant cv4s90	5	141½	141½	141½	.....
130	100	GtNoPap cv4¼s91	8	130	130	130	.....
61	56⅛	Gt NRy 3⅛s90N	10	59⅜	59⅜	59⅜	.....
88	75	Gt West Unit 6s87	6	81	80½	80½	−1
112	93	GrnGiant cv4¼s92	11	111⅛	111⅛	111⅛	− ⅞
102⅞	81½	Grolier cv4¼s87	17	88	87	87	−1

MARKET DIARY

Issues traded	1,571	1,560	1,590	1,613	1,578	1,566
Advances	726	731	695	584	570	640
Declines	601	606	670	807	770	692
Unchanged	244	223	225	222	238	234
New highs, 1968	94	93	83	95	81	105
New lows, 1968	19	12	16	19	6	2

DOW-JONES CLOSING AVERAGES

		----TUESDAY----	
	1968	—Changes—	1967
Industrials	955.31	+ 5.35 +0.56%	904.36
Railroads	271.05	— 0.50 —0.18%	248.14
Utilities	130.14	— 0.16 —0.12%	125.32
Composite	340.41	+ 0.69 +0.20%	319.41

Ex-dividend of Columbia Gas System Inc., 38 cents, lowered the utility average by 0.13.
The ex-dividend lowered the composite average by 0.04.

OTHER MARKET INDICATORS

		1968	Change	1967
N.Y.S.E.	Composite	58.20	+ 0.13	52.80
	Industrial	60.89	+ 0.12	55.24
	Utility	45.30	+ 0.06	43.24
	Transportation	55.38	+ 0.28	50.74
	Financial	77.20	+ 0.57	52.64
Standard & Poor's Industrial		113.01	+ 0.25	103.40
American Exchange Price Index ...		$30.77	+$0.09	$22.55
N.Q.B. Over-Counter Industrial		418.21	+ 1.49	339.83

Volume of advancing stocks on N.Y.S.E., 6,810,000 shares; volume of declining stocks, 5,280,000. On American S.E., volume of advancing stocks, 3,380,000; volume of declining stocks, 2,230,000.

MOST ACTIVE STOCKS

	Open	High	Low	Close	Chg.	Volume
Occiden Pet	42¾	42⅞	41	41⅜	—1¼	255,000
Freept Sul	40¾	40¾	38½	39⅜	—1⅛	175,000
Am Motors	14⅜	14⅜	13⅞	14⅛	— ⅛	160,000
Am Tel Tel	54¾	55¼	54½	54⅞	+ ¼	155,600
St Reg Pap	41⅞	42⅛	40¾	41⅞	— ⅛	150,300
Boeing	57⅜	57⅝	56½	56½	—1	138,400
Mad S Gar	11⅛	12½	11	12¼	+1¼	109,900
Caro Pw Lt	37¼	37¼	35¾	36⅛	— ⅞	105,100
Grant WT	40⅜	40⅜	39¾	39⅞	— ½	94,300
Lionel Corp	10⅞	10⅞	10¼	10⅜	— ½	85,500

Average closing price of most active stocks: 34.67

corporation there is a column that shows the year's high and low prices. This is called the *range*. Early in the year—e.g., January—the range is given for the previous year. Later, in February, the range covers all of the previous year and the current year to date. During March, the range for the previous year is dropped, and only the current year is quoted. The range column is important because it shows how a stock stands on any given day as compared with recent months.

The abbreviated name of the issue is usually followed by the dividend rate being paid on the stock. This dividend figure is only an approximation. Occasionally, the dividend figure is followed by a letter such as a or e. These apply to special explanations about the dividends that are given in footnotes at the bottom of the tabulation.

To save space, the day's sales are shown in units of 100. For example, sales of 15,000 shares would be indicated as 150. Four prices are shown for each listed security, as follows. The *open* is the price at which the opening sale of the day was made. The *high* is the highest price at which the stock sold during the trading session that day. The *low* is the lowest price for the day. The *close* is the last or final sale for the day. The *net change* is the difference between the closing price for that day and the closing price for the previous day. It is not the difference between the day's high and low.

Net change is affected by dividend payments. When directors of a corporation vote to pay dividends, a certain date is set as the *date of record,* or the date that the books are closed. All stockholders on the books of the corporation at the record date are entitled to receive the declared dividend. A stock is said to sell *ex-dividend* after the list of stockholders is copied from the stock record books. According to New York Stock Exchange rules, a stock goes ex-dividend on the third full business day before the list of stockholders is made up. When a stock goes ex-dividend, it may fall in price by the amount of the dividend.

All stocks in the newspaper stock tables are considered common stocks unless otherwise specified. Preferred stocks are reported by inserting pf after the name of the issue and before the annual dividend figure. For an example, refer to page 180, under Acan.

The sections "Other Market Indicators" and "Most Active Stocks" contains a number of interesting statistics, including: the volume (number of shares) traded; the number of stocks that advanced in price, declined, and remained unchanged; and details concerning the stocks that had the most active trading. This information is important because many experts believe that a genuine rise in prices must be accompanied by a corresponding increase in the volume of shares sold. The *average daily volume* varies in different periods. In 1957, the average daily volume was about 2.2 million shares. In 1966, the daily average was approximately 7.5 million, a substantial increase.

NYSE commission rates

The minimum commission schedules for NYSE transactions for non-members are as follows.

Minimum Non-Member Commission Rates on Stocks, and Warrants Selling at $1.00 per Share and Above.

On single transactions not exceeding 100 shares based upon the amount of money involved the following rates apply:

Money Value	Commission
If less than $ 100	As mutually agreed
$ 100 to $ 399	2% plus $ 3.00
$ 400 to $2,399	1% plus $ 7.00
$2,400 to $4,999	½% plus $19.00
$5,000 and above	1/10% plus $39.00

Odd lots—(less than a unit of trading). Same rates as above, less $2.00.[16]

Minimum commissions—(notwithstanding above, each transaction is subject to the following): Minimum commission on any single transaction of 100 shares or less will not exceed $75, with a maxi-

---

16/ The lowered commission rate is compensated for due to execution of the transaction at a price that includes the odd-lot differential.

mum charge of $1.50 per share. Where $100 or more is involved, the minimum commission is $6.00 per transaction.

To determine the commission charge to be made on a transaction involving multiples of 100 shares, e.g., 200, 300, 400, etc., shares, multiply the applicable 100 share commission by 2, 3, 4, etc., respectively as the case may be.

Minimum Commission on Bonds
for N.Y. Stock Exchange
Price per $1,000 (principal) Bond

Less than $10	*$10 and above but under $100*	*$100 and above*
$0.75 ea.	$1.25 ea.	$2.50 ea.

Competition normally forces all firms to charge the minimum rates.[17] The aforementioned commissions are paid by both buyer and seller of a security. The seller of securities on the NYSE also pays transfer taxes and a National Securities Exchange (SEC) registration fee.

An excise tax is levied by the state of New York on all transfers of beneficial ownership of securities that take place within the state. A federal excise tax on transfers no longer exists (1968).

New York State Transfer Taxes

$0.01¼   per share under $5
$0.02½   per share between $5 and $10
$0.03¾   per share between $10 and $20
$0.05   per share $20 or more

The National Securities Exchange registration fee is 1/500 of 1 percent of the value of sales of nonexempted securities; for example:

100 shares sold at $40		$4,000.00
Less:		
Brokerage commission $39.00		
New York State tax 5.00		
SEC fee.............................. 0.08		44.08
Net Proceeds to Seller		$3,955.92

17/ A revision to the minimum rates has been proposed to the SEC by the NYSE, which would allow quantity discounts. It appears likely that the minimum commission rates of the New York Stock Exchange will be reduced for quantity purchases (e.g., 10,000 or more shares) which will benefit mutual funds and other large buyers of securities. A revised policy concerning "give-ups" is also expected to be agreed to by the NYSE and SEC.

8 | Review questions

316. A broker acts as .... in securities transactions.
1. an agent
2. a trustee
3. a principal
4. all of these

317. An over-the-counter broker gets paid for his services in securities transactions by ....
1. charging a commission
2. marking up the prices of securities
3. neither of these
4. both of these

318. A sale price that includes the dealer's markup is called ....
1. a market price
2. a bid price
3. an asked price
4. a high price

319. Securities prices are set by ....
1. the Securities and Exchange Commission
2. the law of supply and demand
3. the NASD
4. the Federal Reserve Board

320. A sale in which the seller does not own the securities he sells but borrows them to make delivery is called a ....
1. short sale
2. long sale
3. cash sale
4. none of these

321. A long sale is one in which ....
1. the seller does not own the securities he sells
2. the customer is allowed a long time to pay

3. the seller owns the securities he sells
4. the seller is allowed a long time to make delivery

322. An order that is to be executed as soon as possible at the best possible price is called ....
1. a limit order
2. an open order
3. a market order
4. a stop order

323. An order that becomes a market order as soon as the market price of the security reaches a certain specified price is called a ....
1. market order
2. stop order
3. GTC order
4. limit order

324. An order that can be executed only at a specified price or higher if it is an order to sell, or at a specified price or lower if it is an order to buy is called ....
1. an FOK order
2. an open order
3. a limit order
4. a GTC order

325. An order that is to be held on the books of the broker or dealer until it is either executed or canceled by the customer is called ....
1. a market order
2. an FOK order
3. a GTC order
4. a stop order

326. An FOK order ....
1. must be executed immediately or canceled

2. is good until canceled by the customer
3. must be executed at the limit price or better
4. becomes a market order when the price of the security reaches a specified amount

327. According to a rule of the Securities and Exchange Commission, no short sale of a security on a national securities exchange may take place at a price ....

1. lower than the price that security last sold at on the exchange
2. higher than the price that security last sold at on the exchange
3. the same as the price that security last sold at on the exchange
4. none of these

328. .... transactions that have taken place on the floor of the New York Stock Exchange are printed on the ticker tape.

1. All
2. Only odd-lot
3. Only round-lot
4. None of these

329. Unless otherwise indicated, all stocks printed on the ticker tape are ....

1. common stocks
2. speculative stocks
3. preferred stocks
4. growth stocks

330. If no volume is printed before the price of a security on the ticker tapes, this indicates that the amount traded was ....

1. 50 shares
2. 100 shares
3. 200 shares
4. 400 shares

331. The symbol 8s printed before the price on the ticker tape indicates that .... shares were traded.

1. 8,000
2. 80
3. 8
4. 800

332. In terms of dollars and share volume of business, the American Stock Exchange is more important than ....

1. the over-the-counter market
2. the New York Stock Exchange
3. all the regional changes combined
4. none of these

333. On the American Stock Exchange ....

1. only listed securities are traded
2. only unlisted securities are traded
3. only SEC-registered securities are traded
4. both 1 and 3
5. both 2 and 3

334. The practice of making a profit from simultaneous or nearly simultaneous transactions in securities, made possible because a security may be selling at different prices in different places, is called ....

1. arbitrage
2. a straddle
3. short selling
4. dollar cost averaging

335. National securities exchanges are subject to ....

1. federal regulation
2. self-regulation
3. state regulation
4. all of these

336. The newspaper quotations on over-the-counter securities are averages of prices taken from ....

1. all broker-dealers in the over-the-counter market
2. a few broker-dealers in the over-the-counter market

3. 85 percent of broker-dealers in the over-the-counter market
4. none of the above

337. If a customer gives a broker-dealer an order to buy securities, the broker-dealer may fill the order by ....

1. selling shares from his own inventory to the customer if he has the security in inventory
2. buying the securities, marking up the price, and reselling them to the customer on a dealer basis
3. acting as the customer's agent in finding a seller for the securities and arranging a sale
4. all of these

338. Subject market prices are ....

1. actual prices at which securities can be bought or sold
2. subject to confirmation
3. the subject of controversy
4. none of these

339. Securities listed on national securities exchanges ....

1. cannot be sold in the over-the-counter market
2. are often sold in the over-the-counter market as well as on the exchanges

340. The over-the-counter market is ....

1. an auction market
2. an exchange market
3. a negotiated market
4. none of these

341. If a broker-dealer has a security in inventory, he ....

1. owns shares of the security
2. is committed to buy and sell shares of the security
3. is considering purchasing shares of the security
4. none of these

342. A broker-dealer who is known to be ready and willing to buy or sell shares of a security at all times is said to ....

1. hold a position in the security
2. work out the market for the security
3. make a market in the security
4. hit the bid on the security

343. The prices at which a security can actually be bought and sold are called ....

1. subject prices
2. bid prices
3. firm prices
4. asked prices

344. Checking the market means ....

1. hitting the bid
2. making a market in a security
3. calling other broker-dealers on the telephone to obtain price quotations
4. reading the newspaper quotations on securities

345. Unless a broker-dealer states to the contrary, the prices he quotes are assumed to be ....

1. subject market prices
2. firm market prices
3. workout market prices
4. none of these

346. Wholesale prices for over-the-counter securities are published in ....

1. the pink sheets
2. *Time* magazine
3. *Life* magazine
4. none of these

347. The informally organized market consisting of broker-dealer houses throughout the country is called ....

1. the broker-dealer market
2. the over-the-counter market
3. the exchange
4. the stock market

348. The exchanges are primarily
....
1. auction markets
2. negotiated markets
3. both of the above
4. neither 1 nor 2

349. Any transaction that has not
taken place on an exchange is said to
have taken place ....
1. by private negotiation
2. by competitive bidding
3. in the over-the-counter market
4. none of these

350. The over-the-counter market is
primarily ....
1. an organized market
2. an auction market
3. a negotiated market
4. a subject market

351. The room where securities transactions take place on the New York
Stock Exchange is called the ....
1. post
2. floor
3. trading room
4. stock room

352. At the New York Stock Exchange, the power to make rules and regulations governing the conduct of members and to take disciplinary action
against members is vested in ....
1. the board of governors
2. the board of directors
3. the advisory council
4. the district commission

353. In order to conduct business on
the floor of the New York Stock Exchange, an individual must ....
1. be a floor trader
2. be a registered representative of the
NASD
3. own a seat on the exchange
4. none of these

354. The price of a seat on the New
York Stock Exchange during 1967 was
approximately ....
1. $ 1,250
2. $ 15,000
3. $400,000
4. $150,000

355. A floor member of the New
York Stock Exchange who specializes in
making a market for one or more listed
securities is called a(n) ....
1. odd-lot dealer
2. specialist
3. floor broker
4. floor trader

356. The price at which an odd-lot
transaction in a given security takes
place on the floor of the New York
Stock Exchange is based upon ....
1. the last odd-lot transaction in that security
2. the next round-lot transaction in that security
3. the last sale of that security that took
place at a price higher than the last preceding different sale price
4. none of these

357. A security that has met certain
minimum requirements and has been accepted for trading on an exchange is
called ....
1. a registered security
2. a listed security
3. a good security
4. an over-the-counter security

358. A price quotation for a security
must include ....
1. both the bid price and the asked price
2. both the quotation spread and the size of
the market
3. both the public offering price and the underwriters' spread
4. both the base price and the dividend rate

359. The charge an odd-lot dealer makes for his services is called a ....

1. base price
2. commission
3. differential
4. quotation spread

360. Under the Monthly Investment Plan of the New York Stock Exchange, ... can be purchased.

1. only unregistered securities
2. only unlisted securities
3. both listed and unlisted securities
4. only listed securities

361. Under the Monthly Investment Plan of the New York Stock Exchange, ...

1. the minimum investment is $400 per month, and the maximum investment is $1,000 per month
2. the minimum investment is $40 per quarter, and the maximum investment is $1,000 per month
3. the minimum investment is $40 per month, and the maximum investment is $100 per month

362. Unless a broker or dealer states to the contrary, the amount of securities represented in a firm price quotation is usually ....

Refer to page 260 for correct answers.

1. 5 shares of stock or 100 bonds
2. an odd lot of stock and a round lot of bonds
3. 100 shares of stock or 5 bonds
4. a round lot of stock and an odd lot of bonds

363. The prices quoted in the pink sheets represent ....

1. firm bids and offers
2. approximate prices at which brokers and dealers may expect to buy or sell securities
3. approximate prices at which the public may expect to buy and sell securities
4. none of these

364. In the pink sheets published by the National Quotations Bureau, the letters BW mean ....

1. broker wanted
2. bonds wanted
3. bids wanted
4. bad weather

365. All stockholders of a corporation who are on the books of the corporation at the .... are entitled to receive a declared dividend.

1. payment date
2. program date
3. declaration date
4. record date

9 | National Association of Securities Dealers (NASD)

Each person who enters the investment banking and securities business as a registered representative of a member of the National Association of Securities Dealers must certify, among other things, that he will comply with all provisions of the bylaws, Rules of Fair Practice, and related interpretations. He—no less so than his employer—thereby assumes, under the association's standards of business conduct, full responsibility for his actions.

Knowledge and understanding of the associations's rules are essential if a registered representative wants to build a career in the business, and wants to avoid involving himself and his employer in disciplinary action by the association. However, the task of learning these standards of conduct and abiding by them is not difficult. Association standards have evolved from the actual business practices of responsible firms in the business over a period of many years. Further, the existence of the NASD makes possible enforcement of these rules by responsible men who know the problems that all in the business must contend with, and who are qualified to differentiate between what is reasonable and unreasonable. They are themselves registered representatives with a vast collective experience in all phases of the securities business.

The background and status of the NASD

In 1933, when many industries were adopting National Industrial Recovery Act codes of fair competition, the investment banking business established its own code of fair practice. In 1935, the NIRA was declared unconstitutional, but the securities business code was continued under the auspices of the Investment Bankers Conference Committee, later the Investment Bankers Conference, Inc. In 1938, Congress adopted the *Maloney Act,* which amended the Securities Exchange Act of 1934 by adding a new section, 15A, covering regulation of the over-the-counter market. The Maloney Act provides for such regulation by national securities associations registered with the SEC. The National Association of Securities Dealers, Inc., is the only association registered under Section 15A of the Securities Exchange Act of 1934, and since 1939 the NASD has been the self-regulatory arm of the over-the-counter business. The Maloney Act provides for self-regulation of the over-the-counter market through rules designed to promote just and equitable principles of trade.

In the over-the-counter market, the NASD has powers similar, in many respects, to those of an exchange over its trading floor and its members, and like those of the SEC for regulating business transacted by non-NASD broker-dealers.

The purposes of the NASD as stated in the *Certificate of Incorporation* are as follows.

1. To promote through cooperative effort the investment banking and securities business, to standardize its principles and practices, to promote therein high standards of commercial honor, and to encourage and promote among members observance of Federal and State securities laws.

2. To provide a medium through which its membership may be enabled to confer, consult, and cooperate with governmental and other agencies in the solution of problems affecting investors, the public, and the investment banking and securities business.

3. To adopt, administer, and enforce rules of fair practice and rules to prevent fraudulent and manipulative acts and practices, and in general to promote just and equitable principles of trade for the protection of investors.

4. To promote self-discipline among members, and to investigate and adjust grievances between the public and members and between members.

The bylaws of the NASD

There are 15 articles in the NASD bylaws. Of particular importance are the articles discussed below.

Article I concerns membership. In general, any broker or dealer who is authorized to transact in and whose regular course of business consists of transacting in any branch of the investment banking or securities business in the United States is eligible for membership in the NASD. The firm must first be registered with the SEC and state authorities, if necessary. Membership in the NASD has never been required by law, though the SEC has urged that membership be made compulsory for all broker-dealer firms engaged in an interstate over-the-counter business.

Since the law authorizes NASD regulations that prevent NASD members from giving discounts, commissions, or concessions to nonmembers, non-NASD members are practically precluded from engaging successfully in underwriting or in most over-the-counter business. Approximately 600 firms engaged in the securities business are not NASD members. Most of these firms are: (1) exchange members not engaged in over-the-counter business; (2) dealers who sell real estate, insurance, and savings and loan shares; or (3) retailers of a single mutual fund group whose underwriter is not an NASD member. Such nonmember dealers do not transact business in the majority of mutual funds, whose underwriters are NASD members. Banks by definition are not broker-dealers, and thus are not eligible for membership in the association.

Brokerage firms that want to join the NASD must:

1. First register with the SEC.
2. Have a minimum capital of $5,000 or $2,500, as applicable.
3. Have their principals pass a written NASD examination for principals.
4. Have other associated persons pass a written NASD examination for registered representatives.

There are certain statutory bars to NASD membership. Applicants not eligible for NASD membership or registration as a representative, except by order of the SEC, include:

1. Broker-dealers who have been and are suspended or expelled from a registered securities association or a national securities exchange for acts inconsistent with just and equitable principles of trade.
2. Persons subject to an SEC order denying or revoking broker-dealer registration.
3. Persons who have been convicted within the preceding 10 years of a felony or misdemeanor involving embezzlement, fraudulent conversion, misappropriation of funds, or abuse or misuse of a fiduciary relationship.
4. An individual who has been named a cause of a suspension, expulsion, or revocation, or one whose registration as a representative has been revoked by the NASD or a registered stock exchange.
5. Broker-dealers who have a partner, officer, or employee not qualified for membership, or one who is required to be but is not registered.

In addition to the above-mentioned statutory bars to membership, certain permissive bars also exist. These include qualification standards with respect to training, experience, and such other qualifications as the NASD Board of Governors finds necessary and desirable. For admission to membership, as opposed to registration as a representative of a member, certain financial responsibility standards must be met and maintained.

It is important to understand the meaning of the terms "broker," "dealer," "investment banking or securities business," and "member."

The term *broker* means any individual, corporation, partnership, or other legal entity engaged in the business of effecting transactions in securities for others, but banks are not included.

The term *dealer* means any individual, corporation, partnership, or other legal entity engaged in the business of buying and selling securities for his own account. Not included, however, are banks or any persons who buy or sell securities for their own accounts other than as a part of a regular business.

The term *investment banking or securities business* means a broker's or dealer's business of underwriting or distributing issues of securities, or of purchasing securities and offering the same for sale as a dealer, or of purchasing and selling securities on the order and for the account of others. This term does not include transactions on organized securities exchanges. Thus, a broker who handles only stocks traded on the New York Stock Exchange and who is registered with the exchange need not be an NASD member.

The term *member* means any broker or dealer admitted to membership in the NASD.

As mentioned previously, the two categories of registration with the NASD are principals and representatives. All persons associated with a member who are designated as principals must be registered and must pass a qualification examination, which is more difficult and comprehensive than the examination for registered representatives. Persons required to pass the principal's exam include those active in the conduct of the members' business who are: (1) sole proprietors of a member firm, (2) partners, (3) managers of offices of supervisory jurisdiction, (4) officers, and (5) directors.

Any person who was registered with the NASD in the functions 1 to 5, above, on or before October 1, 1965, is not required to pass the exam unless his registration as a principal has been terminated for a period of two years or more.

Registration of representatives, which is required by Schedule C of Article I of the bylaws, is described further in this chapter under Article XV of the bylaws.

Article I further provides that NASD membership may be terminated only by formal written resignation. Resignations do not normally take effect until 30 days after receipt by the Board of Governors, until all indebtedness to the NASD is paid in full, and until any pending complaints against the member are settled.

Article I provides that each branch office of a member shall be registered with the NASD. Since fees to the NASD are based upon (1) income (0.07 percent of gross), (2) number of branch offices ($30 each), (3) number of registered representatives ($3.00 each), and (4) a basic membership fee of $85, the importance of branch office registration becomes obvious.

Members must notify the NASD of the opening and closing of branch offices. A branch office includes corporate subsidiaries of the member and is any office: (1) located in the United States, (2) owned or controlled by the member, and (3) engaged in the investment banking or securities business.

Criteria used in determining whether a business location is a branch office include: (1) a substantial part of expenses, such as rent or taxes, are paid by the member; and (2) the member lists the location, in a telephone directory or other publication, as an office. NASD District Committees have the right to determine that an office is a branch office. A branch office may or may not also be an office of supervisory jurisdiction, as described later in this chapter under Article 27 of the Rules of Fair Practice.

Article I of the bylaws prescribes that application for membership be made to the NASD Board of Governors on prescribed forms, which, among other things, contain:

1. Agreement of the applicant to comply with the NASD Certificate of Incorporation, bylaws, rules and regulations, and decisions of the Board of Governors or other authorized committees.

2. Agreement to pay dues, assessments, and other charges.

3. Agreement that the NASD, its offices, employees, and board of governors shall not normally be liable to the applicant for official actions.

Membership applications are cleared through the appropriate NASD District Committee before approval and must be submitted with a non-refundable application fee, an assessment report describing branch offices, a financial statement, and resume of principal's experience. The application requires the appointment of an executive representative, normally the proprietor, partner, or corporate officer, who represents the member firm, votes, and acts for the member in NASD affairs.

NASD members must designate one district executive for each district where the member maintains a branch office, except for the district where the member's main office is located. At the main office, the member's executive representative suffices. The district executive representative is entitled to one vote on all district matters.

The NASD Board of Governors issued a ruling, described later in this chapter, that provides for disciplinary action when (1) misleading data is submitted in the application for membership of a firm, or its representatives, or (2) representatives have not been properly registered with the NASD.

Article III of the bylaws deals with dues, assessments and other charges imposed on the members, and provides for disciplinary action in the event of failure to pay. The NASD Board of Governors or president, after 15 days' notice in writing, may suspend or cancel a membership for failure to pay dues, assessments, or other charges, or for failure to furnish information requested in connection with determining such charges. The NASD president must suspend any member who fails to apply for registration as a representative of any person within 15 days after request.

Article IV describes the organization and administration of the NASD. It establishes the Board of Governors as the governing body; and establishes 13 Local District Committees, comprised of up to 12 members, elected for 3-year terms, as agents of the Board of Governors in administering the rules and regulations on a local level. The 23-man NASD Board of Governors includes 21 governors elected by the districts and one governor-at-large, each of whom serves a 3-year term. The board and the NASD president manage the affairs of the NASD and may:

1. Propose to the membership changes in the bylaws or Rules of Fair Practice.
2. Make regulations and issue orders, resolutions, interpretations, decisions, and so on.
3. Prescribe maximum penalties for violations of the bylaws, NASD rules and regulations, and orders, decisions, and directions of the NASD Board of Governors or authorized committee.
4. Select officers, counsel, and other employees.

When the Board of Governors is not in session, the affairs of the NASD are administered by the Executive Committee, composed of five or more members of the board. Disciplinary action taken by the Executive Committee is not binding until approved by the board.

The board is advised on matters of local policy by its Advisory Council, which consists of the chairmen of the 13 District Committees. Each district is also represented on the board by one or more representatives who are elected to 3-year terms.

Members of the NASD Board of Governors and District Committees serve without pay.

Article V provides for the election by the NASD Board of Governors of a chairman, selected from among the governors. It also provides that the board select a chief executive officer, the NASD president, to manage and administer the affairs of the NASD.

Article VI of the bylaws prescribes that each District Committee appoint a District Business Conduct Committee (DBCC), of up to 12 members, at least one of whom is also a member of the District Committee. Such DBCC's may also appoint Local Business Conduct Committees, as they deem necessary. In actual practice, the District Committee also functions as the District Business Conduct Committee. Please refer to the organization chart below.

13 districts covering the United States

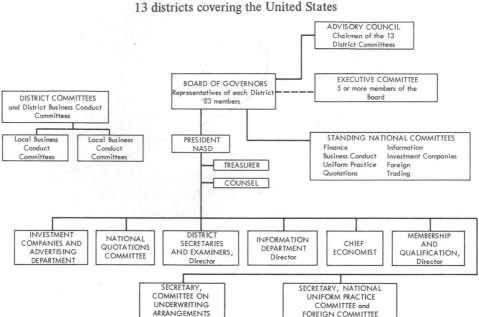

Article VII provides for the establishment of Rules of Fair Practice, and empowers the Board of Governors to prescribe penalties for violations as well as to interpret the rules. A full discussion of the Rules of Fair Practice follows later in this chapter.

Article VIII of the bylaws prevents *use of the name* of the association except as authorized by the board.

It is permissible to indicate membership in the association, as follows.

1. As a matter of record, in trade directories or other business listings.
2. For identification on letterheads, booklet covers, advertising, sales literature headings, market letters, and others, as long as the association's name is in a smaller size type and with less emphasis than that used for the firm's name.
3. On the door or entranceway of a member's principal and registered branch offices, in the form "Member, National Association of Securities Dealers, Inc."

4. In institutional or any other type of general print, as long as:
   a) Use is solely and exclusively for identifying the firm as a member.
   b) It is used only in proximity to and in conjunction with the firm name.
   c) It carries no implied or specific indication of NASD approval of the securities or services discussed in the advertisement.
   d) It is separate and apart from the primary text material in the advertisement.
   e) It is always in a smaller size type and has less emphasis than the firm name.
5. On confirmation forms in the following language: "This transaction (if over-the-counter) has been executed in conformity with the rules and regulations of the Uniform Practice Code of the National Association of Securities Dealers, Inc."

It is prohibited to use the name of the NASD in a fraudulent or misleading manner in connection with the promotion or sale of any specific security or in connection with any other aspect of the member's business, or to imply orally, visually, or in writing that the NASD endorses, indemnifies, or guarantees any member's business practices, selling methods, or class or type of securities offered. Any violation of the above will be considered a violation of the Rules of Fair Practice, which are described later in this chapter.

Article IX provides for adopting additions, alterations, or amendments to the bylaws on proposal of any member of the board, by resolution of a District Committee, or by petition of any 25 NASD members. After approval by the board, the change must be approved by a majority of the membership.

Article XV of the bylaws concerns registration of registered representatives. This article is of great importance to every registered representative and every candidate for registration as a registered representative, because the article defines "registered representative," gives registration requirements, outlines the procedures to be observed in registering representatives, states the steps required for termination of registration, and makes clear that NASD Rules and bylaws are binding on individuals as well as members. Application for registration is made through the member firm on a prescribed form, which contains acceptance of the bylaws, agreement not to hold the NASD liable for official actions, and personal history data. The application must be accompanied by an application fee of $25, and if applicable an examination fee of $20 for prospective registered representatives and $25 for prospective registered principals.

The term "registered representative" means every officer and every partner of a member, and every employee or representative of a member:
1. Who is engaged in the managing, supervision, solicitation, or handling of listed or unlisted business in securities.
2. Who is engaged in the trading of listed or unlisted securities.
3. Who is engaged in the sale of listed or unlisted securities on an agency or principal basis.
4. Who is engaged in the solicitation of subscriptions to investment advisory or to investment management services furnished on a fee basis.
5. Who has been delegated general supervision over foreign business.
6. Who is engaged in training persons for the above functions.

Employees are *not* required to be registered representatives if work is confined solely to: (1) exempted securities; (2) commodities, if the employee is registered by a national commodities exchange; (3) trading on a national securities exchange, if the employee is registered by the national securities exchange.

Additionally, registration is not required for: (1) persons whose activities are solely and exclusively clerical or ministerial; (2) persons who serve only as nominal corporate officers or who have participated only in the capital of the member as investors; (3) foreign associates, who to be so classified must be neither a U.S. citizen, nor resident in the United States, her territories, or possessions, nor may business be conducted by the individual with U.S. citizens, residents of the United States, her territories, or possessions. Several other minor requirements also pertain to foreign associates.

Otherwise, no member shall permit any person to transact in any branch of the investment banking or securities business as a representative of a member unless such person be registered with the NASD as a registered representative of that member. This is a significant restriction in that it *prohibits the use of unregistered* trainees and office personnel as order takers or salesmen. Before an individual may become a registered representative, he must pass a written examination administered by the NASD, and sign an agreement to abide by the NASD bylaws, rules, regulations, decisions, and penalties. This agreement is included as part of the NASD application form for registration as a registered representative.

Registration as a registered representative may be voluntarily terminated at any time by formal resignation in writing to the Board of Governors. The resignation does not take effect until 30 days after the Board of Governors receive the written resignation or so long as there is any complaint or action pending against the registered representative.

Registered representatives may not transfer their registration or any right arising therefrom. This means that a representative changing from one employer to another must terminate his registration and reregister with his new employer.

Any representative whose most recent NASD registration has been terminated for a period of two years or more must pass a qualification examination for representatives before the filing of a new NASD application for membership. The qualification exam covers the subjects described in this book.

By informal agreement among the Board of Governors of the Federal Reserve, the Federal Deposit Insurance Corporation, and the NASD, bank employees or directors of banks that are members of the Federal Reserve System and FDIC are not allowed to become engaged in the securities business due to possible conflicts of interest that would be likely to develop.

No person may be registered as a representative who:

1. Is subject to an NASD order that suspends or revokes his registration.
2. Is subject to an SEC order that revokes or denies his broker-dealer registration.
3. Was named as a cause of a suspension currently in effect, or of an expulsion or revocation by the SEC or the NASD.

4. Is subject to a National Securities Exchange order revoking or suspending his registration for conduct inconsistent with just and equitable principles of trade.
5. Has been convicted within the preceding 10 years of a felony or misdemeanor involving the purchase or sale of a security, or of any felony or misdemeanor that the NASD finds has involved embezzlement, misappropriation of money, fraud, or abuse of a fiduciary relationship.

A second category of registration is that of principals. Principals include those who are engaged in the management of a member's business, such as sole proprietors, partners, officers, managers of offices of supervisory jurisdiction, and directors of corporations.

The examination for principals, for which up to three hours is allowed, includes essay-type problems as well as multiple-choice questions. The two-hour examination for registered representatives includes 125 multiple-choice questions similar to those at the end of each chapter in this textbook.

The minimum passing grade is 80 percent. Applicants who fail the examination must undergo a waiting period before they may retake the test, as follows:

Failures	Waiting Period
First failure	30 days
Second failure	60 days
Third and subsequent failures	90 days

The application fee is $25 for each application filed with the NASD, plus an examination fee of $20 for registered representatives and $25 for principals. The subjects covered in the NASD tests are described in the NASD pamphlet *Study Outline for Qualification Examinations for Registered Representatives and Registered Principals,* which is available for 15 cents from the NASD, Executive Office, 888 Seventeenth Street N.W., Washington, D.C. 20006.

The examination for registered representatives may also be combined, at a single session, with the exam for full or limited registration with the New York, American, and Pacific Coast Stock Exchanges. The exam for principals is also coordinated with the exam for members and allied members of these three exchanges. Several states also coordinate their exams with the NASD.

Examinations are conducted in approximately 70 cities throughout the United States, and in various U.S. embassies and consulates abroad. After a prospective registered representative has submitted his application for registration, through the member firm he wants to become associated with, a certificate of admission to an examination center is mailed to the member firm by the NASD. Details of times and places for exams are stated in a schedule, which accompanies the certificate of admission.

Rules of Fair Practice

The Rules of Fair Practice are a code of ethical conduct. Adopted under the bylaws by the association membership, the rules govern members' and registered representatives' dealings with the public and other members.

The 28 sections of Article III of the Rules of Fair Practice spell out the rules that have been adopted by the membership to promote and enforce just and equitable principles of trade, to prevent fraudulent and manipulative acts and practices, to provide safeguards against unreasonable profits or unreasonable rates of commission or other charges, to protect investors and the public interest, and to collaborate with governmental and other agencies in the promotion of fair practices and the elimination of fraud. It should be noted that while the rules frequently use the term "member" in their language, a registered representative of a member is under the same duties and obligations as a member under the Rules of Fair Practice. Important sections of the rules include the following.

Section 1. A member, in the conduct of his business, shall observe high standards of commercial honor, and just and equitable principles of trade. This section is the keystone of the Rules of Fair Practice.

Within this framework, it is a violation for a member to directly or indirectly publish, circulate, or distribute any advertisement, sales literature, or market letter that the member knows or has reason to know contains any untrue statement of a material fact or is otherwise false or misleading. Such advertisements, literature, and so on will be considered as governed by section 1, if they involve: (1) an offer to purchase or sell a security, (2) the offering of securities analysis or investment advice, or (3) offers of employment as a registered representative.

Sales literature relating to investment companies is governed by the SEC Statement of Policy and is excluded from this section. Also excluded are materials not for public use, tombstone ads, and announcements relating solely to personnel changes of the member.

Each item of advertising and sales literature and each market letter must be approved in writing, before use, by an official of the member designated to supervise such matters.

Disciplinary actions have been taken in violation of Article III, section 1, in the following cases:

1. Failure to register salesmen.
2. Allowing salesmen to engage in securities transactions before registration.
3. Exaggerated and misleading advertising and sales literature.
4. Failure to promptly remit dividends.
5. Free-riding and withholding, discussed later in this chapter.

Section 2. In recommending to a customer the purchase, sale, or exchange of any security, a member shall have reasonable grounds for believing that the *recommendation is suitable* for such customer upon the basis of the facts if any, disclosed by such customer, about his other security holdings and about his financial situation and needs. In this connection, please refer to the Board of Governors interpretations of this section, concerning "Fair Dealing with Customers," "Breakpoint Sales," and "Selling Dividends."

The guideline on *fair dealing* with customers points out several types of selling practices that have resulted in NASD disciplinary action against members and salesmen in violation of section 2. These include such activities as:

1. Recommending speculative low-priced securities without knowledge of or an attempt to ascertain the customer's financial position, as in high-pressure telephone campaigns.
2. Excessive activity, or churning—the practice of brokers who induce a customer to buy and sell securities repeatedly without proper justification.
3. Trading in mutual fund (i.e., investment company shares, especially on short-term basis).
4. Fraudulent activity, such as use of fictitious accounts.
5. Abuse of discretionary authority, as in excess of the authority granted.
6. Unauthorized transactions as, for example, placing an order for a customer that he has not requested.
7. Private transactions, such as a registered representative's canceling transactions from his employer.
8. Misuse of customer funds or securities.
9. Activities that violate civil and criminal laws.
10. Recommending purchases in amounts beyond the financial means of customers.

The Board of Governors has issued a policy concerning the *sale of dividends* and distributions of investment companies in connection with section 2 of the rules. It is essential that investors understand the difference between dividends paid from net investment income and distributions paid from realized security profits. If an investor buys shares shortly before an ex-dividend date, he should understand that no advantage accrues by reason of his purchase in anticipation of a distribution, since the amount of such distribution is included in the price he pays for the shares. The net asset value of a mutual fund always is reduced on the ex-dividend date by the exact amount of the declared dividend. Therefore, a prospective buyer who purchases shares before a dividend is declared would be paying for that dividend in the purchase price.

An NASD policy in connection with section 2 of Article III of the rules prohibits *"breakpoint sales"*—that is, the sale of investment company shares in dollar amounts just below the point at which the sales charge is reduced on quantity transactions. Such sales, which allow the dealer to share in the higher sales charges applicable on transactions just below the breakpoint, are contrary to just and equitable principles of trade. Investment company underwriters and sponsors, as well as dealers, have a definite responsibility in such matters, and failure to discourage and discontinue such practices will not be countenanced.

Section 3. Any *charges* for services performed for customers, such as collection of dividends, be reasonable and not unfairly discriminatory between customers.

Section 4. In the over-the-counter market, principal transactions must be effected at a *fair price*. When the member acts as an agent, the commission or service charge must be fair.

Since the important question of what constitutes a fair price is not easily answered, it is necessary to examine the NASD markup policy, also known as the NASD *5 percent policy*. The basic policy is: "It shall be deemed conduct inconsistent with just and equitable principles of trade for a member to enter into any transaction with a customer in any security at any price not reasonably related to the current market price of the security or to charge a commission which is not reasonable." Some general considerations regarding the 5 percent policy include the following.

1. The 5 percent policy is a guide, not a rule.
2. Markups may not be justified on the basis of expenses that are excessive.
3. The markup over the prevailing market price is the significant spread from the point of view of fairness of dealings with customers in principal transactions.
4. A markup pattern of 5 percent or even less may be considered unfair or unreasonable under the 5 percent policy.
5. Determination of the fairness of markups must be based on consideration of all relevant factors, of which percentage markups is only one.

Some of the relevant factors are as follows.

1. *The type of security involved.* For example, a common stock transaction customarily receives a higher percentage markup than does a bond transaction of the same size.
2. *The availability of the security in the market.* In the case of an inactive security, the cost and effort of buying or selling the security may have a bearing on the amount of markup justified.
3. *The price of the security.* The percentage markup generally decreases as the price of the security increases.
4. *The amount of money involved.* A small transaction may warrant a larger percentage markup to cover expenses of handling.
5. *Full disclosure.* While disclosure to the customer before the transaction does not of itself justify a markup or commission that is unfair or excessive in the light of all other circumstances, it is still a factor to be considered.
6. *The pattern of markup.* Each transaction must stand on its own. However, when reviewing transactions of a member attention is paid to any apparent pattern of markups.
7. *The nature of member's business.* There are differences among members in the services provided to customers. To some degree, the costs of these services and facilities are properly considered in determining fairness of markups.

The 5 percent policy applies to the following types of transactions in the over-the-counter market.

1. *A riskless or simultaneous transaction.* This is a transaction in which a member buys a security to fill an order for the same security received from a customer.

2. *A sale to a customer from inventory.* The amount of markup should be determined on the basis of the bona fide current market. The amount of profit or loss to the member due to market appreciation or depreciation of his inventory does not ordinarily enter into determination of the amount of fairness of the markup.
3. *Purchase of a security from a customer.* The markdown must be reasonably related to the prevailing market price of the security.
4. *Agency transactions.* The commission charged must be fair in the light of all relevant circumstances.
5. *Sales to or through a member, with the proceeds used to purchase other securities from or through the member.* This is viewed as one transaction. In such cases, the profit or commission on the liquidated securities must be taken into consideration in computing the markup on the securities purchased by the customer.

The NASD markup policy does not apply to the sale of securities when a prospectus or offering circular is required to be delivered and the securities are sold at the specific public offering price. Thus, the sale of new issues and of open-end investment company shares are not covered by the policy.

Section 5. Members are prohibited from circulating fictitious reports about transactions in securities. The quotation of bid or asked prices unless such quotations are bona fide is also prohibited. If nominal quotations are used, the member must clearly indicate that. Further description of procedures involving price quotations are given later in this chapter.

Section 6. Members are prohibited from making an offer to buy or sell any security at a *stated price* unless willing to consummate the transaction. NASD members must clearly identify quotations as subject if the member is not prepared to buy or sell a normal trading unit, as is required when a firm quotation is given.

Section 7. Selling syndicates and selling groups are required to clearly reveal in their agreements how much and to whom concessions may be allowed. The agreement must also specify the public offering price of the securities or the formula for determining it.

Selling syndicate is an investment banking term used when a group of investment bankers form a syndicate and commit themselves to purchase an underwriting with their own money, hoping to eventually resell it to the public. A selling group differs from the selling syndicate in that the selling group does not purchase an issue with its own money, but merely acts as sales agents on a best-efforts basis.

Section 8. A member of a selling syndicate or a selling group must allow a fair market price for securities taken in trade, or must sell them for the customer on an agency basis.

Section 9. No member may make use of information obtained through his fiduciary capacity as paying agent, transfer agent, or trustee.

Section 10. No member may directly or indirectly influence or reward any employee of another firm without prior written consent of the employer. This also applies to employees of firms not in the security business.

Section 11. Members may not directly or indirectly influence any newspaper, investment service, or similar publication on any matter that may effect the market price of a security. This does not, of course, apply to paid advertising.

Section 12. A member, at or before completion of each transaction, must disclose by written *confirmation* to the customer whether he is acting as broker or dealer. When a member is acting as a broker, he must furnish or be prepared to furnish information about the identity of the other purchaser or seller, the date and time of the transaction, and the source and amount of commission received by the member from all sources. When a member acts as a dealer, he is not required to disclose his profit on a transaction.

In effect, for each transaction disclosure must be made concerning whether the member is acting as: (1) a broker for the customer and the other party to the transaction, (2) a broker for the other party, (3) the customer's broker, or (4) a dealer for his own account.

Additional data required on confirmations is described later in this chapter, under sections 9 to 11 of the Uniform Practice Code.

Special rules apply to confirmations issued to customers in connection with "third-market" transactions. *The third market* is one in which several NASD firms, which are not also New York Stock Exchange members, make a market in various securities listed on the exchange. The special rules apply to NASD members who act as brokers for their customers in effecting a third-market transaction. Transactions on the third market are often at the most recent price quoted on the exchange plus or minus a small differential. Suggested legends for confirmations issued by the NASD member who effects a third-market transaction for a customer are as follows.

1. When a purchase is made for a customer: "The securities (e.g., 100 shares) were purchased from a dealer who confirmed the transaction at a price of $20 plus 1/8. However, the 1/8, or $12.50 (for 100 shares) is paid by us out of our commission."
2. In a sale for the customer: "These securities (e.g., 100 shares) were sold to a dealer who confirmed the transaction at a price of $20 minus 1/8. However, the 1/8, or $12.50 (for 100 shares) is paid by us out of our commission."

Both the dollar amount and the fractional differential must be shown, and the dollar amount must be the total amount absorbed by the member who executed the retail transaction for his customer.

Special rules also apply to transactions in securities that may be subject to the interest equalization tax. These regulations are discussed later in this chapter, under the "Good Delivery" section of the Uniform Practice Code.

Section 13. Written disclosure to a customer is required of a member in control of or by an issuer of securities before any contract is executed with the customer.

Section 14. A member who is participating in, or has financial interest in, a primary or secondary distribution (underwriting) must furnish to customers written notification of this fact before completion of the transaction when:

1. The member acts as an agent for the customer, or receives a fee from him for financial advice.

2. The customer is purchasing a security in which the member is participating or has a financial interest.

Section 15. A *discretionary account* is one in which the customer gives the broker or dealer discretion, either entirely or within specified limits, in the purchase and sale of securities, including selection, timing, and the price to be paid or received. No member or registered representative may exercise any discretionary power in a customer's account unless such customer has given prior written authorization to a stated individual or individuals, and the account has been accepted in writing by the member.

Discretionary orders must be approved promptly and in writing by the member, and discretionary accounts must be reviewed at frequent intervals to detect and prevent transactions that are excessive in size or frequency in view of the financial resources and character of the account. Records of transactions in discretionary accounts must be maintained for two years by the member.

Sections 16 and 17. These sections pertain to members who are participating in or who are financially interested in primary or secondary distributions. Section 16 prohibits representations to a client that offerings are being made *at the market,* unless the member has reason to believe that such a market exists other than that made by him. Section 17 prohibits members from paying someone else (e.g., another broker) to solicit anyone to make purchases on an exchange that would facilitate a primary or secondary distribution.

Section 18. The use of manipulative, deceptive, or other fraudulent devices to induce the purchase or sale of securities is banned. Misleading sales literature, breakpoint sales, and violation of various other sections of the Rules of Fair Practice could also be a violation of section 18.

Section 19. Members may not make *improper use* of a customer's securities of funds, or hypothecate (pledge) or lend more of a customer's securities as collateral than is fair and reasonable in view of the indebtedness of the customer to the member. Hypothecation is the pledging of customers' securities to lenders as collateral in order to obtain loans.

Members may not borrow or lend a customer's securities without first obtaining written permission. If a member has permission to lend a customer's fully paid for securities, which are in excess of the customer's indebtedness, such securities must be segregated and clearly identify the customer's interest in those securities. SEC rules on hypothecation adopted under the Securities Exchange Act of 1934 have a number of important provisions, which can be summarized as follows.

A broker or dealer may not hypothecate or pledge securities carried for the account of his customers:

1. In such a way as to permit the securities of one customer to be commingled with the securities of other customers, unless he first obtains the written consent of each such customer.
2. Under a lien for a loan made to the broker or dealer in a way that permits such securities to be commingled with the securities of any person other than a bona fide customer.

3. In such a way as to permit the liens or claims of pledges thereon to exceed the aggregate indebtedness of all such customers in respect of securities carried for their account.

This section also provides that no member may guarantee a customer against loss, or share in profits or losses of a customer, except in certain rare cases.

Section 20. Noncash or installment purchases of securities by customers from a member are prohibited, except:

1. When acting as agent, the member must actually buy, take delivery and hold the security for as long as he remains obligated to deliver the security to the customer.
2. When acting as principal, the member must actually own the security at the time of the transaction and continue to hold it for as long as he is under obligation to deliver it to the customer.
3. As provided by regulation T, the member is prohibited from hypothecating securities held under section 20 in amounts in excess of the customer's indebtedness.

Section 21. Books and other records, correspondence, memos, and so on must be maintained in conformity with federal and state laws and NASD rules. Additional requirements for customer records include maintenance of the following information: name; address; age; signature of registered representative introducing the account; signature of officer, partner, or manager accepting the account; and notation if the customer is employed by another member. A file or record of customer complaints and action taken with regard to such complaints must be maintained in each office of supervisory jurisdiction. Chapter 5, concerning the Securities Act of 1934, further details records that must be kept by members.

Section 22. A member must disclose to a bona fide customer, on request, information concerning the member's financial condition. Members are also required, in certain circumstances, to furnish their financial statements to other members.

Sections 23 to 25. These important sections contain the provisions concerning the discounts, concessions, and allowances on transactions between members. *No NASD member is permitted to deal with any nonmember broker or dealer except at the same prices, for the same commissions or fees, and on the same terms and conditions as are accorded to the general public by the member.* Thus, only NASD members may receive price concessions, discounts, and so on from other members. Since most underwritings, mutual fund underwriters, and over-the-counter business is transacted by NASD members, loss, suspension, or denial of NASD membership imposes a severe economic penalty.

Selling concessions, discounts, or other allowances are allowed only as a consideration for services rendered in distribution, and in no event shall be allowed to anyone other than a broker or dealer actually engaged in the investment banking or securities business. Sales to persons other than such brokers or dealers must be made at a net dollar price, without allowing a discount. Thus, no member may give a selling concession, discount, or commission to:

1. The public.

2. Nonmember brokers or dealers, even though they are registered with the SEC.
3. Bank or trust companies.
4. A member of a national securities exchange that is not an NASD member for an over-the-counter purchase.

No member may join with any nonmember (including a member of a national securities exchange) in any syndicate or group for distributing securities to the public, and no member may buy or sell any securities from any nonmember except at the same price accorded to the general public. There are three exceptions.

1. Commissions may be paid to nonmember broker-dealers in foreign countries who are ineligible for membership, provided the foreign broker agrees that in making sales to purchasers within the United States of securities acquired as a result of such transactions, such sales will be made without any selling concessions or discount.
2. Members may join with nonmembers or banks to distribute exempted securities, which are U.S. government obligations or obligations guaranteed by the U.S. government.
3. Members may allow discounts to nonmembers who are members of a registered securities association. However, the only such association at present is the NASD.

Sections 23 to 25 allow the following type of transaction: A member may pay a commission to a member of a national securities exchange for executing an order on the exchange, even though the exchange member is not an NASD member.

Section 26. The *investment trust rule* applies exclusively to the activities of members in connection with the securities of open-end investment companies. There are several important restrictions registered representatives should be aware of.

No member may purchase open-end investment company securities at a discount from the public offering price from the underwriter of the securities unless the underwriter is also a member. Thus, if the underwriter of XYZ Fund is a nonmember, no NASD firm may receive a commission from the underwriter for selling XYZ shares.

No member who is an underwriter of the securities of an open-end investment company may sell any such securities to any broker or dealer at any price other than the public offering price unless:

1. The broker or dealer is also a member.
2. There is at the time of sale a written sales agreement in effect between the parties.
3. The sales agreement contains the following.
   a) The member shall not withhold placing customers' orders so as to profit himself as a result of such withholding.
   b) No member shall purchase open-end investment company securities of which it is the underwriter, except to cover purchase orders already received.
   c) No member shall purchase open-end investment company securities from the underwriter other than for investment, except for the purpose of covering purchase orders already received. This means that a dealer may not buy shares from the underwriter to hold in his inventory for resale at a profit.
   d) No member who is an underwriter shall accept conditional orders for open-end

investment company securities on any basis other than at a specified definite price. Orders for purchase at a "best-of-day" or "next-advance" price must be refused.

e) If the open-end security is tendered for redemption within seven business days after confirmation by the underwriter of the original purchase, the broker will refund to the underwriter the full concession he received.

f) No member may purchase open-end shares from a customer at a price lower than the current bid price.

The minimum price at which a member may purchase open-end investment company shares from the issuer is the net asset value.

Underwriters are required to calculate the public offering price at least once each business day at the closing of the New York Stock Exchange. The public offering price for open-end investment company securities normally is calculated twice daily, at 1 p.m. and at the close of trading on the New York Stock Exchange.

NASD rules require that the price calculated on the basis of the 1 p.m. price is effective from 1 p.m. until 4.30 p.m. The price calculated at the close of trading is effective from 4.30 p.m. until 1 p.m. of the next business day. Thus, no orders may be accepted after the time of price change at the earlier price, except for telegrams that are date-stamped at a time when an earlier price was in effect. Mutual fund (open-end investment company shares) must normally be redeemed by the fund at net asset value on any day the New York Stock Exchange is open.

Section 27. Each member shall establish, maintain, and enforce written procedures in order to properly supervise the activities of registered representatives and associated persons. In these *written supervisory procedures,* the member designates offices of supervisory jurisdiction, which are offices responsible for reviewing activities of representatives in that office and/or other offices. A partner, officer, or manager must be designated in each office of supervisory jurisdiction to be responsible for this function. Appropriate records must be kept for carrying out the member's supervisory procedures.

Each member must designate to the NASD both its branch offices and offices of supervisory jurisdiction. A branch office would be considered an office of supervisory jurisdiction only if designated as such and only if specified supervisory activities are assigned to it under the member's written procedures. If an office falls within the definition of both a branch office and an office of supervisory jurisdiction, it must be reported to the NASD in each category.

Each member must review and endorse in writing on an external record all transactions and correspondence pertaining to the solicitation or execution of any securities transaction. A member must review the activities of each office, periodically examine customer accounts to detect and prevent irregularities or abuses, and make inspections at least annually of each office of supervisory jurisdiction.

Each member should *ascertain by investigation* the good character, business repute, qualifications, and experience of any person prior to certifying his application to the association.

Section 28. This section concerns transactions for personnel of another member. If a registered representative seeks to open an account with another member, that member must promptly and in writing notify the employer member of that fact. An employer member may require duplicate copies of confirmations or monthly statements from the executing member.

Article II of the Rules of Fair Practice defines such terms as NASD, the corporation, bylaws, member, customer, selling syndicate, and selling group.

Article IV requires members to keep in each office for customers' information a copy of the NASD: (1) Certificate of Incorporation, (2) bylaws, (3) Rules of Fair Practice, (4) Code of Procedure, and (5) interpretative rulings issued by the Board of Governors.

Any person or any District Business Conduct Committee (DBCC) has the right to file a complaint against a member with the DBCC itself or any other DBCC, if such a person believes a member to be in violation of the Rules of Fair Practice. Business Conduct Committees, the Board of Governors, and members of such committees are empowered: (1) to require members against whom a complaint has been made to report orally or in writing on such matters, and (2) to investigate the books and records of such members. No member may refuse to make any report requested under this article, nor may any member refuse to permit such inspections. If a member refuses to furnish such information, he may be suspended by the NASD president after 15 days' notice in writing.

Article V of the Rules of Fair Practice provides that District Business Conduct Committees, the NASD president, or the Board of Governors may impose the following penalties on any member or person associated with a member: (1) censure; (2) fines up to $1,000; (3) suspensions of membership or registration for a definite period; (4) expulsion or suspension from membership, or revocation or suspension of registration as a registered representative (may be levied, after seven days' notice, for failure to pay a fine); (5) payment for the cost of proceedings.

If a person's registration is suspended, revoked, or canceled, he may not be continued in the employ of the member in any capacity whatsoever. Such punitive actions are reported by the NASD to other members as well as to the press.

In order to discover unethical practices or violations of NASD rules, to obtain useful statistical information, and to gain knowledge, the NASD makes surprise examinations of member firms pursuant to resolutions of the Board of Governors.

1. The NASD has the right to require written reports and inspect books and records. This right is also delegated to NASD district and local Business Conduct Committees.

2. After 15 days' notice is given to a member that information is required by the NASD, the member may be suspended by the president of the NASD for failure to furnish such information.

3. Filing misleading information with respect to membership or registration as a registered representative, including information that is incomplete or inaccurate so as to be misleading, may be cause for disciplinary action.

4. A member may be suspended for failure to register personnel or pay fees.

Article VI of the Rules of Fair Practice requires the NASD secretary to furnish members with a current list of member firms.

Code of Procedure

The NASD Code of Procedure describes how complaints for alleged violations of the Rules of Fair Practice shall be handled. It makes clear that first jurisdiction for violations of the rules is with the District Business Conduct Committees (DBCC), and that the role of the Board of Governors is that of an appellate and review body. If a complaint against a member firm is filed with a DBCC, the member firm (respondent) is notified of the charges made by the complainant. The respondent must reply to the charges in writing to the DBCC within 10 days.[1] Then, either the complainant, the respondent, or the DBCC may request a hearing before the DBCC itself to further investigate the matter. The DBCC may dismiss the complaint because it finds there was no violation of law or NASD rules. Or the DBCC may impose a penalty, which the respondent may either accept or appeal to the Board of Governors within 15 days of the date of the decision. The Board of Governors, after reviewing the decision of the DBCC and giving opportunity for another hearing, may either concur, increase, reduce, modify, or cancel such disciplining action. In addition, the Board of Governors may return the case to the DBCC for further proceedings.[2] Action taken by the Board of Governors may be appealed to the SEC, which may concur or reduce the penalty but may not increase it. The decision of the SEC may be appealed to the federal courts. Penalties do not become effective until the expiration of all periods of appeal or review.[3]

1/ The DBCC may institute a shortened "Summary Complaint Procedure" if it feels that: (*a*) the facts are not in dispute; (*b*) a violation of the rules has occurred; and (*c*) following the normal complaint procedure is not appropriate.

If the respondent accepts the DBCC offer of "Summary Complaint Procedure," hearings are waived and the maximum penalty for all alleged violations may not exceed censure and/or a fine of $500 for each respondent. Offer by the DBCC of a summary must: (*a*) be in writing; (*b*) specify the charges; and (*c*) specify the penalty deemed appropriate. Acceptance by the respondent, which must be within 10 business days after the date of complaint, constitutes admission of the violations, acceptance of the penalties, and a waiver of all appeal rights to the Board of Governors. The Board of Governors may, however, institute review on its own initiative. If a summary is rejected, normal complaint procedure is followed.

2/ Even though no appeal is made, the National Business Conduct Committee reviews every district decision to determine whether the district's ruling should be reviewed by the Board of Governors. In the case of appeal to the BG, a subcommittee of the BG holds a hearing, unless it is waived. Following such hearing, the subcommittee recommends action to the National Business Conduct Committee, which then makes a recommendation to the BG, who ultimately, by vote, make disposition of the case.

The bylaws provide that the BG may deny membership to an applicant or summarily cancel the membership of a member if the board believes the applicant or member (or person associated with the member) is subject to certain disqualifications. Should the applicant or member disagree, a Membership Continuance Request may be made. The board's handling of such membership continuance cases is in a manner similar to that of appeals from DBCC decisions.

3/ If no appeal is made from a DBCC or SEC decision, such decision does not become effective until 30 days after the date of the decision. Notice to NASD members and the press of expulsion, or other must be made: (*a*) thirty days after the decision of the DBCC if no appeal is made to the BG, (*b*) thirty days after the decision of the BG.

In general practice, the District Committees also function as the DBCC. District Committees may employ a district secretary and such other employees as may be necessary. The DBCC is empowered to examine the books, records, and business practices of member firms.

Moral and legal obligations of a registered representative

In addition to understanding the ethical standards and rules of the association, Securities and Exchange Commission, and Federal Reserve Board, the registered representative must realize his moral obligations and his responsibilities under law to his customer and to his employer.

In all dealings with customers, the registered representative is placed in a position of trust. He is bound morally, ethically, and legally to serve the best interests of his customer. Many of his obligations are specifically covered in the association's Rules of Fair Practice.

However, a registered representative also acts on behalf of his employer. In other words, he is an agent of his employer (his principal). This principal to agent relationship is based upon good faith under law; each has responsibilities to the other.

An employee may not act adversely to the interests of his employer by acquiring a private interest of his own in opposition to the interests of his employer. The object of these rules is to secure faithfulness on the part of the agent to his principal. For example, a registered representative could not sell his own property to his employer without disclosing that it was his own property. A sale of this kind would be voidable by the employer, regardless of whether the transaction was fair or not. Neither could a registered representative sell his own property to his customer without informing his employer. In this instance, an employer would have recourse against the registered representative. Further, an agent must never act for a third person whose interests are contrary to those of his principal.

The total effect of the law of agency as it applies to the registered representative requires that he serve his employer as instructed with all his skill, judgment, and discretion, and that he keep his employer informed of all facts coming to his knowledge that affect his employer's business, rights, and interests.

The law also covers a principal's responsibilities to his agent. A principal is obligated to compensate and indemnify his agent for services rendered on his behalf according to his instructions. He is liable to his agent for his own conduct as well as to third parties for the conduct of his agent as long as his agent is acting within the scope of his duties. In summary, the law requires the relationship between principal and agent, or employer and employee, to be one of mutual trust and confidence.

Beyond the legal obligations that exist between employer and employee are their moral obligations to each other. Fulfillment of these obligations is a necessity for building a career in the securities business. A reputation for honesty, integrity, and fairness is one of the most valued assets that can be acquired in the securities business by a firm and a registered representative.

There is an effective way of stressing the importance of knowing and understanding the standards under which the securities business operates, and of realizing the moral and legal obligations of registration. Let us consider the procedure that must be followed by a registered representative whose registration has been revoked by the NASD, SEC, or a registered securities exchange, and who wants to reenter the securities business as a registered representative with an NASD member.

The representative must first find a firm that is willing to employ him. A new application for registration as a registered representative must be filed by the member, disclosing the applicant's past history in the securities business. The application is referred by the executive office of the association to the appropriate District Committee.

The applicant's prospective employer may then request a hearing before the District Committee, during which all the facts and circumstances regarding the applicant's history are discussed for the record. His prospective employer must report the type and kind of supervision that will be exercised over the applicant's activities. The District Committee makes a recommendation to the NASD Board of Governors, requesting either that the employer be continued in membership with the applicant employed as a registered representative, or that the application for registration be denied and the membership of the prospective employer be canceled if the applicant is employed. Next, the Board of Governors must consider the recommendation of the District Committee and the record of the hearing at the district level. The respondent also has an opportunity for another hearing before the Board of Governors.

If the Board of Governors believes that the prospective employer is capable and prepared to supervise the activities of the applicant in a satisfactory manner, the board must then recommend to the SEC that the employer be continued in membership with the applicant as a registered representative. The SEC must then study the record and the recommendation of the Board of Governors. If the Commission is satisfied that the applicant should be permitted to reenter the business and that he will be properly supervised, it will issue an order directing the association to continue his employer in membership with the applicant as a registered representative. Only if the Board of Governors does not act favorably on the request for registration may the applicant appeal directly to the Securities and Exchange Commission.

The applicant may not be registered again until and unless a favorable decision is rendered by the Securities and Exchange Commission. Furthermore, he must go through this procedure every time he changes his employer.

The above procedure is not, and is not intended to be, a simple one. However, a registration is never revoked without due cause. Experience has clearly shown that a registration need never be revoked if representatives learn the standards of the securities business and conduct themselves in accordance with their position of trust.

Uniform Practice Code

Article XIV of the NASD bylaws authorizes the Board of Governors to adopt a Uniform Practice Code (UPC). The UPC is designed to make uniform the customs, practices, usages, and trading techniques employed in the investment banking and securities business. The administration of the code is delegated to the National Uniform Practice Committee and District Uniform Practice Committees.

All over-the-counter transactions in securities between members, except transactions in exempted securities, such as government bonds and municipal issues, are subject to the Uniform Practice Code, unless the parties agree that certain or all sections of the code shall not pertain. Thus, any contract between members is governed by the UPC, unless the members have stated otherwise. If a situation arises that is not covered by the code, decisions are made by the National Uniform Practice Committee for interdistrict trades, and for all other trades by the appropriate District Uniform Practice Committee.

Refusal to abide by the rulings of the Uniform Practice Committee is considered to be conduct inconsistent with just and equitable principles of trade, that is, violation of section 1, Article III, of the Rules of Fair Practice, and is subject to disciplinary action. Important sections of the Uniform Practice Code are as follows.

Section 4 concerns *delivery of securities*. This refers to the length of time allowed a seller to deliver securities to the buyer on exchange contracts. In every securities transaction, there are several dates of importance.

1. *Trade date* is the date on which a transaction was effected.
2. *Settlement date* is the date on which a transaction is effected or accomplished, e.g., the date on which securities are delivered and paid for.
3. The *delivery date* is the date on which the securities should be delivered to the customer. Types of deliveries include: (*a*) cash, (*b*) regular way, (*c*) seller's option, (*d*) buyer's option, and (*e*) delayed.

A "good delivery" of a security by a seller means that the security is in such form that ownership of record may be easily transferable.

The seller has a varying amount of time to make delivery of the securities sold, depending on the type of transaction, as follows.

Cash transactions require delivery on the day of the transaction. Cash transactions frequently occur at the end of the year when sellers, for tax reasons, want to consummate a transaction quickly. Thus, on the trade date in a cash transaction the security must be delivered to the office of the purchaser. Confirmations must be exchanged, and the security must be paid for.

Regular-way or *normal* transactions require delivery on the fifth business day, not counting weekends or holidays, following the date of the transaction. This type of transaction is the most common. For example, if the trade date is Friday, the delivery date would normally be the following Friday. The buyer is not obligated to accept delivery before the delivery date. However, he may accept an earlier delivery, at his option.

Delayed delivery transactions require delivery on the seventh calendar day following the date of the transaction. If the delivery date so determined is a weekend or holiday, the delivery date becomes the next business day.

Seller's option transactions require delivery on the date the option expires, which may be as long as 60 calendar days after the trade date. Delayed or seller's option contracts are requested by sellers who know that it will take them time to obtain their securities for delivery. The seller under a seller's option contract may make delivery at any time after five business days from the trade date have expired, but must first give one day's advance notice.

Buyer's option transactions give the buyer the option of receiving securities at his office on the date the option expires. If the seller wants to deliver before that date, the buyer must agree to such early delivery.

When, as, and if issued (WAII) or when, as, and if distributed (WAID) contracts relate to securities that have not been issued, or when the distribution date may not have been determined. The type of securities to be issued is known—for example, when a stock split has been authorized but not yet effected. Delivery dates are determined by the NASD District Uniform Practice Committees. If no date is declared by the committee, the securities may be delivered one day after written notice is given to the seller. All trades in when-issued securities, including any profits or losses, are canceled if the securities are not issued.[4]

In both short sales and security transactions on a when, as, and if issued or distributed basis, the broker may be required to *mark to the market.* For example, broker X sells short 100 shares of stock ABC to broker Y. Broker X borrows stock from broker A to deliver to Y. In consideration of the loan from A, X deposits the value of ABC stock for the credit of A. If ABC stock rises in value, broker A will be partially unsecured and will have the right to require broker X to deposit additional money. This adjustment is called marking to the market. Conversely, if the ABC shares fell in price, broker X could demand a refund of a proportionate part of his deposit.

Section 5 concerns transactions in stocks that are ex-dividend or ex-rights. There are four significant dates to consider.

The *declaration date* is the date when the board of directors gives notice that a dividend has been declared. When the dividend is announced, a record date is given.

Record date is the date fixed by the issuing corporation for the purpose of determining the stockholders entitled to receive dividends or rights, or to vote on company affairs. On this date, a list is made of all stockholders to whom a dividend will be paid at a later date.

The *ex-dividend or ex-right date* is the date on and after which a seller is entitled to receive a dividend or right issue previously declared. In other words, stock purchased ex-dividend is bought by the buyer without the dividend. The ex-dividend or ex-right date is a date specifically designated by the Uniform Practice Committee. Normally, this date will be the *fourth business day* preceding the record date if the record date falls on a business day, or the fifth business day preceding the record date if the record date falls on a nonbusiness day. However, if the committee does not receive definitive dividend information sufficiently in advance of the record date, the ex-date designated

---

4/ The NASD recommends use of a standard form contract for WAII and WAID transactions. If such forms are not used, the member will be deemed to have executed a special contract, which will not be subject to the ruling and interpretations of the National Uniform Practice Committee. Deposits made with members against orders for WAII or WAID securities must be segregated from other funds of the member, and may be used for no purpose whatsoever other than to secure such contracts.

will be the first full business day practicable in all the circumstances—normally the first full business day following public notice of the dividend declaration.

For stock of an open-end investment company, the ex-dividend date is the date designated by the issuer or its principal underwriter. This is usually the day after the record date. Note that the ex-date for mutual funds does not follow the normal custom for stocks.

The *payment date* is the date the company or its agent actually pays the dividend. For example, a dividend of $1 per share is declared on November 1, 1967, payable on December 10, 1967, to stockholders of record on November 15. The stock would normally trade ex-dividend, that is, without the dividend, as follows.

Record date	Wednesday	November 15
First day preceding	Tuesday	November 14
Second day preceding	Monday	November 13
Weekend	Sunday	November 12
Weekend	Saturday	November 11
Third day preceding	Friday	November 10
Ex-date is the fourth day preceding	Thursday	November 9

Thus, the stock would trade ex-dividend on the fourth business day preceding the record date.

Note that in a regular-way transaction a buyer of the stock on Thursday, November 9, would neither take delivery nor become the stockholder of record until Thursday, November 16, as follows.

Trade date, ex-date	Thursday	November 9
First day after trade	Friday	November 10
Weekend	Saturday	November 11
Weekend	Sunday	November 12
Second day after trade	Monday	November 13
Third day after trade	Tuesday	November 14
Fourth day after trade	Wednesday	November 15
Delivery date, fifth day after trade	Thursday	November 16

Thus, a buyer of a stock on the ex-date in a regular transaction will not receive the dividend, because he is not the stockholder of record on the record date.

Section 6 relates to bond trading. When bonds are traded without accrued interest, they are said to be *traded flat*. Also, when a bond is in default or some doubt exists about the payment of the next coupon due, the bond is traded flat. The Uniform Practice Code provisions on ex-interest apply. When stock is traded flat, it is termed ex-dividend. Rules for ex-interest transactions in bonds are similar to those for stocks traded ex-dividend.

Sections 9 to 11 concern confirmations. Written confirmations must be exchanged on the day of a cash transaction, and/or on or before the first business day following a transaction for all transactions other than cash. Confirmations should contain an accurate description of the security, including such things as common, preferred, participating, coupon rate, and dividend rate. The requirement to exchange confirmations, mentioned above, does not apply to transactions cleared through the National Over-the-Counter Clearing Corporation.

Section 13 allows the seller of a security to require the purchase money, paid on delivery of the security sold, to be by certified check, cashier's check, bank draft, or cash.

Section 14 provides that the federal transfer tax (now obsolete) and state transfer stamps be paid for and provided by the seller of a security. If the seller fails to furnish the required state transfer stamps, the buyer may provide them and deduct the cost from his payment.

Sections 15 to 18 concern units of delivery. A certificate for more than 100 shares is not a good delivery and may be refused by the purchaser. If a contract is for more than 100 shares, delivery must be in certificates from which units of 100 shares can be made. If the contract is for 100 shares or less, either one certificate for the exact number of shares or certificates totaling the exact number of shares may be delivered. The following are examples of good and unacceptable deliveries.

If a sale of 400 shares is made, a good delivery would be: 4 certificates for 100 shares each; 8 certificates for 50 shares each; 8 certificates—4 for 85 shares each, and 4 are for 15 shares each. In the same sale of 400 shares, an unacceptable delivery would include: 2 certificates for 200 shares each; 5 certificates for 80 shares each; or 10 certificates for 40 shares each.

Sections 17 to 18 provide that the trading units for bonds, or certificates of deposit for bonds, shall be in denominations of $500 or $1,000, unless otherwise agreed.

The unit of trading for stock rights and warrants is normally 100 rights or warrants. Normally, one stock right will accrue for each share of issued stock, and one warrant will represent the right to purchase one share of stock.

Buy in and sell out

When a delivery is late, incomplete, in wrong units, or otherwise unacceptable, the seller has the responsibility for straightening out the situation. If the seller fails to deliver securities within the period set by the contract, the buyer may buy the securities elsewhere at the seller's expense, after giving notice to the seller and waiting one day.

Failure of the seller to make proper delivery allows the buyer the right to *buy in*. A buy-in occurs when the unsatisfied buyer buys the securities necessary to complete a transaction, but makes such purchase for the account and risk of the seller who failed to complete the original transaction. A buy-in may take place after the first business day following the date delivery was due, with the following qualifications.

1. Written notice of buy-in must be delivered to the seller at his office prior to 12 noon, his time, of the day preceding execution of the proposed buy-in.
2. The buy-in notice must contain the necessary details of the transaction.
3. The buyer must accept any portion of the undelivered securities up until the time the buy-in may be closed.

If the seller fails to complete the transaction after notice, the buyer may close the transaction by making a cash purchase for the portion of the contract on which the seller has defaulted.

When a buy-in is executed, details of the transaction must be given promptly, by telephone or telegraph, to the defaulting seller. A written copy of such details must be furnished to the secretary of the National Uniform Practice Committee.

If before the closing of a buy-in the buyer receives notice from the seller that the securities (including actual certificate numbers) are in transit, the buyer must defer closing the transaction for at least seven calendar days from the date delivery was due under the buy-in. The closing of a buy-in may be deferred for a specified period by a member or representative of the National Uniform Practice Committee.

The buy-in procedure described above pertains primarily to stocks or bonds. It does not apply to contracts for warrants, rights, convertible securities, called securities, cash contracts, or contracts that include guaranteed delivery on a specified date.

Failure of the buyer to accept delivery according to the terms of the contract allows the seller the right to *sell out*. Thus, the seller may, without notice, sell out all or any part of the securities called for by the contract in the best available market for the account and liability of the buyer. Notice of the details of sell-out must be given to the defaulting buyer on the day of execution of the sell-out, with a copy to the secretary of the National Uniform Practice Committee.

Drafts

Sections 19 through 23 deal with drafts. A draft, sometimes called a bill of exchange, is an instrument drawn by one person (the drawer-seller), ordering a second person (the drawee-buyer) to pay a definite sum of money to a payee (seller) on sight or at a specified future date.

Often, delivery of securities to the buyer is accompanied by a draft. These drafts must be accepted by the drawee on any business day during business hours. The acceptance of a draft (and delivery) prior to the settlement date is at the option of the buyer. Failure to accept a draft in which no irregularities exist shall make the buyer liable for payment of interest and other expenses incurred due to the delay.

Good delivery

Securities must be delivered in such form that the owner of record may be easily transferred. There are several requirements for good delivery, depending on a variety of circumstances surrounding the sale.

To be a good delivery, any registered security, e.g., common stock, must be accompanied by an assignment, and a power of substitution when that is required. A power of substitution provides for the appointment of an attorney.

An assignment shall be executed on the certificate itself, or if on a separate paper there must be a separate assignment for each certificate. *Signatures* to assignments or powers of substitution *must coincide exactly with the registration on the face of the certificate.* For example, if a stock is registered in the name of Lawrence Rosen, the assignment may not be signed Larry Rosen.

Each assignment, endorsement, alteration, or erasure shall bear a signature guarantee acceptable to the transfer agent or registrar.

Each signature to an assignment or power of substitution must be witnessed by an individual and dated. A certificate with either the assignment or power of substitution witnessed by a person since deceased is not a good delivery.

A certificate with an assignment or power of substitution executed by a person since deceased, or by a trustee, guardian, infant, executor, administrator, assignee, or receiver in bankruptcy, agent or attorney, or with a qualification, restriction, or special designation is not a good delivery, except for certificates registered under a Gifts to Minors Act.

In order to reregister stock in the name of a deceased person to street name for delivery to a buyer, the transfer agent normally requires:

1. A certified copy of the deceased's will.
2. A certified copy of the court order that appoints the executor.
3. A death certificate.
4. A tax waiver from the state, showing that state taxes have been paid.
5. The stock certificate signed by the executor and witnessed.

A certificate with an inscription to indicate joint tenancy or tenancy in common shall be a good delivery only if signed by all co-tenants. A certificate registered in the names of two or more individuals or firms shall be a good delivery only if signed by all the registered holders.

To repeat, the Uniform Practice Code provides that certificates delivered must be properly endorsed. The assignment should be executed on the certificate itself or on a separate paper. The signature must exactly coincide with the face of the certificate and must be witnessed. An assignment separate from the stock certificates that permits assignment or transfer is called a *stock power.* Its wording closely resembles the phrasing on the back of the stock certificate. A certificate with a properly endorsed stock power attached is negotiable. Bearer certificates or bonds do not require an assignment in order to be negotiable.

To transfer certificates, an unmarried woman must use the prefix Miss. If the certificate does not show the prefix Miss, she must sign an acknowledgement and have it notarized. Again, of course, this is subject to any state laws that may restrict her rights. An acknowledgement is a notarial statement that the notary knows the parties named, and that they have appeared before him and executed their signatures.

A certificate in the name of a widow must be accompanied by an acknowledgment executed before a notary public.

In some states, a certificate in the name of a married woman is not a good delivery. These states provide that such certificates must be signed by both husband and wife, with an acknowledgement. A certificate in the name of a married woman shall be a good delivery, except when state laws restrict her rights.

The stock or bond certificate must be in good condition. If it is mutilated, the transfer agent, a company officer, or bond trustee must certify that the certificate is valid.

Other requirements for good delivery include two items previously mentioned: (1) the time of delivery, and (2) the number or quantity of shares represented by each certificate.

A security that has been called is not a good delivery unless the entire issue has been called.

A temporary certificate is not a good delivery when permanent certificates are available.

A certificate in the name of a corporation or institution shall be a good delivery only if the statement "proper papers for transfer filed by assignor" is placed on the assignment and signed by the transfer agent. Should the transfer agent's books be indefinitely closed for any reason, a certificate in the name of a corporation must be accompanied by an assignment signed by an officer of such corporation other than the corporate secretary, together with:

1. A signature guarantee by a member bank of the Federal Deposit Insurance Corporation.
2. An acknowledgement.
3. A copy of a corporate resolution, certified by the secretary, authorizing the officer to effect such transactions.
4. A certificate and acknowledgement executed by a corporate officer, certifying that the officer who signed the assignment actually is an officer and that his signature is genuine, as of the date of execution.

Coupon bonds must have all unpaid coupons attached. Acceptance of cash in lieu of missing coupons shall be at the option of the purchaser.

A coupon bond endorsed to a party shall not be a good delivery unless the sale specified an endorsed bond. A registered coupon bond shall be a good delivery only if it is registered "to bearer."

Normally, when a bond is sold the sale takes place at a point in time between interest payments. The seller of the bond has owned the bond for part of the interest period. Yet, the bond, if registered, will normally be reregistered in the name of the buyer before the next record date, and the buyer will receive interest for the full period. To make the situation equitable, the price the buyer pays for an interest-bearing security is adjusted as follows.

1. If a cash delivery, interest is added to the bond price for the period up to but not including the day of the transaction.
2. If a noncash delivery, interest is added for the period up to but not including the fifth business day following the date of the transaction.

Bond interest is computed on the basis of a 360-day year; every calendar month is considered to have 30 days; and every period from a particular date in one month to the same date in the following month is considered to be 30 days. Thus, the number of elapsed days should be computed in accordance with the following examples.

From the	To the	Of the	Number of Elapsed Days Is
1st	30th	same month	29
1st	31st	same month	30
1st	1st	following month	30
1st	28th	February	27

When interest is payable on the 30th or 31st of the month:

From the	To the	Of the	Number of Elapsed Days Is
30th or 31st	1st	following month	1
30th or 31st	30th	following month	30
30th or 31st	31st	following month	30
30th or 31st	1st	second month following	1 month 1 day

When certain documents, such as a license, clearance certificate, or affidavit of ownership, are required by law, or there are other government regulations in connection with the purchase, sale, or transfer of a security, a good delivery does not take place unless accompanied by the required documents.

The *interest equalization tax* (IET) is levied on the purchaser (if a U.S. citizen or resident) of certain foreign equities and debt obligations. The tax was imposed to aid the unfavorable U.S. balance of payments. Exempted from the tax are transactions in securities that were owned by U.S. citizens or residents before July 19, 1963.

When a broker sells a foreign security (or debt instrument), he must disclose at the time of execution of the contract, that the buyer is subject to the interest equalization tax if such is the case. If the confirmation issued by the selling broker fails to state "buyer is subject to interest equalization tax" (a clean IET confirmation), it shall be conclusive proof that the selling broker has proper documentation to indicate that the transaction is not subject to IET.

Proper documentation in a participating selling member's[5] possession includes

---

5/ Participating members include NASD members who with regard to the IET agree to comply with the Internal Revenue Code provisions and those of the NASD. A nonparticipating member in connection with the sale of a foreign security must state: "Buyer subject to IET," or must provide a Treasury Validation Certificate.

(among other items outlined in the NASD Manual) a statement from the seller, executed under penalty of perjury (unless the seller is the member dealer and a U.S. person), on which the selling member relies in good faith, indicating that the seller is a U.S. person and is the owner of all foreign stock or debt obligations carried in the records of the member for such person, and one of the following.

1. At July 14, 1967, the selling member carried the foreign security in its records (on a trade date basis) for the account of the seller, and reported such holding to the Treasury Department in connection with such NASD member firm's agreement to abide by NASD and Treasury rules.

2. After July 14, 1967: (*a*) the selling member sold the foreign security to its customer, who is now desirous to sell it; or (*b*) the selling member, acting as broker, acquired the foreign stock for its customer (the seller), and the IET was not payable; *and* (*c*) the foreign stock has since been continuously carried on the member's books for the account of the seller; or (*d*) the seller delivers to the selling member the identical stock certificates or evidences of indebtedness so acquired.

3. The selling NASD member receives from its customer (the seller) stock that was registered in the name of the seller before July 19, 1963, by participating custodian, which acted as transfer agent or registrar in registering such stock.

4. The selling member receives a validation certificate from the Treasury Department.

5. The selling member withholds from the proceeds of the sale, with the consent of the seller, an amount equal to the IET that would be imposed on the purchaser.

When a member dealer sells a foreign security out of his inventory, and such stock was acquired from a non-U.S. person, the confirmation sent by the selling member must contain the designation "Interest Equalization Tax—Dealer Transaction." The following statements, one of which must be checked by the buying member and returned to the selling member, also must be made.

1. "We represent that these securities are being purchased for the account of a customer who is not a U.S. person, or that these securities were resold on the date of purchase or the next business day in the case of stock or within 30 days after the date of purchase in the case of a debt obligation, to a person other than a U.S. person."

2. "The purchaser of these securities was a U.S. person, or these securities were not sold on the date of purchase or the next business day in the case of stock, or within 30 days after the day of purchase in the case of a debt obligation, to other than a U.S. person. We will, upon demand, reimburse you for the IET payable by you because of your purchase of these securities. It is agreed by the parties to the purchase and sale of the securities represented by this confirmation that the statement checked above shall be considered a provision of the contract effectuating the transaction."

Records clearly indicating the nature of all transactions in foreign securities must be maintained by both buying and selling members.

Section 48 of the UPC concerns due bills. For the distribution to be made, a security sold before it trades ex-dividend, ex-interest, or ex-rights, and delivered too late for transfer on or before the record date, must be accompanied by a due bill (or due bill check in the case of a cash distribution). The due bill allows the purchaser of the security to collect the dividend, interest, or rights from the seller.

Section 50 concerns transfer fees. The party at whose instance a transfer of securities is made—e.g., seller—shall pay all transfer fees and service charges of the transfer agent. In addition, the seller pays the costs of delivery, including insurance and postage.

Reclamations

When delivery of a security is made and some type of irregularity exists in connection with such delivery (e.g., the wrong security or an incorrect number of shares), the buyer has the right to return the security and the seller has the right to reclaim it. The term *reclamation* refers to the claim to such right to return or right to reclaim.

When a security is returned or reclaimed, the seller (the party who originally delivered the security) must either: (1) give the security in proper form for delivery; or (2) return the money amount of the contract, in which case he shall be considered to have failed to deliver. (The right to buy in may then become effective.)

The right of reclamation is subject to time limitations, as follows.

1. Reclamation due to "not a good delivery" where "good delivery" may be obtained without charge must be made within 15 days of original delivery.
2. Reclamation due to delivery of the wrong (incorrect) security may be made without time limit.

These cases serve to illustrate several types of reclamations. For a complete discussion of the time period allowed for reclamation in connection with various other types of transactions, the Uniform Practice Code should be consulted.

Registration of securities may be in the name of the owner. Securities held in the name of a broker rather than in his customer's name are said to be carried in a *street name*. This occurs when the securities have been bought on margin or when the customer wants the broker to hold the security.

District Uniform Practice Committees settle any disputes with respect to technicalities of a transaction that arise between members in their district. The National Uniform Practice Committee settles interdistrict disputes.

Interpretations, policies, and explanations

These guidelines are published by the NASD to enable members to better understand the rules of the NASD. The important policies not previously discussed are as follows.

Free-riding and withholding is the subject of an NASD policy issued in extension of section 1 of the Rules of Fair Practice. Failure to make a bona fide public offering, at the public offering price, of a hot issue acquired by a participant in a distribution is known as *free-riding and withholding*. A *hot issue* is an issue that on the first day of trading sells at a substantial premium over the public offering price.

Failure to make a bona fide public offering when there is great demand for an issue can be a factor in artificially raising the price. Not only is such failure in contravention of ethical practices, but also it impairs public confidence in the ethics of the securities business.

The NASD interpretation is that members have an obligation to make a bona fide public offering, at the public offering price, of securities acquired by a participation in any distribution. With the exceptions noted below, if a member either has unfilled orders from the public for a security or has failed to make a bona fide public offering of the securities acquired by participation in a distribution, it would be a violation of Article III, section 1 of the Rules of Fair Practice to:

1. Withhold any of the securities in the member's account.
2. Sell any of the securities to any officer, director, partner, employee, or agent of the member, or to members of the immediate family of any such person.
3. Sell any of the securities to any account in which any person specified under 1 or 2 has a beneficial interest.

   Exception: A member may withhold for his own account, or sell to persons in categories 2 and 3 above, part of his participation in an offering acquired as described above if the member is prepared to demonstrate that the securities were withheld for bona fide investment in accordance with the member's normal investment practices, or were sold to such other persons in accordance with their normal investment practice with the member, and that the aggregate of the securities so withheld and sold is insubstantial and not disproportionate in amount as compared to sales to members of the public. *Normal investment practice* is the individual's history of investment through his account with the member.

4. Sell any of the securities to any person in the securities department of, or whose activities involve or are related to the function of buying or selling securities for, banks, insurance companies, or any other institutional-type accounts, or to a member of the immediate family of such persons.

   Exception: A member may sell part of the securities acquired as described above to persons in category 4 if the member is prepared to demonstrate that the sales made to such persons are for bona fide investment and are in accordance with their normal investment practice with the member, and that the aggregate sales to such persons are insubstantial and not disproportionate in amount as compared to sales to other members of the public.

5. Sell any of the securities to any other broker or dealer at or above the public offering price.

   Exception: A member may sell part of the securities to another member if the buyer represents to the selling member, and is prepared to demonstrate, that such purchase was made to fill orders, as an accommodation and without compensation, for bona fide public customers at the public offering price. If such accommodation order is filled for any person in categories 2, 3, or 4, the member who fills the order for such person must represent to the selling member, and be prepared to demonstrate, that such sale was for bona fide investment and in accordance with the normal investment practice of such person with the member.

An *advertising* interpretation issued in extension of Article III, section 1 of the Rules of Fair Practice sets standards for advertising, sales literature, market letters, and recruiting advertisements, and requires advertising to be filed for review at the NASD executive office in Washington within five business days after its initial use, with certain exceptions. Members are required to maintain a separate file of such literature for three years from the date of each use. This interpretation does not include mutual fund advertising and sales literature, which is covered by the Statement of Policy.

Another policy concerns *continuing commissions*. The payment of continuing commissions in connection with the sale of securities is not improper so long as the recipient remains a registered representative of an NASD member. However, payment of continuing commissions to registered representatives after they cease to be employed by a member of the association, or payment to their widows or other direct beneficiaries, will not be deemed in violation of NASD rules provided bona fide contracts call for such payment.

An interpretation concerning *arranging loans* points out that a broker-dealer is prohibited from granting or arranging for credit to enable customers to buy or carry open-end investment company shares, because such shares are both new issues and unlisted.

The interpretation concerning *prompt payment* by members for investment company shares requires members to transmit payments to underwriters (or custodians) promptly after the date of the transaction. If payment is not received within 10 business days for transactions involving more than $100, the underwriter must immediately notify the association's office in the district where the dealer's office is located.

The *"special deals"* interpretation provides, in brief, that an investment company underwriter may not give a member or a registered representative of a member anything of material value in addition to the discounts or concessions called for in the prospectus. Material value is interpreted to mean gifts that exceed $25 per person in value during any one year. Members are required to file, within five days after use, details of sales contests or incentives involving mutual fund shares.

Registered representatives of an NASD firm assume both a moral and a legal obligation to comply with all NASD requirements. They must always bear in mind their responsibilities to their firm and to their customers.

Another subject of NASD policies concerns the contractual plan *reinstatement privilege*. Most contractual plans allow an investor to sell up to 90 percent of his holdings and later replace such investment without sales charges.

The NASD will consider it a violation for a member to:

1. Encourage a planholder to use the replacement privilege more frequently than one time per year.
2. Use the replacement privilege within six months of his last investment.
3. Use the replacement privilege within 90 days of the withdrawal.
4. Use the withdrawal privilege to provide temporary funds for other investments.
5. Use the privilege to take advantage of fluctuations of the net asset value of the mutual fund.

Personnel of other members is the subject of an NASD interpretation. If an employee of another dealer wants to place an order, the dealer who accepts the order must send written notice to the employer of the customer, stating that his employee has opened an account.

Procedures for over-the-counter quotations

Each NASD District Quotations Committee establishes standards concerning the distribution of price quotations to the press or news media. Such standards must be at least as stringent as those established at the national level by the Board of Governors and the National Quotations Committee. National NASD minimum requirements for a security prerequisite to its price being quoted include the following.

1. When price is first quoted, it must be $1 bid or greater.
2. Issues that fall below 50 cents bid will be deleted.
3. Sufficient investor and interdealer interest is necessary.
4. Dividend declarations must be published and filed with the NASD Uniform Practice Committee at least 10 days prior to the record date.
5. The company must publish financial statements at least annually, and supply them to stockholders and the NASD.
6. The company must promptly disclose to news media any significant developments.

Quotations supplied to the press by the NASD do not represent actual transactions. The price quotations are bids and offers quoted by over-the-counter dealers to each other (interdealer), and do not include retail markup, markdown, or commission.

NASD members are prohibited from reporting transactions or quotations, unless the member believes them to be bona fide.

When an NASD member is making a firm trading market in a security, the member is expected to buy or sell a minimum of a normal trading unit of such security.

Summary

The bylaws, rules, regulations, history, and *raison d'être* of the NASD are complicated. However, they become simplified when remembered in the context of the four basic purposes of the NASD, as stated at the beginning of the chapter.

1. To promote the investment banking and securities business, to standardize its principles and practices (through the Uniform Practice Code), to promote therein high standards of commercial honor (through the Rules of Fair Practice), and to encourage and promote among members observance of federal and state securities laws (through the Code of Procedure for Handling Violations and Complaints).
2. To provide a medium through which its membership is able to confer, consult, and cooperate with governmental and other agencies.
3. To enforce rules of fair practice to prevent fraudulent and manipulative acts, and in general to promote just and equitable principles of trade for the protection of investors.
4. To promote self-discipline among members, and to investigate and adjust grievances between the public and members and between members.

9 | Review questions

366. The controlling factor when offering securities to an investor should be
....
   1. the interest on the investment
   2. the interest of the salesman
   3. the interest of the firm
   4. the interest of the investor

367. The Board of Governors may prescribe penalties applicable to members and/or registered representatives for violation of the association rules, including: ....
   1. censure and fines and costs of proceedings
   2. suspension
   3. expulsion
   4. all of these

368. A member participating in an initial offering of a security who fails to make a bona fide public offering of the security and instead retains his allotment for himself or his family or his employees or employee profit sharing plan is said to be ....
   1. straddling
   2. beating the bid
   3. free-riding
   4. churning

369. A member must be diligent in determining that the execution of a transaction for a partner, officer, or employee of another member will not be adverse to the interests of the other member. The executing member can fulfill this obligation by ....
   1. checking with the salesman
   2. notifying the employer-member prior to execution
   3. talking to his own partners
   4. checking with the SEC

370. Complaints for violation of the association's rules may be filed with district committees by ....
   1. members of the public
   2. other members of the association
   3. other District Committees or any aggrieved person
   4. all of these

371. ABC Company, an NASD member dealer, wants to purchase mutual fund shares from the sponsor corporation at a discount from the public offering price. ABC Company may have the discount if ....
   1. sponsor corporation is also an NASD member
   2. there is a sales agreement in effect between ABC Company and sponsor corporation
   3. both 1 and 2
   4. none of the above

372. A fund's underwriter is not permitted to sell a fund's shares if the public offering includes a sales charge that is
.... :
   1. unfair
   2. more than 5 percent
   3. both 1 and 2
   4. neither 1 nor 2

373. NASD members must maintain the public offering price when selling fund shares to ....
   1. other NASD members
   2. nonmembers of the NASD
   3. both 1 and 2
   4. neither 1 nor 2

374. NASD member underwriters normally calculate the public offering price of a fund share ....
   1. once each business day

2. twice each business day
3. once a week
4. once a month

375. An NASD member underwriter may give special discounts or concessions to NASD member dealers in addition to those stated in the fund's prospectus. ....

1. true
2. false

376. NASD member underwriters may accept orders for fund shares on the basis of ....

1. the current offering price
2. the best-of-the-day price
3. the next advance
4. none of these

377. An effect of the requirements of the Securities and Exchange Act of 1934 and of regulation T is to bar broker-dealers from granting credit to enable customers to buy ....

1. on margin
2. on a margin of less than 80 percent
3. on a margin of less than 75 percent
4. the securities of open-end investment companies.

378. Recommendations to a customer about the purchase, sale, or exchange of a security must be based upon reasonable grounds for believing that ....

1. the stock is a good growth stock
2. the dividends or interest due on the security have always been paid regularly
3. the recommendation is suitable for the customer, considering his financial situation and needs
4. all of the above

379. When members handle discretionary accounts ....

1. transactions effected for it must not constitute churning of the account

2. the member must get the approval of the customer before he makes any decisions the member considers major decisions
3. a record must be kept of only major transactions
4. none of these

380. A member must deal with a nonmember ....

1. as it would deal with a member as long as the nonmember is registered with the SEC
2. as it would with a member if the nonmember is a bank or trust company
3. as it would deal with a member of the general public
4. only if given permission by the local DBCC

381. In a cash account, the customer is expected to pay ....

1. in cash
2. promptly
3. at the discretion of the broker-dealer
4. within 30 days

382. An account in which the broker or dealer extends credit to a customer for the purchase of securities is called a ....

1. cash account
2. discretionary account
3. margin account
4. debit account

383. An account in which the customer gives the broker or dealer power to decide on such matters as price or timing is called a ....

1. cash account
2. discretionary account
3. safety account
4. margin account

384. A salesman for ABC Company, NASD member dealers, finds that a prospective customer thinks that both dividends and capital gains distributions are

paid from the fund's investment income. The salesman ....

1. need not explain the distinction because it is not important
2. must explain to the customer the difference between a dividend and a capital gains distribution
3. neither of the above

385. Sales made by dealers in amounts just below the breakpoint so as to share in higher sales charges are considered by the NASD as being ....

1. in accord with just and equitable principles of trade
2. contrary to just and equitable principles of trade
3. neither of the above

386. When a delivery is late, incomplete, in wrong units, or otherwise unacceptable, the responsibility for setting things right lies with ....

1. the seller
2. the buyer
3. the NASD
4. none of these

387. An assignment may be necessary to transfer the ownership of ....

1. all bonds
2. bearer bonds
3. common stock
4. none of these

388. A power of substitution ....

1. transfers ownership
2. provides for the appointment of an attorney
3. allows the seller to substitute one security for another
4. none of these

389. A when, as, and if contract specifies ....

1. the kind of security to be traded
2. the date of the transaction

3. neither 1 nor 2
4. both 1 and 2

390. A .... type of contract does not specify the time within which a security must be delivered.

1. buyer's option
2. regular-way
3. delayed delivery
4. when, as, and if

391. A regular-way contract normally requires that delivery be made within ....

1. two days after trade date
2. five days after trade date
3. five business days after trade date
4. none of these

392. Registration with the NASD is not required of ....

1. the manager of a securities office of a member
2. an investment counselor who works for a member
3. a broker who handles only stocks traded on the New York Stock Exchange and who is registered with the exchange.
4. all of the above

393. A member who participates in the primary or secondary distribution of an issue of securities must not represent to his customer that he is trading the securities at the market unless the member ....

1. has engaged in the practice of free riding
2. has reasonable grounds to believe that a market for the security exists other than that he himself makes
3. is selling the security at a price not related to the current market price of the security
4. is selling the security in the over-the-counter market rather than on an exchange

394. The seller fails to deliver securities within the period set by a contract;

the buyer may buy the securities else-where (buy in) ....

1. at his own expense
2. without notice to the seller at the seller's expense
3. at the seller's expense, after giving notice to the seller and waiting one day
4. none of the above

395. A member must disclose to a customer, at or before the completion of a transaction, whether ....

1. the member is acting as a broker or dealer in the transaction
2. the member is receiving a larger markup or commission than it did on the last comparable transaction it completed
3. both of the above
4. neither of the above

396. Information about a member's financial condition as disclosed in its most recent balance sheet must be ....

1. mailed to all customers at each quarter
2. sent out with each confirmation of a transaction
3. made available to any regular customer if he requests it
4. divulged only to the NASD and SEC

397. Paying for publication in a news-paper finance column of a report de-signed to influence the market price of a security would be considered ....

1. failure to buy or sell at a stated price
2. inducing the purchase or sale of a secu-rity by a deceptive or manipulative device
3. neither of the above
4. both 1 and 2

398. A member may not offer to buy or sell a security at a quoted price unless ....

1. the member is fairly sure it can obtain the assets to buy with or the securities to sell before any offers are accepted

2. the member is sure that the stated prices will allow a high profit
3. the member is fully prepared to buy or sell at the quoted price
4. all of these

399. Charges for services a member may render to its customers, such as col-lection of interest and dividends, must be ....

1. no more than the cost to the member
2. certified by the member as necessary and reasonable
3. reasonable and not unfairly discrimina-tory between customers
4. none of the above

400. The Rules of Fair Practice state that all transactions in securities must be executed at prices that are fair, consider-ing all relevant circumstances. This means that ....

1. commissions must not be more than 2.5 percent
2. a broker may figure his costs, but not charge for his experience, in his commis-sion
3. the conditions prevailing in the market with respect to the security at the time of the transaction will affect the markup or commission
4. a member must always disclose the amount of its markup or commission be-fore the transaction is effected

401. The Board of Governors has is-sued an interpretation with regard to markups and commissions that states ....

1. any markup of 5 percent or less will be considered fair and reasonable
2. the overly large or excessive expenses of a member may legitimately be covered by large markups and commissions
3. the fairness of markups is based on con-sideration of all relevant factors, of which the percentage of markup is only one
4. all of the above

402. The Maloney Act is ....

1. another name for the Securities and Exchange Act of 1934
2. an amendment to the Securities and Exchange Act of 1934 which provides for self-regulation of securities exchanges
3. an amendment to the Securities and Exchange Act of 1934 which provides for the supervision of the over-the-counter securities market by national securities associations
4. none of these

403. To .... is not a purpose of the National Association of Securities Dealers.

1. provide a medium through which its membership may consult with governmental and other agencies and to promote self-discipline among members
2. adopt and enforce rules of fair practice in the securities business
3. foster increased financial rewards for firms
4. investigate and adjust grievances between public and members

404. The NASD is ....

1. the enforcement branch of the SEC organization
2. a corporation empowered by federal law to require its members to maintain certain high standards
3. an association run by securities dealers to interest the public in securities
4. none of these

405. A member firm of the NASD may not employ a representative unless such representative is registered with the NASD. Ordinarily registration entails ....

1. filing an application with the NASD
2. paying prescribed fees when the application is submitted to the NASD
3. passing a qualification examination
4. all of these

406. No one may be a registered representative of an NASD firm who ....

1. was named as a cause of suspension currently in effect, or of an expulsion or revocation by the NASD or SEC
2. is subject to an order of a national securities exchange revoking or suspending his registration for conduct inconsistent with just and equitable principles of trade
3. has been convicted within the preceding 10 years of a felony or misdemeanor involving purchase or sale of any security.
4. any of the above choices

407. NASD registration may be ....

1. transferred from one representative to another
2. terminated only if there is no complaint pending that involves the registered representative
3. terminated, effective immediately on receipt by the Board of Governors, of the written termination
4. none of the above

408. In executing a transaction with a customer who is known to be an employee of another member, a registered representative must ....

1. determine that the transaction is not adverse to the interest of the member with whom the customer is associated
2. refuse to open an account for a registered representative who works for another member
3. neither of these

409. No member shall give anything of value to any employee of another person for the purpose of influencing or rewarding the actions of such employee in relation to the business of his employer without ....

1. the knowledge and approval of the NASD
2. the knowledge and approval of the SEC
3. the consent of the other employer
4. any of these

410. Advertising and sales literature for any securities or services offered by a member may ....

1. employ come-on techniques, and make flamboyant and misleading statements
2. use the name of the NASD as a reference
3. state that the advertiser is approved by the SEC
4. be factual and informative

411. The terms "free riding" and "withholding" refer to ....

1. excessive activity in a discretionary account
2. identical orders to buy and sell placed at the same time by the same person
3. the failure of a member, while participating in a distribution of securities, to make a bona fide public offering at the public offering price
4. an attempt to stabilize the market price of a security made by a member who is participating in the distribution of a security

412. In determining whether or not a member is guilty of free riding, the NASD ....

1. does not take into account the normal investment practice of the individual
2. takes into account the normal investment practice of the individual

413. A member participating in the primary or secondary distribution of securities may purchase some of the securities for his own account, provided ....

1. his firm holds a position in the securities
2. the amount purchased is not excessive according to the provisions of the prudent man rule
3. he has made a bona fide public offering of the securities, and the amount he purchases for his own account is not excessive in view of his normal investment practice
4. none of these

414. According to the NASD Rules of Fair Practice, selling group and selling syndicate agreements must contain ....

1. the date of the public offering
2. the first ex-dividend date for the security
3. the public offering price or the formula for determining it
4. an indication of interest

415. There are 13 NASD District Business Conduct Committees because ....

1. some districts elect a DBCC and some do not
2. only 13 of the District Committees allow the Board of Governors to appoint a DBCC for their district
3. each District Committee must appoint a DBCC
4. none of these

416. A member may not offer or give anything of value to a person for publishing or circulating in any newspaper or similar publication a report intended to ....

1. advertise the services of a member
2. have an effect on the market price of a security
3. none of these

417. An applicant for NASD membership as a broker-dealer may ....

1. wait to send in its application for SEC registration until after it has received its NASD membership
2. not be granted NASD membership until it has been registered by the SEC
3. not be registered by the SEC until it has received its NASD membership
4. none of the above

418. No broker-dealer may be granted or continued in membership in the NASD if ....

1. any partner, officer, or employee is not qualified for membership under any of

the limitations of the bylaws of the NASD

2. it has been expelled or suspended by the NASD or a national securities exchange
3. the SEC has suspended or revoked its SEC registration, or has suspended or expelled it from the NASD or an exchange
4. all of the above

419. After a complaint about a violation of the Rules of Fair Practice has been filed with a DBCC, ...
1. the SEC is notified of the complaint
2. the respondent is notified of the complaint
3. neither of the above choices
4. both 1 and 2

420. If a hearing is held by the DBCC, it must have been ....
1. requested by the complainant
2. requested by the respondent
3. requested by either or both the complainant and respondent or initiated by the DBCC itself
4. none of the above

421. A DBCC may not state in a normal procedure complaint the decision that ....
1. the complaint is dismissed because the DBCC finds a violation as charged in the complaint was not committed
2. the respondent shall be suspended from membership in the NASD
3. the respondent shall be suspended from membership in the NASD and there shall be no right to appeal this decision
4. none of the above

422. After the DBCC has reached a decision, the respondent or complainant may request the Board of Governors to

review the case, or the Board may review it on its own initiative. This sequence of steps is in accordance with the ....
1. Rules of Fair Practice, Section V
2. Uniform Practice Code
3. Code of Procedure
4. Statement of Policy

423. After reviewing the decision of the DBCC and giving opportunity for another hearing, the Board of Governors may ....
1. uphold the decision of the DBCC
2. reverse the action of the DBCC and dismiss the complaint
3. increase, reduce, modify, or cancel the penalty imposed by the DBCC
4. any of these

424. The Board of Governors may prescribe as a penalty ....
1. suspension or expulsion from membership
2. fine or censure
3. all of these
4. none of the above

425. Membership in the NASD is open to ....
1. all persons who want to buy and sell securities
2. all broker-dealers who are engaged in transacting any branch of the investment banking business under the laws of any state and/or the laws of the United States
3. all brokers or dealers authorized to transact any branch of the investment banking or securities business in the United States, under the laws of any state and/or the laws of the United States, except those who are excluded by statutory or permissive bars to membership
4. none of these

Refer to page 261 for correct answers.

10 | Internal Revenue Code

In addition to the securities laws and regulations, there is another important area of federal jurisdiction that affects investors. This area is taxes, which are fully outlined in the Internal Revenue Code.

There are some basic aspects of the code that every registered representative should be familiar with.

The income tax

Income tax calculations are made on a form called a return. A return must be filed by every citizen of the United States and every resident of the United States, who has gross income of $600 or more (or $1,200 or more for those who have reached age 65). A return must be filed even though the individual's exemptions and deductions are such that there will be no tax liability. Normally, returns must be filed by April 15 of each year with the District Director of Internal Revenue for the district where the taxpayer resides or maintains his principal place of business. Citizens abroad and citizens of U.S. possessions file with the Director of International Operations, Internal Revenue Service, Washington, D.C. 20225.

Taxpayers who have income only from salary, wages, interest, and dividends may file on Form 1040, a single-sheet, two-page form. Those who have other sources of income are required to file, in addition to Form 1040, one or more of the following supplementary forms.

1. *Schedule B,* used for reporting income from rents, royalties, pensions, annuities, partnerships, estates, and trusts.
2. *Schedule C,* used for reporting income from a personally owned business, practice, or profession, such as a sole proprietorship.
3. *Schedule D,* used for reporting income from the sale or exchange of property (capital gains and/or losses).
4. *Schedule E,* used for reporting income from farming.

A very simple return may normally be filed on Form 1040A, which is like an IBM punched card, if an individual's gross income (or that of husband and wife for a joint return) is less than $10,000, and consists entirely of wages on which tax was withheld and not more than $200 total of nonwithheld wages, dividends, and interest.

It is usually advantageous for a husband and wife to file a joint return, because the effect of the joint return is to divide the total taxable income by two. The rate of tax is determined on the basis of the split income, and the final amount due is then multiplied by two. The advantage of filing a joint return is due to the progressive or increasing rate of taxation as taxable income rises. For example, tax rates for 1967 on individuals filing separate returns were as follows.

Taxable Income	Amount of Tax	Rate of Tax on Excess
$	....	14%
500	70	15%
1,000	145	16%
1,500	225	17%
2,000	310	19%
4,000	690	22%
6,000	1,130	25%
8,000	1,630	28%
10,000	2,190	32%
12,000	2,830	36%
150,000	90,490	70%
200,000	125,490	70%

DETERMINATION OF TAXABLE INCOME

Gross income:

Salary		$ 9,000.00
Capital gains (50% of long-term gains)*		1,000.00
Dividends after exclusion		200.00
Interest		200.00
Total Income		$10,400.00

Deductions from gross income:

Entertaining employees and customers $390.00		
Passport fee, business trip 10.00		−400.00
Adjusted gross income (AGI)		$10,000.00

Less: Standard deduction (10% of AGI, maximum $1,000) or itemized nonbusiness expenses (charitable gifts, certain taxes, interest, investors' expenses, medical expenses) .... −1,000.00

Less: Exemptions ($600 per eligible person, including self) .... −600.00

Taxable Income .... $ 8,400.00

* Include 100 percent of short-term capital gains, if any.

Computing the tax

An individual's taxable income of $8,400 is taxable according to the rates shown on page 236.

Tax on $8,000 . . . .$1,630
Tax on $400 at 28% 112
Tax Due $1,742

However, from the tax due the following are deducted.
1. Tax withheld during the year.
2. Estimated tax paid.
3. Retirement income credits.
4. Investment tax credits.
5. Foreign tax credits.

A thorough discussion of taxes is beyond the scope of this book. Tax counsel should be consulted on tax matters. An excellent reference source published by Commerce Clearing House is *U.S. Master Tax Guide*. The above "tax due" amount does not include a temporary surtax of 10 percent which is effective for 1968 tax returns.

Dividend exclusion of $100

Income in the form of wages or interest from savings accounts is treated as ordinary income. However, income from dividends is handled differently, and such income may receive special treatment, because dividends are a distribution of corporate earnings, and these earnings have already been subjected to a federal corporate income tax. Therefore, to compensate for this double taxation of dividend income special tax treatment (the dividend exclusion) is made available to the taxpayer.

The government formerly allowed a $50 dividend exclusion, which simply meant that the first $50 of dividends received by a person during the year was not taxable.[1] If, for example, an investor held three securities, each paying him $100 in dividends, he would have reported $300 less the $50 exclusion, for a total taxable amount of $250. This $250 would then be included in his gross income. In certain circumstances, a husband and wife filing a joint return would have enjoyed a $100 exclusion. The exclusion applies only to dividends received from American corporations. The 1964 tax laws increased the exclusion to $100 per person and $200 for husband and wife.

The *dividend tax credit* was a second relief from double taxation. The government allowed a 4 percent dividend tax credit, which worked as follows. If dividend income after deduction of the exclusion was $250, the investor was usually allowed to deduct 4 percent (e.g., $10) from the total tax due the government that year. The 1964 tax law decreased that amount to 2 percent for 1964, and it is now eliminated. The dividend tax credit no longer exists.

1/ The dividends that may be excluded must be eligible dividends. For example, dividends received from real estate investment trusts and certain exempt corporations, among others, are not eligible.

Capital gains tax

In addition to taxes on ordinary income (e.g., dividends), there is also an income tax on capital gains. Capital gains arise when something is sold at a profit. In order to qualify for capital gains treatment, such sales must not be in the normal course of one's business. The gains are not normally realized and taxable until a sale is made. A sale must normally take place to establish a capital gain or capital loss.

If a sale was made within six months of the time the property was acquired, the gain is *short term* and is taxed as ordinary income. If the sale was made more than six months after the time the property was acquired, then the capital gain is a *long-term capital gain* and is subject to a maximum tax of 25 percent. The capital gains tax is either a flat rate of 25 percent or the amount that would result from adding 50 percent (half) of the gain to ordinary income for the year, whichever is the lesser amount.

Consider the following example. If an investor has a long-term capital gain of $1,000 and is in the 60 percent income tax bracket, then he would pay $250 in taxes (25 percent) on this portion of his income because the maximum tax on long-term capital gains is 25 percent. It would be disadvantageous for this investor to take half of the gain, $500, and include it as ordinary income, because that $500 would be taxed at his bracket rate of 60 percent.

If he has a long-term capital gain of $1,000 but is in the 30 percent income tax bracket, then he would pay only $150. In this case, he adds 50 percent, or half, the capital gain amount ($500) to his gross income. The tax on the additional $500 of income at his bracket rate of 30 percent is only $150.

In order to qualify for long-term capital gains treatment, an investor must have owned property for more than six months. However, there is an exception to this rule. Long-term capital gains distributed by mutual funds are reported as long-term gains by the shareholder, regardless of how long he has held his fund shares. Mutual funds report to their shareholders the breakdown of distributions into long-term or short-term capital gains. Thus, an investor in mutual funds might receive long-term capital gains distributions after owning the fund shares for a period of only one month. The status of distributions paid by mutual funds is based on the period for which the fund has held the security in its portfolio, and not how long the investor has held the fund shares.

To repeat, *short-term* (six months or less) *gains* are taxable as ordinary income, and *long-term* (more than six months) *gains* are taxed at half the rate for ordinary income, or at 25 percent, whichever produces the lesser tax.

The date on which a transaction takes place toward the end of the year may be crucial in determining whether a capital gain or loss is includable in the current year's income tax return or must be postponed until the following year. The rules are:

1. To establish a *loss,* a security may be sold up to and including the last day of the year.
2. To establish a *gain,* the proceeds must have been available to the seller by the last business day of the year. Thus, for a regular-way transaction, the last trade date at

year-end is often before Christmas. If Thursday, December 21, is the trade date, the settlement date in a regular-way transaction will be Friday, December 29. Gains from any regular-way sales on December 22 or later are taxable in the following year.

When a security is sold at a loss, the loss may not be taken for tax purposes if a substantially identical security is purchased within 30 days before or after the sale date (total 61 days). If a substantially identical security is repurchased 31 days after the sale, one may claim the tax loss. When a loss is disallowed, as explained above (a wash sale loss in tax terminology), the cost basis for the acquired stock is adjusted. If the quantity of new securities purchased is equal to the quantity of securities sold and loss disallowed, the adjusted new basis on the new securities is determined as follows.

The basis for new securities (B) equals the cost of the retained securities (R) plus the acquisition price of the securities sold (A) less the sale price of the securities sold (S). Thus, the formula is:

$$B = R + (A - S).$$

For example:

> 1/1/61 buy 100 XYZ for $3,000 ($A$)
> 1/10/68 buy 100 XYZ for $2,500 ($R$)
> 1/25/68 sell 100 XYZ for $2,400 (which were bought 1/1/61) (S)

Thus, B, the basis for the 100 shares still owned is:

> $2,500 ($R$) + ($3,000 (A) − $2,400 ($S$)), or $3,100.

The loss is, of course, disallowed on the sale.

If the investor had sold the 100 shares purchased on 1/10/68, a normal short-term loss of $100 would be allowed. The sale of stock bought less than 30 days previously does not become a wash sale because another lot is held that was bought more than 30 days before the sale.[2] When a security is sold for a gain, there are no restrictions on repurchases.

Investors may have as many as four different types of capital gains and losses. These are: (1) long-term capital gains from sales made more than six months after the purchase; (2) long-term capital losses from sales made more than six months after the purchase; (3) short-term capital gains from sales made six months or less after the purchase; (4) short-term capital losses from sales made six months or less after the purchase.

The procedure for handling such transactions for federal tax purposes is complicated, but a step-by-step analysis may simplify the situation. Total the sum of (1) all long-term capital gains minus all long-term capital losses, and (2) all short-term capital

2/ The wash sale loss provisions do not apply to people who conduct a trade or business in securities. However, such people are not allowed long-term capital gains.

gains minus all short-term capital losses. These two figures represent the net long-term gain or loss and net short-term gain or loss.

If the net long-term total is a plus and the short-term total is a minus, net them. If the result is a long-term gain, it is favorably taxed. If the result is a net short-term loss, $1,000 of it can be used to offset ordinary income, and any excess can be carried over indefinitely as a short-term loss.

If the net long-term total is a loss and the short-term total is a gain, net them, too. If the result is a long-term loss, $1,000 may be used to offset ordinary income this year, and the rest may be carried over indefinitely as long-term capital loss.

If both totals are gains, they are treated separately. The long-term gain is favorably taxed, and the short-term gain is taxed as ordinary income. If both totals are losses, they are also treated separately. First, $1,000 (using short-term loss first) can be employed to offset ordinary income. Anything left is carried over indefinitely to future years' returns as long- or short-term loss, as the case may be.

The capital gain or loss procedure for individual taxpayers (not corporations) may be better understood by referring to the following table. First determine the amount representing net long-term gains minus long-term losses, and the amount representing the net of all short-term capital gains minus short-term losses.

Case	A If net long-term gains minus losses are	B And net short-term gains minus losses are	C And the sum of A plus B is	Then, the gain or loss in C is taxable as
1	plus	minus	a gain	long-term gain
2	plus	minus	a loss	short-term loss
3	minus	plus	a gain	short-term gain
4	minus	plus	a loss	long-term loss
5	plus	plus	treat the two gains separately	
(a)	(1) plus			long-term gain
(b)		(2) plus		short-term gain
6	minus	minus	treat the two losses separately	
(a),	(1) minus			long-term loss
(b)		(2) minus		short-term loss

In cases 1 through 4, the net long-term and net short-term amounts are opposites (plus and minus or vice versa). Note that if the sum of columns A and B, shown in column C, is a gain, the gain is of the same character (i.e., long-term or short-term) as that of the column where a plus appears. If the sum in column C is a loss, the loss is of the same character as that in the column where a minus appears.

In cases 5 and 6, both the long-term and short-term items are plus, or both are minus. In both cases, each item is treated separately; a long-term gain is treated as such, and a short-term gain retains its character. We have previously discussed the tax treatment of both long- and short-term gains.

Capital losses fall into two categories: long-term, from the sale of an asset held longer than six months; and short-term, when a sale is made within six months.

Capital losses must first be used to offset capital gains. If capital losses exceed capital gains, the excess up to $1,000, using short-term losses first, can be deducted from the ordinary income of that year. Any unused losses can be carried forward—as short- or long-term losses, as the case may be—to be used in the same way in future years. For example, a taxpayer sells six securities during the year, as follows.

Security	Period of Time Held before Sale	Gain (Loss)	Type of Gain or Loss
A	2 months	300	Short-term gain
B	8 months	(200)	Long-term loss
C	3 months	(400)	Short-term loss
D	2 months	(300)	Short-term loss
E	7 months	800	Long-term gain
F	9 months	400	Long-term gain

The first step in determining the taxable income is to break down the transactions into long term and short term, and obtain the net gain or loss in each category.

Long Term			Short Term		
Security	Gain	Loss	Security	Gain	Loss
B	...	200	A	300	...
E	800	...	C	...	400
F	400	...	D	...	300
Total	1,200	200	Total	300	700
Net	1,000 gain		Net		400 loss

Mr. Trader, then, has a $1,000 long-term capital gain and a $400 short-term capital loss. The sum of these is plus $600, which is treated as a long-term capital gain.

Short sales and options

A short sale results in a short-term gain or loss, regardless of the length of time between the date of the short sale and the closing out of the sale.

Sales against the box may produce either short- or long-term gains and losses, depending on the holding period of the stock in the box.

The cost of an option is normally added to the price of the stock purchased through exercise of a call. The cost of an option to sell is normally deducted from the sales proceeds derived from exercising a put. However, gains and losses from exercising a put are normally short term, as in short sales.

When options are sold (as opposed to exercised), they are treated like any other security for purposes of determining capital gains and losses.

Stock dividends and rights

Unless a stock dividend or right is received in lieu of cash, the amount is not included as income on its receipt.[3] Its tax status is determined on sale of the stock dividend or rights, or on exercising them.

The basis of stock dividends or rights is allocated in proportion to the fair market value on the date of distribution. Exception: If rights are distributed and their fair market value is less than 15 percent of the stock in respect of which they are issued, the basis of the rights is zero, unless the taxpayer elects to allocate a portion of the basis of the old stock. For example:

Mr. Investor buys 100 XYZ at $65 cost $6,500
He later receives 100 rights, which allow him
the right to buy 50 shares of XYZ at $100
per share.
On the day of the rights distribution:

1. The original 100 shares have a fair market
value of $120 each $12,000
2. The 100 rights have a fair market value of
$10 each 1,000
3. The basis allocation is then $13,000

4. Basis of old shares equals:

$$\frac{\$12{,}000 \text{ old shares}}{\$13{,}000 \text{ total}} \times \$6{,}500 \text{ (cost)} = \$6{,}000.$$

5. The basis of the rights is:

$$\frac{\$1{,}000}{\$13{,}000} \times \$6{,}500 = \$500.$$

If the rights were sold for $1,000, the reportable gain is $500. If the rights are exercised to buy the new stock, the basis of the new stock is the subscription price (50 shares at $100, total $5,000) plus the cost basis of the rights ($500), total $5,500.

3/ A distribution is in lieu of cash if: (*a*) it is made in discharge of preferred dividends for the current or preceding year, or (*b*) there is an option for the stockholder to receive either stock, cash, or other property.

For determining the long-term or short-term nature of gains and losses involving rights, the following rule applies. The holding period of nontaxable stock dividends and stock rights includes the holding period of the stock on which the dividend or rights are distributed; the holding period of the stock acquired by the exercise of rights starts at the date on which the rights were exercised.

Commissions

The commissions paid when purchasing a security are part of the cost price and may not be deducted from income as an expense. The commission paid when selling a security is to be treated as a deduction from the sales proceeds and may not be treated as an expense.

Bonds

If a bond is originally issued ($980) at a discount ($20) from the stated redemption price ($1,000), when the bond is sold by the original purchaser any gain due to the original issue discount may be ordinary income and not capital gain.[4] If at the time of original issue there was no intention to call the bond before maturity, the discount is apportioned over the entire period to the maturity of the bond. If the bond is sold before maturity, only a pro rata part of the original discount is treated as ordinary income. Any gain in excess of that amount could be long-term capital gain.

If, at the time of original issue there was an intention to call the bond before maturity, the discount is not prorated, and the entire gain due to the discount is treated as ordinary income. For example, Mr. Investor buys a $1,000, 10-year bond from the issuer for $850. The issuer had no intention of calling the bond before maturity. A year later, Mr. Investor sold the bond for $910. The portion of the $60 gain that is ordinary income is 1/10 times the $150 original discount, or $15. Of the $60 gain, $15 is ordinary income. Long-term capital gain is $45.

In the case of bonds purchased at a premium, whether at original issuance or from another investor, the premium ($200) is the amount of the bond's cost basis ($1,200) that exceeds the redemption value ($1,000).

The investor who owns taxable bonds may elect to amortize the premium over the life of the bond by deducting the pro rata portion from interest income for the year. The amount of premium, so amortized, reduces the cost basis of the bond by the same amount. For tax-exempts, the premium must be amortized. Amortization of premium is not allowed for any portion of the premium due to a convertible feature of the bond. The amount of premium that is a result of a convertible feature may be determined by comparing the bond price to that of similar quality nonconvertibles selling on the open market.

4/ If the amount of the original issue discount is less than 0.25 percent of the redemption price at maturity times the number of years to maturity, the discount will be considered to be zero.

For example, Mr. Investor buys a 6 percent, $1,000 nonconvertible bond for $1,020. The bond matures in 10 years. He may elect, if it is a taxable bond (and must elect if it is tax-exempt), to amortize the premium at the rate of $2 per year. The $2 per year is deductible on his tax return. At maturity, his cost basis will be $1,000.

When bonds are traded flat, the purchase price and cost basis are the same. If accrued interest in default at the time of purchase is paid later, the part representing accrued interest is treated as a return of capital. For example, Mr. Investor buys a 4.5 percent bond for $900 flat. Accrued interest of $90 was in default at the time of purchase. Later in the year, he receives an interest payment of $135. Income is $45, and $90 is a return of capital, which reduces his cost basis from $900 to $810.

When taxable bonds are sold between interest dates, the accrued interest up to the date of sale is taxable to the seller. Interest after the date of sale is taxable to the buyer. Both the seller and buyer ignore the accrued interest in determining the selling price and cost basis. For example, Mr. Investor sells Mr. Smith a 6 percent, $1,000 bond for $1,025. Accrued interest to the date of sale is $25. When Mr. Smith receives his $30 interest check, he should report only $5 as income. Mr. Investor reports $25 as interest, and treats the sale price as $1,000. The cost basis for Mr. Smith is also $1,000.

If a bond is purchased with coupons detached, when the bond is sold later, and if there is a gain, the portion representing the artificial discount due to detached coupons is treated as ordinary income.

When a corporation issues bonds at face value, there is neither a gain nor a loss. If bonds are issued at a premium, the premium is amortized over the life of the issue, and the annual pro rata amount is income to the corporation. When bonds are issued at a discount, the discount is amortized over the life of the bond, and the pro rata annual amount is treated as an expense.

Corporate 85 percent dividend credit

In corporations, dividend income from investments in the securities of other corporations may be treated differently than direct business income or dividend income to individuals. Eligible dividends received by a corporation are subject to an 85 percent deduction, so only 15 percent of the dividend income is taxable.[5] This is called the 85 percent dividend credit for corporations.

Corporate tax

For purposes of taxation, the Internal Revenue Code treats both corporations and other entities as corporations, including certain trusts, partnerships, and associations. Generally, it is disadvantageous to be taxed as a corporation, and competent legal counsel should be consulted to avoid unnecessary taxation through careful planning. In

---

5/ Eligible dividends include only those received from other U.S. corporations, which are subject to income tax and, in certain rare cases, dividends from foreign (non-U.S.) corporations. In certain cases, dividends received by a corporation from nonconsolidated affiliates are allowed a 100 percent deduction.

the special case of some closely held (10 shareholders or less) corporations, known as tax-option or subchapter S corporations, election may be made to be not subject to the corporate income tax. Then, shareholders include in their personal returns their proportionate shares of the corporation's taxable income—as in a partnership.

Corporation taxable income is computed in a manner similar to that of individuals' income. However, corporations do not have an adjusted gross income. Capital losses of corporations may not be offset against other income. Such capital losses may be offset against capital gains only during the five years after the year in which the loss occurred.

Every U.S. corporation that is not exempt must file a corporate income tax return (usually Form 1120) by March 15. Corporations on a fiscal-year basis must file by the 15th day of the 3rd month following the close of the fiscal year. The fiscal year is a corporation's accounting year. Due to the nature of a particular business, some companies do not use the calendar year for their bookkeeping, although most do. Some, such as department stores, customarily use a fiscal year on February 1 through January 31 of the next year. Other companies may run from July 1 through the following June 30.

Rate of corporate tax

Corporations pay tax at the rate of 22 percent on the first $25,000 of taxable income, and 48 percent of taxable income over $25,000.[6] An additional accumulated earnings tax may be imposed on corporations that avoid income tax by an unreasonable accumulation of earnings (in excess of $100,000) not distributed to shareholders. The rate of additional tax is 27.5 percent on the first $100,000 of such unreasonable accumulation, and 38.5 percent on the excess.

A similar additional tax, at a 70 percent rate, is imposed on undistributed personal holding company income. A personal holding company is a corporation: (1) whose stock is more than 50 percent owned directly or indirectly by 5 or less individuals; and (2) that has at least 60 percent of its adjusted income derived from dividends, interest, rents, and royalties.

Regulated investment companies

Mutual funds may qualify as regulated investment companies under the provisions of subchapter M of the Internal Revenue Code if they disburse or pass on at least 90 percent of their dividend income. If they qualify, there is no tax on the interest and dividends received by the fund that are, in fact, distributed. If 5 percent of the dividends received by the fund were retained, the fund would pay tax on that amount. Of course, the fund shareholders who receive a portion of this net investment income must pay taxes as individuals.

Additionally, in order to qualify the fund must be a domestic (U.S.) corporation (not a personal holding company) registered under the Investment Company Act of

6/ These are the rates in effect on February 1, 1968. These rates do not include the 10 percent temporary surtax which is effective for 1968 returns.

1940 for the entire taxable year as a management company or unit investment trust, and must maintain a specified portfolio diversification.[7] If the fund did not disburse at least 90 percent of its earnings, it would be subject to the corporate income tax like any other corporation, but regulated investment companies are exempt from the corporate income tax. This is called *conduit theory* of taxation for mutual funds.

By qualifying as a regulated investment company and distributing 90 percent of net investment income to shareholders, the fund pays no federal corporation tax on dividends, except for any undistributed or retained income. The fund is also exempt from federal taxation on realized capital gains that have been distributed to shareholders; such capital gains distributions to shareholders are taxed to the shareholders themselves as long-term gains. If realized capital gains are retained by the fund and not distributed, they are taxable to the fund. The special tax treatment for regulated investment companies avoids the normal corporation income tax, which in January, 1968, was 22 percent of the first $25,000 of income, and 48 percent of income over $25,000.

Other taxes on individuals

In addition to income taxes, individuals also must pay federal estate tax, gift tax, transfer tax, and interest equalization tax.

Federal estate tax

Estate taxes are levied on the taxable estate of a deceased person. A U.S. citizen may leave one half of his estate to his spouse without being subject to the estate tax. In addition, there is a $60,000 estate tax exclusion; that is, up to $60,000 of the estate of a U.S. citizen is not taxed under the present federal estate tax. Thus, a U.S. citizen may leave an estate of $120,000 and have no estate tax liability if at least one half of the estate is left to the spouse. Property in an estate may be valued at either the time of death or one year later, whichever time yields the lesser estate value.

Federal gift tax

There is also a federal gift tax. However, substantial gifts may be bestowed before one becomes subject to the gift tax.

There is an annual gift exclusion of $3,000 ($6,000 if the donor is married, and both he and his wife are U.S. citizens) for gifts to any one person. This means that the donor may give every year up to $3,000 each (or $6,000 if his wife is also a U.S.

7/ At least 50 percent of the fund's assets must consist of cash, cash items, or securities limited to not more than 5 percent of its assets in securities of any one issuer, and not more than 10 percent of the outstanding voting securities of that issuer. At least 90 percent of the fund's gross income during any taxable year must be earned in the form of dividends, interest, and capital gains from the sale of securities. Not more than 30 percent of its gross income may be derived from the sale of securities held for less than three months.

citizen) to any number of other persons without filing a gift tax return. If he gives over $3,000 (or $6,000, if applicable) to any one person in one year, the excess over this amount is a taxable gift, and the donor must file a return, reporting all such excess amounts (taxable gifts) made during that year.

The return is due at the same time as the income tax return, ordinarily on or before April 15 of the following year. Aside from this, there is no relationship between the income tax return and the gift tax return; that is, gifts, whether or not taxable as such, are not deductible for income tax purposes, unless they are gifts to charity or similar donations.

Even when taxable gifts are reported as described above, no tax is payable until the donor has used up his entire lifetime exemption of $30,000 of taxable gifts (this is also combined with his wife's lifetime exemption, if his wife is also a U.S. citizen, to become $60,000 for the two together, no matter which of them actually makes the gifts). This $30,000 (or $60,000, where applicable) is a single exemption, covering the donor's entire lifetime of taxable gifts; it is not an annual exemption.

Also, the exemption is cumulative; that is, if $15,000 of taxable gifts (amounts in excess of the annual $3,000 or $6,000 exclusions) are reported in one year on the first gift tax return the donor has ever filed, and a further $15,000 of taxable gifts in the aggregate are reported in subsequent years, he has then used up his entire lifetime exemption (the amounts are doubled for the U.S. citizen husband-and-wife). From that point on, he can still give individual gifts of up to $3,000 ($6,000, where applicable) a year to any number of persons without reporting the gifts, but any excess over this amount to any person (taxable gift) must be reported on a gift tax return, and the applicable tax must be paid.

The federal government currently taxes gifts at rates ranging from 2.25 percent to 57.75 percent which are three-quarters of the estate tax rates (1968). Since the gift tax rate is lower than the estate tax rate, many people prefer to make gifts during their lifetime to avoid the higher estate taxes at death. However, the government has ruled that any gift made in the three years before death may be considered to have been in *contemplation of death,* and therefore may be taxable, not at the gift rates, but at the estate tax rates.

For purposes of determining estate tax and the new cost basis to the heirs, securities held until death currently are valued at their current value at the time of death or one year after the time of death. These securities (of a decedent) are not subject to income (capital gain) tax.

Transfer taxes

Federal transfer taxes formerly were imposed on the transfer of securities from one person to another. The rate was 4 cents per $100 of value. This tax no longer exists. However, many states, including New York, still impose transfer taxes. Transfer taxes are paid by the seller of securities and not by the buyer.

Interest equalization tax

In order to help the United States deficit balance-of-payments situation, an interest equalization tax is currently imposed on U.S. citizens or residents who buy foreign securities or debt instruments. The tax (1968) is generally 18.75 percent of the amount invested, and is payable at the time a purchase is made. Certain exemptions from the tax are made for purchases of new issues of Canadian corporations and for investments made in certain less-developed countries.

Since gift, estate, and other taxes are every bit as complex as income taxes, investors should consult qualified experts to avoid costly mistakes.

State and local taxes

In addition to the federal taxes, most states also impose income taxes and inheritance taxes. Further, subdivisions of the state levy city or county taxes, such as real estate taxes and personal property taxes.

FICA, unemployment, and self-employed taxes

Under the Federal Insurance Contribution Act, employers were required in 1966 to withhold 4.2 percent from each payment of wages up to a cumulative total of $6,600 paid to the employee during the year. This is the employer's share of the tax and represents the combined total of social security (3.85 percent) and medicare (0.35 percent). The employer pays an additional 4.2 percent on behalf of the employees. Beginning in 1967, the social security rate increased to 3.9 percent and medicare to 0.5 percent, making the combined FICA rate 4.4 percent.

Employers who have 4 or more covered workers pay unemployment taxes in the amount of 3.1 percent of the first $3,000 of wages of such workers.

A combined tax rate (1967) of 6.4 percent—5.9 percent for social security and 0.50 percent for medicare—is levied on up to $6,600 of income of most self-employed persons.

Conclusion

Taxes are extremely complicated, and qualified experts must be consulted. This chapter attempts only to touch the highlights of the more important taxes. We have mentioned several items that may be of interest to the investor who seeks to reduce taxes, including tax-exempts and certain contractual plan investments[8] in mutual funds. Other ventures available for the investor who can afford the cost and risks include real estate (tax shelter is obtained through the combination of high interest payments and accelerated depreciation), oil ventures (intangible drilling costs and depletion provide the tax shelter), and cattle purchase (cattle are depreciated over a short life span).

8/ See Chapter 4, "Mutual Funds and the Investment Company Act of 1940."

10 | Review questions

426. Of the taxes that affect investors and their investments generally, the most important one is the ....
   1. estate tax
   2. gift tax
   3. income tax
   4. transfer tax

427. Dividends and interest received by an individual from taxable securities are classed for tax purposes as ....
   1. capital gains income
   2. corporate income
   3. ordinary income
   4. none of these

428. An individual's ordinary income is taxed at a rate ....
   1. not exceeding 25 percent
   2. based on the amount of his gross income
   3. based on the amount of his taxable income
   4. of 22 percent or 48 percent, depending on whether the amount to be taxed is over $25,000

429. The $100 exclusion is allowed ....
   1. to reduce capital gains income
   2. to all individual taxpayers
   3. to compensate for the double taxation of dividends
   4. none of these

430. The double taxation of dividends involves ....
   1. the corporate income tax and the personal income tax
   2. the taxation of dividends received by two persons in the same family
   3. a double tax on certain bonds
   4. the dividend and interest income from stocks and bonds

431. The term "tax-exempt" as used in tax-exempt bonds means that ....
   1. no taxes of any kind are levied against them
   2. interest received from such bonds is not subject to the federal income tax
   3. profits from their sale are not taxable
   4. none of the above

432. The interest from a .... is subject to the federal income tax.
   1. Kentucky Turnpike bond
   2. U.S. savings bond
   3. Louisville sewer bond
   4. New York Port Authority bond

433. A capital gain occurs when ....
   1. a security is sold
   2. a security has a paper gain
   3. a security is sold for less than was paid for it
   4. none of the above

434. A long-term capital gain or loss results from the sale of a security held for ....
   1. less than six months
   2. six months or less
   3. six months or more
   4. more than six months

435. A net long-term capital gain is taxed ....
   1. at the same rate as a net short-term capital gain
   2. at the same rate as one's dividends and interest
   3. at a rate not less than 25 percent
   4. at a rate not higher than 25 percent

436. A net short-term capital gain is taxed ....

1. at the same rate as a net long-term capital gain
2. at the same rate as one's dividends and interest
3. at a rate not less than 25 percent
4. at a rate not higher than 25 percent

437. If at the end of a year an individual has

$12,000 of long-term gains,
$10,000 of short-term gains,
$18,000 of long-term losses,
$ 6,000 of short-term losses,

he has, for tax purposes, a net capital ....

1. gain, long term, of $2,000
2. loss, long term, $2,000
3. gain, short term, of $2,000
4. loss, short term, of $2,000

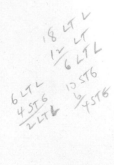

438. Capital losses that exceed capital gains may be deducted from ordinary income in an amount that does not exceed ....

1. $ 1,000
2. $10,000
3. $ 500
4. $ 10

439. The rate not used in reference to the corporate income tax is ....

1. 22 percent
2. 48 percent
3. graduated rate
4. none of these

440. A gift of securities made within three years of the donor's death ....

1. is never taxed at the deceased's estate tax rate
2. is not taxed at the estate tax rate when it can be proved that the gift was not made in anticipation of death
3. is always taxed at the gift tax rate
4. none of these

441. When securities pass to an estate, any accrued gains ....

1. are taxed at a rate not higher than 25 percent
2. are passed on to the heir without the gain's being subject to the income tax
3. may be subject to both the estate tax and the income tax
4. none of these

442. Tax and legal questions should always be referred to one's ....

1. registered representative
2. securities analyst
3. attorney or accountant
4. sister-in-law

443. The term .... describes the manner in which regulated investment companies are taxed.

1. conduit treatment
2. triple taxation
3. unfairly
4. none of these

444. The qualifications for becoming a regulated investment company are stated in ....

1. section 26 of the Investment Company Act of 1940
2. regulation U of the Federal Reserve Board
3. subchapter M of the Internal Revenue Code
4. Securities Act of 1933

445. An investment company is given conduit treatment ....

1. always
2. only if it qualifies as an open-end management company
3. only if it qualifies as a regulated investment company
4. none of these

446. "Regulated investment company" refers to ....

1. the restrictions imposed on the managers of an investment company

2. the tax status of an investment company
3. neither 1 nor 2
4. both 1 and 2

447. In order to qualify as a regulated investment company, an investment company must ....

1. be registered under the Investment Company Act of 1940 for the entire taxable year
2. observe certain regulations concerning diversification of portfolio
3. distribute at least 90 percent of its net investment income, exclusive of capital gains
4. all of the above

448. A regulated investment company pays taxes on ....

1. its total investment income
2. its net income
3. its retained income
4. none of these

449. A fund shareholder's dividends are usually taxed as ....

1. dividends in the same way as those from other U.S. corporations
2. estate gains
3. tax-exempt interest
4. gifts

450. A fund shareholder is taxed on his long-term capital gains ....

1. at a minimum rate of 25 percent
2. at a maximum rate of 25 percent
3. at a maximum rate of 20 percent
4. at a maximum rate of 40 percent

Refer to page 261 for correct answers.

451. A mutual fund investor reports .... on his federal personal income tax form.

1. dividends received
2. capital gains distributions received
3. both 1 and 2
4. neither 1 nor 2

452. If an investment company retains its capital gains, ...

1. the company does not pay taxes on these gains
2. the company pays the taxes on these gains on behalf of its shareholders

453. A U.S. person who dies, leaving a total estate of $40,000, would ordinarily expect his estate to pay a federal estate tax of ....

1. $ 1,000
2. $10,000
3. $ 5,000
4. $0

454. A U.S. person who gives his daughter a gift of $3,000 worth of securities during a year would pay a federal gift tax of approximately ....

1. $750
2. $100
3. 4 percent
4. $0

455. The interest equalization tax may apply to ....

1. all interest
2. the acquisition of foreign stock or debt instruments
3. dividend receipts
4. none of these

General review questions

456. A corporation's intangible assets include ....
1. brand names
2. good will
3. patents and trademarks
4. all of these

457. Which of the following statements are (is) true? ....
1. The term "bid wanted" (or BW) means a security is being offered for sale, and prospective buyers are requested to submit a bid for it; the term "offer wanted" (or OW) means the security referred to is being sought for purchase, and anyone who wants to sell is requested to submit an offer.
2. Offered firm means that the seller has made an offer good for the period of time specified by the seller or until rejected.
3. Firm bids or firm offers are prices at which a dealer is committed to buy or sell securities.
4. All of these are true.

458. Which of the following statements is (are) false? ....
1. When a customer inquires how a security is quoted, it is sufficient if you tell him how your firm is offering that security.
2. A market order is an order to buy or sell at the best obtainable price prevailing in the market when the order is entered.

3. An open order is an order entered at a specific price and is good until canceled.
4. A good 'til canceled order is an order entered at a specific price and is good until canceled.

459. When a bond is trading flat, ...
1. it is selling at a discount
2. it is selling at face value
3. it is selling without accrued interest
4. the buyer is entitled to all interest due

460. An income bond is one that ....
1. guarantees a specific amount of interest annually
2. provides a fixed rate of income return
3. shares with preferred stock in distribution of income
4. may be secured as to principal, but has claim for interest only in event earnings are available

461. Included among the requirements for listing a stock on the New York Stock Exchange, among other things, is (are) ....
1. the number of shares outstanding and the number of shareholders
2. the demonstrated earning power of the corporation after taxes
3. the amount of net tangible assets
4. all of the above

462. In discussing with a prospective customer the features of a contractual systematic investment plan, ... must be taken into consideration.

1. the financial ability of the prospect to continue payments to completion
2. the age of the prospect
3. the prospect's investment objective
4. all of the above

463. The maximum total sales load that may lawfully be charged on contractual investment plans is ....

1. 50 percent of total payments
2. 8 percent of total payments
3. 9 percent of total payments
4. 50 percent of the first 12 payments

464. The XYZ stock can be bought in New York at $10 per share and sold in London at $10.50 per share. A simultaneous purchase of the stock in New York and sale of the same stock in London would be considered ....

1. leverage
2. hedging
3. arbitrage
4. put and call

465. Which of the following mutual funds are most volatile? ....

1. a diversified bond fund
2. a balanced fund
3. an income fund
4. a common stock growth fund

466. Which of the following relating to the Statement of Policy is true? ....

1. The Statement of Policy forbids any representation that investment company shares generally have been selected for investment by fiduciary groups or institutions, and the SOP on investment company sales literature requires that reference be made to a prospectus for information on the sales charge and other facts.

2. Capital gains distributions may never be included with ordinary income in computing a percentage yield or dollar return on investment company shares.
3. In computing rates of return on investment company shares on the basis of dividends paid in the last 12 months, all of these elements must always be present and shown: current offering price, income dividends paid, asset value change in period, disclaimer as to future results.
4. All of the above are true.

467. If a corporation must borrow money for a short time, it ....

1. goes to a commercial bank
2. goes to an investment banker
3. issues bonds
4. gives a stock dividend

468. Dividends are ....

1. contractual payments required of all corporations
2. pro rata distributions among outstanding shares, usually paid in cash
3. adjustments necessary to change the par value of common or preferred stock
4. interest paid to holders of common stock on the basis of shares owned

469. Which of the following statements are (is) true? ....

1. Payments of dividends are required of all corporations.
2. Dividends can be paid only out of current earnings.
3. Annual dividends per share can never exceed annual earnings per share.
4. None of these is true.

470. The A.A.A. Corporation, whose stock is selling at $100, declares a 4 for 1 stock split. The purpose of the split is probably ....

1. to give each stockholder a greater interest in the assets and earnings of the company
2. to increase the earnings ratio per share by 25 percent

3. to create a wider distribution of its shares by stimulating investor interest by reason of the lower price per share
4. none of these

471. The holders of .... of a corporation have prior claim to share in the assets of the corporation in the event of a liquidation or bankruptcy.
1. preferred stock
2. treasury stock
3. bonds
4. common stock

472. The XY Motor Corporation declares a dividend to holders of record July 15, payable August 1. The likely ex-dividend date is ....
1. July 11
2. July 16
3. August 2
4. August 16

473. Which of the following statements are (is) true? ....
1. In a bull market, all securities rise in value.
2. Bear market refers to a period when common stocks in general are rising.
3. During a bull market, common stock prices, in general, are rising.
4. The Dow Jones Averages are a weighted average of all the securities listed on the New York Stock Exchange.

474. Which of the following statements are (is) false? ....
1. Churning, or excessive activity in customers' accounts, is subject to disciplinary action under the Rules of Fair Practice.
2. Shares of open-end investment companies are proper vehicles for in-and-out trading.
3. When recommending that a customer purchase a particular security, all essential information about the security must be supplied.
4. None of these is false.

475. Investing fixed amounts of money at regular intervals is ....
1. dollar averaging
2. averaging the dollar
3. dollar cost averaging
4. market averaging

Each of the regulatory agencies referred to in questions 476 to 480 derives its authority from a federal law and/or amendments thereto. Identify the source of the agency's authority from the following federal laws:
1. Investment Company Act of 1940 and/or Securities Act of 1933 and/or Securities and Exchange Act of 1934.
2. Federal Reserve Act
3. Internal Revenue Code
4. Interstate Commerce Act

476. The agency with which a broker-dealer must register in order to deal in securities ....

477. The agency authorized to set margin requirements ....

478. The agency authorized to prescribe rules of fair practice for members of the association of over-the-counter dealers ....

479. The agency that determines the tax status of distributions from investment company shares ......3..... .

480. The agency that issued the Statement of Policy governing sales literature ......1...... .

481. Supervision over the transactions and correspondence of registered representatives of broker-dealers is the responsibility of ....
1. the NASD District Committees
2. the SEC Division of Enforcement
3. the broker-dealer with whom the registered representative is associated
4. the Department of Justice

482. The 5 percent markup policy is a guide and not a rigid rule. In determining the fairness of a particular markup, ... would be taken into consideration.

1. the type of security involved
2. the availability of the security in the market
3. the price of the security and the amount of money involved in the transaction
4. all of these ✓

483. In ...., the 5 percent markup policy is not applicable.

1. a transaction in which a member sells a security to a customer as agent for another member
2. a transaction in which a member purchases a security from a customer
3. a sale of securities when a prospectus is required to be delivered and the securities are sold at the specific public offering price ✓
4. all of these

484. Which of the following appears to conform to the Statement of Policy? ....

1. The customer is not informed that a lower sales charge would apply to a $25,000 purchase, when he wants to purchase $24,000 of a certain fund.
2. An advertisement states that "The ABC Mutual Fund provides liberal and continuous dividends for your retirement. Send for the prospectus for particulars about the sales charge and other information."
3. "The XYZ Mutual Fund invests in growth stocks. $10,000 invested in this fund 10 years ago is worth $30,000 today. Prospectus on request."
4. "The A.A.A. Mutual Fund seeks to provide better-than-average income. Send for the prospectus for particulars about the sales charge and other information." ✓

485. Persons who are registered representatives, as defined by the bylaws of the NASD, and who must register with the NASD include ....

1. every officer of a member
2. every partner of a member
3. every employee of a member who is engaged in the managing, supervision, solicitation, trading, handling, or sale of listed or unlisted securities
4. all of the above ✓

486. The amount by which the market value of a security or portfolio of securities exceeds, at a given time, the cost price is the ....

1. profit margin
2. net realized appreciation
3. unrealized appreciation ✓
4. capital gain

487. An investment objective, as distinguished from investment policy of an investment company, would be ....

1. better-than-average current income ✓
2. 90 percent of assets invested in common stocks
3. the fund's investment in special situations with good growth potential
4. 2 and 3

488. Margin requirements are established by the ....

1. SEC
2. Interstate Commerce Commission
3. Federal Reserve Board ✓
4. Congress

489. Retained earnings would be found ....

1. on the assets side of the balance sheet
2. on the liabilities side of the balance sheet ✓
3. on the assets side of the profit and loss statement
4. on the liabilities side of the profit and loss statement

490. The net worth of a corporation is ....

1. the total shares outstanding
2. the total value of its assets
3. its total assets less its total liabilities ✓
4. the capital stock less the outstanding indebtedness

491. The advantage of the corporate form of business organization over the partnership or single proprietorship is ....

1. in general, the ability to raise large amounts of capital
2. limited liability of stockholders
3. continuity of existence irrespective of stockholders' death or transfer of interest
4. all of these

492. The .... is not considered a current asset.

1. inventory
2. cash
3. machinery
4. accounts receivable

493. When interest rates in general rise, the price of bonds tends to ....

1. rise
2. fall
3. remain unchanged
4. show no relationship

494. A charter from the .... is necessary in order to form a corporation.

1. Federal Trade Commission
2. Interstate Commerce Commission
3. state
4. SEC

495. Working capital is usually used to buy ....

1. new machinery
2. materials or inventory
3. new factory
4. any of these

496. In general, a corporation assumes the least risk when it obtains funds from ....

Refer to page 261 for correct answers.

1. a commercial bank
2. sale of bonds
3. sale of preferred stock
4. sale of debentures

497. The XYZ Corporation 5 percent bond ($1,000 face value) is quoted at 101 7/8. This means that a purchaser, in addition to commissions, must pay ....

1. $1,010.88
2. $ 101.88 plus accrued interest
3. $1,018.75 plus accrued interest
4. $1,018.75

498. If a bond is selling at a premium, the yield to maturity is ....

1. less than the rate stated on the bond
2. more than the rate stated on the bond
3. the same as the stated rate
4. indeterminable

499. The price-earnings ratio of a corporation is commonly used to determine ....

1. the risk involved in an investment in the company's stock
2. the reasonableness of the market price of a security
3. the ratio of profits to sales
4. the income on capital employed by the company

500. The fee paid to the management company of a mutual fund is ....

1. part of the acquisition cost paid by shareholders
2. an operating expense of the fund
3. part of the custodial fee paid by the fund
4. none of these

Answers to review questions

Chapter 1

1.	3	15.	3	29.	3	42.	2	55.	2
2.	4	16.	2	30.	2	43.	1	56.	1
3.	3	17.	2	31.	2	44.	3	57.	3
4.	4	18.	2	32.	1	45.	4	58.	3
5.	4	19.	2	33.	2	46.	3	59.	1
6.	4	20.	1	34.	1	47.	3	60.	3
7.	3	21.	1	35.	2	48.	3	61.	1
8.	1	22.	1	36.	4	49.	3	62.	2
9.	2	23.	4	37.	1	50.	1	63.	1
10.	3	24.	4	38.	2	51.	1	64.	3
11.	2	25.	2	39.	4	52.	3	65.	2
12.	4	26.	1	40.	2	53.	2	66.	3
13.	1	27.	4	41.	2	54.	2	67.	3
14.	4	28.	2						

68.	3	74.	1
69.	1	75.	1
70.	3	76.	3
71.	3	77.	1
72.	2	78.	3
73.	3	79.	4
		80.	4

Chapter 2

81.	1	86.	4	91.	4	96.	2	101.	2	106.	3
82.	4	87.	3	92.	2	97.	2	102.	2	107.	3
83.	3	88.	2	93.	3	98.	4	103.	4	108.	2
84.	2	89.	2	94.	3	99.	3	104.	4	109.	1
85.	1	90.	1	95.	2	100.	2	105.	1	110.	3

Chapter 3

111.	2	116.	2	121.	2	126.	1	131.	2	136.	2
112.	3	117.	1	122.	2	127.	3	132.	1	137.	3
113.	1	118.	3	123.	4	128.	1	133.	2	138.	1
114.	3	119.	3	124.	3	129.	3	134.	1	139.	2
115.	4	120.	2	125.	2	130.	3	135.	1	140.	2

Chapter 4

141.	4	151.	2	161.	1	171.	2	181.	2	191.	3
142.	4	152.	2	162.	2	172.	2	182.	2	192.	1
143.	2	153.	2	163.	2	173.	2	183.	2	193.	3
144.	3	154.	3	164.	1	174.	1	184.	4	194.	2
145.	1	155.	3	165.	2	175.	3	185.	2	195.	2
146.	3	156.	2	166.	3	176.	2	186.	1	196.	1
147.	1	157.	1	167.	1	177.	2	187.	3	197.	2
148.	3	158.	2	168.	2	178.	3	188.	1	198.	1
149.	2	159.	1	169.	3	179.	2	189.	1	199.	1
150.	1	160.	1	170.	4	180.	3	190.	2	200.	2

201.	3	208.	1	215.	3	222.	3	229.	2	235.	2
202.	4	209.	3	216.	1	223.	2	230.	2	236.	2
203.	2	210.	2	217.	2	224.	2	231.	1	237.	2
204.	2	211.	1	218.	2	225.	2	232.	3	238.	2
205.	2	212.	1	219.	2	226.	1	233.	2	239.	3
206.	2	213.	2	220.	1	227.	1	234.	1	240.	1
207.	1	214.	2	221.	3	228.	4				

Chapter 5

241.	4	246.	2	251.	4	256.	3	261.	1	266.	2
242.	2	247.	4	252.	3	257.	3	262.	3	267.	3
243.	1	248.	4	253.	3	258.	1	263.	2	268.	2
244.	4	249.	3	254.	4	259.	3	264.	3	269.	1
245.	4	250.	2	255.	3	260.	2	265.	3	270.	3

Chapter 6

271.	4	276.	4	281.	3	286.	1	291.	3
272.	3	277.	2	282.	1	287.	1	292.	2
273.	1	278.	2	283.	3	288.	3	293.	2
274.	4	279.	3	284.	1	289.	3	294.	3
275.	4	280.	1	285.	3	290.	4	295.	2

Chapter 7

296.	2	301.	4	306.	4	311.	4
297.	3	302.	4	307.	2	312.	4
298.	1	303.	3	308.	4	313.	2
299.	4	304.	1	309.	1	314.	4
300.	2	305.	4	310.	2	315.	2

Chapter 8

316.	1	325.	3	334.	1	342.	3	350.	3	358.	1
317.	1	326.	1	335.	4	343.	3	351.	2	359.	3
318.	3	327.	1	336.	2	344.	3	352.	1	360.	4
319.	2	328.	3	337.	4	345.	2	353.	3	361.	2
320.	1	329.	1	338.	2	346.	1	354.	3	362.	3
321.	3	330.	2	339.	2	347.	2	355.	2	363.	2
322.	3	331.	4	340.	3	348.	1	356.	2	364.	3
323.	2	332.	3	341.	1	349.	3	357.	2	365.	4
324.	3	333.	3								

Chapter 9

366.	4	376.	1	386.	1	396.	3	406.	4	416.	2
367.	4	377.	4	387.	3	397.	2	407.	2	417.	2
368.	3	378.	3	388.	2	398.	3	408.	1	418.	4
369.	2	379.	1	389.	1	399.	3	409.	3	419.	2
370.	4	380.	3	390.	4	400.	3	410.	4	420.	3
371.	3	381.	2	391.	3	401.	3	411.	3	421.	3
372.	1	382.	3	392.	3	402.	3	412.	2	422.	3
373.	2	383.	2	393.	2	403.	3	413.	3	423.	4
374.	2	384.	2	394.	3	404.	2	414.	3	424.	3
375.	2	385.	2	395.	1	405.	4	415.	3	425.	3

Chapter 10

426.	3	431.	2	436.	2	441.	2	446.	2	451.	3
427.	3	432.	2	437.	2	442.	3	447.	4	452.	2
428.	3	433.	4	438.	1	443.	1	448.	3	453.	4
429.	3	434.	4	439.	3	444.	3	449.	1	454.	4
430.	1	435.	4	440.	2	445.	3	450.	2	455.	2

General review

456.	4	464.	3	472.	1	480.	1	487.	1	494.	3
457.	4	465.	4	473.	3	481.	3	488.	3	495.	2
458.	1	466.	4	474.	2	482.	4	489.	2	496.	3
459.	3	467.	1	475.	3	483.	3	490.	3	497.	3
460.	4	468.	2	476.	1	484.	4	491.	4	498.	1
461.	4	469.	4	477.	1	485.	4	492.	3	499.	2
462.	4	470.	3	478.	1	486.	3	493.	2	500.	2
463.	3	471.	3	479.	3						

Bibliography

Amling, Frederick. *Investments.* Englewood Cliffs, N.J.: Prentice-Hall, Inc., 1965.

Badger, Ralph H.; Torgerson, H.; and Guthmann, H. *Investment Principles and Practices.* 5th ed. Englewood Cliffs, N.J.: Prentice-Hall, Inc., 1961.

Board of Governors of the Federal Reserve System. *Federal Reserve Act.* Washington, D.C., 1966.

———. *Federal Reserve Bulletin,* Washington, D.C., February, 1966.

———. *Federal Reserve System.* 4th ed. Washington, D.C., 1961.

Bogen, J. I. *Financial Handbook.* New York: The Ronald Press Co., 1965.

Casey, William J. *Mutual Funds and How to Use Them.* 4th ed. New York: Institute for Business Planning, Inc.

———. *Mutual Funds Desk Book.* 2d printing. New York: Institute for Business Planning, Inc.

Cohen, J. B., and Zinbarg, E. D. *Investment Analysis and Portfolio Management.* Homewood, Ill.: Dow Jones-Irwin, Inc., 1967.

Crane, Burton. *The Sophisticated Investor.* New York: Simon and Schuster, Inc., 1959.

Dice, Charles, and Eiteman, W. *The Stock Market.* 3d ed. New York: McGraw-Hill Book Co., 1952.

Engel, Louis. *How to Buy Stocks.* Boston: Little, Brown and Co., 1962.

Farrell, Maurice L. *The Dow Jones Investor's Handbook.* New York: Dow Jones & Co., Inc., 1966.

Gerstenberg, Charles W. *Financial Organization and Management of Business.* 3d ed. New York: Prentice-Hall, Inc., 1959.

Graham, Benjamin, and McGoldrick, C. *The Interpretation of Financial Statements.* New York: Harper & Bros., 1955.

Graham, B.; Dodd, D.; and Cottle, S. *Security Analysis, Principles and Technique.* 4th ed. New York: McGraw-Hill Book Co.

Jacobs, Raymond H., and Kohn, E. *Securities,* Vols. 1 and 2. Washington, D.C.: Kalb Voorhis & Co., 1964.

Karrenbrock, W. E., and Simons, H. *Intermediate Accounting.* 3d ed. Cincinnati, Ohio: South-Western Publishing Co., 1958.

Klise, Eugene S. *Money and Banking.* Cincinnati, Ohio: South-Western Publishing Co., 1955.

Loeb, G. M. *The Battle for Investment Survival.* 3d ed. New York: Simon and Schuster, Inc., 1957.

Loll, Leo M., and Buckley, J. G. *The Over-the-Counter Securities Markets.* Englewood Cliffs, N.J.: Prentice-Hall, Inc., 1961.

Loss, Louis, and Cowett, E. M. *Blue Sky Law.* Boston: Little, Brown and Co., 1958.

Miller, Donald E. *The Meaningful Interpretation of Financial Statements.* New York: American Management Association, Inc., 1966.

National Association of Securities Dealers, Inc. Manual. New York: Commerce Clearing House, 1967.

National Association of Securities Dealers, Inc.

NASD and the Registered Representative. Washington, D.C., 1964.

———. *Over-the-Counter Trading Handbook.* Washington, D.C., 1960.

———. *Training Guide.* 4th printing. Washington, D.C., 1963.

———. *What You Must Know.* Washington, D.C., 1964.

Poole, Kenneth E. *Public Finance and Economic Welfare.* 2d printing. New York: Rinehart & Co., Inc., 1957.

Public Policy Implications of Investment Company Growth. House Report No. 2337, 89th Cong., 2d sess. Washington, D.C.: U.S. Government Printing Office, 1966.

Roberts, Edwin A. *The Stock Market.* New York: Dow Jones & Co., Inc., 1965.

Samuelson, Paul A. *Economics, an Introductory Analysis.* 5th ed. New York: McGraw-Hill Book Co., 1961.

Securities Acts Amendments of 1964. Chicago: Commerce Clearing House, 1964.

Securities Act Handbook. 4th ed. New York: Appeal Printing Co., Inc., 1965.

Stabler, C. Norman. *How to Read the Financial News.* 10th ed. New York: Harper & Bros., 1964.

Straley, John A. *What About Mutual Funds?* New York: Harper & Bros., 1958.

U.S. Master Tax Guide. Chicago: Commerce Clearing House, 1967.

Wiesenberger, Arthur. *Investment Companies 1967.*

Wyckoff, Peter. *Dictionary of Stock Market Terms.* New York: Popular Library, Inc.

Index

A

Accountant's opinion, 54
Accounts payable, 38
Accounts receivable, 31, 34
Accrued liabilities, 38
Accrued wages payable, 30
Accumulation plans, 102-3
Acid test, 48
Acknowledgment, 218-19
Active crowd, 176
Active trading of bonds, 176
Acts
 Investment Company Act of
  1940 (the '40 Act), 91,
  107-12,126
 Securities Act of 1933 (the
  '33 Act), 121-25, 138
 Securities Exchange Act of
  1934 (the '34 Act),
  124, 138
Adjustment bonds, 12
Advertising interpretation, 224
Agent, 165
All-or-none basis, 160
Alphabet bonds (E & H), 14
American Depository Receipts
 (ADR), 18
American Stock Exchange, 172-
 74
Amortization, 12
Analysis, 54-85
Annual report, 55, 97, 110
Appreciation, 97, 100-101
Arbitrage, 177
Arranging loans, 224
Asked price
 mutual funds, 98
 over-the-counter, 168
Assets, 29-30
Assignment, 218
Associated person, 132
"At-the-market" transactions
 (NASD), 205
Auction market, 171
Authorized stock, 9
Automatic reinvestment of divi-
 dends, mutual funds, 105
Automatic withdrawal plans, 105
Average, or index, 80

B

Baby bonds, 10
Balance sheet, 29, 33
Balance of payments, 76
Balanced fund, 94
Bank stocks, 64-65
Banker's acceptance, 78
Bankruptcy, 2
Basis points, 18
BD (broker-dealer) form, 124
Bear market, 80, 82
Bearer bonds, 13
Bearer certificate, 19
Beneficiary, 104
Best efforts agreement, 160
Bid price, mutual funds, 99
"Bid Wanted" (BW), 167
Blue chips, 72
Blue List, 17
Blue-sky (state) laws, 148-49, 159
Board of directors, 1, 4
Board of Governors, Federal Re-
 serve System, 124
Board of Governors, NASD, 195
Board of Governors, New York
 Stock Exchange, 174
Boiler room, 179
Bond(s), 10-20, 243
 adjustment, 12
 alphabet (E & H), 14
 anticipation notes, 17
 bearer, 13
 callable, 9
 closed-end, 12
 collateral trust, 12
 convertible, 11
 coupon, 13
 debenture, 12
 federal agency, 15
 full-faith-and-credit, 15
 fund, 94
 general mortgage, 12
 general obligation, 15
 government, 13, 57-59
 income, 12
 "and interest," corporate issues, 176
 limited obligation, 15
 limited open-end, 12

 mortgage, 12, 60
 municipal, 13, 15-17
 open-end, 12
 points, 18
 and preferred stock fund, 94
 quotations, 18, 20
 ratings, 60
 ratio, 48
 real estate mortgage, 60-61
 refunding, 13
 registered, 13, 19
 revenue, 12, 15
 rolling stock, 13
 savings, 14
 secured, 11
 serial, 12
 sinking fund, 12
 special assessment, 15
 state, 16
 statutory authority, 16
 tables, 17
 traded flat, 215
 trading, 215
  active, 176
  cabinet, 176
 treasury, 14
 unsecured, 11
 U.S. government, 14
 yield, 17
Book value, 39, 53
Books and records, 110-11, 130-32
Brand names, 38
Break-even point, 49
Breakpoint sales, 201
Breakthroughs, 82
Broker, 124, 165, 193
Broker-dealer registration, 137
Bull market, 80, 82
Buy in, 216-17
Buyer's option, 214
Buying syndicate, 158-59
"BW" (Bid Wanted), 167

C

Cabinet trading of bonds, 176
Call loans, 75, 78
Call option, 177
Callable bonds, 9
Callable Preferred Stock, 9

Callable provision, 9
Capital, 39-40
Capital gains
    and losses, 238-41
      mutual funds, 245-46
      tax, 238-41
Capital markets, 77
Capital stock, 10
Capital structure, 39, 64
    of a mutual fund, 93
Capital surplus, 39
Capitalization, 39
Capitalization ratios, 48
Cash, 34
Cash dividends, 7
Cash flow, 64
Cash transactions, 171, 213
Censure, 136
Certificates of deposit, 77
Changing number of shares of
    funds, 93
Charges for services, 201
Churning, 127
Civil law, 211-12
Closed-end bonds, 12
Closed-end funds, 92-93, 108
Closed-end investment company,
    91-93
Closing (last) price, stock, 181
Code of Procedure, 210-11
Collateral trust bond, 12
Combined annual gain, 17
Combined or overall coverage, 53
Commercial paper, 78
Commission broker, 174
Commission rates, 182-83
Commissions (taxes), 243
Common stock, 62; *see also*
    Stock(s)
    analysis, 62
    authorized, 9
    classified, 6
    fund, 94
      diversified, 94
    outstanding, 33
    ratio, 48
    unissued, 9
Comparisons with market index
    (Statement of Policy), 144-
    45
Competitive bidding, 158, 160
Conditional orders, 207-8
Conduit taxation, 246
Confirmations, 167, 204, 216
Consolidation, 70
Contemplation of death, 247
Contingencies, 34
Continuous investment plans, 103
Continuing commissions, 224
Contractual plan, 103, 146, 224
Conversion parity, 11
Conversion privileges, mutual
    funds, 105
Convertibility, 11
Convertible bond, 11
Convertible preferred stock, 8
Cooling period, 124, 159

Copyright, 38
Corporate bond analysis, 59-61
Corporate 85% dividend credit,
    244
Corporate securities, 5
Corporate taxes, 244-45
Corporations, 3-10
Cost averaging, 56, 145
Cost of sales, 41
Coupon bond, 13
Coupon rate, 17
Coverage of senior charges, 53
Cumulative preferred stock, 8
Cumulative voting, 6
Current assets, 32, 34
Current liabilities, 34, 38
Current ratio (or working capital
    ratio), 47
Current yield, 17-18
Custodial services, 105-6, 144
Custodian or custodian bank, mu-
    tual funds, 105-7, 144
Custodian charges, mutual funds,
    105-6
Custodian fee, mutual funds, 106
Custodians, 105-6, 144
Cyclical industries, 72

D

Date of record, 181
Dealer, 124, 165, 193
Dealing with nonmembers, 206
Debenture bond, 12
Debt-equity ratio, 48
Deceased person, 218
Deceptive acts, 127
Declaration date, 214
Defensive industries, 72
Defensive issue, 72
Deferred charges, 38
Deficit, 41
Deficit spending, 76
Deflation, 74
Delayed delivery, 171, 213
Delegated duties fee, 106
Delist, 173
Delivery date, 213
Depletion, 37
Depreciation, 31, 37, 41
Depression, 74
Differential, 175
Dilution, 11
Directors, 1, 4
Disciplinary cases, NASD, 200
Disclosure
    of control, 204
    of financial condition, as bro-
      ker or dealer, 206
    of participation or interest in
      primary or secondary
      distribution, 204-5
    of prices and concessions, 203
Discount, 17
    closed-end funds, 93
Discount rate, 74
Discretionary accounts, 127, 178,
    205

Diversification, 91
Diversified common stock fund,
    94
Diversified management compa-
    nies, 108
Dividend distribution, 105
Dividend exclusion and credit,
    237
Dividend income, double taxation
    of, 237
Dividend payout ratio, 51
Dividend return, 51
Dividend per share, 51
Dividends, 6, 181-82, 201, 214
    payable, 39
Dollar cost averaging, 56, 145
Domestic corporation, 4
Dow Jones Averages, 81
Dow Theory, 82
Drafts, 217
Dual listing, 172
Due bills, 221-22
Due diligence meeting, 159

E

Earned surplus, 39, 42
Earnings
    on invested capital, 52
    per share, 51, 62
Economics, 74
Equipment, 32
Equipment trust certificate, 13
Equity, 9, 29
Establishing gain or loss, 238
Ethics, 211
Ex-dividend, 182
Ex-dividend date, 214
Expense ratio, 106
Explanation of risks, 122, 144

F

Face amount certificate compa-
    nies, 107
Factor of safety, 59
Failure to register personnel, 200
Fair commissions, 202
Fair Practice Rules (NASD), 200-
    210
Federal agency bonds, 15
Federal Deposit Insurance Corpo-
    ration, 65
Federal estate tax, 246
Federal funds, 77-78
Federal gift tax, 246
Federal Reserve System, 74-75
Fiduciary, information received,
    203
FICA (Federal Insurance Contri-
    bution Act), 248
FIFO, 35
Filing literature, 146-47, 224
Fill or kill, 170
Financial companies, 67
Financial securities, 64-68
Financial statements, 29-42

Fire (property) and casualty in-
  surance companies, 66-67
Firm bid, 167
Firm commitment, 160
Firm market, 167
Firm offer, 167
Firm prices, 167
Fiscal measures, 76
Five percent policy, 202-3
Fixed asset to net worth ratio, 54
Fixed assets, 32, 37
Flat trade, 215
Floating debt, 16
Floating supply, 80
Floor, 174
Floor broker, 175
Floor trader, 174
Foreign corporation, 4
Form X-17-A-5, 127
Formula plans, 56
Franchise, 68
Fraudulent devices, use of, 123,
  127-28
Free-riding and withholding, 222
Front-end load plans, 103
Frozen account, 133
Full and fair disclosure, mutual
  funds, 121
Full-faith-and-credit bonds, 15
Fully managed fund, 96
Fully paid plans, 104-5
Fund appreciation, 100
Fund objective, mutual funds,
  94-95
Fundamental analysis, 63
Funded debt, 40

G

General obligation bond, 15
General mortgage bond, 12
Gift tax, 150
Gifts
  in contemplation of death,
    247
  to minors, 149-51
Give-ups, 178
"Good delivery," 213, 217-22
Good 'til canceled, 170
Goodwill, 37
Government bonds (U.S. govern-
  ments), 13, 57-59
Government regulations (SEC
  Statement of Policy), 143
Governments, 13-17
Growth funds (mutual funds), 94
Growth industries, 72
Growth stock, 72
Guaranteed bonds, 13
Guaranteed stocks, 9, 13
Guarantees, prohibition, 206

H

Hedging, 177
High price, 181
Highest sales charge, 145

Holding company, 4
Hot issue, 160, 222
Hypothecation, 126, 205

I

Income, or yield, 17
Income bond, 12
Income fund, 95
Income statement, 29, 40-42
Income stocks, 72
Income tax, 235-44
Indenture, 10
Indexes, 80
Indication of interest, 123
Industrial securities, 62-64
Industry performance against
  company performance,
  145
Inflation, 74
Information for analysis, 54-55
Insiders, 128
Insurance stocks, 65-67
Intangible assets, 34
Internal Revenue Code, 235-48
"And interest," 176
Interest charges, 11
Interest coverage, 53
Interest equalization tax, 77,
  220-21, 248
Interest rates, 78, 79
Interstate Commerce Commis-
  sion, 70
Intrinsic value, 73
Inventories, 34-35, 167
  LIFO-FIFO, 35
Inventory valuation, 35
Inventory turnover, 52
Investment, 34
  analysis, 56
  banker, 157, 193
  characteristics, 56-57
  companies, 91, 108
  v. speculation, 63-64
  in subsidiary, 37
Investment Advisers Act of 1940,
  126
Investment advisory agreement,
  mutual funds, 96
Investment Company Act of
  1940, 91, 107-12, 126
Investment company stocks, 67-
  68
Investment trust rule, 207

J

Joint tax return, 236
Junior securities, 8

L

Last (closing) price, 180-81
Leasehold improvements, 38
Leaseholds, 38
Ledgers, 110
Legal list, 148

Legal reserve requirements, 75
Letter of intent, 102
Level charge plan, 103
Leverage, 49
  ratio, 49
  stock, 49
Liabilities, 29, 38-39
  and stockholders' equity, 38-39
Life insurance companies, 65-66
Life insurance feature, 104
LIFO, 35
Limit order, 168
Limitations upon use of the Asso-
  ciation's name, 196-97
Limited obligation bond, 15
Limited open-end bond, 12
Liquidation value, 144
Liquidity, 47
Listed securities, 172
Literature, sales, 143-47, 200
Load (sales), 92, 98, 102-4, 207
Loans
  by banks, 75, 134
  to brokers, 80
Local taxes, 248
Long position, 178
Long-term capital gains and
  losses, 238-41
Long-term debt, 34, 39
Low price, 181

M

Maintain an orderly market,
  174-75
Make a market, 167-68
Maloney Act of 1938, 124, 191
Management claims (Statement of
  Policy), 145
Management companies, 108
Management company (sponsor),
  96-97
Management fees, 106
Management of funds, 96-97
Managing underwriter, 157
Manipulation, 127
Manipulative acts, 127
Mark to the market, 214
Market order, 168
Market value, 10
Margin, 124, 133
Margin of profit, 52
Marketable securities, 34
Marketing new issues of securities,
  157
Matched orders, 127
Maturity date, 10, 14
Mergers, 70
Methods of issue and redemption
  of funds, 92-93
MIP (Monthly Investment Plan),
  179
Misleading information as to
  membership and registra-
  tion, filing of, 200, 205,
  209
Monetary measures, 76

Money and banking, 74-79
Money market, 77-79
Monthly Investment Plan (MIP), 179
Mortgage bond, 12, 60
Municipal bonds, 13, 15-17
Mutual funds, 91-112
   asked price, 98
   automatic reinvestment of dividends, 105
   bid price, 99
   capital gains, 245-46
   capital structure, 93
   conversion privileges, 105
   custodian or custodian bank, 105, 107, 144
   custodian charges, 105-6
   custodian fee, 106
   distribution, 98-99
   financial statements, 99-101
   full and fair disclosure, 121
   fund custodian, 105-7
   fund objectives, 94-95
   fund purchases and services, 102-5
   growth funds, 94
   investment advisory agreement, 96
   Investment Company Act of 1940, 107-12
   net asset value, 98-101
   objectives, 94-96
   offering price, 98
   penalty of front-end load plan, 103
   premium, 93
   prospectus, 121
   redemption price, 99
   registration statement, 122
   sale of open-end fund shares, 101-2
   sales charge, sales load, 92
   structure, 96-97
   underwriter, 98
   withdrawal plan, 105, 146

N

NASD (National Association of Securities Dealers), 191-225
   Advisory Council, 195
   application for membership, 194
   bars to membership, 193
   Board of Governors, 195
   branch office, 194, 208
   breakpoint sales, 201
   bylaws, 192-99
   Certificate of Incorporation, 192
   charges, 201
   Code of Procedure, 210-11
   commingled securities, 205
   confirmation, 204, 216
   customer records, 206
   delivery of securities, 213

   Executive Committee, 195
   fair dealing, 201
   fair price, 202
   foreign associates, 198
   high standards, 200
   improper use of securities, 205
   "at the market," 205
   markups (percent) policy, 202
   member, 194
   Membership Continuance Request, 210 f.
   penalties, 209
   personnel of another member, 209, 224-25
   price concessions, 206
   price quotation, 203
   principals, 194, 199
   qualification examination, 198-99
   recommendations and suitability, 200-201
   registered representative, 197
   registration of representatives, 197
   Rules of Fair Practice, 200-210
   sale of dividends, 201
   sales agreement, 207
   selling group, 203
   selling syndicate, 203
   stated price, 203
   Summary Complaint Procedure, 210 f.
   third market, 204
   Uniform Practice Code, 212-22
   use of name, 196
   written supervisory procedures, 208
National Quotation Bureau, Inc., 166-67
National securities associations, 128
National securities associations, 128
Negative asset, 32
Negotiated market, 166
Negotiated underwriting, 160
Net asset value, mutual funds, 98-101
Net Capital or 20 to 1 Rule, 126-27
Net change, price, 181
Net investment income, 100
Net long- or short-term gain, 238-41
Net long- or short-term loss, 238-41
Net prices to persons not in investment banking or securities business, 206-7
Net profit, 41
Net quick assets, 48
Net tangible assets value, 53
Net unrealized appreciation, 97, 100-101
Net worth, 39, 53

New capital, 146
New York Stock Exchange, 171-74
New York Times averages, 82
Newspaper quotations, 203, 225
Nominal yield, 17
Noncumulative preferred stock, 8
Noncumulative voting, 6
Nondiversified fund, 94
Nondiversified management companies, 108
Nonmembers, dealing with, 206
No-par, 9
Nonresident-owned (NRO) companies, 95
Notes receivable, 34

O

Objectives, mutual funds, 94-96
Obsolescence, 37
Odd-lot dealer, 175
Odd lots, 80
"Offer Wanted" (OW), 167
Offering circular, 123
Offering price, mutual funds, 98
Offerings, "at the market," 127
Open-end bond, 12
Open-end funds, 92-93
Open-end investment company, 91-93
Open market operations, 75
Open orders, 170
Opening price, 181
Operating costs, 41, 106-7
Operating income, 41
Operating profit, 40-41
Operating ratio, 52
Ordinary income, 237
Organization expense, 38
Other assets, 34, 38
Outstanding stock, 9
Over-the-counter, 165-83, 225
Overall coverage, 53
Overlapping debt, 16
"OW" (Offer Wanted), 167
Ownership, of shareholders, 4

P

Paid-in capital, 10
Par value, 9
Parity, 11
Participating preferred stock, 8
Partnership, general and limited, 3
Passing of securities at death, 246
Patent, 38
Payment date for dividends, 215
Penalty of front-end load plan, mutual funds, 103
Performance charts and tables (Statement of Policy), 146
Periodic payment plans, 103
Periodic reports, 128
Perpetual existence, 4
Personal holding company, 245

Pink sheets, 166, 167-68
Plan completion insurance protection, 104
Plant and equipment, 32
Points, stocks and bonds, 18, 179
Post, 175
Preemptive right, 7.
Preferred dividend coverage, 53
Preferred stock, 8, 61
    analysis, 61
    callable, 9
    convertible, 8
    cumulative, 8
    fund, 94
    noncumulative, 8
    participating, 8
    ratio, 48
Premium, 17
    mutual funds, 93
Prepaid expenses, 34
Preservation of records, 110-11, 132-33
Previous bid, 168, 169
Price-earnings ratio, 51-62
Primary distribution, 157
Prime rate, 74
Principal (dealer), 165
Private offering, 158
Private placement, 158
Procedures for over-the-counter quotations distributed in the press or by radio or television as a public service, 225
Profit and loss statement (statement of income), 40
Prompt payment, 224
Property dividend, 7
Proprietor/proprietorship, 2-3
Prospectus, mutual funds, 121
Protective provisions of bond issues, 60
Provisions for taxes on income, 39
Proxy, 6
Proxy statements, 128-29
Prudent man rule, 148
Public offering price, 98, 102, 206-7
Public Utility Holding Company Act of 1935, 125
Public utility securities, 68-70
Publication of purchases or sales, 203
Purposes of the NASD, 192
Put option, 177

Q

Qualification examination, 137, 198-99
Quantity discounts, 102
Quick asset ratio, 48
Quotations
    bonds, 18, 20

    over-the-counter, 168, 169-70, 179, 225
    stock market, 179-82

R

Railroad securities, 70-71
Range for the year, 179-82
Rates of return (Statement of Policy), 143-44
Rating scales, bonds, 60
Raw materials, 34
Real estate, 71-72
Real estate mortgage bonds, 60-61
Realization of gains or loss, 238
Recapitalization, 70
Receiver's certificates, 13
Recession, 74
Reclamations, 222
Recommendations, 129
Record date, 214
Record of transactions, 130
Redemption (Statement of Policy), 144
Redemption price, mutual fund, 99
Red herring, 123, 159
Refinancing, 70
Refunding bond, 13
Regional exchanges, 172-73
Registered bond, 13, 19
Registered representative, 197
Registered stock, 19
Registrar, 5, 105
Registration as broker-dealer, 137
Registration fee, stock sales, 183
Registration statement, mutual funds, 122
Regular way transaction, 167 f., 171, 213
Regulated investment companies, 245-46
Regulation A (of the '33 Act), 123
Regulation G (effective March 11, 1968), 75
Regulation Q, 77
Regulation T (of the '34 Act), 75, 133
Regulation U (of the '34 Act), 75, 134
Reorganization, 70
Reprints (Statement of Policy), 145
Reserves, 34
Resistance level, 83
Restricted management fund, 96
Retained earnings, 39, 42
    statement, 41
Return, 17-18
Revenue bond, 12, 15
Reverse stock split, 10
Rewarding employees, 203
Right of NASD to require written reports and to inspect books and records, 209

Rights, stock, 2
Rights of accumulation, 105
Risk, 122, 144
Rolling stock bonds, 13
Round lot, 175, 216

S

Safety of capital (Statement of Policy), 144
Sale price (offering price) of investment fund shares, 98, 102, 206-7
Sales, 41
Sales charge (sales load), mutual funds, 92
Sales commissions (Statement of Policy), 145
Sales to inventories ratio, 52
Sales literature, 143, 224
Sales to net working capital ratio, 53
Savings bonds, 14
Schedule D, 235
Seat on New York Stock Exchange, 173
SEC (Securities and Exchange Commission), 121, 124-38
SEC Statement of Policy, 143-47
    comparisons with market index, 144-45
    management claims, 145
    performance of charts and tables, 146
    reprints, 145
    safety of capital, 144
    sales commissions, 145
Secondary distribution, 157
Secured bonds, 11
Securities, 1
    classification of, 72-73
Securities Act of 1933, 121-25, 138
Securities acts summarized, 138
Securities Exchange Act of 1934, 124, 138
Self-employed taxes, 248
Seller's option, 171, 178, 213-14
Selling and administrative expenses, 40-41
Selling against the box, 177
Selling charges of funds, 92
Selling concessions, 202, 206
Selling dividends, 201
Selling group, 203
Selling group member, 159, 203
Selling out, 216-17
Selling syndicate, 158-59, 203
Senior securities, 8
Serial bond, 12
Settlement date, 213
Settlements, 171
Sharecost averaging, 145
Sharing in accounts, 206
Short interest, 80
Short position, 178

Short sale, 177-78
Short sales and options, taxation, 241-42
Short-term capital gains and losses, 238-41
Signature guarantee, 218
Single payment plans, 104-5
Sinking fund, 12
Sinking fund bond, 12
Solicitations of purchases on an exchange to facilitate a distribution of securities, 205
Sources of financial information, 54-56
Special assessment bonds, 15
Special cash account, 133
Special deals, 224
Special situations, 73
Special situations fund, 95
Specialist, 174-75
Specialized common stock fund, 95
Specialized funds, 95
Splits, 10
Sponsor, 98
Spread, 178
Stabilization, 160
Standard minimum, 47
Standby, 160
State bonds, 16
State charter, 3
State laws (blue sky), 148-49
State taxes, 248
State transfer taxes, 183
Stated value, 9
Statement of changes in net assets, 100
Statement of income, 29, 40, 41
Statement of Policy (SEC); see SEC Statement of Policy
Statutory authority bonds, 16
Statutory voting, 6
Stock(s), 5-10; see also Common stock and Preferred stock
    authorized, 9
    bank, 64-65
    certificate, 5
    delivery, 213
    dividend, 7, 242-43
    exchanges, 171-83
    growth, 72
    guaranteed, 19
    income, 72
    insurance, 65-67
    investment company, 67-68
    leverage, 49
    noncumulative voting, 6
    outstanding, 9
    points,179
    power, 218

price, closing (last), 181
quotations, 179-82
registered, 19
registrar, 5, 105
rights, 2, 7, 242-43
    value of, 7
split, 10
treasury, 9
unissued, 9
values, 9
watered, 178
yield, 17
Stockholder privileges, 5-8
Stockholders' equity, 34, 39
Stop-loss-limit, 170 f.
Stop order, 123, 170
Straddle, 178
Street name, 5, 218, 222
Subject market, 167
Subject price, 167
Subordinated debentures, 13
Summary complaint procedure, 210
Supervision, 129
Surplus, 39
Suspension, 195
Swap funds, 95
Switches, 145-46
Syndicate, 157-58

T

Tape readers, 83-84
Tax anticipation bills or bonds, 14
Tax anticipation notes, 17
Tax exempt securities, 15
Tax-free exchange funds, 95
Taxation, 4, 235-48
Technical analysis, 79-80
Temporary certificate, 219
Term loans, 39-40
Ticker tape, 176
    symbols, 176
Tombstone advertisements, 147
Total asset value, 99
Total sales to inventory ratio, 52
Trade date, 171, 213
Traded flat, bonds, 215
Trademark, 38
Trading
    on the equity, 49
    by insiders, 128
Transactions between members and nonmembers, 206
Transactions for personnel of another member, 203
Transfer agent, 5, 105
Transfer fees, 222
Transfer tax, 216, 247

Treasury bills, 14
Treasury bonds, 14
Treasury certificates, 14
Treasury notes, 14
Treasury stock, 9
Trust Indenture Act (1939), 125, 126
Trustee in bankruptcy, 71
Types of orders, 168, 170

U

Underwriter, 157
Underwriter, mutual funds, 98
Underwriting agreement, 157, 159
Underwriting spread, 160
Unemployment taxes, 248
Uniform Practice Code, NASD, 212-22
Uniform Securities Act, 148
Unissued stock, 9
Unit investment trusts, 103, 107
Unit of trading, 216
Units of delivery, 216
Unlisted trading, 172-73
Unrealized appreciation, 97, 100-101
Unsecured bonds, 11
U.S. government bonds, 14

V

Volume of shares sold (volume of sales), 80, 84
Voluntary (open) account, 103
Voluntary plan, 103
Voting, 5, 6
Voting trust certificate, 10

W

Wages payable, 30
Warrants, 7
Wash sale, 127, 179
Watered stock, 178
Weighted average cost, 35
"When, as, and if issued," 214
Withdrawal plans, mutual funds, 105-46
Working capital, 29, 47, 64
Working capital (current) ratio, 47
Written confirmation, 127
Written procedures, 129

Y

Yield, 17-18
    to maturity, 17